Praise for
THE VANISHING DEEP

A Texas Tayshas Reading List Pick
An Apple Most Anticipated Book
A Isinglass Teen Readers' Choice Award Long List Pick

"This riveting YA thriller . . . is among the most exciting stuff being put
out in the genre right now."   —*Entertainment Weekly*

"An immersive, fast-paced story about survival, grief, guilt, and second
chances."   —*School Library Journal*

"Tensions [are kept] high as the characters explore a detailed, inventive,
lovingly crafted world . . . the narrative's sea legs come through deep, reso-
nant characterizations and the characters' intense emotional inner lives. A
seaworthy stand-alone."   —*Kirkus Reviews*

"[In] this fast-paced ecological thriller . . . Scholte builds palpable suspense
through Lor and Tempe's alternating narratives while offering timely com-
mentary on sustainability and responsible stewardship of land and sea."
                                                 —*Publishers Weekly*

"Scholte's intricate world building stands out from the usual run of post-
apocalyptic novels, with a particular emphasis on the effects of a world
steeped in overconsumption and an eco-apocalypse . . . Readers will be left
with deep questions about personal sacrifice and emotional closure."
                            —*The Bulletin of the Center for Children's Books*

D0110951

Praise for
FOUR DEAD QUEENS

AN INDIE BESTSELLER
AN AMAZON BEST BOOK OF THE MONTH
A BLUE SPRUCE BOOK AWARD NOMINEE
A TEXAS TAYSHAS READING LIST PICK

"A good, devious mix of some of the best fantasy and murder mystery that YA has had to offer." —*Entertainment Weekly*

"Checks all the boxes for an addictive read." —*Refinery29*

"A darkly delicious tale . . . perfect for fans of both fantasy and murder mysteries." —Kerri Maniscalco, #1 *New York Times* and *USA Today* bestselling author of the Stalking Jack the Ripper series

"[An] exciting fantasy debut . . . stunning." —*Paste*

"An action-packed romance." —*Booklist*

"A cinematic thrill ride brimming with murder, mayhem, and twists that will shock you . . . Absolutely riveting." —Sarah Glenn Marsh, author of the Reign of the Fallen series

"Enticingly twisting." —*The Bulletin of the Center for Children's Books*

"A triumphant, exciting debut that will keep readers guessing all the way to the final chapter." —Beth Revis, *New York Times* bestselling author of *Give the Dark My Love*

"Scholte's stand-alone debut marks her as an author to watch." —*Kirkus Reviews*

"An intrigue-heavy adventure in a world filled with characters whom readers will want to revisit." —*Publishers Weekly*

"Takes unexpected turns, has complicated characters who develop over time, and ends unpredictably." —*School Library Journal*

THE
VANISHING
DEEP

Also by Astrid Scholte

LEAGUE OF LIARS
FOUR DEAD QUEENS

THE
VANISHING
DEEP

ASTRID SCHOLTE

G. P. PUTNAM'S SONS

G. P. Putnam's Sons
An imprint of Penguin Random House LLC, New York

First published in the United States of America by G. P. Putnam's Sons,
an imprint of Penguin Random House LLC, 2020
First paperback edition published 2022

Visit us online at penguinrandomhouse.com

THE LIBRARY OF CONGRESS HAS CATALOGED THE HARDCOVER EDITION AS FOLLOWS:
Names: Scholte, Astrid, author.
Title: The vanishing deep / Astrid Scholte.
Description: New York: G. P. Putnam's Sons, [2020] | Summary: "Seventeen-year-old Tempe brings her dead
sister back to life for twenty-four hours in hopes of unraveling the truth behind their parents' death"
—Provided by publisher.
Identifiers: LCCN 2019039244 (print) | LCCN 2019039245 (ebook) |
ISBN 9780525513957 (hardcover) | ISBN 9780525513964 (ebook)
Subjects: CYAC: Death—Fiction. | Experiments—Fiction. | Secrets—Fiction. | Grief—Fiction. |
Family life—Fiction. | Science fiction.
Classification: LCC PZ7.1.S336533 Van 2020 (print) | LCC PZ7.1.S336533 (ebook) | DDC [Fic]—dc23
LC record available at https://lccn.loc.gov/2019039244
LC ebook record available at https://lccn.loc.gov/2019039245

Book manufactured in Canada

ISBN 9780525513971

1   3   5   7   9   10   8   6   4   2

FRI

Design by Samira Iravani
Text set in LTC Cloister

For Andrew—
I would cross the ocean for you.

THE
VANISHING
DEEP

Palindrome—*a word, number, phrase, or sequence of symbols or elements whose meaning can be interpreted the same way both forward and in reverse.*

We begin as we end; we end as we begin.

That is life.

It's the middle we must hold on to.

CHAPTER ONE

TEMPEST

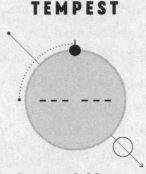

Sunday, 8:00 a.m.

I DIDN'T WANT to resurrect my sister because I loved her.

I didn't want one final goodbye, to whisper words left unsaid or clear my conscience of any slights between us. I didn't want to hear her voice say my name, *Tempe*, one last time.

I wanted to soothe the anger that scorched through me. An anger that had a life of its own, taking hold within me, propelling me to action—even on the days when I was exhausted from the early-morning dive, even when I'd had enough of this scrappy life.

I wanted to drown memories of her long dark hair, curling in the water as she dove deeper ahead of me, always knowing where to search next. I wanted to extinguish memories of her dancer limbs twirling above her head as storms raged nearby. I wanted to forget her now-silenced bell-like voice once and for all.

As much as the thought of her name angered me, the thought of never hearing it again angered me even more.

Her name had begun to fade in the two years since her death, like the last rumble of thunder in a storm. In the beginning, friends—all Elysea's—would say *your sister*, as if saying her name would send a fresh wave of tears down my already flushed cheeks. Then, as days turned into weeks, her name was said soft and tentative, signaling to me that it was time to start moving on. To get out of bed, to live my life.

When weeks turned into months, people stopped speaking about her altogether. As though she never existed.

Then I'd heard something that changed how I felt about her, transforming my grief to anger.

So now I *needed* to hear her voice one last time. I needed the truth. And for that, I needed to resurrect her.

Neither of us could rest until then.

The boat shifted with the waves; I adjusted my footing so I didn't fall into the sea. The *Sunrise* had been my parents' transportation to work. Small, but swift. The shell-colored deck was triangular, with two "wings" underneath the stern of the boat, which hooked down and into the water to keep balance at high speeds. A cramped cabin was suspended below, its belly dipping into the sea like an overfed familfish.

I gazed at the deep blue waters. From above, you could see a slight turbulence beneath—a hint of something other than sand, salt and sea.

A sunken city—one that I had scavenged for years, and from which I had never returned empty-handed. My deeply tanned olive skin spoke of the years I'd spent on and under the water, searching for scraps.

Today would be my last dive here. Elysea had found this site when I was twelve years old, and after five years, I knew every twist and turn of the labyrinth of steel, glass and stone. There was only one room left untouched. And I wasn't leaving until I explored it. After that, I would need to find a new dive site and hope it hadn't already been ravaged like so many sunken cities in this section of the sea.

I tightened the straps of my flippers, made from blunted blades of Old World knives. The rusty, thin metal sheets shrieked as I flexed my foot to test the movement.

"Oh, shut up," I said. The flippers were my mother's, and I couldn't afford new ones. I wouldn't waste Notes on anything other than reviving my sister, or topping off my breather.

One last dive, I thought as I put the breathing tube in my mouth and pulled the pliable transparent dome over my head. As I clipped it onto the neck of my diving skin, the dome inflated.

One final goodbye. Another memory to shelve, another link to Elysea forever severed. The thought should've brought a wave of sadness, but I felt only cold, steely determination. Soon I, too, could forget Elysea's name.

I took a shallow breath to check the gas levels of the small cylinder attached to my belt.

My breather beeped twice.

Oxygen low.

I yanked the dome off and spat out my breather. Aside from food, diving gas was the most expensive commodity. It allowed us to search for relics from the Old World—for anything useful in the new one. My dive finds barely covered the costs of living on the Equinox Reef and what was left went toward my sister's resurrection. I was hoping I could unearth something from the remaining room to fund topping off my breather and allow me time to locate a new ruin, without having to dip into my savings.

I placed the breather back in my mouth and pulled the dome over my face. The levels would have to be enough.

I rattled some black stones with iridescent blue spirals in my palm, like miniature swirling galaxies. I dropped one into the ocean, saying a prayer to the Gods below, to allow me to enter their world, their sacred sanctuary—and survive it. It was a childish habit. When Elysea and I were young, we'd thought it was the will of the Gods below who took souls from boats in a storm and the air from the lungs of divers. We didn't realize it was simply chance, bad luck or unskilled diving. The perils of our world.

Together, we'd learned to conquer the ocean. Or so I'd thought. Until Elysea had drowned, almost exactly two years ago.

Before I allowed any further doubt to muddy my mind, I grabbed my oilskin bag, clipped it to my diving belt and tilted backward off the boat.

The water was cold, but only my fingertips were cool, the

rest of my body protected by my diving skin—a material made of thin, rubbery blue plates stitched together like fish scales, which I always wore under my clothes. I kicked my weighted metal flippers, which coaxed me downward.

Take shallow, steady breaths. I couldn't help but hear my sister's voice in my head. She'd taught me how to dive, after all.

"The free fall is easy," she would say. "Save your air for the return trip. When you'll need it. Just follow me into the dark, Tempe." She never called me by my full name—Tempest—saying it was too harsh for her little sister. "Temp*ee* sounds sweeter," she'd said.

I could barely remember the little girl I'd once been.

A plume of bright light shone from the corner of my eye—my map to the world below. I kicked toward it as I fell. Before long, my vision was illuminated by shades of blue, purple and pink, dotted along shafts of rusted metal. Since the Great Waves around five hundred years ago, bioluminescent coral had grown along the city ruins, lighting the way toward the ocean floor, like Old World lights on cobbled streets, or the stars in the night sky. A sunken constellation.

The sight never failed to take my breath away. And even though the building was long dead, it glowed with life. It was beautiful.

I followed the path downward.

When I passed a red-brown metal turret, I took a slight turn to the left. Rusticles, like fossilized seaweed, dripped from every edge. The holes that were once doorways and windows into a lively world were now the soulless eyes of a watchful, watery tomb.

A lost city. A drowned society. The perfect harvest.

My breather beeped again. I took shallower breaths, hoping the Gods were in favor of my presence. Many divers had searched for the Gods below. A temple, a shrine, a palace. *Anything*. But they'd remained undiscovered. It gave naysayers ammunition to doubt the deities' existence.

But in a world made almost entirely of water, we needed our guides. The Old World believed in the Gods above and followed the stars to journey across the land. But with hardly any land remaining, it was pointless to look to the sky. The water was our master.

I wished we'd begun with the lower levels of the building when we'd initially discovered this site. But it had been my first dive. Elysea had wanted to start closer to the surface, even though I'd argued that I was ready. She'd only been two years older than me, but after our parents' deaths, she'd acted more like my guardian than my sister. Back then, I'd barely fit into my mom's abandoned flippers.

"You'll grow into them," Elysea had said, fastening them as tight as she could around my then-small feet. "It's better that they're big so you can use them for longer."

I hadn't argued, excited to be included on the dive.

After five years, I was now one of the best divers on our home of the Equinox. While other kids went to school, sailed with their parents, swam with their friends, danced with their siblings, I dove. And dove and dove.

There was nothing on the surface for me now.

I dove deeper, keeping my breaths shallow to save gas.

As much as I missed diving with Elysea, I liked being by myself. With nothing but the waters to guide me, the Gods below protecting me, and the quiet to soothe my restless mind. My anger.

Elysea had been lucky to find this ruin. It must've broken free from a larger cluster of buildings during the Great Waves. Most sunken cities were overcrowded with divers, and few relics were left to be found. Not this building. This ruin was all mine.

The dive site was located close to the isle of Palindromena, and most divers steered clear of the brutal waves that crashed against the jagged coast. Too many people drowned there. Plus, those who lived on the Equinox were superstitious. The island was cloaked in mystery and tainted by death.

But I wasn't afraid of Palindromena. The facility had always been a specter in my life, but never touched me directly, like a looming shadow.

When I reached the ocean floor, I darted through a knocked-out window. Coral had grown around the frame, lighting the entrance. Many people believed the Gods below were to thank for the coral that had appeared in the years since the Great Waves, showing the way to sunken treasures. Without the

Gods, and their coral, the Old World would've been lost to the ocean.

My breather let out another warning beep. I had to be quick.

The building's ground floor had been a row of tiny shops, all interconnected. More coral bloomed inside, illuminating the rooms. The first shop was some kind of eatery. Tables tipped upside down, slivers of ceramic plates and glass cups were now debris in the water.

I rushed through the room, keeping my eye out for anything I might've missed. Anything *valuable*. Old cups were interesting, but not worth many Notes. I needed something useful for more diving gas and to fund Elysea's resurrection.

Down here, skeletons were as common as the yellow familfish that traveled in schools of hundreds up near the Equinox. Coral had grown in the gaps of disintegrated bone, piecing together the skeletons and fortifying them from further decomposition. They floated through doorways and rooms as though they continued to live and breathe, while their flesh and muscle had long peeled away.

I was twelve when I first saw a glowing patchwork skeleton, providing fuel for a week's worth of nightmares. Now they were friends. I'd given them names, backgrounds, personalities. It made it less creepy. *Slightly.*

I'd never made friends easily, but down here, the skeletons didn't have a choice.

I nodded to Adrei. His red-and-pink calcified skull rested on the café counter, his bony hand beside his face as though

I'd caught him deep in thought. On the ocean floor, there was little movement, no currents or fish to disturb him. As I swam by, my flippers rippled through the water and his luminous fingers rattled, as if to say hello.

I continued on to the next room.

"Hey, Celci," I said to a skeleton stuck floating between two corridors. I'd named her after my old aunt, who'd passed away from crystal lung when I was a child. I still remembered her teeth too large for her face, like this skeleton. I gently nudged Celci as I passed, moving her into the next room to be with Adrei. Even the dead shouldn't be alone.

The shop next door had been a bookstore; I passed without a second look. The room had been sealed before I'd forced open the door. While I'd managed to salvage some books, the rest had quickly broken down and clouded the room. The books I'd already retrieved weren't worth much; as soon as they were brought to the surface, the pages began to decompose in the humid salty air. Perhaps it would've been better to leave them down here, their words trapped within the pages, their untold stories safe.

So much of our history had disappeared. Most of the tales of the Old Gods had been forgotten, giving rise to the New Gods. People believed the Old Gods had turned away from us and our selfishness and didn't warn us of the impending waves.

When the Great Waves hit, people struggled to hold on to their faith.

It wasn't until the coral began blooming that people believed we weren't alone. We hadn't been abandoned by the Gods after all. Like the stars in the sky, the coral would guide us to supplies submerged below.

We could survive this new world with the remnants of the past.

My mom had believed in the Gods below, but my father hadn't. Did Dad's lack of faith cause their deaths? Did he misread the churning waters and darkening skies that became the vicious storm that destroyed their boat? But then, Elysea—

My breather let off a few frantic shrieks. *I hear you*, I thought. *But I'm not done yet.*

I arrived at the last untouched room and jimmied the door open with my diving pliers. I held my breath, not only to save diving gas but in anticipation. But I couldn't see anything inside. I snapped off a piece of coral from the door frame and swam into the room.

I let out a disappointed breath.

Bits of once-colorful material hung in threads from rusted poles, fallen from the ceiling.

A clothing shop.

I'd hoped the room, located at the back of the building, had been protected from the impact of the waves, like the bookshop had, but the shop's window faced an internal courtyard. And the glass was long gone.

I shifted old bits of clothing around in hopes of finding jewelry, trinkets, *anything*. But the Great Waves had drained all life from this room.

My breather started beeping more insistently. I had minutes left and I still needed to start my staggered ascent to avoid decompression sickness. I was going to have to buy more diving gas and hope it didn't take too long to find another dive site.

Then something caught my eye. Something nestled within a patch of bright pink coral. Something green. A rare color, certainly down here.

I swam through the shop's missing window and glanced up. Part of the building had collapsed onto itself, sealing the courtyard within. No wonder I'd never seen it.

But that wasn't what had caught my attention.

I swam forward, my heart beating in time with the increasing beeps of my breather. *It can't be. It can't be.*

When my fingertips touched the waxy green surface, I took in a dangerously deep breath. My breather started wailing, but it barely registered.

It was a plant. A *plant*! Thank the Gods below!

My breaths came in gasps now. A plant would be worth hundreds, thousands, of Notes.

I would be ready. Ready to go to Palindromena. At last, ready to say a final goodbye to Elysea.

My hands hovered over the plant, scared it would disintegrate at my touch.

How was this possible? Sure, some divers found plants, but most were a kind of seaweed. This was different. Seaweed couldn't grow down here in the dark. This was a land plant. And somehow it had survived.

I pushed debris away from the plant. Something had fallen on top of it and covered most of the foliage. Something organic, from the soft and granular feel of the debris. A tree! It must've fallen in the waves and protected the plant from decomposing.

I took in an excited breath, only to come up short. The breather's beeping had turned into a constant shriek.

I was out of air.

I shoved my fingers into the soil and dug around for the roots. *There.* I gave the plant a gentle tug, and it came up easily. A few leaves and branches snapped off. If I could get this plant to the surface intact, it would be a miracle.

A burn began to build in my chest as I pulled a transparent sleeve from my bag and wrapped it around the roots. Heat seared through me, shooting down my veins and bubbling at my lips.

Air. I need air.

I wouldn't be able to make it back through the shops and to the surface. I needed a quicker way out.

I glanced up. It was my only chance.

Tucking the plant under my arm, I kicked my flippers. Hard. The burn began to flame in my muscles.

Surface. Now.

I swam upward, reaching the blockage that had sealed in the courtyard. It was a section of plaster knocked askew from a nearby wall. I shoved the plaster with my shoulder, hoping it would give way and lead me up and into the light.

This building had been good to me. Surely it wouldn't let me down. Not now.

The breather stopped beeping, no longer needing to warn me. I was either dead or at the surface. Still, I had time. Years of diving experience had expanded my lungs. I held the small amount of oxygen in my chest. I had a few minutes left.

The plaster began to break free as I rammed into it, fragile from the hundreds of years of being submerged. I tore at the wall until I saw the glimmer of the sun. The surface!

I swam through the opening, but there wasn't time for a steady ascent. When I made it to the surface, I would have to take a recompression pill to neutralize the bubbles that were currently forming in my muscles and bloodstream. But that was the least of my problems.

The small amount of oxygen in my lungs was gone. My lungs were done. My legs were done.

I thought of Elysea. This was how she'd felt in her final moments. All around her, blue. All around me, blue. The burn. The ache. The terror.

But no one would find me down here. There was no one left *to* find me. I should've stayed down with Adrei. I didn't want to die alone, like my sister had.

I kicked and kicked, but the light seemed too far away. I heaved for another breath, but there was nothing left. I spat out the breather inside my dome, defeated.

This was it, my last moments. I thought of Mom and Dad.

And Elysea—even after everything she'd done. I hoped I would see them again, in whatever happens after death.

As my vision dimmed, my stubborn lungs tried one last time, heaving in a breath.

Air! I almost choked on it. Of course! A small amount of air had been used to inflate the dome.

My lungs expanded in relief. And the breath of oxygen was gone.

But it was enough.

I pushed for the surface.

CHAPTER TWO

LOR

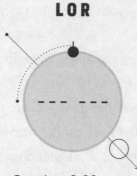

Sunday, 2:00 p.m.

I TRIED to ignore the bodies as they watched me from their tanks. I failed. Every damn time.

I hated this place. I hated the smell. I hated the dim lighting. I hated everything it stood for. Most of all, I hated death. But I didn't hate the bodies. It wasn't their fault they'd gotten caught up in Palindromena's scientists' scheme to save the planet. They believed they held our future in their hands because they sustained the crops. If the crops died, we all died.

I should've been used to this place by now. I'd been working, and living, down in Palindromena's basement, the Aquarium—as other employees affectionately called it—for two years. But I'd never get used to the dead.

The island of Palindromena had been named after the facility, which had developed a process to revive those who had died from drowning, if only for twenty-four hours. Most people wished for a last opportunity to say goodbye to their loved ones, and Palindromena could provide it, if you could afford

15

the fee of three thousand Notes. Those who did fork over the Notes claimed it was worth it, but the price had always seemed like extortion to me.

I knew the other employees thought the procedure was a miracle, allowing for more time—a gift from the Gods below—but there was nothing miraculous about the revival process. In the end, death was a bastard. And he never played fair.

Then why did I choose to surround myself with the dead?

I didn't deserve to be with the living.

It was time to admit defeat and get out of bed. I'd been awake since early this morning, after a routine nightmare. After two years of the same dream, you'd think it would lessen the impact. But I always woke yelling Calen's name. There was no relief, not even in sleep. Not that I deserved it. My unconscious mind loved reminding me of what I'd done. Last night was no exception.

When I'd finally faded into the numbness of sleep around four in the morning, *that* day rose bright as a sunrise. And it was as though it were only yesterday and not two years ago.

I was out on the cliffs of Palindromena. Rock climbing was the only time I felt completely myself. I wasn't "island boy." I was just Lor. On a climb, I could set my own pace, path and destination. A feeling of control that otherwise always felt out of reach. No one controlled my movements, no one set expectations. It was something that was all mine. Something I wanted. Unlike the island of Palindromena, which I felt held captive by.

16

My best friend, Calen, was not as confident a climber, but he was always by my side, matching my movements. Sometimes he looked different—his hair short or black or brown, rather than long and blond—and sometimes I knew I was dreaming, but he was always there. In every dream. Every night.

We'd been best friends since we were young, exploring the island while our mothers worked together. While most Palindromena employees lived on the nearby Equinox and traveled by boat each day, our families stayed at the island cottages to keep a close watch on the facility. Calen eventually moved to the Equinox to attend school there, and I stayed behind with my mother. I'd promised my grandparents that I would look after her once they were gone. I was all she had left.

Calen would visit every weekend, often bringing across friends from the Reef to see the infamous Palindromena. And while he'd become more interested in girls and boats and parties, I wanted to conquer the island. The last remaining challenge was Hallowed Mountain—the tallest of the island's cliffs. At an almost invert angle toward the top, climbing was strictly off-limits. But that didn't deter us.

In the dream, as in real life, our friends watched from below. They called out to us as an ominous cloud circled the island.

"We should climb down," Calen said, the fear visible in his eyes.

But just as I had two years ago, I said, "We're almost there. We'll make it to the top before the storm hits."

I kept climbing, desperate to see the world beyond the island. And Calen was tethered to me. But I was wrong.

We didn't make it.

The rain cloud broke, pummeling us with warm water. I wiped my face with the back of my hand and something salty coated my lips. I glanced down. My hands were coated in blood.

I looked to Calen, but the blood rain hadn't touched him. As he pulled himself up to my level, his grip slipped. Blood had coated the rock. He scrambled for a moment, trying to find a purchase, before falling. Below us, our friends screamed.

I quickly closed the rope belay to halt Calen's descent. I jerked as the rope pulled tight, his weight nearly wrenching me from the cliff.

"Hold on!" I cried as he dangled helplessly beside me.

He didn't respond, his face impassive, his eyes devoid of any life. That was when I realized the truth.

I was dreaming. And Calen was already dead. Still, I was desperate to change the outcome.

I tried to take in the rope and pull Calen back toward the rock's face, but my hands couldn't form a grip, they were too slick with blood.

"This is your fault," Calen said, his face still crushingly placid.

"No, no, no, no!"

But the rope went slack. And, as always, Calen was gone, falling to the water below, near where our friends watched on in horror.

I'd been stupid. Arrogant. Childish. Egotistical. Convinced I could climb any surface on the island. That I could conquer Palindromena. Then the world.

All it had taken was one wet, slippery rock. A long fall to the water. And one of my closest friends had died. Because of my arrogance. Because of me.

When I'd woken up, it had been a relief to be back in the Aquarium. I didn't close my eyes again, knowing I would only return to that cliff.

I rolled out the tension from my shoulders and reached for a book from the shelves behind my bunk. The library had been my grandparents' when they were still alive. A vast collection from the Old World. Stories about places you could travel on foot or by rover—and not by boat. Life was different back then. It wasn't about survival. It was about living. Truly living.

This damned new life was for the dead.

For today's diversion, I selected a book on the wonders of Old World architecture and how the government instructed cities to build taller structures to accommodate overcrowding. Some Old World buildings rose thousands of stories into the air. Of course, these were the first to topple in the Great Waves.

Then I began my daily routine of walking the aisles of the Aquarium to check for any leaks, my book never far from my face. There were hundreds of people who had drowned down here, awaiting the possibility of a final farewell with their loved ones. Due to the turbulent ocean, perilous dives and frequent storms, most deaths since the Great Waves were due to drowning and, therefore, suitable for revival. The facility would keep the bodies for ten years, then dispose of them. As one of the few remaining islands, space was at a premium. Palindromena couldn't house the dead forever.

Even if your loved ones couldn't afford to revive you, or if you'd died in a manner other than drowning, the facility owned your body after death. It was part of the arrangement with the Conservators of the Reefs. In exchange for providing human subjects for scientific research, the Reefs received fresh produce and vital medicine for life on the water. A fair trade, right? After all, what did you need your body for once you were dead?

As I walked the glowing aisles, I kept my eyes trained on my book, trying to avoid any movement in my periphery. While the dead wore their hair under a tight translucent cap, some strands would inevitably escape and float around their faces like seaweed. The luminous tank water was made from crushed coral, which prevented the bodies from decomposing. They bobbed up and down in the liquid, seemingly reanimated.

Worst of all were their eyes. Open, they watched with colorless irises, pupils contracted to a pinhole. As I turned a corner, one of those eyes blinked.

I stumbled backward, dropping my book and crashing into a cart of chemicals behind me. The bottles clanged and rolled onto the floor. Luckily, none shattered.

The entire basement echoed my mistake. The corpse laughed.

"Raylan!" I snapped, realizing the face belonged to someone standing behind an empty tank and not inside it. I picked up my book and shoved it into my back pocket. "What in cursed waters do you think you're doing?"

Raylan stepped out from behind the tank, then doubled over in laughter. His tawny-brown skin was highlighted by the illuminated tanks, his cropped curly hair appearing a bluish black. "You should've seen your face!" He clutched his chest and bugged out his eyes in a ridiculous imitation of me. He was wearing the typical Warden uniform of a beige T-shirt with the Palindromena logo of two hands cupping a leaf printed on the front. He'd added some Reef flair by looping a black cord around his neck with a giant garseal tooth dangling from it. It looked more like a weapon than jewelry and contrasted with his easy grin, which was usually at my expense.

"Playing with the dead isn't funny, Ray." But I couldn't suppress my joy at seeing him. Someone to talk to other than the deceased. Although Ray was eighteen, with only a year separating us, he seemed so much younger than me. I assumed that was the consequence of guilt and the dead as my constant companions. "Why are you screwing around down here?" I asked.

"I brought you some fish cakes," he said, holding out a small metal container as though it were some sort of peace offering. "Thought you might want to try my latest batch."

I forced myself not to snatch the container out of his hands and devour the entire contents. Ray's fish cakes were the best thing in this sodden world.

"Thank you," I said with my mouth full of fish, because I couldn't help myself. "They're amazing."

He grinned. "I made them for the party last night. You should've come."

My shoulders tensed and I swallowed roughly. "I told you, I was busy."

"Busy? Doing what?"

"Doing what I always do: guarding the basement." I hated lying to him, but I couldn't tell him why I was down here. My friends had seen everything that day. *I'd* forced Calen to climb that mountain, and didn't listen when he wanted to climb down. While my subconscious mind liked to add some gory details, my dreams were annoyingly accurate. I often wondered if the memory would ever fade, or if I'd be forced to relive that day for the rest of my life.

While I couldn't hide from what happened, I *could* hide from everyone who knew me. So I'd disappeared from the world.

Ray studied me for a moment before asking, "Why don't they ever let you have a night off? I know the Director can be intimidating, but I'm sure she'd understand. You need a life outside this place."

But that was exactly the point of being down here. I couldn't—*wouldn't*—leave the Aquarium. I didn't deserve to have a life beyond this damp, dim basement. I didn't deserve to enjoy the world outside when I'd stolen it from Calen. In truth, I also didn't deserve Ray's friendship, even though I couldn't seem to push him away.

When he'd first come down to the Aquarium six months ago, he'd been looking for somewhere to hide out after his first revival. The grief of the patient's family had been too much for him. While my initial instinct had been to ignore Ray, I'd found myself stepping out of the shadows to console him. I told him it was this place, it drew death toward us like the tide to the shore. And all we could do was wait for tomorrow and hope it would be brighter.

Ironic, considering I would never allow myself to leave the basement. Living down here, away from—*almost*—everyone, was my penance.

"I have a life," I said finally. "And I need the money." It was a thin excuse, and not at all true, but I hoped he'd accept it. As he usually did.

"For what? More Old World books? I think you've got those covered." He chuckled. "*Covered*, get it?"

"That's not funny." Although I smiled. It was impossible not to when Ray was around.

He slapped my bare forearm. "You're so pale you're beginning to look like them!" He was from one of the Reefs—the Equinox—and his ochre-brown skin had further deepened from years on the water.

"Thanks for the support, Ray." I'd heard that from him before. *As pale as a corpse.* Or my favorite: *wearing the skin of the dead.*

His smile faded. Had I kept him at a distance for too long? After all, we'd been friends for six months; eventually my evasiveness was going to wear thin. So I said, "Maybe next time." Even though that could never happen.

"Great!" Luckily, he was easy to appease. I worried about the day he would push for more answers.

"So how was the party?" I asked, changing the subject.

"The best." He beamed. Whenever he spoke about the Equinox, he got that look on his face. "I met this really cute guy. You should've come! There were lots of nice girls there."

"Uh-huh," I said noncommittally. I wasn't even sure I'd remember how to talk to a girl, let alone flirt with one.

Ray followed behind me, his footsteps heavy as he shuffled along. A few years ago, he'd been in an accident. Two angling boats had collided, and his left foot had been caught between them, shattering the bones in his ankle. While he got around well enough, I'd often see him grimacing in pain at the end of a long day.

"You doing okay?" I asked.

"Me?" He gave me his trademark grin, the gap flashing between his front teeth. "I'm always good, bud."

While I knew he didn't like talking about his accident, I hated seeing him in pain. Not the pain of his injury, but losing the one thing that made him who he was.

Ray's passion for the ocean could be traced back to his ancestors who were seafarers even before the Great Waves. Ray used to be a spearfisherman, spending more hours deep below the surface than above it. But he didn't want to go back into the ocean after his accident, knowing he wouldn't be able to swim as he once did. He needed the balance of two strong feet to work deep-sea flippers, or so he'd told me. And for that, he would have to heal the damaged tendons in his foot, and the best place to research healing was Palindromena.

While scientists had found a way to repair damage to the brain and lungs after drowning, it wasn't permanent; the tissue would return to its previous state after only twenty-four hours. When Ray wasn't working as a Warden, he spent most of his free time helping out in the medical division, hoping there was a way to apply what the scientists had learned about repairing the brain and lungs to heal injured cells and tissue of the living.

"Who was your client today?" I asked, changing the topic.

"A really nice lady," Ray said fondly. Despite being constantly surrounded by death, he still empathized with the clients and patients. I wondered if that would fade, in time. A common consequence of working in this place was that you began to see death as something ordinary—something that happened every day. Something that didn't destroy families and futures.

"And the patient—the revived?"

"Her son." This time his voice was definitely soft. "Drowned six months ago. The mother wanted me there with her at the end."

"Really?" Usually the clients wanted to be alone with their revived loved ones.

"I explained that wasn't the way it worked. We don't want patients to realize what's happening. And you know I don't like being around the revived." He made a face. "It creeps me out."

I raised my eyebrow. "How many times do I have to tell

you that the revived don't smell? They're alive, completely. For twenty-four hours." Until they weren't.

"They smell different to me." He tapped his nose. "My mother says I have a sense for these things."

"Your mother is afraid of her own shadow."

He held a finger up, opened his mouth to argue, then said, "Fair point."

Ray had told me that his mother still believed in the Old Gods. She hated Palindromena and how they used the dead for money. She had visited just after Ray started here, begging him to quit his job and return to the Equinox. But she'd spent only an hour on the island before retreating to her boat. She claimed the whole place reeked of death. It was probably the smell of the crops she found so unfamiliar.

Still, she wasn't wrong. This island was death, and death was this island. They couldn't be separated from each other.

I didn't believe in the Gods below or the Old Gods. It was a waste of time. We determined our own fate. No one knew that better than I did.

"So while I'm here . . ." Ray cleared his throat. "I need to ask you a favor."

"No," I said, without looking at him.

"Oh, come on!" He slung an arm around my shoulder. He had to stand on his toes to reach. "It's an easy favor, bud."

"Somehow I doubt that." From what Ray told me, he was always getting into trouble. His casual honesty went against Palindromena's penchant for secrets.

"It is. I swear on the Gods below." The cockiness had leeched from his voice. His open face was surprisingly cautious.

He was worried about my reaction. This couldn't be good.

"Come on, then," I said. "Out with it."

His eyes darted to the furnace behind me. We'd found ourselves at the back of the Aquarium, where the previously revived bodies were stored before being buried at the temple at the bottom of the sea. With little land left, it was an honor to be buried there, but few could afford the price the facility set, which created a divide between the people who lived on the Reefs and the workers on the isle who could afford it.

The dead couldn't be revived a second time; their hearts couldn't take it. If relatives couldn't afford to move their loved ones to the temple, they would be destroyed in the furnace. Luckily, that wasn't part of my job description. Nessandra, the Director of Palindromena, took care of body disposal.

"Umm," Ray said, his eyes landing on everywhere but me. "I have a client tomorrow—"

"Absolutely not." I jammed my hands into my pants pockets, putting two and two together.

"Come ooonnnn. It's just one client. One measly client. All you have to do is babysit. It's easy. Everything is automated." He grinned and tapped the screen on the metal echolink on his wrist. The technology of a Warden: it tracked a patient's revival. I hated the sight of them.

"Great, then you can do it tomorrow." I started walking again.

Ray stumbled. "I need you to welcome the client, make sure they're calm and—"

"I do tank maintenance, I'm not a Warden. And you know it's against the rules." As a Warden, you were responsible for the patient for the duration of their revival. You were to ensure they didn't realize they were once dead or leave the facility. Working at Palindromena was a coveted position, as you would earn five times more than any other profession. But the job came with a steep price. Which Ray was well aware of as a trainee Warden. "I can't believe you're even asking me this. Nessandra would have your head."

"We don't have to tell the Director," he said softly.

Nessandra, or the Queen of Death, as the employees called her, had strict rules to protect her company from any critics on the Reefs. Aside from Ray, she was the only person who knew I was down here. I couldn't jeopardize my one refuge.

"No." I faced death enough down here; I wouldn't see it up close as a Warden. What Palindromena was doing was wrong. They masqueraded as a company that cared about your loss. But they didn't. Your grief was merely a means to a profitable end. And everyone paid the price. The dead *and* the living.

"*Please*, Lor," Ray said, his voice low, imploring.

I stopped walking and turned. It wasn't often Ray was serious. "What's going on?"

His brow furrowed. "A doctor is visiting the Equinox from the Northern Reefs. I booked an appointment with her weeks ago." He took a breath. "She specializes in rehabilitation."

I glanced at his left foot. Before coming to Palindromena, Ray had seen every doctor within two thousand miles. No one had a solution. And while Ray was hopeful he could heal his foot here, this was the first time he had mentioned *rehab* rather than researching a remedy. Was he preparing to move on? Did he realize there was another future out there for him, that he didn't have to be stuck in the past? He didn't have to be like me?

"I wasn't supposed to be rostered tomorrow," he said, "but a revival was just booked in. I'm the most suitable, as I'm a similar age to the client and all the other young Wardens are busy. You know I wouldn't ask if I didn't have to, but I'm already in deep shit with the Director. I can't lose my position here."

Part of the mystery to Palindromena was intentional. Scientists wanted the process to seem mystical and blessed by the Gods below. Last week, Ray had been put on probation for telling a client that if you took a body out of the tanks for more than a few hours without being revived, then it would start to decompose and liquefy in front of your eyes. The more years since their death, the quicker the decomposition; it was something I'd once told him in passing. Raylan hadn't meant to scare the client, but his loose lips had lost Nessandra a precious customer. Many people on the Equinox already didn't trust Palindromena. And word of mouth was everything. They had to feel their deceased loved ones were safe here, and that their taxes were being well spent.

"I'm sorry," I said. "But I can't leave my post." For years, Calen had been my one connection to the world outside the island. Now that he was dead, it was like that world no longer existed.

Ray was the only reminder of what lay outside the basement walls.

"Please." He pressed his palms together, almost in prayer. "It's twenty-four hours and then you can return to this dingy basement and hide away from life."

I crossed my arms over my chest. "I'm not hiding."

"Really? Then why don't you ever leave the Aquarium?" There was a challenge in his voice.

I'd always thought I'd fooled him. Perhaps I didn't give him enough credit.

"Of course I leave." I forced a laugh. "I leave all the time. Don't be ridiculous."

"Lor," he said slowly, carefully, "I've seen your bunk in the back."

I wanted to snap at him, to tell him to get out. Tell him that he was wrong. I didn't live down here. But I faltered, the lies not forming.

"I won't tell anyone," he said quickly, realizing my fear. "I'll keep your secret. I understand if you don't want to talk about it."

I huffed. He didn't understand at all. How could he? I'd spent the last six months lying to him—my friend. A friend who was asking for my help.

I could see the desperation behind his eyes as his chance to see this doctor was slipping away. I knew what it felt like to be haunted by your past. I wished I could free him of it.

I should have said no. I should have pushed him away. Never seen Ray again.

But the thought of a silent future that stretched out for years and years burrowed a cavernous hole within me. I needed something to hold on to. And that was Ray.

If I showed him that I could leave the Aquarium, perhaps I could keep our friendship for a little while longer. I knew I couldn't keep up this charade forever, but at least I would have tomorrow.

"Fine," I said. "I'll cover for you. Just this once."

His face lit up. "Seriously?"

I nodded like it was nothing. Like stepping out of this self-imposed prison wasn't an insult to Calen's memory. When he died, I'd promised to never forget him. And that I would pay for taking his life.

"Thank you!" Ray slapped my back. "Just pretend to be me for twenty-four hours. Your job as a Warden is to guide the client through the revival process and be there in case anything goes wrong. And it won't. Smooth sailing, bud. Smooth sailing."

Only time would tell if I'd live to regret this.

CHAPTER THREE

TEMPEST

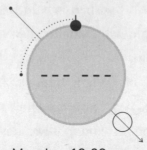

Monday, 10:00 a.m.
Two hours before revival

I STILL COULDN'T BELIEVE my plant had been acquired by the Equinox Conservators for a staggering four thousand Notes. Normally, I had to beg someone to take my found goods off my hands. Soggy books, shards of plates, shreds of material—none of that was worth much. But a plant . . . A plant was everything. It was worth more than I'd managed to cobble together in the past five years combined. Elysea would've been proud.

While I didn't think the plant would produce anything edible, it meant something had survived down there. It would give the Conservators hope. While the crops on Palindromena fed the nearby Reefs, including the Equinox, there wasn't enough to feed the growing populations. We needed to find an alternative food source. And if plants could live underwater, then we wouldn't be tied to the island of Palindromena.

The Equinox had been struggling for years now. While we

were the closest Reef to Palindromena, we needed something to trade for food. All the nearby dive sites had been pillaged dry. In the next few years we'd only be living off fish and seaweed hauled from the deep. Adequate, but not very satisfying. Not compared to the Reefs farther south, which still had sunken cities at their fingertips, allowing them to pay for root vegetables, rice, fruit and herbs. All grown on Palindromena.

I wasn't sure how the Equinox would survive into the next decade. But that wasn't my problem. At least, not right now.

When I'd brought the plant to the midday auction yesterday, the Equinox Conservators were elated. They peppered me with questions.

Did you find more land?

Where did you find the plant?

Are there more plants?

Take us there. Now!

Okay, so they weren't all questions.

I gave them the coordinates of the dive site, knowing I had no need to return.

While the citizens of the Equinox were expected to do the physical work, if there was anything ever *truly* valuable, then the Conservators would shut down the site and send in their own team to ensure proper care was taken with an object's retrieval. My building would be crawling with conservation divers within the hour. Not that there was anything left to find.

I wished my little plant well when I handed it over. While

the waxy green plant should mean more to me than the dyed woven sheets of seaweed in my hand, they didn't. Notes were all that mattered now.

Most of the Notes would go toward reviving Elysea. Every decision I'd made in the last two years was about reviving my dead sister. I wasn't sure who I'd be once I left the memory of her behind. I wasn't sure who I *wanted* to be.

I shook my head. I'd worry about tomorrow later. Today, I had a date with Palindromena.

I hadn't slept at all last night. My body was fueled by anticipation. I was going to see Elysea again. I'd finally get the truth about my parents.

Once back in my quarters, I tipped the Notes from my bag onto the bed. I counted three thousand Notes and shoved them into my clam jewelry box. I flittered my fingers across the remaining one thousand. No more scavenging for moldy seaweed and fish scraps from the canteen's trash.

I placed the jewelry box in my oilskin bag and took one more look around the room. I may have removed most of Elysea's personal belongings, but she was still frustratingly present. She'd painted the rusted metal walls green with seaweed paste, to remind us of the times when there were entire forests and not a few trees left on the remaining islands. Of a time when there had been fields of flowers. But that was centuries ago. Blue was our reality now. Water our home. Green had disappeared into its depths. Or so I'd thought, until I'd found that plant.

34

Even the way the glasses were positioned on the narrow metal shelves reminded me of her. She was always reprimanding me for placing the cups right side up, claiming her prized coffee tasted salty from the dust in the air. If the cups were placed upside down, salt-dust couldn't collect in them.

I hadn't understood the issue. Why was salty coffee bad? Everything in our world was not only awash in blue, but crystallized in salt. Everything was crunchy, crusty, dry, hard. Our mother had taught us to shake the crystal dust from our blankets each evening before climbing into bed, although you couldn't prevent the salt from lining your lips overnight and gluing your eyelids shut.

Now I grabbed her favorite shell mug and flipped it so salt could collect in the glass. Elysea wasn't ever coming back to reprimand me. No one was.

I left my quarters and headed toward the crowded harbor.

The sun was high in the sky, and the air was already thick with humidity and salt, like breathing through a wet blanket. My lungs dragged, feeling dull and heavy, like holding my breath underwater. I brushed tendrils of dry, briny black hair behind my ears.

I walked along one of the rusty gangplanks that was once the skeleton of an Old World building. After the Great Waves, survivors from all over the world congregated on the few remaining islands, uniting various cultures. But they soon realized that the land was best saved for growing crops, and so the Reefs were built from bits and pieces of sunken Old

35

World cities hauled from below. Now large anchors tethered the floating metal structure to the land my ancestors once called home.

Around fifteen thousand Reefs existed today, with each zoned to the closest island in a five-hundred-mile radius. Anything beyond that was too far for crops to travel before they perished. And the Equinox was the biggest Reef of its kind, home to over ten thousand people.

I passed by the center of the Equinox, a circular building that housed the Conservators' hall on the bottom floor with an atrium for the communal canteen above it. On the roof sat a towering lightning rod, which generated power for the turbines beneath the Equinox—our only form of electricity. Branching off from the main building were several sprawling residential arms, each cluttered with metal houses. The houses had curved roofs like the back of a spoon, to aid in the collection of rainwater, used for drinking and washing.

Kids, younger than school-age, were dotted along the edge of the gangways that crisscrossed between the residential arms, fishing rods dangling from their small hands. They'd be lucky if they caught a minuscule sugarfish. You had to leave the harbor to catch anything decent; the fish were afraid of the whine of the turbines.

All the older kids attended the composite Equinox school—an open-air classroom bolted onto the side of the Conservator hall. The classroom was packed; you could hardly see the metal grate the children were sitting on. I overheard the teacher mention the name *Ilani* as I walked by. The Ice Nation.

My ancestors had once lived close to Ilani, and it was, therefore, one of the first lands to be submerged. Before then, the Old World had been on the brink of war, with land at a premium and every nation grossly overpopulated. The only untouched land was locked beneath a slab of ice—Ilani—and it had once covered more than a third of the planet.

The governments all came to an agreement to unlock the land and end the global population and resource crisis. Their plan had been to defrost a portion of Ilani, but the flare bomb had been too effective. The ice melted entirely, raising the ocean globally and killing billions.

Some people could say the governments got exactly what they wanted in reducing the population. But I wouldn't dare insult the dead by saying such things.

When I was at school, I saw pictures of the land my ancestors once lived on, and it was difficult to grasp something so vast and dry. Different regions had existed across the enormous continent with millions upon millions of buildings cluttering its surface.

Now there was nothing left of that land, aside from the fifty new islands that had been created when the Great Waves struck. They were once mountains, or cliffs, that had managed to keep their heads above water. Most islands were now owned by private research facilities—in hope of finding a way to prolong our life upon this waterlogged world.

One such island was Palindromena—my destination for the day.

I'd grown up a child of Palindromena employees; my dad had been Head Warden, managing the revival program, and my mom had been the Lead Botanist, tending to the few crops left to feed this part of the world. Even though my parents had worked there, neither my mom nor my dad would speak about their work in any detail. Mom used to tell me not to dwell on death and only think of the light, placing a flower behind my ear—a flower she had pulled from the fields on Palindromena.

Not long after, she had died in a storm along with my father. And Elysea had drowned three years later. I wished Mom had told me more about the place I was soon to visit. It might have quelled the panic spiking up my spine.

The *Sunrise* stood out among the hundreds of moored boats in the harbor. While most vessels were made from scraps of land vehicles from the Old World, the *Sunrise* was sleek and shiny. An expensive boat provided by Palindromena. A parting gift from my dead parents. They'd been on our old dive boat the night they were caught in a storm and thrown into the side of the Equinox. I suppose you could say I was lucky they'd taken the older boat. But I didn't believe in luck; I believed in the Gods below and what they determined for my future. Why they had chosen to take my parents *and* my sister, I wasn't sure.

Today, I hoped to find that out.

While I had sold everything belonging to my family, I

couldn't bear to part with the *Sunrise*. Too many memories were attached to this boat, like the barnacles that clung to its belly. When we were young, my parents took my sister and me out at sunset to watch the silvery garseals leap through the air. And after my parents died, Elysea and I spent our days with our feet dangling in the water, imagining a different life. A better one.

Letting go of the *Sunrise* would sever all ties with my past. I needed the *Sunrise*'s steady pulse beneath my feet, like a heartbeat.

I climbed onto the boat's deck and started the engine. The *Sunrise*, like most vessels, ran on solar power. As I left the dock, a vibration was automatically sent through the waves—a signal that would transmit to the Watchtower. No one entered or left the Equinox undetected.

"Equinox Watchtower," a woman's smooth voice called over the transmitter before I had even shifted from the dock. "Equinox Watchtower to pier B20. Acknowledge."

"This is Quicksilver *Sunrise*," I said. "I acknowledge."

The Watchtower tracked the comings and goings of boats, ensuring the weight of the floating metal island could support ten thousand people. Weight restrictions needed to be upheld, down to how many fish were farmed each day and how many children a family could have. The Conservators wouldn't risk sinking the Equinox to the bottom of the ocean like the buildings of the past.

If a family had more than two children, they had a choice:

try to survive on their own, untethered to any Reef, or hope another Reef accepted new residents. Either way, they had to leave the Equinox.

"What is your destination today, *Sunrise*?" she asked.

"Palindromena," I said with a heavy sigh. I waited for her response. Most people on the Equinox either disliked or feared the facility. While they needed the island's produce and medical supplies, like recompression pills, they thought bringing back the dead was against the Gods' wishes. Both Old and New. But unless we learned how to grow crops underwater, those on land held all the power.

"Right." Her voice was curt. I was just another person giving Palindromena exactly what they wanted. More money. And a further hold on the Equinox's future. "What time will you return?"

"Before tomorrow evening."

"The time is noted," the woman said. "We will expect you then."

She didn't have to say it. If I failed to return on time, no one would come looking for me. If my boat was snagged in a storm, if I was thrown into swirling waters, if I found myself caught between a creature's teeth, that was not their problem. Many people disappeared in the waves as they searched to improve their lives. The ocean between the Reefs was unpredictable, with storms looming on nearly every horizon. It was easy to meet a watery end.

There were also the stories of something *other*. Something in the water whose hunger couldn't be satisfied. But they were merely stories. The sea was dangerous enough on its own; it didn't need the creative minds of those half drunk on ragar at the Spring Tide to fashion new reasons to fear the ocean.

If I didn't return to the Equinox tomorrow night, my death would be noted, my belongings seized and my rooms reassigned to someone else. No one would bat an eyelid. In fact, the Conservators would see it as further proof that you shouldn't engage in Palindromena's services.

"Acknowledged," I said to the Watchtower.

"Sail away, then, *Sunrise*."

Once I cleared the moored boats within the harbor, I looked back to the Equinox. The numerous suspended residential arms that connected to the circular Conservator hall made the structure look like the body of a sea creature with long-reaching tentacles. Even with its enormous anchors, there was a subtle sway to the floating city.

South of the Equinox, I could see a line of blinking silver buoys that comprised Palindromena's sonar perimeter and ran their territory's boundary. While other islands used tracking systems to monitor boat activity, Palindromena used theirs to detain any vessels that crossed from other regions. In the decades before the perimeter, boats would travel to Palindromena, ambush the workers and steal crops for themselves. Since then, Palindromena enforced a law that only facility-built boats with embedded sensors could journey through their demarcation line; any other vessels would be met with their weaponized fleet.

Beyond the silver buoys lay the only ungoverned passage of ocean, called the Untied Sea. Ruled by Remorans, ruthless nomads who ransacked vessels for parts and left a trail of sunken boats in their wake, you'd have to be incredibly desperate or stupid to cross it.

I turned back to the direction of Palindromena. The striking island could be glimpsed through the salty haze. Four sheer cliff faces punched up from the water like determined fingers, as if the land had reached for the sky with its final breath. In its "palm" were the crops that fed all the nearby Reefs. Mom used to talk about *her* plants for hours, as though they were her children. How they each needed different amounts of water, sunlight and feed. When I was little, I wanted to be a botanist like her. I liked the idea of bringing something new into the world.

I gritted my teeth and swallowed down the memory. Today I would have my answers. I would find out what happened to my parents.

I couldn't help but wonder if somehow Elysea knew I was coming, and whether she sensed my fury.

CHAPTER FOUR

TEMPEST

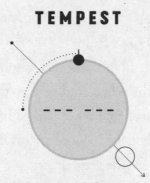

Monday, 11:00 a.m.
One hour before revival

AFTER AN HOUR of sailing, I approached Palindromena's dock. My heartbeat reverberated through my body like the boat's engine beneath my feet.

Whump. Whump. Whump. Whump. Whump.

I worried my heart might give in, but if this was to be my last moment, then what better place to die? For who knew life and death more intimately than Palindromena?

While the Equinox didn't care about missing citizens, Palindromena did. They were responsible for searching their territory for anyone who had met a dire end. Palindromena's retrieval boats were stationed at various points around the sonar perimeter and would scour the ocean nightly to pull bodies from the water. They would then preserve the bodies in tanks, and wait for their loved ones.

Like Elysea. But not my parents. An entire night had passed before the remains of their boat had been found, and by then, their bodies were gone. Most likely, they had been devoured by some sea creature.

And it was all Elysea's fault.

Four months after Elysea died, I'd found out she'd seen our parents before their boat had crashed into the side of the Equinox. A fact she'd never told me. I had to hear it from her best friend, after Elysea had died. More importantly, she'd told him she was responsible for the accident.

She was the reason my parents were dead.

Today I would find out exactly what happened.

I said a quick prayer to the Gods below, hoping my heart would hang in there—long enough to see Elysea's face one more time. I bit the inside of my cheek, summoning my fury to burn away any thrill of excitement; I wouldn't allow sentiment to distract me from what I needed.

As I drew into the dock, spindly metal arms moved through the water to guide my vessel. Palindromena was expecting me, reading the pulse of my boat as clearly as the light of the coral below.

The pier was made of polished recycled metal, similar to the *Sunrise*. The mass of silver was blinding in the sunlight. I cut my engine and lifted a hand to block the glare. While I couldn't see any signs of the facility behind the sheer cliff face, the building couldn't be far. The whole island wasn't more than ten miles in diameter.

The pier was cluttered with other vessels, including two bulky retrieval boats with nets on either side of the hull. I shivered, thinking how Elysea had been scooped from the water by the same kind of vessel. No doubt my parents had kept the harsh truth of Palindromena from us so that we didn't dwell on the dangers of the ocean and how death was a mere breath away.

When the *Sunrise*'s hull nudged the pier, the steel arms steadied the boat against the tide.

A woman with glossy black hair in a blunt bob approached my boat. She wore a beige pantsuit almost the same color as her sandy complexion. In the near-midday heat, her cheeks bloomed with pink.

I felt underdressed in my threaded-seaweed wrap dress that didn't cover much of my diving skin.

"Hello," the woman said. Her brown eyes narrowed as she read from a digital tablet. "Tempest Alerin?" She was probably checking my appearance against the paperwork I'd filled out yesterday with the Palindromena rep.

I'd been lucky an opening had been available on such short notice. Immediately after I'd sold my plant, I'd visited the rep's boat located not far from the Reef. The Conservators didn't allow Palindromena business to be run on the Equinox. After I'd given the rep all of my details, they'd provided a welcome pack to study overnight. It contained information to help me fool Elysea into thinking she was alive. Such as the date she died, the weather, and the latest news at the time. It was like peeking into the past. A past I wished I could return to. So I could stop my sister from getting on that boat.

"That's me," I said, grabbing my oilskin bag.

"I'm Selna." She gave me a warm smile as I stepped onto the pier. "Welcome to Palindromena. Here." She held out two opaque pills. "They're Land Legs. They'll help with the stationary sickness."

I glanced down at my legs, confused. But then I felt a pull toward the side. I stumbled, and Selna caught my arm.

"Happens all the time," she said, and pressed the Land Legs into my hand. "They dissolve under your tongue. It will help." She patted my arm as I attempted to stand upright. "Trust me."

Aside from recompression pills, I wasn't used to seeing medicine. Even though Mom had worked at Palindromena, she believed only in what the earth provided: fish eggs for immunity and dried seaweed powder to fight off crystal lung. She wouldn't allow Dad to bring any medicine into our quarters.

I held one pill up to the sunlight. "What's in it?"

"Magic," Selna replied with a smile and a wink.

I hadn't believed in magic since I was five years old, when I thought schools of flarefish were sunken shooting stars. I would sit on the edge of the deck with my parents, my feet dangling in the water, watching as they swam by. Since my parents died, the light of the flarefish now blended into the darkness—meaningless, like the constellations our ancestors had once revered.

"Do you have the payment?" Selna asked.

"Yes." I handed her the Notes from my jewelry case. I'd never see that amount of money again.

She counted the Notes, then typed something on her tablet.

"Come," she said, tucking the tablet into her pants pocket. She led the way from the pier toward the mass of green in between the rock faces.

I tried to follow, but nearly fell backward into the boat. Selna smiled but said nothing else. A few stumbling steps later, and I placed the pills under my tongue.

Selna led me to a parked rover, similar to Old World land vehicles. Two arms reached out on either side with pipes connecting to a rusted tank in the back. A crop feeder. Had my mom driven one of these? Why did it seem familiar?

"Climb on in," Selna said, noticing my hesitation. I did as I was told.

I coughed as the rover kicked up dirt along the dry road leading away from the beach. The thrum of the engine was similar to the hum of the *Sunrise* beneath my feet. It was somewhat reassuring.

"First visit to the land, eh?" Selna spoke loudly over the engine.

I wanted to reply, but my response was caught in a wheeze.

"Don't worry, the dust will pass soon."

She was right. We made a turn and entered a vast field of crops.

An obsidian dome sat nestled in the cliffs behind the crops, a black pearl held within the island's clutches. But that wasn't what attracted my attention. I'd never seen so much green. Except in my dreams.

Mom used to call them dreams of the forgotten—memories inherited from our ancestors, passed down through our bloodline to remind us of our history. How else would I know the crisp smell of a forest? Or the sight of a vast meadow covered in purple flowers?

Dad didn't believe in my dreams, or the Gods below. "How do we know what Tempe dreams is what the Old World looked like? How do we know she sees green as you see green?" He had touched my forehead with a laugh. "Maybe what she sees is barnacle pink."

Mom would then shush him and tuck me back into bed, telling me to continue to dream of days gone by. "One day we'll return to that world," she would whisper against my cheek. "Be happy in your dreams, Li'l Tempe."

And for a long time, I was.

Once we reached the dome, Selna pulled the rover to a stop. This was it. Palindromena.

I couldn't see anything through the tinted glass. I swallowed a few times to wet my dry throat.

"There's nothing to fear," Selna said, coming around to help me off the rover. "We're here to support you through this time."

But I wasn't afraid. At least, not in the way she thought I was. I wasn't afraid of saying goodbye to Elysea. I was afraid I wouldn't get what I came for.

Selna ushered me through security and into the high-arched foyer. I halted, shocked by what towered in front of me.

"It's beautiful, isn't it?" Selna asked, backtracking. She pressed her palms together. "Praise the Gods below for protecting our island."

I covered my mouth with my hand, speechless.

At the center of the dome-shaped foyer was a sprawling tree, its black branches spiraled out like arms, pointing to different levels of the building that split off from the foyer. The branches were curved, so different from the Equinox's mess of sharp metal edges. And the air smelled different.

No salt, I realized.

I took in a deep breath, enjoying the clear air as it traveled easily through my lungs. All year round, the humidity was like breathing through a wet rag. In here, I felt lighter, buoyant—similar to the joy of a dive.

Flowers and vines knotted around the towering white columns and across sparkling tiled walls. Was this where Mom pulled flowers for me? Through the tree's foliage I could glimpse the blue sky through the glass ceiling. Green and blue together again.

Just like my plant.

"How?" I rocked back on my heels. "How did this tree survive?"

Selna gave me a coy smile. "We'll explain in orientation."

Before I could look around any further, she directed me toward a dimly lit theatre. As soon as I entered, the screen came to life, words appearing in red.

A dying planet.

A booming soundtrack crashed all around me.

"Take a seat," Selna whispered, gesturing to an empty chair. A few other people sat in the theater, enraptured by the flickering screen.

The video went on to depict the tragedy of the Great Waves, which all but destroyed modern society. Buildings fell, technology failed, animals perished, and we were forced to scavenge for what little remained to build a new world atop the ocean.

But the New World is not unkind.

I scoffed at that. Tell that to my parents, my sister and everyone who lost their lives because of the turbulent sea.

With the rising water rose a new power. The Gods below. They have blessed our island. They have given us Palindromena. They have offered a new beginning. Death is no longer the final goodbye.

I knew the spiel. Late at night, I'd overheard Mom and Dad having heated arguments over Palindromena's belief that the Gods below were to thank for the ability to bring back those who had drowned. Dad said he'd never seen any evidence of these submerged deities that Palindromena claimed kept their island safe from destruction. He said the revival process was science, and nothing more.

I wondered if they had time to think of the Gods below when their boat upturned, sending them into the waters? Or were their last thoughts of their treacherous daughter? Did they even have time to think of me?

The remainder of the video focused on the stages of grief and how I would feel when faced with my loved one, temporarily alive, but it didn't reveal anything about how the revival process *actually* worked. Although I already knew the water in the tanks ensured the bodies didn't decompose after death.

After the video, Selna left me alone in a waiting room adjoined to Elysea's "recovery room." Paintings of happy, smiling faces surrounded me. Families coming together. Loved ones reunited. I turned away, feeling my body sway and my head pound. Were the Land Legs wearing off?

I had only been there for a few minutes when another woman entered. She was fair-skinned with short blond hair, fine features, high cheekbones and wide-set blue eyes. She was strikingly beautiful, if a little severe-looking.

She smoothed her palms down her crisp white jacket. "Tempest Alerin," she said. "I haven't seen you since you were about this"—she held her hand near the top of her black pants—"high."

"I'm sorry?"

"You don't recognize me?"

I shook my head.

"Forgive me." She pressed her lips together. "You must've been too young to remember. I worked with your parents." *Mom and Dad used to bring me here?* "I'm Nessandra," she added, "the Director of Palindromena."

"Really?" When my parents spoke of their boss, I always imagined someone white-haired and weathered. A scientist in a lab coat.

But she appeared untouched by the sun. She didn't spend

her days on boats and diving for scraps. Palindromena was clearly flourishing. Making money from the dead, like my parents had.

"It's true." She smiled. "I'm blessed to be in charge of this entire operation." Pride brought warmth to her voice and color to her pale cheeks.

"Oh." I was unsure what else to say. I wasn't expecting to meet anyone as important as the Director of Palindromena. I hoped she wouldn't see through my guise of a grieving sister. I couldn't imagine interrogations were part of the company's motto.

"I wanted to say hello when I heard you were coming in." She gently took my hands in hers. "I'm so sorry for your loss."

I nearly asked whose death she was referring to, but I didn't think she'd appreciate my dark humor. "Thank you."

"I'm sure you'll find what you're looking for here." When I stared blankly, she added, "Closure."

I didn't like the way her blue eyes darted across my face, studying me. I pulled my hands free and tucked them under my arms.

"It's not what you expected, is it?" She gestured around us. "Palindromena?"

"No." I couldn't remember coming to the facility when I was younger, although apparently I had. Were all my dreams of forests simply memories of this tree and the crops outside?

"Ahh." She noticed my focus on the tree through the open door. "She's a beauty, isn't she? The last black-bark tree, and over five hundred years old. My parents built the facility around her; they were the founders of Palindromena," she said, her eyes full of memories. "Fifty years ago, they discovered a protein in coral that not only prevented dead organic matter from further decomposition, but even showed signs of repairing the damage. And this healing was increased tenfold if you reset the life cycle of an organism by restarting its heart." She smiled at me as though I understood. I didn't. "Did you know trees have a pulse?" she asked.

"They have a heart?"

She laughed, but not unkindly. "No, but some trees have a heartbeat." She placed her hand over her chest. "Like how blood moves through us, fluids are pumped around the tree over a twenty-four-hour cycle. This is all controlled by a command center of cells, similar to our brain. While trying to revive dead crops, my parents found that when they restarted a tree's pulse, the command center came back online. The 'brain' was healed. However, the renewed life lasted only for the duration of one day-night cycle. And twenty-four hours is not long enough for trees to bear fruit." She laughed again.

When I didn't join in, she continued. "And so my parents turned their thoughts to other implementations, where twenty-four hours of life would be a precious time and not a disappointment. Still, we don't give up. We will continue until there is no relapse. For plants and, maybe one day, for our patients."

Both Palindromena and the Reefs wanted the same thing: to grow crops underwater. But neither was succeeding.

"But this is not what you're here for, is it?" the Director said. It was clear she enjoyed telling the story, regardless of how many times she'd told it. "Are you ready for the most precious twenty-four hours of your life to begin?" She pointed to a door behind me with the number sixteen on it.

I didn't know how to respond to that.

"Of course you are." She smiled, but it didn't reach her eyes. Did she find my silence unnerving? "Your Warden will be here any moment, and he will be by your side for the entire twenty-four hours. His name is Raylan Bassan. He's from the Equinox, like you. Perhaps you know each other? He used to be a spearfisherman," she whispered conspiratorially, as though that would impress me. "One of the best."

I didn't know anyone called Raylan. Both Elysea and I hadn't had much to do with kids our age after we'd left school when our parents died. Regardless, I didn't want anyone with me. I needed to speak with my sister alone.

She must've misread my silence. "You have nothing to fear, Tempest."

I gave some kind of shrug and nod at the same time.

"Now," she said, her face settling into a look of consternation, "you must promise me you'll do your best to ensure your sister does not know she died."

"Why?" Although I wasn't planning to tell her.

"It's less traumatic for everyone involved," she said. "Imagine how you would feel if you found out you had twenty-four hours to live."

"What's she going to think happened? Our parents worked at Palindromena. Won't she figure it out?"

"When she wakes, the doctors will tell her there's been an accident. They'll explain she was in a coma for a few days and has to stay in the Equinox infirmary for observation. Her room is set up to appear as though she hasn't left the Reef."

"And that works?" I couldn't believe that, not when everyone on the Equinox knew about Palindromena. "She won't suspect the truth?"

"We revive people from all over the world," she said. "Most people don't know our services as intimately as those who live on the Equinox. For patients who have grown up close by, we give them something to forget their most recent memories. They won't remember what happened in the last few hours of their life. Elysea won't remember drowning. Trust me."

I hoped she'd remember the night of my parents' deaths; otherwise, what was the point of all this? "What if she does figure it out?"

"Then the scientists will sedate her to ensure she is not panicked. Obviously, it's not ideal, as we want you to make the most of your time together. While it's easiest for everyone that she doesn't find out the truth, I assure you, we are prepared for any situation. We're here to take away your grief." She smiled gently. "And one day, I hope to eradicate death altogether so there will be no more suffering." I could tell she'd also lost someone; pain was reflected in her eyes.

That was a world I would like to live in.

"Wait here," she said, her mood shifting. "Your Warden will be with you shortly."

"Thank you."

She squeezed my hand. "You remind me so much of your mother." The way she said it, I was certain she meant to be reassuring, but it only made me miss her.

"Thank you," I repeated.

She gave me an understanding nod. "Tempest, your Palindromena journey begins now."

CHAPTER FIVE

LOR

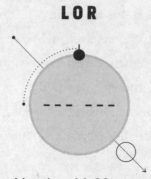

Monday, 11:00 a.m.
One hour before revival

MONDAY. The day I would finally step out of the shadows of the Aquarium. If I could first convince myself to get out of bed.

I didn't move from my bunk when Nessandra left a bowl of berries near the entrance. She was always leaving me meals before she started work, knowing I wouldn't go upstairs to the employee cafeteria. Just because I used the basement as my hideout didn't mean I approved of what her company did. Like always, I'd pretended to be asleep when she visited.

I'd avoided speaking to her for nearly two years. She'd forced me to go through a revival with Calen, saying it would help us say goodbye—something she never had the chance to do with her parents. But the fear in Calen's eyes when he realized what was going to happen would haunt me for the rest of my life. Knowing you had twenty-four hours before oblivion was never an easy fate to accept.

Fear was the last emotion he ever felt. And while it was easy to blame Nessandra, it was *my* fault.

Today went against everything I'd vowed two years ago. I'd promised myself I'd remain down here, out of sight, living with the nonliving, until the end of my days as penance. But Ray was asking for my help. This time I would listen. I would put Ray's well-being before my own, like I should have with Calen. I would do better.

Because there were only around fifty Wardens—and I was bound to be noticed as not one of them—Ray had run through the prerevival procedure with the scientists last night. They had set up the echolink for the revival and provided a digital tablet with information on the patient's death. Ray had left both pieces of technology behind. I'd stashed them under my pillow, hoping to wake the next morning and find them gone. Our deal merely another bad dream.

But I hadn't fallen asleep, and my pillow was still lumpy.

Eventually I sat up on my bunk and pulled the echolink and tablet from their hiding place. I stared at the echo's inky-black screen for a few seconds, building up the nerve to put it on. This would mean no going back. I hesitated, holding it above my wrist, my mind warring against me. I'd worn one only once before. The day I'd said goodbye to Calen.

Before then, I believed in the revival program and the Gods below. Growing up on the island, I'd only ever heard of the wonders of Palindromena; I'd never questioned what they did. But after the accident on Hallowed Mountain, I couldn't stomach what *this* place put people through. I wanted to smash the echo into a thousand pieces.

But this wasn't just about me. I'd recognized the haunted look in Ray's eyes. I couldn't let him turn into me. Sad, bitter and lonely. Ray needed today. He hadn't had hope for a long time. And sometimes that was all you needed to get through the day.

I bared my teeth as two pins along the underside of the metal band pierced my skin and tapped into my bloodstream. A circle of blue light illuminated the edge of the screen as it connected to my pulse.

Before the Great Waves, electricity ran through the earth— lighting homes and streets. But now we only had the sun, the wind and the water to generate power. And our bodies.

While trying to revive those who had drowned, Palindromena scientists had discovered people were their own form of electricity. By tapping into the bloodstream, your pulse could be utilized not only to keep your body alive, but to power small devices like the echolink. It was more reliable than the sun. Unless you were dead, of course.

I didn't want to look at the screen for too long. I'd pretend it was jewelry and nothing more. I quickly changed into the beige Palindromena T-shirt Ray had "borrowed" for me and shoved the digital tablet into my back pocket, behind a book.

Ray's parting words last night had been to keep my head down and everything should be all right. It was hardly reassuring.

I reminded myself that I was doing the right thing. Ray

wanted nothing more in this world than to return to spearfishing. The desire to hunt ran in his blood. About a decade ago, his father had caught a mammoth garseal, which the entire Equinox feasted on for one night, and the leftover flesh was traded with Palindromena for valuable medicine, like recompression pills. Ray's father had been crowned a hero.

The story of the garseal had been told over and over again for Ray's entire childhood, until it became a part of him, as though it were his own memory. No one could've blamed Ray for losing all sense when he saw a leviathan shadow dip beneath his boat. He'd been so focused on the creature, he didn't see the approaching vessel until it was too late.

I hoped today Ray would start to move on. Not that I didn't understand his desire to return to the past. I wished I could go back to the cliffs two years ago.

But I couldn't go back, and I didn't want to go forward either. Yet here I was, about to take a step out into the world.

It was easier to forget what I'd done down here, even though I was surrounded by the dead. By returning to the world above, I would be reminded of how things used to be. How I would count down the days until the weekend, when I would see Calen and his friends from the Equinox. How we would race rovers along the sand, toast fish over a beach bonfire and talk late into the evening about the world beyond the island. I'd had dreams of traveling the world. Or, at the very least, dreams of leaving the island. Now I didn't even want to leave the basement.

I *should* forget this deal with Ray. The client would show up, and no Warden would be there to assist her. The appointment would be canceled, and Nessandra would reschedule. But Ray would be punished. He'd likely be fired, and his future—and the past he so wanted to be reunited with—would be ripped away for good.

I couldn't take that from him.

I grabbed a strip of white cloth from the supply cupboard and headed upstairs before I lost my nerve. I made a makeshift bandana out of the cloth to cover my sandy-blond hair and concealed the lower part of my face with a germ mask. It wouldn't be unusual for a Warden to wear a mask; protecting clients and patients was Palindromena's number one priority.

I took a deep breath. My hand rattled the handle as I opened the door. I had to do this. For Ray. It was the right thing. The unselfish thing. I'd return to the Aquarium in twenty-four hours, and everything would be as it should be.

"Don't be a coward," I whispered to myself.

I forced my legs to stop shaking and walked toward the main foyer. My movements were stilted, as though my body had forgotten how to walk. I clenched my fists. I could do this.

I squinted on entering the foyer, the sun streaming in through the glass front wall and ceiling. I'd forgotten how bright it was in here. I stood still for a moment. Memories of the sun seared through my mind, so vivid I could feel it blistering my skin.

My mother had always reprimanded me for not wearing long-sleeved T-shirts. My fair complexion meant I burned easily and quickly, but I enjoyed the feeling of the sun on my skin.

"Excuse me," a woman said, brushing by me.

I darted to the side.

I couldn't allow myself to be lost in my memories.

The Wardens had gathered around the black-bark tree. As a kid, I'd loved trees. I'd spent countless hours climbing what few trees were left on the island. I'd started climbing cliffs when I grew bored.

The Wardens' breathy voices echoed throughout the room. My wrist vibrated, letting me know my client awaited my arrival.

"Wake those from the darkest depths," the Wardens chanted. "Bring them into the light. Let them have their final goodbyes before they descend back into your watery embrace. We trust in you. We follow you. Forevermore."

A Warden with a deep brown complexion and long curly hair noticed me pass by, but he only smiled in response. I moved quickly toward the recovery rooms before anyone could approach me. Even with my mask and bandana, I couldn't afford to have anyone look at me too closely. Only Ray and Nessandra knew I was down in the basement. And I wanted to keep it that way.

As I approached door sixteen—my posting for the next twenty-four hours—I heard a familiar voice carry from down the hallway.

Nessandra.

Shit. I couldn't let her see me. My mask and bandana would never fool her. I ducked back around the corner.

As she told the client that the next twenty-four hours were precious, I ground my teeth. The revival program was a sham. It didn't help anyone. Not the dead, nor the living.

I remained hidden behind the wall until I heard the *click-clack* of Nessandra's footsteps disappear down the corridor. Only then did I approach my client.

Tempest Alerin.

CHAPTER SIX

TEMPEST

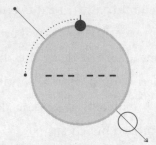

Monday, 11:30 a.m.

Thirty minutes before revival

I BOUNCED MY FOOT in time with the ticking clock on the wall. While it had only been a few minutes, it felt like hours since the Director left me waiting for my Warden.

I uncurled my fingers again and again, aiming to release some tension. After so many years of hearing about Palindromena, it still felt foreign. I couldn't picture my parents walking these hallways. I couldn't even imagine their faces. Sometimes I worried I'd forget them entirely. Time washing away the memories, as it did with everything else.

Finally, the door to the corridor opened and a tall boy stepped inside. I felt like a freshly caught fish, passed from one fisherman to the next.

From what I could see of him, the boy looked a few years older than me, the rest of his face covered by a mask. His skin was the same pearly shade as the Director's, with a smattering of freckles across his nose.

His bright blue eyes caught mine. For a moment, we stared at one another.

"Hi," he said eventually, holding out his hand. It trembled slightly. "I'm L—" He swallowed audibly. "Lucky to be your Warden."

I pursed my lips in response. *Lucky, all right.* He didn't look happy about it. Even though most of his face was hidden, I could see his clenched jaw.

He was much younger than I expected. I'd imagined all Wardens were like my father, a tall thin man with a jovial smile. He'd had the ability to be calming without patronizing, give advice without preaching, and make you feel as though you'd been friends for all your life. I'd admired his talent for conversing with people he'd just met when I couldn't hold down a single friend for an entire school year.

Too quiet. Too serious. Too sensitive.

I was never what people wanted me to be.

Elysea, and her best friend, Daon—who'd been forced to hang out with me because he was so besotted with my sister—were my only friends. And on the worst nights, when I used to lie in bed staring at the ceiling, I'd wonder how I could be different—more friendly, *better*—and I wondered if Elysea was my friend at all. Or simply had to spend time with me because she was my sister.

Had I been a burden to her?

"Raylan," my Warden said, breaking the silence. "I'm Raylan Bassan. Tempest, is it?"

"Tempe," I corrected him, finally agreeing to shake his hand. I knew I had a habit of making people feel uncomfortable, but I'd long ago discovered that if you stayed quiet a moment longer than expected, people would reveal more than they intended. And sometimes I needed that extra time to collect my thoughts.

Raylan watched as our hands connected, my suntanned light brown fingers against his pale ones. On his wrist sat a decorative metal band with a circular embedded black screen. The screen was blank aside from a circle of blue. I dropped his hand with a gasp.

An echolink.

I hadn't seen one since my father was alive. It was something only Wardens wore to track the dead's revival. When we were kids, it had both fascinated and terrified Elysea and me. Dad never even let us touch it.

"It's not for kids," he'd say.

"What does it do?" I would ask.

And every time, he'd give my mom a knowing look before saying, "Nothing you need to concern yourself with."

Elysea and I used to believe the echolink wielded the power of life and death itself, and if you touched it, your heart would turn as black as the round screen, a cavernous hole inside your chest. As kids, we used to dare each other to sneak into our parents' room while Dad was asleep and touch the screen. We'd always flee before we got too close.

Raylan cleared his throat, and I glanced away from his wrist.

"I'm here to assist you through the duration of your sister's revival."

What did this boy know of grief and death? His hand had been soft in mine, weak. I didn't need him.

I arched my eyebrows, waiting for him to get on with it.

"Have you been given your Land Legs?" His voice was slightly muffled by the mask.

"Yes." I decided to throw him a bone. "When I arrived on the island."

"Good" was all he said. He didn't seem much more talkative than me. I thought Wardens were supposed to be comforting? Again I thought of my dad and how he'd made everyone feel important and *seen*.

I'd lost count of how many nights Dad had sat by my bedside after a bad day at school. I would tell him about the kids who called me names, who claimed I was tainted by the dead because my parents worked at Palindromena while most parents worked on dive sites, out on boats or as anglers. One year, my classmates had spread a rumor that I'd been born in a tank—a science experiment gone wrong.

My dad would tell me that they made fun of what they didn't understand, of people who were different. Special. And that it was their fear that made them lash out. He'd tell me that I was his beautiful flarefish, who brightened the darkest seas. I doubted he'd say that now.

I pushed back the memory and focused on Raylan.

"The recovery room is through here." He pointed to the

door behind me. "That's where your sister will be for the entire time she's revived."

I wished I'd had one last moment with my dad. To tell him how much I loved him. But Elysea had taken that from me.

"I've been through all of this," he said, gesturing around him. "I know it's a difficult time."

"You lost someone?" I asked, watching the grief tug at his features. Did Palindromena require Wardens to go through the revival program? I supposed it would create empathy with clients. Perhaps he did know grief intimately, how it tainted every waking moment and how, after those blissful hours when you were asleep and managed to finally forget, it made the waking hours all the more painful.

Had my father gone through this process with someone he'd loved, seeing he was a Warden? He'd never said, and both his parents and older sister had died from crystal lung, and couldn't be revived.

Raylan nodded. "The procedure allowed me to have some more time with a friend."

I could see, or rather sense, his sadness. "Was it worth it? Seeing them again?"

He let out a stuttering breath, which echoed in his mask. "Yes."

That was hardly convincing.

He fiddled with his bandana, his fingers trembling slightly as though he were nervous.

"How many revivals have you overseen?" I asked. He was acting as though *he* were the one about to go through the next twenty-four hours. Then again, it could have been me making him so jittery. While my dad thought I was his special flarefish, everyone else said I looked people too long in the eye, or not long enough. Kids thought I was odd because I was so quiet and serious and still. They didn't know what I was thinking. So they assumed I was thinking the worst.

They would circle me, throw sand in my hair and chant, *water witch, water witch, water witch,* as they ran around. They wanted protection from the Gods below. Protection *from* me.

But I'd never wished them ill. Often, I hadn't even been thinking about them at all—I'd been trapped in my own mind, wondering how I could approach these kids who already seemed to hate me. How I could make them see I was just like them. And during that quiet deliberation, they had decided I was strange and creepy and wanted nothing to do with me.

"I've overseen ten revivals," Raylan said. I'd almost forgotten my question.

"Is ten a lot?" I'd never asked my dad how many he'd overseen in his lifetime. I hadn't thought there was a time limit to ask questions. I'd thought I had my entire adult life to know and enjoy my parents. To ask the things you never thought of as a child. But I'd never considered my parents as anything other than the people who loved and raised me. I didn't get to know them as Minda and Deren—as the couple who had met because of Palindromena and fallen in love. Now it was too late.

"Yes," Raylan said, snapping me out of my thoughts. "I've only worked here for six months."

"You're from the Equinox?" That was what Nessandra had said, but Raylan didn't look familiar. Now that I was closer, I could see a slight stubble on his jaw behind his mask. He must've been a few years above me in school, and I'd dropped out when I was twelve, after my parents died. With no more money coming in, Elysea and I took to diving so we could pay our taxes. Taxes that had kept Elysea in a tank for the last two years.

"Yes," he said.

I eyed his fair skin confusedly. Most people who lived on the Reef couldn't remain that pale from the constant sun exposure.

"I know what you're thinking—paler than a bonefish, right?" He held out his arms, and I gave him a weak smile. "I guess that's what happens when you spend most of your time inside, studying to become a Warden."

"Right." Although I wasn't sure I'd ever met anyone as fair. Even the classrooms on the Equinox were exposed to the elements.

"It's nearly noon," Raylan said, gesturing toward the recovery room behind us. He seemed eager to get rid of me. "Noon is when Palindromena revives patients," he explained. "It's a bit of an in-joke, as the word *noon* is a palindrome."

It wasn't funny, so I simply nodded.

"A palindrome is a word or sentence that can be reversed and still have the same meaning forward or backward," he explained. "The facility is named Palindromena, as death is reversed, giving life, and then the patient returns back to death."

I let out an annoyed breath. "I know why it's called Palindromena."

He squared his shoulders and cleared his throat. I was definitely making him uncomfortable, but I didn't care.

"Right, so, your sister will be brought to this room." He pointed again to the recovery room behind me. "And I'll remain in the waiting room." He gestured to where we were standing. "In case you need me."

"For twenty-four hours?" I asked. "Don't you sleep? Eat?" When he didn't flinch, I added, "Piss?"

He laughed, almost reluctantly. "Not if you need me."

Okay. That seemed a bit overkill, but what did I know? Maybe people needed the constant support? The orientation video had said I might go into shock when I saw my sister. But shock was not a part of my plan. Shock would be a distraction.

"Are you ready to go in?" He had his thumb over the face of his echolink; was he signaling the scientists to wake

Elysea? I wished Dad had explained the details of the procedure.

I imagined my sister lying placid on a bed, lips blue, milky eyes staring blankly at the ceiling. And barnacles covering her skin like a rash. What would move first? Her eyes? Her fingers?

Something clawed at my chest. *Fear. It's only fear.*

When I finally managed to nod in agreement, my mouth parched, Raylan touched the screen of his echolink and a second blue circle appeared. He closed his eyes as if in thought. His shoulders slumped for a moment.

When he opened them, he said, "She's on her way."

CHAPTER SEVEN

LOR

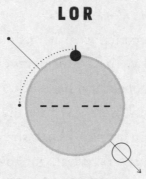

Monday, 11:50 a.m.
Ten minutes before revival

ONE LOOK from Tempest Alerin and I wanted to run back down to the Aquarium.

Her eyes tracked my every movement. Discerning and severe. I felt seen. A feeling I hadn't had in almost two years. Sure, Ray came to visit, but this girl was looking at me. Really looking.

Her eyes were a warm brown, but there was no warmth behind them. Her narrow jaw was set. She was thin; her collarbone stuck out, and her cheekbones were sharp. Her olive complexion was deepened from her life on the water, her long hair the color of a starless sky. She was one of the most beautiful girls I'd ever seen. In another life, my old life, I might have even asked her out.

I wasn't sure what to expect from a client, but something was off about her demeanor. Something simmered beneath her. Something I couldn't put my finger on.

I shouldn't be doing this. I'm going to get caught. She's going to real-ize I'm not a trained Warden.

Or maybe I'd forgotten what it was like to converse with people other than Ray. To have their eyes on mine. Their hand in mine. I'd nearly dropped it at her touch. Her hand was small, but the grip was firm. Until she spotted my echolink. From the shocked expression on her face, I knew she must've realized the echo symbolized her sister's revival. But how? She wasn't acting as though she'd been through all this before.

Then the moment had passed and it was as though noth-ing fazed her. As though she wasn't about to see her dead sis-ter. While her gaze was intense, she appeared to be concealing her true emotions. Was she worried about crying in front of a stranger? She didn't appear to be sad. She didn't seem . . . anything, really. But she had to be feeling something. No one could face grief so fearlessly. Or heartlessly.

"Is she already awake?" Tempest asked. She wasn't reacting how Ray had explained a client would. I'd expected tears, I'd expected excitement, I'd expected nerves. I hadn't expected her.

She was too calm. Too in control. It was unnerving.

"Yes," I said, rotating my wrist to loosen the tension. The echolink felt like an anchor. I didn't want to look at its screen; I didn't want to look at the two circles, knowing what they meant. "Elysea will be here soon."

I pressed a panel beside the door to open it. The door slid shut behind us as we entered the recovery room. There was a narrow bed in the middle of the space, and a window at the back showed the ocean, rather than the rock wall the facility had been carved into. The view Elysea Alerin would expect to see if she awoke in the Equinox's infirmary after an accident. A cruel ruse, like this entire operation.

While I hated being a part of this, my eyes greedily took in the scene—something other than the dark and damp of the Aquarium.

Tempest surveyed the room silently, her hands clasped behind her back.

Why didn't she say anything?

I pulled the digital tablet from my back pocket and quickly scrolled through her sister's file for something to do.

DECEASED: ELYSEA ALERIN

AGE: SEVENTEEN

MOTHER: MINDA, DECEASED

FATHER: DEREN, DECEASED

SIBLING: TEMPEST, TWO YEARS YOUNGER

CAUSE OF DEATH: DROWNED. PULLED FROM THE WATER BY THE RETRIEVAL BOATS. MOST LIKELY SWEPT OFF HER BOAT IN THE STORM THE NIGHT BEFORE.

DEATH STATUS: GOOD CONDITION.

BODY PRESERVED SIX HOURS AFTER DEATH.

APPROVED FOR REVIVAL.

Included were dozens of images of Elysea. Dead. Eyes unfocused. Brown hair around her shoulders. Skin chalky. Lips blue.

I clicked off the screen before Tempest saw.

To break the silence, I pointed to a silver tray and said, "There's some food for your sister when she wants it. And if you need anything else, press the button at the door, and I'll unlock it from the other side."

"Okay." Her voice was distant.

My wrist buzzed, sending a shock down my arm. I glanced at a door to the adjoining room. The entrance to the revival wing. A light above the doorway flicked from red to amber.

"Your sister is almost here," I said. Tempest's face paled. It was the first time she'd shown any concern, and I found myself taking a step toward her. "It will be all right."

She darted away like a frightened fish. "I'm fine."

I should've left, but I didn't want her to do this alone.

"I know what you're going through," I began, but she wasn't listening anymore; her eyes were locked on the amber light.

"What's taking so long?" she asked.

"She'll be here in a few moments." I wished I could stay, in case she needed me. But Ray had been clear: leave before the patient arrives. Conceal the truth.

Still, I found it difficult to move my feet. Was it because the mere smell of this room reminded me of two years ago, when I'd last seen Calen?

I shook the images of his lifeless body from my mind and focused on Tempest. Her eyes were glazed and unblinking.

"There's a bathroom over there." I pointed to a narrow door in the corner. "And if you want to talk, I'll be outside. Otherwise, you'll be alone in here."

"Alone?"

Did she want me to stay? "With your sister, of course."

She pressed her lips together and turned back toward the door.

"Once Elysea enters," I said—Tempest visibly flinched at her sister's name—"the countdown will begin." I pointed to the clock on the wall. "We will take her away moments before the twenty-four hours is up." She wouldn't have to see her sister die again.

I finally managed to move back to the waiting room. "Good luck, Tempest."

She tore her focus from the amber light to glance at me briefly before I exited.

I had a feeling her face would haunt me long after she was gone.

CHAPTER EIGHT

TEMPEST

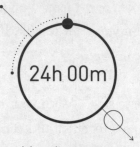

Monday, noon

MY BREATHS SOUNDED louder and louder in my ears until they blended into a swooshing sound, like the sound of the ocean. The last sound Elysea ever heard.

Elysea.

My only sibling. My sister who had taught me to dive. My sister who had sung me to sleep while storms shook the walls of our quarters. My sister who had made life feel somewhat whole again after our parents died.

And yet she was a girl of secrets and lies. I needed to see her one more time. I needed to hear her say the words.

I'm the reason Mom and Dad are dead.

I swallowed down all emotion. I was strong. I could do this. This was the moment I'd worked for. All my long days at the dive site, surviving on scraps. Surviving, alone.

Don't falter now, Tempe. Don't fall apart. Remember why you're here. Remember the pain she caused. You deserve the truth.

My legs started to tremble, and the more I focused on them *not* trembling, the more they did. I dug my fingernails into my palms.

I can do this.

The amber light turned to green.

My sister. Here. Alive.

Nothing happened. Then I heard a click from behind me. I spun. The clock on the wall had begun turning. Which could only mean that—

"Hello, Tempe."

My sister stood in the open doorway.

She looked exactly as she had the day she'd drowned. Her lips pink, her cheeks rosy against her olive skin, her chestnut-brown hair falling in glossy waves down her back. Not only did she look alive, she looked well. It was hard to imagine her as anything *but* alive. As though the past two years were merely a horrid nightmare.

"Hello, Elysea." My voice shook a little.

"I hope I didn't scare you," she said, stepping toward me.

My sister rising from the dead? No, nothing scary about that.

I took a few steadying breaths. I couldn't crumble. Everything I had been planning for years was right in front of me. I had to disconnect. This wasn't my sister, not my *real* sister— this was a means to an end.

"Did they tell you what happened?" I asked.

Confusion clouded her face. She glanced at the pale blue

gown she was dressed in and fiddled with the infirmary bracelet around her wrist. "The doctor told me I was in a boating accident two days ago and I've been in a medically induced coma since then."

"You drowned."

She coughed, as if she could remember water filling her lungs. Perhaps she could. My chest burned with sympathy.

"Almost," she amended with a smile.

"Right," I said quickly. "You *almost* drowned."

She moved over to the bed and climbed onto it. "I feel a tad hazy"—she tapped her forehead with jittery fingers—"but the doctor said that was a product of the coma. Otherwise, I feel fine."

"That's good."

"Are *you* okay?" She pulled her knees to her chest, her long infirmary gown bunching around her ankles. "You're looking at me strangely."

"I was worried."

"Of course!" She brought her palm to her forehead. "You must have been terrified, thinking you were left alone. I'm so sorry."

"Yes, I'm in shock." I knew I sounded distant but I didn't know how to act normal without lowering my walls.

Was now the right time to ask about Mom and Dad? Perhaps I only needed a few minutes of the twenty-four hours? Then why did the words feel like a dead fish on my tongue?

Elysea squeezed her eyes shut. It was better when she wasn't watching me. It was easier to lie.

"I wish I could remember." Her voice was soft. *"What happened?"*

"You were out two nights ago. Your boat was found over-turned." The truth was the easiest.

Her green eyes flashed open—as vibrant as the plant I'd found. "Why was I out by myself?"

Wasn't that the million-Note question? But Nessandra had said Elysea's last memories would be blurry. I hoped she hadn't forgotten anything else.

"How did they find me? The Conservators don't search for missing boats." There was fear behind her eyes. She knew. *No.* She couldn't.

I took a breath and recited the story I'd prepared.

"There was another boat nearby." Even though it was dangerous being out at night, that didn't mean people wouldn't take the chance. After all, flarefish only glowed in the moonlit water, like ghosts beneath the surface. One plump fish could feed ten people. It was worth it. Es-pecially with Equinox's recent struggles. "They found you." The Palindromena retrieval boat had found her body, even-tually. "You were very lucky." I smiled. I hoped it looked genuine.

"Oh." Her forehead smoothed. "They resuscitated me?"

I nodded and looked away, unable to take her gaze. The

room was hot. Too hot. I wished there was a real window to open. I wished I wasn't wearing my diving skin beneath my dress; the thin, rubbery plates didn't breathe.

"Why are you so far away?" Concern lined her voice.

I needed to do better. I had to convince her she was alive and that she would *stay* alive. If she suspected the truth, I'd lose my advantage.

I gave her a rueful smile. "You know me. I hate the smell of the Equinox infirmary. And you reek of it."

She laughed her crystal-bell laugh. "Come here, Li'l Tempe."

I groaned at the nickname. "I'm not little," I mumbled, shuffling over to her. And I wasn't. I hadn't been shorter than Elysea since I was twelve. Two inches of height was the one obvious physical trait that differentiated us. But if you looked closer, we were quite dissimilar. I took after our dad with his brown eyes, black hair and longer nose, whereas she had Mom's eyes and round cheeks.

I sat on the edge of her bed and held out my hand, ensuring my fingers didn't shake. It had been over two years since I'd seen her. Two years since I'd touched her skin. I didn't know what she'd feel like.

When her warm fingers enclosed mine, I let out a shuddering breath.

"It's all right," she said, tears in her eyes. "I'm not going anywhere." Not like Mom and Dad—she didn't have to say it.

Only she *had* left me. And it was worse that she didn't even know it.

She felt the same, looked the same, smelled the same. A part of me was annoyed. I wished she were different; it would make this easier. It would feel less like my heart was being stomped on.

Remember, she lied to you. You're alone because of her.

"I can't wait to leave this place," she said with a sigh and a wiggle of her toes. "You're not the only one who hates the infirmary." When I was learning to dive, I'd spent many hours being patched up by Equinox doctors with Elysea by my side. Palindromena had done a great job of replicating the ward. "I want to go back to our quarters," she said. "I want to dance tonight."

I couldn't help but picture Elysea back on the Equinox, seeing how life had moved on in the years she'd been dead. Her best friend, Daon, was in a new relationship. Her room empty, all possessions sold for what little they were worth. Her dance class now led by her understudy. And I, well, I wasn't the same. Not because she'd died. But because I'd heard something I couldn't unhear. A truth.

It was only four months after she'd died when Daon told me the secret Elysea had kept from me until her last breath. She'd been out on the ocean the night our parents died. She was responsible for their deaths. It not only changed how I felt about Elysea's death but tarnished all memories of her. My grief ignited into rage, and over the years, it had burned me up inside, until there was nothing left but cinders.

Before that, I would've given anything for more time with my sister. Now I was only desperate for the truth.

"Where's Daon?" she asked, as if she'd read my mind. "I thought he'd be here."

I shrugged. "Busy with work. You know how he is."

She smiled, and something plucked at my heart. She cared about him, but not in *that* way. But she'd never told him how she really felt, worried she'd lose him as a friend.

I'd often wished she had told him the truth. But who was I to tell her what to do? I had hoped she would eventually tell him on her own. Then she'd died.

She squeezed my hand. "Thank you for being here."

I nearly laughed at the absurdity of it all. *I* was the reason *she* was here.

How did people do this? How did they look at their deceased loved ones, now whole again? How did they pretend that for twenty-four hours they were merely visiting and would return home another day? A day that would never come?

Did they keep their loved ones awake all night, needing every second? Wouldn't that give the truth away? Or did they watch them sleep, wishing and hoping those stolen moments could extend into a future that would never be?

I understood the need to keep up the ruse. I didn't want to lose my time with her.

Elysea had once meant everything to me, and even with my heart hardened from the last two years, I hadn't been prepared for this. I didn't think I would want to be near her, touch her. But she was the same. She was Elysea. My big sister and, for the last few years, my guardian.

I stared at our entwined hands. Mine were darker than hers from the two additional years spent on the ocean. I dropped her hand and hid mine in the folds of the bed blankets, hoping she hadn't noticed the difference.

"I nearly lost you." I didn't have to fake the crack in my voice, remembering the moment I'd been told she had been lost. I didn't leave my bed for two weeks. Daon had brought food every day, forcing me not to give up, telling me that Elysea would want me to be strong.

"I'm sorry," Elysea said, her mouth downturned. "I never should've gone out. I can't remember anything from the past two days." I wished she did. Now that I had her here, I also wanted to know why she did it. Why she risked going out at night and unknowingly sacrificed herself.

"Like Mom and Dad," I said.

"What?" Her head snapped up. "*No*, this was different."

"How can you say that?" I studied her face, waiting for something to give. "Do you know why they went out the night they died?" I let the line dangle there, hoping she'd take the bait. "You always said you didn't."

She turned her face away. "No, I don't know." *Liar.*

"You said you discovered their deaths the next morning, when we woke to find them gone." I took a breath. "But you lied. You were there with them. Don't deny it."

"What are you talking about?" Her soft, soothing voice had turned hard and defensive. She looked like Mom when she was angry.

"Daon told me your little secret." I leaned closer, wanting to spit the words at her. "You were on the water that night, but only you came home."

The accusation hung over us like a snapped mast, poised to crush us both. I was shaking from anger, but Elysea was still. Still as death.

I couldn't take the silence anymore. "You were responsible for their deaths!"

"No." She shook her head vehemently. "That's not what happened."

"Then tell me!"

I thought my words would unleash a barrage, and all the secrets she'd hidden for years, the secrets she had taken to her grave, would come pouring out. But she didn't say anything. Not at first. Her startled eyes locked onto mine with such intensity that I knew I was in trouble.

"Why are you asking me this?" She arched her eyebrows. "Why now, after all these years?"

"Daon told me while you were . . . in a coma. He told me you saw them that night and that you were responsible for their deaths."

Tension had begun to build in her shoulders, drawing them higher. Her breaths came rapidly.

"Why are you asking me this now?" she asked again, her eyes dodging around the room as though she didn't want to focus on me.

"Because"—I leveled my voice—"I need to know exactly what happened to them. Why did you tell Daon the truth but not me? Your sister! They were *my* parents too!"

Her eyes landed on mine. "What day is it, Tempe?"

I could feel us both hold our breath. The silence ricocheted between us. We knew the moment we were rising to, like the crest of a wave, soon to crash. The moment of truth.

She knew she was dead. My leverage was gone.

CHAPTER NINE

LOR

23h 30m

Monday, 12:30 p.m.

EACH MINUTE that passed while I wasn't down in the Aquarium scratched at my skin like tiny needles. At first, I thought I was having an allergic reaction to the natural light beaming down from the glass ceiling. Then I realized it was anxiety.

I'd never been an anxious person. I used to spend my days suspended thousands of feet above the ragged coastline, secured only by my fingertips and toes. Being calm and steady was a necessity for survival. Today I felt hot and jittery and had tingles spiking up and down my arms. I hoped I wouldn't pass out.

I practiced the breathing exercises I'd learned from climbing. Slowly my hands stopped shaking and the feeling of pinpricks receded.

I wasn't dying. At least, not today.

Half an hour passed, and my eyes adapted to the sun, as though it was only days, not years, since I'd seen sunlight. I remembered how after only a day outside, freckles would appear across my shoulders and arms. I remembered the ache that would build in my muscles as I pulled myself to the top of the cliff.

I would sit up there for as long as I could, the world appearing far more interesting than the island I was tied to. Ironic that I would end up retreating to the basement. While I wasn't a fan of the ocean and the stormy seas surrounding the isle, I had once dreamed of traveling the world—or what was left of it. I wanted to visit the Islands Cavalcade, the party islands, located just outside Palindromena's reach and influence. Or see the Roving Reefs to the west, which never moored and continued scouring the seas for supplies, a race against time.

I wanted to go somewhere my family hadn't been. I wanted to be free.

Now I never could be.

While my freckles had almost completely faded away in the past two years, the memory of Calen and my last climb remained.

I tried reading my book, but I was too agitated, my eyes not focusing on the faded old text.

I rolled my shoulders. I wasn't used to sitting for lengths at a time. It was better to keep moving in the Aquarium. Let the faces in the tanks blur.

There weren't any noises coming from the other waiting rooms. What did the other Wardens do while they waited? Were they like Ray, researching as much as they could about life and death on their tablets? Or did they squander their time, not realizing how precious life truly was?

No matter how hard I tried, I couldn't get Tempest's face out of my head. And sitting here with nothing to do wasn't helping. Now I knew why Ray would visit so often; this wasn't the most riveting job.

I took in a deep breath. At least the air didn't reek of chemicals up here. People who suffered from respiratory issues applied to work at Palindromena, in hopes the clean air would ease their symptoms. But Palindromena had countless applications; they only accepted those who excelled on the entry exam. Like Ray.

"It doesn't hurt that I supply the island with ragar," he'd once argued. While I'd never tasted the fermented seaweed drink, I'd heard it was very popular. Still, Ray was downplaying his intelligence. He'd been researching how to repair dead cells and nerves for months before he was offered the Warden traineeship.

While Ray had a secure future here, he didn't want it. He wanted the ocean. He wanted to follow in his father's footsteps. He wanted to reconnect with his ancestors. Being in the ocean was a part of who he was and he said he felt like half himself without it. Training to be a Warden was a stopgap, a way to earn Notes while learning from the world's best doctors and scientists. He was an optimistic little pain in the ass. But sometimes his optimism worked against him. He still hoped to return to his old life. Yet today was the first step in moving forward. I hoped the doctor had some plan for rehabilitation.

I tapped my fingers against the face of the echolink. Without anything else to do, I thought of my own future. I knew the best thing to do would be to leave Palindromena and go somewhere no one knew my name or face, and never return. But I couldn't. What right did I have to live out my dreams when I'd taken Calen from his? That would be turning my back on Calen and my culpability in his death. And while I couldn't hide out in the basement forever, I wouldn't leave the island.

If I had only twenty-four hours left in this world, what would I change? What *could* I change?

It didn't matter. I would never leave this place. I'd never have more than this life. I had my work and my daily visits from Ray, and that was enough to get by. Most days.

A part of me envied the clients in these rooms. They were here because of passion or love—even pain. I couldn't remember what any of those felt like.

The digital tablet in my lap pinged and the screen came to life.

Tell me you haven't screwed up. A message from Raylan.

I huffed a quiet laugh.

How was the doctor? I asked.

I waited for a few minutes before his message appeared.

She was cute. You'd like her. You should come to the Equinox. How's your client?

I sucked in a breath. That meant the appointment hadn't gone well. *Shit.*

She's cute too.

There was no point in pushing the subject. You couldn't force Ray to talk when he didn't want to. Something we had in common.

Good, he wrote back. Twenty-four hours will fly by!

I wasn't so sure about that.

Are you heading back now? I asked.

Soon. His reply came quickly. Decided to see the family while I'm here. Could be a while. You know how my mom gets.

I wished I was there for moral support. While his mother loved him, she would give him a hard time for leaving his family. She couldn't understand why he wanted to work for Palindromena. She didn't understand his obsession with healing his injury so he could return to the fishing fleet. She thought being with the family was more important.

You got this, bud? Ray asked.

A part of me wanted to tell him about Tempest's strange behavior, but I didn't want him to worry. I was probably just overanalyzing everything. I didn't know this girl. I didn't know what was strange for her, or what was normal.

I got this, I sent back.

CHAPTER TEN

TEMPEST

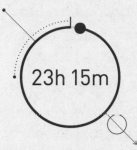

23h 15m

Monday, 12:45 p.m.

NO, NO, NO, NO, NO. Elysea couldn't suspect the truth. Not after everything I'd sacrificed to be here. She'd been back for less than an hour.

I eased away from her. I remembered the day she'd drowned as though it were yesterday. The Equinox authorities knocked at my door, informing me of her passing, their faces grave but not surprised. With dive finds increasingly rare, people acted more and more reckless. Some tried for a better life, setting off for another Reef. Others crossed the Untied Sea, hoping to uncover new dive sites, and were never seen again. They were probably lying in the belly of some beast, their bones a splinter in the creature's teeth.

It took me a moment to remember Elysea had asked me today's date.

"Twenty days from full lunar tide," I said without flinching, remembering the information Palindromena had given me to study last night after I'd filled out their forms. "You've been in a coma for two days."

She grabbed my hand in hers. "You've been working the wreck?" Her eyes searched mine, but for what? Did she believe me? "While I was asleep?"

I nodded, ignoring my jangling nerves. "Adrei says hi."

She gave me a slight smile and leaned back into her pillows. "I don't want to fight with you, Tempe." She sounded exhausted all of a sudden.

"Of course not." As far as she was concerned, I was still her loving fifteen-year-old sister. But so much had happened in the two years she was gone. Fury reignited within me.

But I couldn't scare her away again. I'd pushed her too hard, too fast. I had to assure her that everything was all right.

I couldn't fail at this.

I moved in beside her. "You feel okay?"

As soon as I said it, I realized that it was something I should've asked from the beginning. I wasn't acting like the caring sister I used to be. I wasn't sure I remembered that girl. The Equinox had no use for her. *I* had no use for her. But Elysea did.

"I don't feel any pain." She smiled. "I imagine that's good. No lasting injuries?"

I squeezed her shoulder. "You'll be back dancing at the Spring Tide in no time."

As soon as I said the words, something burned at the back

of my eyes. I'd come here determined to find answers, but I hadn't prepared myself for the impact of seeing my sister alive. How could I?

You'll be in shock, the video had said.

Palindromena was right after all. I'd planned for this moment, but I couldn't plan how my sister would react. What she'd say and how it would make me feel.

She was still my sister.

For the first time, I let that sink in. She wasn't some stranger, some revived *thing* who wore my sister's face. This was Elysea. And even though she was responsible for the death of my parents, I loved her.

And I was lying to her.

Why did people come to Palindromena? This was painful, far too painful. How did Raylan do this every day? How had my father?

"Tempe?" Her voice was timid. "Are you crying?"

I'd cried only a few times in my life, and most of them were against my sister's shoulder. I couldn't help but lean into her.

"I've missed you," I said.

Her hand curled into my hair. "I'm sorry for scaring you." But tears also lined her voice.

"Tempe?" she asked again.

"Hmm?" I murmured back.

"You always tell me the truth, don't you?" Her voice shook.

I stilled. "Yes." Even though *she* hadn't.

My face was hidden from hers, my hair creating a curtain around me. She smelled like salt and flowers. She smelled like Elysea. The only person who truly understood me. Who never thought I stared too long or was too quiet or too strange. I was always her *Li'l Tempe*.

"Good," she replied. "And I will always tell you the truth."

I pulled away at that. "Then what happened the night Mom and Dad died?"

She gave me a sad smile. "What happened to me?"

"What do you mean? I thought they told you what happened."

"The Equinox doctors?" She arched an eyebrow.

I nodded, perhaps a little too enthusiastically. "Yes."

Her bottom lip quavered. "Tempe." *Oh, Gods below, no.* "Tempe, I'm at Palindromena, aren't I?"

My breath left my lungs. Should I call Raylan in now? If they sedated her, I'd never find out the truth. "What are you talking about?"

Tears formed in her eyes. "Your skin is darker, and your hair a little longer than before." I'd cut my hair yesterday, hoping it would be a similar length to the day Elysea had died, but I had no way of knowing. "And you don't look at me the same. You don't look at me like I'm your sister. You look at me like I'm . . ." She choked on the words, unable to finish the sentence.

I should've known she'd figure it out. We'd known more

about revivals than most. Our childhood had been filled with the word. *Palindromena*.

"Don't be silly." I patted her hand. "You're confused from the accident. You know I don't like the infirmary."

"You said you wouldn't lie to me."

"And you said you wouldn't lie to me." I was not about to let her turn this around. Not after saving for almost two years, after selling everything we'd owned, after diving tirelessly all day, every day. After being alone. This was *my* revival as much as hers. She was not about to ruin it.

"What happened the night our parents died?" I pressed. "You were out there. What did you see? What did you *do*?"

Elysea flew from the bed and ran for the door. She pulled at the door handle but found it locked.

"What are you doing?" I didn't move from the bed. "Why are you avoiding my questions?"

She turned around, tears tracking down her smooth olive skin. "Why are you avoiding mine?"

"Tell me." I was done with this game. I'd waited long enough to hear the truth. I launched off the bed. "What happened that night? What did you do?"

She clutched the material of her nightgown at her chest. "What happened to me? Please, tell me it isn't true. Please tell me I'm really in the infirmary. Tell me I didn't die. I don't want to be dead."

"You're not. You *are* in the infirmary. Look around you!"

She huffed, snot catching in her throat and nose. "You were always such a terrible liar."

My hands clenched at my sides. This was going all wrong. Why couldn't she do what I wanted her to do, say what I wanted her to say, just this once?

I stepped forward. "What were you doing out that night?" Another step. "What did you say to Mom and Dad?" Step. "What did you do?" Step.

She wasn't looking at me; she was studying her hands. "I feel alive, Tempe. But I'm not, am I? Not really."

I was done placating her. "Tell me the truth!"

Tears continued down her cheeks, but she didn't wipe them away. "You first, little sister. What happened? When did I drown?"

I glanced away, unable to meet her eyes. I wasn't her little sister. I was older than her now.

She rushed at me, her hands clutching my arms. Her eyes startled. "Why would you do this to me? Why would you bring me back only to put me away again? Like some discarded thing?"

I stumbled backward. "Stop it! You're fine. You're here. You're alive."

"No." She shook her head. "Nothing about this is fine. You're not acting like my sister." She studied my face. "How long have I been gone? Weeks? Months?"

Pressure built within my chest, like a bubble beneath the

surface, threatening to burst. But I didn't have the energy to argue.

Shock. Yes, it was shock. I wasn't prepared to see my sister again, and I wasn't prepared for her to know the truth. The shock had gotten to me, made me forget my plans. Just like the video had warned me.

I ran for the door and pressed the exit button.

Seconds later, it opened.

I slipped outside, shutting the door, and my sister, behind me.

CHAPTER ELEVEN

LOR

22h 45m

Monday, 1:15 p.m.

A SPARK JOLTED my wrist, letting me know that Tempest had pressed the exit button. She'd only been with her sister for over an hour. I jumped up and unlocked the door.

Tempest's cheeks were flushed, her eyes wet.

"What's wrong?" I asked.

I locked the door behind her. She'd opened her mouth to reply when another voice called from inside the room.

"Let me out! Tempe! Don't leave me in here to die!" It had to be Elysea.

Oh shit. She knew.

Tempest slid to the floor, wrapping her arms around herself.

I stared at her for a long moment, tempted to flee. This wasn't my battle.

I looked at my wrist, where the two illuminated circles were a blaring reminder that I couldn't run now. I had accepted this responsibility the moment I'd put on the echolink. I had promised Ray.

Sliding down beside her, I asked, "Are you okay?" I didn't know how to act as a Warden, but as someone who'd been through this before, I knew how she might feel. As though she were fracturing in two. Her life from before Palindromena and her life after. A life that would not include her sister. It was something Palindromena didn't cover in their little introduction video.

I gritted my teeth. I hated what Tempest was going through. And I hated Palindromena for causing more pain to those already grieving.

Tempest shook her head, burrowing her face in her knees.

Elysea continued yelling and thumping against the door. I wasn't sure if the noise would carry to the other rooms. I had to get this under control. Quickly.

I read through the information on the tablet. It was pretty clear; if a patient realized they were dead, you were to notify the scientists who would sedate them. But there had to be another way. Tempest had already gone through the pain of resurrecting her sister; she should be able to see this through to the end. There had to be some good to come from this.

"You need to convince her she's wrong," I said, reading from the screen. "Tell her she's confused. That she hit her head in the accident."

Tempest didn't shift; I doubted she'd heard a word I'd said.

I should've known I'd screw this up. I wasn't like Ray. I spent my days worrying about the dead—what did I know about the living? Even in my old life, I was never particularly good at reading people. Perhaps that was because I was more focused on what I wanted.

I should've asked Ray to return immediately. But I didn't move. I didn't want to cut the time with his family short because I'd failed.

I let Elysea thump against the door while Tempest cried silently beside me. I wanted to reach out and touch her, reassure her, but I held back. There had to be something else I could do to help.

"I'm sorry," I whispered. I wasn't sure what I was apologizing for. For her loss, for her sister or for not knowing how to make this better.

Only I could. Tempest was grieving, and I knew what that felt like. Grief was the only thing I knew intimately. And it never really went away, no matter what Palindromena professed. It was a bruise that didn't require much pressure to bring pain.

"Tell me what happened in there," I said.

"What happened?" she snapped, looking up. "Elysea died. That's what happened!"

I inched a little closer to her. "Don't waste this time, Tempest. You don't want to regret it."

I had wasted the final hours with Calen. I'd ranted to Nessandra that it was wrong to use the revival process in an attempt to fix what I'd done, when I should've focused on what mattered. On how Calen felt in the hours before his death.

Those wasted hours still haunted me.

"You have to calm your sister down," I said. "You have to lie to her."

Tempest's expression shattered.

How did Raylan do this? I wanted to look away from her tearstained face, but her eyes drew me in like a whirlpool.

"I can't." Her voice was rough from tears. "There's nothing to say that will make it better."

She was wrong. There was *too* much to say when you knew your words, and time, were limited. Now was the time to say everything.

I tried again to ask what happened, but she put her head back on her knees, shielding her face from me. She needed to trust me. She had no one else. But clearly, she didn't trust easily. She must feel so alone.

Except she *wasn't*. Not really. She had her sister, if only for twenty-four hours. And Elysea needed Tempest as much as Tempest needed her. I knew that much. It wasn't fair to either of them. Death had chosen Elysea far too young. Grief had destroyed Tempest's life. And Palindromena played them both for fools.

Tempest didn't need me. These sisters needed each other.

I pulled the mask from my face. First I would show that I trusted her.

"Elysea needs you right now. You're all she has." I realized what had to be done, what I'd been too scared to do. "Don't lie to her, Tempest. Tell her the truth. Tell her what happened."

She looked up at me, confused. "But the Director said—"

"Don't worry about that." My hand hovered near her shoulder. "Tell her you missed her. Tell her how you really feel." The back of my throat began to thicken. I would *not* cry. "Don't let her last moments be alone. If not for you, do it for her. She's scared of dying. But you can help her. You can calm her down. Don't let her last moments be spent in fear."

"Like when she drowned," she whispered. She was fighting herself, her eyes not quite focused on mine.

Fear robbed you of everything. You couldn't see clearly. You couldn't make the most of what was in front of you. I'd been so afraid that day on the cliffs. I'd made a huge mistake, and I continued to pay for it. I wouldn't let Tempest regret her decisions.

Nothing ruined life more than regret.

"Palindromena isn't only for the client. For you," I said. "It's for the revived. This is their last chance to live. Their last chance to see you. You can make this right. Only you can turn this around."

Her brown eyes wavered. "I don't know that I can."

"You can." This time I placed my hand on her forearm. I wanted her to know I was here for her. That I understood. "You're the one person who can. I know you can do this. You're strong. You wouldn't be here if you weren't." And I believed that. She'd come here on her own, somehow paying the ridiculous price the facility required. I thought back to the information I'd read in Tempest's file. "You've survived the last two years without your sister and your parents. You can do this."

"I thought I could," she said, her voice soft and eyes downcast, "but I miss her. I don't want to say goodbye."

Elysea had stopped banging at the door. Somehow, the silence was worse.

I understood wanting to hide from the pain of reality. After all, I'd been hiding in the Aquarium for two years. But we couldn't always hide from the truth. Sometimes we had to embrace what hurt us most. Sometimes we had to do what was right for the other person at the expense of ourselves, like how I was covering for Ray.

"You've already said goodbye," I said gently, not wanting to upset her. "By leaving her alone, you've said your feelings are more important than hers."

"No, I—" she started.

I held up my hand. "I'm not trying to be mean. I'm trying to make you see what's in front of you. You have the chance to be with your sister. One last time. You have the chance for a proper farewell. Did you get that before?"

She shook her head.

"Then don't let this opportunity slip away." I hated that I sounded exactly like a Warden—like someone who believed in the good of Palindromena. But Tempest had come this far; she had to make the most of it. Or she'd never forgive herself.

"Don't live a life of regret." The words rasped in my chest as I said them.

Tempest stared at me, her eyes boring into mine; my heart

thudded. I wanted to know this girl. I wanted to know what would happen with her sister. I wanted to help.

Tempest stood. "Okay," she said, her voice steadying. "I'll go in."

"You're doing the right thing," I said, unlocking the door for her. She reentered without looking back.

I let out a sigh and closed my eyes.

CHAPTER TWELVE

TEMPEST

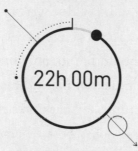

22h 00m

Monday, 2:00 p.m.

I WAS A CRUEL PERSON. Raylan didn't have to say the words;
I could read it on his face. He was horrified by me. I'd always
feared my grief had turned me into someone else, someone my
parents wouldn't recognize. Now I knew the truth.

I was cruel and bitter and unkind.

Perhaps those kids had been right in avoiding me as a child.

Elysea had stopped pounding against the door. The silence
made my chest ache. As though she was already gone from
me. Again.

It was two p.m. I'd wasted nearly two hours of her revival.
I wished I didn't know how much time had passed, but clocks
were everywhere in this place. They didn't want me forgetting
how many "precious" hours remained.

Precious time I could no longer use the way I wanted.

I'd spent years preparing for this moment, all for nothing. All those hours on the dive site, alone. All those Notes
spent. I'd never know the truth of my parents' death.

Elysea wouldn't answer any of my questions now.

She was upset. Angry. At me. And I didn't blame her. I couldn't imagine the shock of discovering you'd died and had only twenty-four hours until you returned to that blank slumber. Still, I needed the truth. Not only had she lied about my parents, but she'd left me that night. She owed me this.

But I also couldn't turn my back on her. Raylan was right. I couldn't let her last hours be by herself. His words had weighed on me like a fishing net, trapping me within. His blue eyes were hard and yet kind. He understood what I was going through.

This was my one chance. My only chance. Elysea couldn't be brought back again. And she still had twenty-two hours left of her short second life.

I would be there for her, but I would also have my answers.

Elysea had retreated to the bed, her arms wrapped around her middle. Her eyes and cheeks were red. Her hair was skewed, as though she had been pulling at it. She was a mess.

"Are you going to tell me the truth now?" she asked, her voice quivering and her body shifting in agitation.

I gave a slight nod. "I'm here to make you a deal."

"What kind of deal?" She looked terrified.

"Tell me about Mom and Dad, and I'll tell you anything you want to know"—I gestured around us—"about this place. About what happened."

"About my death?" Her expression turned stormy.

I hesitated. "Yes."

She let out a shuddering breath. "I knew it. The moment I walked in here. I just knew." She glanced up at me. "You brought me back to find out about what happened to Mom and Dad?" Was that hurt in her voice? Because I didn't just want to spend time with her?

"And why you went out the night you died."

She raked her hands through her hair. "I don't remember anything about that night. I wish I did."

I hoped her confusion would wear off now that I was telling her the truth. I wanted answers about everything.

"Then start by telling me about Mom and Dad."

She drew herself from the bed, as though her limbs were weighed down with anchors, her usually upright dancer's posture wrecked. "What do you want to know?" She approached me as though she wasn't sure how I would react. Was she worried I'd run again?

"Everything," I kept my voice firm.

"You said I was responsible for their deaths?"

"Daon told me that you confided in him. He said you were out diving that night and saw Mom and Dad. He said that you were the reason they were dead."

She surprised me by nodding. Finally, the truth. I braced myself.

"Yes," she repeated slowly, cautiously. "But it's not what you think."

"Then explain!"

She pulled her hair back from her face. Her hands were

red from where she'd been pounding at the door. "I don't want you to hate me."

I raised an eyebrow. "You assume that I love you now."

Her brow crumpled, tears forming in her eyes. "I'm so sorry, Tempe."

I gritted my teeth. "Don't be sorry. Tell me the truth."

A breath tore through her body as though she struggled to breathe. "I was out diving that night. I wanted to find something for your birthday. An Old World necklace, or some pretty stones. I wanted it to be a surprise."

I stilled. My birthday was in a few days; I hadn't thought about it for almost two years. It didn't hold any significance without my family.

Elysea closed her eyes as she continued the story. "When I came up from the dive, Mom and Dad had pulled their boat up next to mine. They had traced the *Sunrise* on their boat's locator, and had stopped by on their way home from Palindromena. But something was wrong. They told me we had to leave immediately."

"Leave?" I asked.

She nodded. "They wanted to leave the Equinox."

"And go where?" The Equinox had been my family's home for generations, and before that, our home had been the land beneath the sea.

"I don't know. They said it was life or death. When I asked them what that meant, Dad said they didn't have time to explain. They told me to take the *Sunrise* home, collect you and then follow them. But I didn't want to. I argued that I loved my life on the Equinox. I loved my dance classes. I"—she gestured to both of us—"*we* were happy there. We were settled. But Mom and Dad promised we would be happy at our new home as long as we were together."

She tugged at her hair. "I didn't know what to do. I was young, I was confused. I was scared. Mom and Dad were acting so strange, so I agreed. They gave me a crude map Mom had drawn to their planned destination."

The *Sunrise* only took three passengers; we never could've journeyed together. But I hadn't seen this map before. I held my breath, and my tongue, waiting for the rest of the story. Waiting to hear how this led to my parents' death.

"When I got home, I was going to wake you up, but you looked so peaceful. You'd had a bad day at school, and you needed to rest," she said. "I went to sleep instead, thinking it wouldn't make much of a difference if we left early the next day. But then—"

"Our parents died in a storm that night, their boat capsizing."

She covered her mouth with her hand. "It's all my fault. If I'd left immediately, like they wanted me to, we never would've been apart."

So that's why she told Daon she felt responsible. She thought we could've saved them if we'd also been out on the water that night.

Something that had been sitting on my shoulders for the last two years began to shift.

"We all could've died in that storm," I said, moving closer. "You saved us, Ely."

"Maybe," she said. Before I could say anything else, she asked, "Are they recording us?"

"What are you talking about?"

"Can they hear what we're saying?" She pointed to the door where Raylan was waiting outside. "Palindromena?"

"No. I don't think so." No one had mentioned anything about recordings. "Why?"

"There's something I need to tell you, but first"—she lowered her voice—"you must break me out of here."

I startled. "Have you drunk too much seawater?"

She grabbed my hands in hers, her eyes holding back tears. "Please, Tempe!"

I pulled from her grasp. "I can't break you out of here. I *won't*."

Her brows pinched together. "Because I lied to you? Because I left you too?" She shook her head. "I'm sorry, Tempe."

"Because there's no way out!" I couldn't even get out of this room without Raylan's permission. "And you'll be dead again tomorrow."

Hope lit her features and she reached for me once more. "But you would break me out, if there was a way?"

I shook her off. "Tell me what you were going to say first."

I could tell my rejection hurt her, but right now, I didn't care. I was sick of the deceit. I'd lived the past two years confused about what had happened to my parents, and my sister.

Elysea twisted her brown hair around her hand, something she did when she was nervous. "You're going to be angry with me."

I doubted I could be angrier, or more confused, than I already was, conversing with my dead sister.

I jerked my chin to indicate she should continue.

"Everything I told you is the truth," she said. "I saw Mom and Dad that night and they wanted us to follow them, but I didn't listen. And then they died." She shook her head. "I've never even said this out loud, as I knew it sounded impossible. But I have to tell you . . ."

I felt like I'd taken in a mouthful of seawater, bubbling in my chest and throat. "Tell me what?"

"Mom and Dad," she said. "They're still alive."

CHAPTER THIRTEEN

TEMPEST

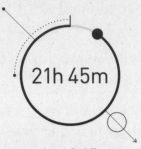

21h 45m

Monday, 2:15 p.m.

OUR PARENTS, alive?

"What are you talking about?" My legs felt like limp sea-weed. "Their boat was nothing but splinters. No one would've survived that."

"That's what I thought too," Elysea said. "Until I found Mom's necklace two years after her death."

"What?" Aside from her wedding band, Mom only ever wore necklaces. I remembered sitting in her lap as a child, twirl-ing a string of blue stones in my hand as she sang to me. She then broke off the cord and the stones fell into my palm.

"For you," she'd said, pressing a kiss to my temple. "For good luck."

I'd kept the stones. And I dropped one into the sea each time I dove, hoping my mom was watching over me.

"The gold necklace with the black pearls," Elysea said. "It was Mom's favorite. She was wearing it the night she disappeared."

"Where did you find it? Near where their boat crashed?"

"No." Her voice was so low I had to lean close. "That's the thing, Tempe. I found it hundreds of miles away. At a dive site. *Our* dive site."

"That doesn't make any sense. How could it have gotten there?"

"Exactly!" She grabbed my arms, and for the first time, her face and posture radiated confidence. "Don't you see? It was a message. A message to us that they were still alive and they want us to find them."

"I don't know ..." Although I wanted to believe in this beautiful fantasy. "Maybe it was a similar necklace?"

She nodded sagely. "I was worried that I was seeing things that I wanted to see. Hoping they had somehow survived. I didn't tell you about what I'd found because I didn't want you to get your hopes up. A few months afterward, I found Dad's echolink."

"No," I said, my breath a whisper. "That's impossible." While a necklace could have floated in a wave, an echolink was attached to the skin. It was highly unlikely to be dislodged, even in a boating accident. I couldn't remember a time when Dad wasn't wearing it. "Where ... ?" I couldn't finish the sentence.

"The same spot." A smile played on her face. "Another message, I'm sure of it. After I found the echolink, I started sneaking out at night to spend time by the dive site, hoping to catch them."

"When was this?" My body started to tremble.

"A month ago." Her hands dropped to her sides. "A month before I died, I suppose."

"That was almost two years ago." Any hope I had left me in a rush. If our parents *were* still alive, why hadn't I found anything of theirs at the dive site?

"Two *years*?" she repeated, stumbling over the words.

"I'm sorry." What else was there to say? "Was that why you were out the night you died?"

"Maybe." She frowned. "I wish I could remember. Still, there has to be some explanation for what I found. They were Mom and Dad's most important possessions."

"Aside from the *Sunrise*."

"Right." She pointed at me. "Which they left behind the night they supposedly died. It can't be a coincidence that both the necklace and the echolink ended up where we dove every day. Perhaps they were still tracking the *Sunrise*?"

"If they're still alive," I said, "why haven't they returned? Why leave us clues like that?"

"I don't know." Her expression hardened. "But there's one way to find out the truth. Break me out of here, and we'll find out together."

"I . . ." Was this all a plot to help her escape? For what purpose? She'd still be dead in less than twenty-four hours. "I don't know."

"Please, don't let me die in here."

"You're already dead." My voice was hushed like sea spray.

Her vibrant eyes didn't shift from my face. "I don't feel dead."

I bit back my retort. *You will be. Soon enough.*

"Please, Tempe. I know I don't have long, but I don't want to be stuck in here for my last hours. I want to go *home*." Her voice broke on the word, and so did the hold on my resolve. A part of me wanted that too.

I wasn't used to seeing my sister broken. Her hair frayed, her eyes glassy. She had always been the calm one. The strong one. She was meant to be reassuring me, not the other way around. I wished we could go back two years. Before she was dead and before everything changed.

"How would we find out if they were still alive?"

"The map," she said with a nod. "It's the best place to start."

I glanced over my shoulder. We couldn't escape without Raylan unlocking the doors. And Palindromena wasn't about to let us walk out the front door, certainly not with Elysea in an infirmary gown. The Director had made it clear Elysea would be sedated if she found out the truth.

But I couldn't leave Elysea here. I, too, wanted to believe that our parents were alive and leaving us messages. If I didn't break her out, I'd always wonder if she were telling the truth. It would eat me up inside.

"Where is this map?" I asked.

"I hid it somewhere safe." Her expression was guarded. It was her only leverage. "Get me out of here and I'll take you to it."

Could I trust her? After all the secrets she'd kept from me?

"I wanted to tell you," she said, reading my hesitation. "I wanted to tell you everything. But I didn't know how. I thought if I told you the truth about the night Mom and Dad left, then you'd leave me too." She exhaled a faltering breath. "But then *I* left. I understand if you don't trust me."

I wanted to. I really did. And I wasn't about to turn away this chance of seeing my parents again, if they were in fact alive.

"Okay. Deal."

Elysea threw her arms around me. "Thank you, Tempe. Thank you."

I pushed her away, not ready to give in to the emotions that threatened to drag me under.

And we were still left with the complication of breaking out. The only window in the room was fake. We had to exit through the front door. Somehow we had to convince Palindromena that we weren't a risk. That Elysea wasn't a patient trying to escape. That she was just another visitor.

"Where's the food?" I asked, looking around for the silver tray Raylan had pointed out earlier.

"Are you hungry?" She sounded incredulous as I approached the silver tray.

I laughed, an almost hysterical sound. "We need to get you some clothes if we're going to walk out of here."

Lifting the tray lid, I found a bottle of rainwater, seaweed chips and a cup of blended sugarfish pudding—Elysea's favorite. It wasn't a coincidence; I'd filled out her preferences last night when I'd applied for her revival.

"Perfect." I opened the milky-green pudding and smeared it down my dress before dabbing some across my lips.

Before she could ask if I'd drunken too much ragar, I ran to the door and pressed the exit button. "Raylan!" I made my voice wobble. "Raylan!"

He opened the door and I slipped through.

"Are you okay?" He hadn't put his mask back on and the concerned look on his face made my insides twist. I didn't want to fool him, but I didn't have any other choice.

I held my hand to my mouth and spoke through my fingers. "It got too much." My voice squeaked. "I threw up."

A small wrinkle of disgust appeared on his nose as he took in my stained dress before his expression settled into one of understanding. "That's okay," he said. "Let's go clean you up."

I braced my hand on the door behind me. "No. I don't want to waste any more time. You're right. Elysea needs me." And now I needed her.

He must've misunderstood the ferocity in my voice as grief, as he smiled empathetically. "I'll get you some clean clothes."

"Please. And no infirmary gowns. I don't want to be mistaken for a patient."

A ghost of a smile appeared on his face. "Of course not."

He let me back into the room without asking any more questions.

Now I had a breakout to plan.

Elysea paced the floor, her hands clutching her sides. "What did you do?"

"I asked for clothes," I said as I searched for anything that could be used to help us escape. All the furniture was bolted down. There was nothing we could use as a weapon. "We're going to have to use the element of surprise."

Elysea shook her head. "I don't want you to get hurt." That was the Elysea I knew. More worried about me than her own well-being.

"I won't." But I wasn't sure how Palindromena's security would react. I'd paid for Elysea's revival. Why did they care where she spent her last hours?

And yet they did. Their insistence I lie to Elysea was proof of that. Although Raylan had told me to tell her the truth—

There was a knock at the door. Elysea jumped.

"The clothes," I said.

Raylan's face was clear of any suspicion when he opened the door. He handed over a pair of loose-fitting water-resistant shorts and a T-shirt with PALINDROMENA on the back.

"Sorry they're a bit big. There's a drawstring to bring the pants together." He shrugged. "They're the only ones I could find. The gift shop is currently closed."

Gift shop? As if this place wasn't extorting enough money from its grieving clients. I swallowed down my retort and accepted the clothing.

I gave him a thin smile so as not to tip him off. "Thanks."

"How are you doing?" His concern appeared genuine.

His eyes dropped to the crusted pudding on my dress. "Any better?"

I felt bad for deceiving him. He'd been nothing but helpful.

"Yes." I backed away. "Much better." There, that answered both questions.

"Stay strong," he said, with a jerk of his chin, understanding my desire to return to my sister.

As soon as the door slid shut, I threw the clothes at Elysea. "Wear these."

She began putting on the too-large shorts without question. After she pulled on the shirt, I explained, "We need Raylan to think you're me."

She frowned. "My hair is longer, and lighter."

"I don't think he'll notice. It will work." I wasn't sure if I was trying to convince myself or her. "Just keep your head down, okay? I need to get him to unlock the door out to the corridor."

She squeezed my hand. "I trust you."

I pushed her toward the door and pressed the button. "Raylan? Can you please open the door again?" I would've liked to have waited longer so he wouldn't be suspicious, but we'd already lost two hours. And I was worried I'd back out if I took more time to think things through.

"Is everything all right?" he asked through the door.

I made sure my reply was steady. "Yes, I need to go to the bathroom."

He paused. "There's a bathroom inside." Was that suspicion in his raised voice?

Elysea twisted to look at me, apprehension clear in her eyes. I held up my hand, signaling her to stay silent.

"Um . . ." I hesitated until the souring smell of pudding invaded my nose. "That's where I threw up. It's quite gross." There. That was a reasonable enough excuse.

"Oh." The tension eased from Raylan's voice. "Sure, one second."

The door clicked and opened.

"Get ready," I whispered to Elysea.

Elysea stepped toward Raylan and into the waiting room. But we still needed Raylan to unlock the door into the corridor. I remained crouched. As the recovery door slid closed, I wedged the food tray into the doorjamb to prevent the locking mechanism from engaging. I paused, waiting for an alarm to go off.

A bated breath.

Nothing.

I peeked through the gap created by the tray. Raylan moved toward the outer door that connected to the hallway. My nails bit into my palms as he pressed the unlock button. The door slid open, and light filtered in from the hallway. I could almost taste the sunlight. And freedom.

"Thank you," Elysea said, her voice lower to mimic mine. She kept her head tilted down so Raylan wouldn't notice the difference between us.

Raylan pointed down the open doorway. "The visitor bathrooms are that—" he began. "Hey, what happened to your shoes?"

Cursed waters! I hadn't thought about that.

Before I could do anything, Elysea stumbled forward and hit the floor. No one was in better control of their body than my sister. Her fall looked real.

"Are you okay?" Raylan crouched beside her, his hand nearing her shoulder. I didn't like using his kindness against him, but I didn't hesitate. I shoved the tray to the side, forcing the recovery room door back open. It slid without grievance.

Raylan glanced up in surprise. He blinked rapidly as he took me in, realizing the girl crouched beside him was not, in fact, me. He reached for the door lock.

Before he could press the panel, Elysea darted into the corridor. I smashed the food tray into the door's panel. It sparked and smoked, and I leaped through the doorway just before the door slid closed behind me, sealing Raylan inside.

"Go, Elysea!" I whispered.

I tried not to think of Raylan's confused face as we took off down the hallway.

———

"Slow down," I said to Elysea. "You look suspicious."

Tension reverberated off her in waves. "Is that a—" she began.

"Tree." I filled in as we passed by the central black-bark that wound itself throughout the building. "The last black-bark in the known world."

Elysea tore her eyes from the tree. "Get me out of here, Tempe."

We walked toward the foyer, with short but quick steps. Was it my imagination, or did the security guards' eyes follow us as we passed by? Did I imagine their hands moving to their belts, their fingers curling around weapons?

When we reached the foyer, I glanced around, but I couldn't see the Director or Selna. No one who would recognize us. We were going to make it. But before we could leave, we had to pass through security.

I took a few calming breaths, reminding myself that Palindromena was more worried about people breaking in than breaking out. Hopefully.

We approached a thin middle-aged man with a curly black beard and skin the color of Palindromena's amber cliffs. He sat at a glossy white desk not far from the entrance. He smiled as we approached. I decided it was best to appear helpful and nonthreatening, although my legs urged me to bolt.

"Tempest Alerin," I said.

The man scrolled through his tablet.

"And her?" He fixed his gaze on Elysea. "I have on my records that you arrived alone."

I glanced at the guards standing watch at either side of the glass door, barring our way out. Batons dangled from their belts.

"I—" But I had nothing.

We were so close to the outside world. So close to being free.

I could only hope that Palindromena wouldn't send me to the Prison Reef for what I'd tried to do. I'd never escape the enclosed floating fortress that was surrounded by a net of starving razorfish.

Think, Tempe, think.

Elysea took a step toward the desk, attempting to look brave and strong, as though she had nothing to hide, but her shoulders were rigid.

This was the moment. The moment we failed. The moment *I* failed. And for the first time, guilt swirled hot in my belly like a sea serpent.

What if everything she believed was true? What if she'd blamed herself for our parents' deaths, only to find messages years later that indicated they were still alive.

I'd brought her back. Back for a sin she didn't commit. Now she was going to spend her last hours in an infirmary room, knowing death called her name. Or maybe Palindromena would end her restored life before she had a chance to return to that sterile infirmary bed. Was that what they really meant by sedation? Was that the punishment for breaking Palindromena's rules? Was that why I'd never heard of any revived patients leaving the island?

I wouldn't allow Elysea to be caught. Not now. She had twenty-four hours; *I* had a lifetime.

Elysea squared her shoulders, ready for whatever happened next. That was when her Palindromena T-shirt caught my eye. She didn't look like a patient; she looked like—

"My Warden," I said, nodding to Elysea.

The guard gave a carefree shrug but checked his data. "My records say Tempest's Warden is a Ray*lan* Bassan," he said, emphasizing the male name. "Oh. That's odd." The two guards at the door looked in our direction at his exclamation.

We were done for. All he'd have to do was glimpse the real Raylan's photo and realize Elysea was not the boy with sandy-blond hair and crystal-blue eyes.

I tensed for his accusation.

He tapped his screen. "Your photo ID is missing for today's revival."

I glanced at my sister. Could we be so blessed by the Gods below?

"It's Ray*la*, actually." Elysea let out an exaggerated sigh. "My name was entered in incorrectly when I first joined Palindromena."

"How annoying," I said with a carefree laugh.

Elysea smiled in response. She was a much better actor than me; all her performances had prepared her for this moment. "Very annoying. And I did take the photo. Technology!" She threw up her hands in defeat. "What can you do?"

"You could call the Director," I suggested, hoping the guard would do nothing of the sort. If I was right, people like Nessandra should not be bothered with insignificant admin issues. I forced myself not to look at my sister. I pretended she was my Warden. Nothing more.

The man scratched his beard and grimaced. "I don't want to cause a fuss." I took in a sharp breath and held it, not wanting to look too relieved. "Where are you headed?" he asked me. "I have you clocked in until tomorrow at noon."

"That's another mistake," I said. "I've decided not to go through with the revival after all. I want to go home."

"Really?" The man looked at me as though I had drunk too much ragar.

"Yes. I'm not ready to say goodbye to my sister. Not yet." Truth rang clear in my voice. No one could argue that I was lying, because I wasn't. I needed my sister with me.

"Fair enough," he said. "Well, you're always welcome to come back." He pressed something on his tablet and the front door opened. The two guards on either side of the glass stepped aside to let us through.

We were almost there.

"Wait," he said before we could leave. "What happened to your shoes?"

Elysea laughed her bell-like laugh, and one hundred different memories of us playing in and around the ocean filled my head. "I'm from Equinox," she said. "Being barefoot helps me balance on the water."

He studied her for a moment before grinning. "I hear you. I only just started working here. I'm still not used to the stillness of land."

I gave him a smile and a wave. "Thank you!"

"I'll be back soon," Elysea called over her shoulder.

We were lucky. Almost too lucky. But I didn't question the Gods below and why they chose today to be on my side. I would take what I could get.

We were halfway to the harbor when an alarm sounded from behind us. Raylan must have escaped and alerted the authorities.

Get out. Get out. Get out, the alarm wailed. Elysea and I were in complete agreement.

CHAPTER FOURTEEN

LOR

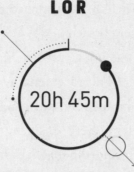

20h 45m

Monday, 3:15 p.m.

I'D FAILED. I'd failed Tempest. And I'd failed Raylan. He had trusted me, and I'd let him down.

I wished I could yank the echolink from my skin. But that wouldn't change anything. As soon as I'd put on the echolink, I'd sealed my fate.

Would Tempest have broken her sister out if she'd known the truth about the revival process?

There was a reason we locked patients in the facility and didn't tell them they were dead. All of Nessandra's blathering about it being best for the patient and the client was simply to cover the truth.

A Warden was connected to their patient.

If anything happened to Elysea in the next twenty-four hours, then it would happen to me. Our lives were intrinsically linked through the echolink, tethered to my heartbeat.

If she died, I would too.

But I didn't care about that. I cared about Ray. It was his future I'd bargained with. *My* future had ended the day Calen took his last shuddering breath.

As a Warden, it was your responsibility to keep your patient safe and secure at Palindromena. I wasn't sure what the consequences would be for Ray, but I knew they'd be dire. It was the price for working here, ensuring the revival program ran smoothly and Palindromena maintained its hold over one of the few islands. The Equinox Conservators were always looking for a reason to question Nessandra's authority; if enough Reefs had doubts over her methods and motives, then they could band together and have her ousted.

I should've realized from the beginning what Tempest was concocting. At times she seemed sad or hurt, but mostly she seemed determined. Focused.

Now I knew why.

She'd always planned to break her sister free.

I looked at my wrist.

3:15 p.m.

I had three options.

1. Call attention to what had happened here, outing me and Raylan and what we'd done.

2. Wait until twenty-four hours had passed and give in to the fate that awaited me.

Or . . .

Well, there were only really two options. And neither was great for me. Even if I stayed silent, the tank with Elysea's name on it would remain empty and Ray's job would be forfeited, at the very least. Because of me. Because I couldn't keep two girls in one room for twenty-four hours.

Unless . . . Unless I found Tempest and brought Elysea back here without anyone knowing what had happened, then Ray's job would be safe. I had around twenty hours. Then I could return to the silence of the Aquarium.

I *had* to get out of this room. I *had* to find those girls.

I pushed at the door, but it wouldn't budge. While Tempest had smashed the internal locking mechanism, there had to be another way to open the door from the outside, without alerting security. I scrolled through my digital tablet, looking for any information on how to unlock the door. The only reference to the doors was if there was a fire. I paused, rereading the passage.

In a state of emergency, such as a fire, the facility's doors will be unlocked, and all employees are to meet outside in the courtyard. The patients will remain locked inside the recovery rooms to ensure they don't learn of their fates. Once the threat has been cleared, all employees must return to their posts.

I studied the ceiling. There was a fire sensor in the middle of the waiting room. Too bad I didn't have anything to burn. The only thing that could catch fire was the tree in the foyer. Or paper.

Of course! My book!

I pulled it from my back pocket and tore out a page. I glanced around the room, searching for something to generate a flame with. But there was nothing in the recovery room or the waiting room. Then I remembered the door sensor. It had sparked when Tempest had destroyed it.

I studied the ruined panel. A few blackened wires curled in on each other. I grabbed the tray Tempest had dropped and took a deep breath.

This is it. My one chance.

I swung as hard as I could and smashed the panel, hoping to find some life left in the electronics.

My efforts were rewarded with a tiny spark. I shoved the paper against the wire and blew against it. While the spark immediately died, the heat began to brown the paper. I pressed my lips together to stop from crying out in joy. Seconds later, the paper began to smoke.

I jumped onto one of the waiting room chairs and held the smoking paper to the sensor.

For a moment, nothing happened. Then I heard the blessed sound of the fire alarm.

I flew to the door and pushed the handle. But the door still wouldn't budge.

Shit. Maybe the outside lock had been busted too.

The alarm echoed off the walls and inside my brain. It was so loud, I almost didn't hear the click of the door unlocking.

Almost.

I pushed at the door again and it slid open. I fled down the hallway, lost in the crowd as the employees exited the building.

———◦———

I ran down to the basement. I tore off the mask and bandana; I was beyond illusions now. The blank faces in the tanks watched me as I headed toward my bunk. I couldn't help but think they were wondering if I would let them escape too—if they were revived.

As much as I hated what Palindromena did, I wasn't on some ridiculous crusade to give everyone their last twenty-four hours in the sun. I was too selfish for that. I always had been. My mother had once said that I only cared about myself. That I worried only about what worried me.

She was right in a way. I was selfish. Grief was selfish. I stayed in this basement mourning the loss of the life I once had. But I'd tried to be different. I cared for the bodies in the tanks like I hadn't cared for Calen. I'd placed my future and dreams behind me.

Tempest had been selfless in her grief. She'd put herself in danger to rescue her sister. To give her the chance to take her last breaths outside this facility. I had to admit her actions took guts.

The back of the basement was quiet and dark. For a moment,

I considered hiding out down here and pretending the last few hours hadn't happened. But pretending wouldn't undo what Tempest had done. The only chance to fix this was to bring Elysea back to Palindromena.

I grabbed a few belongings from my bunk. I wished I had a weapon, but weapons needed to be assigned and checked in at the end of the day by security. That would mean alerting others to the fact I lived down here. If I wanted to return to the basement, I needed to keep my involvement in Elysea's revival a secret.

I left through the rear exit, where the bodies were transported into the building before being homed in their tanks. Palindromena didn't want to parade the dead in front of clients.

I blinked into the sun. The heat rolled over my skin like coarse sand. The alarm continued to sound, echoing across the entire island. I should've run, but my feet were fixed to the ground. The smell of seaweed and soil seeped into me. I could taste the salt on the air. A slight wind ruffled the longer strands of hair around my face. My eyelids fluttered shut and I breathed everything in.

I'd forgotten what it felt like. To be outside. To be alive. Even though I didn't have time or the luxury to enjoy it, my body had a mind of its own. My lungs expanded in relief. My shoes dug into the earth. And my hands twitched, wanting to feel the scrape of rock beneath my fingertips. Wanting to climb to the top of the surrounding mountains.

But I couldn't. If I allowed myself to move on, I was saying that Calen's death meant nothing to me.

The insistent alarm reminded me of why I was out here. I had more pressing concerns. I couldn't keep this from Ray any longer.

I composed a message on my tablet and hit send.

I need you to come back to Palindromena. Now!

CHAPTER FIFTEEN

TEMPEST

20h 30m

Monday, 3:30 p.m.

WITHOUT A LAND ROVER, it had taken about fifteen minutes to run back to the dock. The *Sunrise* bobbed up and down in the water like a lost child looking for his parents in a crowd. I scrambled aboard, pulling off my sweat-soaked and pudding-crusted seaweed dress to reveal my diving skin. I threw the dress into the water.

Blue-black clouds had gathered on the horizon. A storm.

I turned on the boat's engine, the hum soothing my nerves. We were nearly out of there. We were going to make it.

Elysea was fixated on Palindromena behind us. Although we couldn't see the facility from here, we could still hear the wails of the alarm. So far, no one had approached from the dock. Not yet.

"Don't worry," I said, pressing on the accelerator. "I'm getting you out of here." I wasn't sure who I was trying to convince. I couldn't break either of us free from reality.

"Do we know how much time we have?" Elysea asked. "That *I* have."

One problem with leaving Palindromena was that we wouldn't be surrounded by clocks. I looked at the sun behind the brewing storm.

"Only a few hours have passed since you were revived," I said. "We have plenty of time."

Plenty of time for what? For Elysea to prove our parents were still alive? If she was right, would there be enough time to find them? Time for one last reunion?

My lungs stuttered as though I had no more oxygen left in my breather.

"Are you all right?" Elysea placed her hand on my shoulder.

I wanted to say no. I hadn't been all right since her death. "We'll have to move quickly. Before—" But I couldn't say the words.

"Before I die."

I didn't reply. I pulled away from the shore and left Palindromena behind.

Waves lapped up against the bow of the boat and sprayed our legs and feet. I wiped the foam from my cheek. I might as well be swimming.

"Where are we going?" I asked, turning the boat toward the crowded black clouds. "Where's the map?"

"The Equinox," she said, studying the horizon as though our home would suddenly appear. "I hid it somewhere safe."

"Back to the Equinox it is, then." I veered the boat to the right.

"Palindromena will send security after us." She twisted her long hair into a sea snake. "We broke their rules."

"I know."

I checked to see if there was any movement on the beach behind us.

Nothing. Just a thin line of crisp white sand.

But the final echoes of the alarm and the fleet of boats in the harbor were a promise that Palindromena *would* come.

The *Sunrise* wasn't built for many—three people at most—but it was built for speed. The boat cut through waves like a knife slicing through freshly caught familfish.

Let them try to catch us.

Elysea approached the deck. "When did you get so grown up, Tempe?"

I turned to study the ocean ahead. "While you were gone, Ely," I said softly.

I could feel her breath against my neck.

"I'm so sorry," she said. "I'm so sorry I left you."

I cleared my throat before replying, "It's fine." I didn't want to talk about this now. I had to safeguard my last ounce of strength, a buoy in choppy waters.

Elysea's eyes flicked across my face, as though she was looking for something . . . something to show I was still the girl she knew. Still her little sister.

But I wasn't. Her death had forced me to become someone else. Without her, without Mom and Dad, I'd had to grow up fast. I didn't have any other family on the Equinox. There had been no one to take care of me. No one but myself.

I returned to the wheel, not wanting to disappoint her.

"It will take an hour to return to the Equinox," I said.

She didn't reply, sensing my distance. Even though she was back—albeit briefly—I was not about to revert to that little girl she knew. That girl who looked to her older sister for everything. To survive these twenty-four hours, I needed to become the storm, not succumb to it.

I peered at Elysea from the corner of my eye. She'd taken a seat on the stern.

"Why did you keep the map?" I asked. "If you thought our parents were dead?"

Her brows pinched. "It was the last thing they gave me. Of course I wanted to keep it."

"But you didn't share it with me."

"I told you," she said. "I felt guilty for not leaving when they asked me to. Like you, I thought they'd died that night—and I could've been there to save them. I didn't want you to blame me. I didn't want to lose you too."

I gulped, breathing in the salty air. But I needed a clear head, not the mugginess of the sea.

"I'm sorry." She hung her head. "I thought I was doing

139

what was best. I was only fourteen; I made a mistake." Her voice softened. "I'm sorry I kept it from you."

I swallowed down the ache in my chest.

Now that I knew she wasn't responsible for our parents' deaths, it would be harder to let her go.

Palindromena had lied.

Twenty-four hours would never be enough.

CHAPTER SIXTEEN

LOR

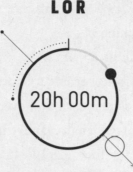

20h 00m

Monday, 4:00 p.m.

I STAYED HIDDEN in the cliff's shadows as I awaited Ray's arrival.

These cliffs were once a treasured place where I'd spent most of my days. Now they loomed like death's shadow. The end of my old life.

After an hour, Ray arrived in his trawler, pulling straight up to the beach.

"What happened?" he asked when I approached. I hated that I'd dragged him back here for this.

"They tricked me," I said.

"What are you talking about?"

"The Alerin sisters. They escaped." I hung my head. "I'm so sorry, Ray."

He let out a string of curses. "Escaped to where?"

"I don't know," I said.

Ray ran his hands down his face. "You know what this means."

"You'll lose your job."

He cursed again. "It's worse than that. My family will lose their home on the Equinox."

"What are you talking about?"

"When I signed up to become a Warden, I promised the Director that I would treat each and every patient as though they were a member of my family. If anything ever went wrong, I would have to pay my life's taxes in full. That's money my parents don't have. They'll have to sell their place on the Equinox to get it. That's one of the reasons my mom hates me working here—she thought the risk was too high. But with my father getting older, and me not being able to spearfish anymore, working here was the only option."

"I don't know what to say," I whispered. "I'm so sorry."

"You're sorry?" He glanced at my wrist and raised his eyebrows. "You're wearing the echolink because of me and now that the patient's gone, you—"

"I don't care about that."

"Do you have a death wish?" he scoffed. "If anything happens to her out there"—he squinted against the glare of the ocean—"you're fish-bait, bud."

"I know." For the next twenty-four hours, Elysea's fate was tied to my own.

I swallowed roughly a few times. I needed water. The sun was hot, and my skin already felt like it was burning.

"We have to alert Palindromena's security," Ray said. "That's the only way we can retrieve her quickly and safely."

"No. You'll lose your job and your family will lose their home. I can't do that to you."

His breaths came raggedly between words. "What else can we do?"

"*We* can find them. *We* can bring them back."

"It's too risky."

"It's too risky not to."

He put his hand on my arm. "You don't want to compromise my future, and I won't gamble with yours. I'm willing to take the chance and hope that Nessandra forgives me. The most important thing is that we get the patient back. And our best chance is with Palindromena's retrieval boats."

"We can't." If Palindromena found out I'd been involved, I'd have to face the consequences of my involvement in Calen's death. I'd have to take responsibility. But I wasn't ready. Not yet.

"Why?" he asked. "What's going on, Lor?" It wasn't often he used my name. Which gave me an idea. I could tell him *something* to help make him understand, without revealing *everything*.

"I'm Lor Ritter," I said with a small shrug, hoping to lighten the moment. "I'm Nessandra's son."

"Nessandra?" Ray blinked. "As in the Director?" I nodded.

"But Nessandra doesn't have a son," he said.

I let out a laugh. Of course she'd never mentioned me. Sometimes I believed Nessandra loved the facility more than me. Her true child. My mother had inherited Palindromena from my grandparents. While they had become uneasy with what they'd created, questioning the morality of it, my mother hadn't.

After my grandparents died while out on the water, my mother had become determined to solve the riddle that was death so no one else would ever lose a parent, child or friend. A seemingly noble cause, but she was willing to sacrifice anyone and everything to get what she wanted.

Ray glanced to the cliffs behind me, as though he could see through to the facility. "Tell me you're joking."

"I wish I was." I envied Ray's childhood. Not only did he have a mother who wasn't the Queen of Death, but he'd gone to school, had friends, enjoyed parties—engaged in normal childish activities. While I spent my younger years staring at corpses as my mother stuck needles into their arms to bring them back to life.

I'd been a constant disappointment, preferring to spend my days out climbing cliffs rather than learning about revivals. I didn't want to inherit Palindromena, and I'd never known my father—my mother had only told me he'd been a fisherman, but he was long gone.

Growing up, I'd been determined to be free of the island and explore the world. Now I was desperate to stay hidden in its basement. But that safe and secure future was at risk.

"Why didn't you ever tell me?" He crossed his arms over his chest. "I don't understand."

"My mother and I don't see eye to eye over her company. We should leave the dead in peace, but my mother believes

Palindromena *brings* peace. She can't know that I let a patient escape. She'll kick me out of the Aquarium, and I don't have anywhere else to go." Hopefully he wouldn't ask why.

Ray pressed his lips together, but stayed silent.

"I didn't mean to let you down, Ray. Let me fix this. I can fix this." I didn't want another friend to suffer because of my mistakes. "You can trust me."

"I never should've asked you to cover for me," he said eventually. "All of this for nothing."

I didn't want to ask, but I couldn't stop the words from coming out. "What happened at the doctor?"

He didn't glance up. "She said a brace would help with my mobility on the Equinox, but I can't wear that in the water without it rusting completely." He was quiet for a moment. "So she suggested aqua therapy to help strengthen my other muscles to ease some pain, but the pressure of deep-sea spearfishing is out of the question."

"I'm sorry." That only left Palindromena and their medical division. He needed his job. "Please let me help you. You can trust me."

Ray didn't reply but turned back to his boat. I didn't blame him for wanting to leave. Would I ever see him again?

"Get in," he called over his shoulder. When I didn't move from the sand, he said, "Well, don't just stand there. We're going fishing."

I stumbled onto the boat. "I really am sorry," I said. "For everything. I should've—"

He held up a hand. "I'm the one who got you into this mess."

"You didn't know I'd be completely incompetent."

His lips twitched. "I should've guessed."

I couldn't help but laugh. It eased some of the tension from my shoulders. Despite everything, he still trusted me.

He shouldn't.

"Let's just find Tempest," I said, squashing that traitorous voice. "They can't have gotten far."

"That's the client?"

I nodded, and he pushed down on the accelerator. The boat lurched away from the coast as though it were a caged beast that had finally been unleashed.

The afternoon sun reflected on the ocean. I kept my eyes downcast, attempting to avoid the direct rays.

"Are you feeling okay?" Ray asked, peering back at me from the deck. He kept his hands at the wheel. "Seasick?"

I shook my head. I felt good. Great, even. Free. And the smaller the island became, the better I felt. I wished I was leaving because I wanted to. I wished I was never coming back.

"What happened exactly, Lor?"

I thought about lying. I thought about telling Ray that I couldn't tell the difference between the two sisters, sticking with the story that they'd tricked me with. But as soon as Elysea stepped out of the containment room, I'd known she wasn't Tempest.

While Tempest had been studying me all morning, I'd been

studying her. I couldn't help it. There was something about her, a mystery that I couldn't quite unravel, a curious puzzle.

So why hadn't I reacted straightaway when Elysea had stepped out the door and not Tempest? I don't know. Maybe I'd been struck by the fact that I was standing in front of a girl who had been dead only hours before. Or maybe I wanted to see what would happen next? Or maybe it was because our lives were connected, which created some kind of affinity with her?

I rested my hands on the side of the boat. My skin was almost translucent. The waves kicked spray into my face, coating my lips with salt. I remembered the taste. From driving land rovers along the beach. I remembered the wind in my hair when I was on the cliffs. I remembered what it was like to live.

Now I knew the truth.

A part of me had wanted Elysea to escape because *I* couldn't.

Ray was watching me with serious eyes.

He deserved the truth.

"I think I let them go," I said.

"*What?*" He nearly pulled the steering wheel off the boat.

I ran a hand through my hair. "One moment I was looking at Elysea, *alive* . . . and I—hesitated, I guess, knowing what was going to happen to her." There was no other way to describe it. And I knew all too well, having been through the revival process with Calen.

"Gods, Lor!" I'd never seen his face flush with anger before.

It made him look younger. It made me feel worse. "You knew I would lose my job!"

"I'm sorry! I wasn't thinking clearly." I hadn't interacted with anyone aside from Ray for two years.

"You got too close," he said with a sigh. "You made it personal. You didn't want to see the girl die."

It wasn't that. I'd been thinking about me and my experience with a revival. How Palindromena tore families apart, not brought them together like they claimed. But Ray wouldn't understand. He'd never been through a revival with someone he loved. I hoped he'd never have to.

"It will be all right." He gave me a tight smile. "We'll find the Alerin girls and return Elysea to Palindromena. Nessandra will never know what happened. Everything will be fine." He looked at the echolink on my wrist. "How much time do we have?"

I glanced at the screen.

"Nineteen and a half hours," I said. "Then we can try to forget this day ever happened."

Ray didn't reply. I could tell there was more he wanted to say, but he stopped himself. That was a first.

"How will we find them?" I asked.

He tapped his bare wrist. "We can locate her using your echo."

"Great. Show me."

He grinned, the old Ray reappearing. "Oh, we don't need that. At least, not yet."

"What are you talking about?"

"I've worked at Palindromena for six months and there's one place each patient wishes they could go once they're revived."

I nodded in understanding.

"Home," we said at the same time.

CHAPTER SEVENTEEN

TEMPEST

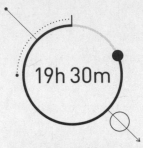

Monday, 4:30 p.m.

I DIRECTED THE *SUNRISE* toward the Equinox harbor. Elysea remained quiet. She was studying our home as though she were trying to commit it all to memory.

A magnetic boom lowered, bringing the boat to a halt before we could travel any farther.

"Equinox Watchtower to Quicksilver *Sunrise*," a voice on the transmitter said, "do you acknowledge?"

I pressed the radio transmitter button. "I acknowledge."

"You've returned early, *Sunrise*. We had you set to return tomorrow afternoon."

I swallowed down my fear. "Yes, there was a change in plans." The Conservators didn't allow Palindromena's security on the Equinox. We should be safe here. *Should.*

After a long, drawn-out moment, the voice said, "Our scans read two bodies on board. Can you confirm?"

Cursed waters. I hadn't thought about that. Hopefully it had been a slow trade day and they'd let us dock.

"Confirmed," I said with a quick glance to Elysea. "A visitor from another Reef." I was going to say Palindromena, but that wouldn't do me any favors.

"Spring Tide is this evening," the voice said. "It's one of our busiest nights. We were not expecting your return so soon."

I knew what she was implying. Weight limits were strict. Two extra bodies might not seem like a lot, but every pound mattered.

Four hours, Elysea mouthed, sensing my panic.

"We're only here for four hours," I added. "Then we'll both be leaving the Equinox until tomorrow, as originally planned."

Elysea touched my elbow to comfort me while we awaited their decision.

"Thank you, Quicksilver *Sunrise,*" the woman said. "I can grant you access to the Equinox until eight thirty p.m., but no longer. If you fail to return to the waters by then, your boat will be released from the pier and sent out into the ocean." A fitting punishment; losing your boat meant losing your income. They were essentially casting us out.

The boom lifted. A red buoy floated out and touched the *Sunrise's* bow before drawing it into the harbor. Once we'd docked, I cut the engine and leaped onto the rusted metal deck with a clang. Elysea remained aboard the boat.

"Hey!" I said. She jerked and looked up at me, as though she'd been caught in thought. "We don't have time to waste, remember?"

Her eyes were glassy and distant. I held out my hand. "Are you feeling okay?" She still had plenty of time left. The orientation video had said it wasn't until the last hour that she should feel sluggish.

She took my hand. "Everyone here thinks I'm dead."

That was what she was worried about? "We'll be in and out before they notice."

Her whole body shook as I helped her onto the dock. Perhaps that wasn't what she wanted. This was her home—the only home she'd ever known—and I was taking her back only to leave again.

And it wasn't only me she had to leave. It was her entire life.

Was it easier for death to strike you down without warning? Or was it better to know when death would strike, so you could use your last hours, months, years, to be with the people you cared about?

Palindromena seemed to think it was the latter.

The harbor was a hive of activity as boats returned for the day. We caught the attention of a few tired divers who hauled their equipment onto the dock. Their brown skin was glistening from the water and their black hair crusted with salt. Their gloomy expressions told the tale of another fruitless dive.

I hoped they didn't recognize Elysea. If they did, would they turn us in to Palindromena for a quick grab at some Notes? Or let us have the remainder of our twenty-four hours in peace?

Most people on the Equinox knew someone who had drowned. Surely they would leave us be. I still didn't understand why it was so important for the revived to spend their twenty-four hours stuck in a hospital room. They should be allowed to go home one final time. Was it because they wanted to control the disposal of the bodies? To be buried in the tomb under the sea, you needed to pay additional Notes along with your yearly taxes. Palindromena was a business, after all. Perhaps they just didn't want to lose their commodities?

Elysea stayed close by my side as we walked through the harbor. "Everything looks the same," she said.

I shrugged. "Nothing changes around here."

She didn't glance at me when she replied, "*You've* changed."

I shrugged again. "It's been two years." I could see my words hurt her. "Where's the map?" I needed to change the topic.

She gave me a sad smile. "Home."

A bitter taste swirled in my mouth. I'd sold nearly everything we owned, and I'd never seen a map. I cast her a sideways glance. "Where exactly?"

"I'll show you." She pressed her lips together, unwilling to say anything more.

This had better not all be a ruse so that she could see the Equinox one last time.

⚒

Elysea moved slowly, almost languidly, wanting to take everything in, until we reached the entrance to our quarters. Then she pushed past me, something ignited within her.

She spun around the main room, her mouth open in shock. "What happened?" She spread her arms wide. "Where are Mom and Dad's things? Where's *everything*?"

"I sold it." Mom and Dad had a few personal items, but otherwise, they hadn't kept much. There were too many weight restrictions on the Equinox.

While it had hurt to part with them, to lose more of my parents, I needed all the Notes I could get.

Elysea stared at the blank walls. "The paintings?"

"Sold."

"Mom's jewelry?"

"Sold."

Before Mom had worked at Palindromena, she'd been part of the Equinox's endeavor to clean up the ocean, retrieving items that were killing the marine life. She had retained a small collection of jewelry from her dives that wasn't worth a lot of money, but she felt helped connect us to our past. She used to say that if we forgot where we came from, we were bound to re-create the same mistakes made before the Great Waves. Such as fighting over land, resources and, worst of all, each other.

"The Conservators took that piece," I said, waving at the blank wall Elysea was mournfully studying. Elysea had always loved that painting of a rainy cityscape; I thought it might make her happy to know it now hung in the Conservatory.

"What about Mom's treasure chest?" Her voice rose as she looked around the empty quarters.

"I sold it. You know there wasn't any treasure in that."

How Mom found the chest had been one of our favorite bedtime stories.

"I was out on a dive," Mom would say, "not far from Palindromena's shores when I found something."

"Treasure!" I'd add in glee, knowing the story so well it could've been a memory of my own.

Mom pointed to me and laughed. "Yes! A treasure chest. I thought the Gods had sent it to me, and that I would find a fortune inside."

"But she only found me," Dad piped in, tickling Elysea's feet as she sat on our bunk. "I'd found the old box washed up on the Palindromena shore, and after finding nothing inside, I'd thrown it back into the ocean."

"And straight into Mom!" Elysea said with a big grin.

"I yelled at him for nearly taking my head off," Mom said. "I told him that I was part of the Equinox's effort to clean up the ocean, and there he was, throwing away Old World relics as if they were trash."

Dad placed his arm around Mom. "She called me an entitled land lover. And I realized I wanted to be insulted by this woman for the rest of my life."

Mom would then kiss Dad until we'd scream at them to stop.

Although Mom loved diving, she'd accepted a job at Palindromena to be closer to Dad. After all, the ocean was unpredictable and dangerous, and they had wanted to start a family.

Mom had always warned us away from diving, but Elysea and I had no choice once we were alone. Neither of us had graduated from school; we had left at fourteen and twelve, respectively, to earn Notes so we could afford to keep our quarters. Even if I *had* graduated, I wasn't interested in training in medicine to work at Palindromena, becoming an Old World historian, learning Conservator politics or owning a business at the market. I liked being underwater; it was the one place I could escape the jeers and mockery of my classmates. It was the one place I felt at peace with who I was.

Elysea's prospects were also limited. She considered the smiles of her students and applause from the audience as compensation enough for her dancing, refusing any payment.

While it had been painful to sell the item that had brought my parents together, it had stones embedded in the lid that were worth a few Notes. I would've sold the metal beams in the ceiling if I could've torn them free.

Elysea put her head in her hands and moaned. "The map was in the treasure chest, along with Mom's necklace and Dad's echolink."

"No. There wasn't anything in there. I checked before I sold it."

She sat on my bed—or what passed for my bed these days, a crate and some blankets. I'd sold my seaweed-threaded mattress months ago. "There's a hidden compartment in the lid," she said.

Desperation washed over me. "No . . ."

"We have to get it back." Her hands started shaking. We could both feel the pressure of the hours counting down, without having to see a ticking clock. "We have to . . ." But the rest of her words were lost in sharp breaths and shudders. She was falling apart.

Elysea had always been the sturdier of us two. She used to joke that her emotions were as stable as her dancer's posture, perfected over years of balancing on her tiptoes. This broken, frantic girl was not the sister I'd known.

I would have to be Elysea's anchor in this, as she'd been mine in the years our parents had been gone. She wasn't in a state to make any decisions. I was the older sibling now. I had to take charge.

"Elysea," I said, trying to get her to focus on me. The window behind her showed a darkening sky. I stripped the concern from my voice. "We will find out who bought the treasure chest. We still have time."

She didn't respond. While she looked at me, her eyes bored through me. And I knew she was seeing her death.

It was coming for her, and there was no way we could hide from it or outrun it.

CHAPTER EIGHTEEN

LOR

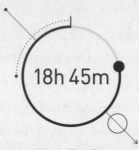

18h 45m

Monday, 5:15 p.m.

RAYLAN'S BOAT APPROACHED the Equinox at five fifteen, as the sun was setting. The anchored Reef was made up of a large central circular metal building with hundreds of smaller connected structures. The metal was rusted from the salty water and air.

The entire structure looked almost skeletal, like the spine of a beached garseal. Behind the Equinox, a storm brewed. The air smelled sharply of seaweed and salt. Not exactly pleasant.

"She's a beauty, isn't she?" Ray asked, directing the boat into the harbor. I'd never seen so many vessels. Palindromena employed two hundred people in total, and it was rare to see everyone together. Even from a distance, I could hear the sound of music, people and *life*. A direct contrast to the quiet corridors of Palindromena and the Aquarium.

My heart rate picked up speed, but it was from excitement, not nerves.

"Yeah." Unsure what else to say.

Of course I knew about the Reefs, everyone did. But I never could've imagined anything like this. In my mind, the Reefs were rafts tied together. Something crude and fragile. Perhaps it was the way my mother spoke about how sophisticated Palindromena was in comparison—how lucky *I* was to live on the dry land, surrounded by advanced technology. I didn't realize until now that I'd believed her on some level.

But the Equinox was a solid, imposing structure. It appeared like something out of a fantasy novel, rising in rusty waves from the water. Determined and brash, daring you to mock it.

For a moment, I forgot all about the Alerin sisters.

Ray beamed with pride as he looked at his home. A feeling I'd never had for Palindromena.

"My ancestors built this place," he said. "They were seafarers before the Great Waves and were always in the water. Because they were the strongest swimmers, they were able to pull wreckages from the Old World to the surface." He frowned for a moment. "The Equinox used to be the most thriving Reef, but, like everything, resources aren't unlimited."

"What will happen once nothing remains below?" I asked.

Ray rubbed his brow. "Either we leave our home or break the Reef apart, draw up the anchors and search for new sites. But if we leave, we'll be abandoning everything we have here. We'll lose our harmonious society."

I'd read about the divisions of the Old World and how they were often at war over land and resources. While the Great Waves were horrific, they had forced everyone to band together for survival. "I'm sorry."

He cocked an eyebrow. "Why are you apologizing?"

"My mother." I sighed. "If she didn't force everyone to pay such high taxes, then the Equinox wouldn't be under so much strain."

He surprised me by laughing. "If it wasn't your mother, then it would be someone else." He nudged me. "That's economy. That's the human race. We give and get nothing for free."

"You sound so cynical," I said. "You sound like—"

"You?" The side of his mouth lifted. "A consequence from hanging out with you, bud."

"I hope everything works out." I meant for the Equinox and for him.

"If I can return to the water," he said, his voice soft, "I'll be able to help my home. I'll be able to fish for something larger than sugarfish." He would follow in his father's footsteps. "I'll protect my ancestors' home; I'll keep the Equinox afloat." He grinned. "Pun intended."

"I know you will." I really wanted to believe that was true, even if it meant not seeing him at Palindromena every day. If that was what he wanted, I wanted it for him.

My mother used to say that change happened. For everyone. People changed; people could enact change. But that was bullshit. Change happened *to* you. Life, and death, they *happened* to you. And there was nothing you could do about it. You either held on for the ride or got swept away in the storm.

Sometimes I wished I believed in the Gods below. But there were too many deadly storms, dangerous accidents and unexplained drownings in these cursed waters. Why would any deity inflict that kind of life on us? Or was it a punishment for the way we'd treated the Old World or each other? Would we always be held accountable? Was it ever possible to break free of the atrocities of the past?

I wish I knew the answer. Perhaps there would be a time when I wasn't haunted by Calen and his final word to me.

Murderer.

Ray's hand descended on my shoulder, jolting me from my thoughts. "We'll find her, bud."

I hoped that was true. For Ray.

"Or are you worried you might take a tumble into the ocean?" He grinned, no doubt thinking about my awkward boarding of the boat. "You can hold on to me if you want." He held his arms out mockingly.

I shoved his shoulder, appreciating his attempt to lighten the mood. "Just steer the boat."

We approached a fortifying boom between two watchtowers, blocking the entrance into the harbor.

The boat shuddered, and the vessel stopped.

"What's going on?" I asked.

"We're being scanned," Ray said, then held a finger to his lips.

A woman's voice crackled over the boat's transmitter. "Equinox Watchtower to incoming vessel. We detect two people on board, when you left with one this afternoon. What is your business? Acknowledge."

"This is *Surf to Turf*," Raylan said, with an embarrassed grin as I shot him a confused look over the boat's name. "We're here on official Palindromena business. We won't be here long."

"What kind of business?" Her voice took on a hard edge. I'd heard the Equinox didn't approve of Palindromena's presence. More so than the other Reefs, they didn't like what my mother was doing back on the isle. I didn't blame them.

"Recruitment," Raylan said suddenly, almost shouting it over the transmitter. "We thought Spring Tide would be a good opportunity to find new recruits."

I gave him a thumbs-up. That was better than anything I could've come up with.

Silence echoed on the other end. Would they send us back to Palindromena? Was this where we failed?

"You are permitted entry till eight thirty p.m.," the Watchtower said. The boom rose, and the boat floated forward. "But we will cut you loose after that. We expect the Spring Tide to be in full swing by nine."

I looked to my echolink. It was five thirty. The Equinox

wasn't too large, and with the echolink, we should find Elysea in no time.

I gave Ray a nod.

"Acknowledged," Ray replied.

A shaft of fading sunlight broke through the sky and hit the water, lighting the aquatic world below. Fish flitted away, and larger forms moved slowly toward darker waters.

The hairs on the back of my neck stood upright. I'd never seen what was beneath the ocean's surface. I'd never seen what was left of the Old World. I instinctively moved toward the edge of the boat for a closer look. When the boat wobbled, I darted back to the center.

Ray snickered at me.

I clenched my teeth. I had to concentrate. Find the Alerin girls. And push thoughts of everything else away. Now was not the time for sightseeing.

"Let's check where Elysea is," Ray said, setting the boat to autopilot mode. He twisted my arm to press something on the echolink's screen. A blinking blue dot appeared. "This is an echolocator—it's connected to Elysea's heartbeat for the duration of the revival. As long as her heart is beating, we can track her." It was then that I noticed the dot blinked in time with a heartbeat. "It looks like she's headed to the east, the opposite end of the harbor. She must be headed to the Spring Tide."

"What's the Spring Tide?"

He grinned. "It's a night market with restaurants and

bars. It's where people hang out on Equinox. It's the only place, really." He chuckled. "It's a great spot to pick up the latest catch and *be* the latest catch." He winked at me.

"Why would they go there?" I watched the blue dot inch across the screen.

"To party? They only have nineteen hours left together before Elysea dies." He shrugged. "That's what I would do. I never used to miss a Spring Tide, but now"—he pressed his lips together—"the crowds make it difficult to maneuver around. And my dance moves aren't quite what they used to be." He chuckled.

"You think they're celebrating?"

"It's better than counting down the hours back at Palindromena."

I wondered what Tempest was thinking right now. Surely, she knew we'd follow them home. Was their escape worth it? Just so Elysea could see the Equinox one last time?

But I knew all too well that grief made you act out of character and in desperation. My mother's business depended on it. Grief was like a cloud; it muddied everything. It sank deep into your bones and weighed you down. And you'd do anything to lighten the load.

Ray headed back to the helm. "We should plan our attack now."

"Attack?" I didn't want to hurt these girls. Although I knew ultimately that I would.

He shook his head at me. "What did you expect? That Elysea would come willingly? That Tempest would let us take her sister after everything she's done to escape?"

He was right. "What do you have in mind?"

"We do whatever it takes." His usual grin was vicious. He wasn't going to let these girls win. There was too much at stake.

I studied the echolocator. "She's stopped moving," I said, looking at the dot on the screen. "Too easy." I forced a smile.

I hoped I was right.

CHAPTER NINETEEN

TEMPEST

18h 30m

Monday, 5:30 p.m.

ELYSEA AND I HEADED toward the far end of the Equinox, behind the circular Conservator hall to an open-air gangway, suspended between two residential arms. The floor was made of mesh, allowing the cool sea breeze in, and a roof of threaded seaweed kept the weather from encroaching on the festivities. Bowls of fluorescent coral hung overhead to light the spectacle that would soon become the Spring Tide—a celebration of the calm tides caused by the sun and moon being at right angles to each other, which occurred twice a year.

Day merchants and traders had already packed away their goods, making way for the labyrinth of small bars and restaurants. The walls separating each merchant were simple sheets of material, permitting various scents to blend together and create the distinct smell that was the Spring Tide. Sardines sizzled on hot plates, flavored seaweed hung from stall ceilings, and clamshells brimmed with hot ragar—a spirit made from fermented seaweed that hit you in the face like the odor of a month-dead familfish.

In the middle of the market sat a circular stage.

For a moment, I wished I could pretend that I was a girl spending the evening with my sister. That we were here for food, dancing and drinks. Perhaps we'd go for a late-night swim afterward, to wash the humidity from our skin, all the while teasing each other for being a guppy and not daring to venture farther into the moonlit water. We'd only be concerned about the creatures we couldn't see, until we were face-to-face with their giant teeth. But those creatures were simply stories. Fantasies. As was this life of a simple Reef girl.

My stomach clenched at the sharp aroma of fish and salt. I hadn't eaten anything all day, aside from the pudding I'd smeared on my lips. As I passed a stall selling dried seaweed, I snapped off a piece and gave half to Elysea. I slipped a Note onto the counter and left before anyone saw me. Everyone at the Spring Tide knew Elysea; we needed to keep a low profile. While I wasn't sure if they'd turn us in to Palindromena's security, it wasn't worth the risk.

A crack of lightning tore through the blackened sky. The customers of a nearby watering hole *ooooh*ed in appreciation. Most humid days ended with a lightning show, another reason there was no wall along one side of the bridge. Free entertainment.

Elysea paused at the stage as it lowered into the sea, halting when a foot of water covered the floor. Preparation for tonight's performance.

I pulled on her arm. "Come on."

We weaved among the stalls, searching for Daon. Elysea had tied a scarf around her head in hopes of concealing her identity. I wished she'd stayed back in our quarters, but she said she didn't want to be left alone. I knew that wasn't the reason. She wanted a glimpse of her old life. I hoped she'd stay quiet.

During the day, Daon sold goods hauled from the sunken world. At night, he poured ragar with a side of the best ceviche on the Equinox. Customers came for the conversation as much as they came for the ceviche. A common saying on the Equinox was that the only people who didn't like Daon were the people who'd never met him.

Positioned at the far edge of the bridge, his bar had the best view of the ocean tide and swirling storms.

"Stay here," I said, pulling Elysea by the elbow into a shadowy corner between stalls.

Her eyes flashed. "I want to hear what Daon says."

"No. You want to see him. But that's not what we're here for."

She worried her lip between her teeth. "Is he well?"

I huffed. I knew it. "Yes, he's fine. Now stay here."

She didn't argue.

"Daon!" I called out over the rising storm as I took a rare open stool at the bar. We were lucky to come at the start of the night; an hour or so later, and drunken patrons would be fighting over the few seats.

"Tempe!" Daon's face lit up as he took me in. "It's been too long!"

His long straw-colored hair was thrown up into a loose bun, a few hairs falling about his sun-bronzed face. His hazel eyes sparkled in the coral-lit light as though he knew a secret you weren't privy to. While Daon had never convinced Elysea to go on an official date, they'd spent their nights at the market, Elysea leading her dance troupe while Daon kept everyone fed and watered. The King and Queen of the Spring Tide.

I worked my finger into a scratch in Daon's old wooden counter. "Yeah, sorry I haven't been around much lately."

He let out a booming laugh as though I'd told him the funniest joke. "You're not my target audience, kid." He pointed to the sign behind him, which said EIGHTEEN AND OVER ONLY. "Unless I missed a birthday?" A cloud crossed his face.

After my parents disappeared, Daon had been like an older brother. And while he'd tried to comfort me after Elysea had died, the constant reminder of her death took a toll on him.

"Nope, still seventeen," I said with a smile, hoping to lighten the mood. "For a few more days."

His expression lifted. "What can I do for you, then?" He pointed at a patron's bowl of thinly sliced raw fish, the tang of citrus heavy in the air. "Ceviche?"

"I don't have time," I said, while my stomach disagreed with me.

"There's always time to eat," he said with a laugh. The sound instantly shifted my mood. And for a moment, the pressure of today fell away.

I glanced behind me to where Elysea was waiting in the shadows, but I couldn't make out her silhouette. "I have to ask you something, Daon."

"You can ask while you eat." He turned away to prepare the ceviche.

My stomach complained again, so I decided to take him up on the offer and keep some for Elysea. Hopefully Daon wouldn't notice when the plate went missing. I reached into my bag for some Notes.

He waved me away with his large fillet knife. "The Alerin girls always have and always will eat free."

I grinned, my mouth already starting to water. "Thank you, Daon."

"No worries!" He pulled a large fresh fish from a tub underneath the bar and threw it onto his small work area with a thump. He sliced quickly through the soft translucent flesh with wide, smooth arcs of his blade. If he were a dancer, then his blade would have been part of the performance. He placed a few pieces of the fish onto a small oyster plate and scattered slices of dried seaweed on top. To finish the dish, he squeezed some citrus juice over the fish. Citrus that no doubt had come from Palindromena's crops.

It was like cold water dousing my shirt, seeping through muscle and skin. For a second, I'd forgotten about Palindromena. I'd forgotten about everything. All that remained was the rumble in my belly and the smell and sight of food.

"I need to ask you something," I repeated while shoveling the food into my mouth. I tried to slow down, but once the fish had hit my tongue, all bets were off.

"Easy there!" Daon said. "You're not supposed to eat the cutlery!" His demeanor changed, brows lowering over his eyes. "When was the last time you ate?" He pinched one of my arms, making me drop my fork.

"Hey! That hurt."

"You haven't been eating enough." His eyes narrowed. "You're skin and bone!"

"What do you call this?" I popped another mouthwatering sliver of fish into my mouth. The tang of the citrus buzzed on my tongue before the flesh melted away. I let out a sigh. Daon's ceviche was utter perfection. I couldn't remember the last time I'd eaten something other than the leftovers I'd gathered from behind the mess hall. And the Equinox never threw out much food—they couldn't afford to.

He gestured to my plate. "That doesn't count."

"Daon," I said, forcing him to focus. I pushed the plate away so I would focus too. "I need to recover something I sold to you."

"You've been diving a lot lately," he said. "A busy mind is a healthy mind, eh?"

Sure, let him think that was my way of coping with Elysea's death. Better than the truth that I'd saved up enough money to resurrect her, and that she was standing mere feet away.

"Do you remember one of my parents' items I sold you? It was a smallish treasure chest." I gestured the size with my hands. "With gems on the lid. It wasn't in great condition. You gave me about five Notes for it."

"You want it back?" I could guess what he was thinking; I'd gotten rid of everything, and now I realized I'd made a mistake. Last year, he'd tried talking me out of it, but I'd been determined.

I pulled the corners of my mouth down in a—hopefully—reproachful look. "Yes. Do you remember who bought it?"

His forehead crinkled for a moment; then he snapped his fingers. "I sold it to Marsa Keena."

My eyebrows rose. Marsa had been a teacher at school, but she'd long since retired. "Why would she want it? The gems are fakes."

He shrugged.

"Okay." At least it was someone I knew. Surely, Marsa would allow me to retrieve the map without too much trouble. "Thank you."

"Anytime, kid," Daon said with a grin.

I made to slip off my stool when someone cleared their throat.

"Tempest Alerin," the voice said from behind me.

I froze. While it was boiling hot under the seaweed roof, goose bumps prickled all over my body.

Gods below.

He'd found me.

CHAPTER TWENTY

LOR

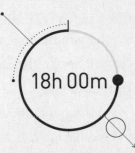

Monday, 6:00 p.m.

ONCE RAY AND I BOARDED the Equinox, we followed the little blinking dot on the echolink to the Spring Tide.

The sun had just set and the night market was lit only by hanging bowls of coral. The atmosphere was thick with people, with little room to breathe. The air was humid, salty and fishy. Thin fabric walls separated a stall selling sweetened sugarfish pudding from its neighbor selling fresh fish entrails. It was both disgusting and fascinating.

Before I'd locked myself away in the Aquarium, I used to eat all my meals at the Palindromena canteen while my mother worked. And even though we had access to the best fresh produce, the portions were small and strict. A few steamed vegetables and a fillet of fish. Nothing was as tasty as Ray's fish cakes or as mouthwatering as the perfume of the Spring Tide.

My senses didn't know what to make of it all.

And it was so loud. People shouted over each other to be

heard. On the island, it was quiet. If someone was talking, you listened. If I hadn't been so concerned that we might lose the Alerin sisters, I would've explored the labyrinth of stalls.

While the Equinox and Palindromena weren't far from each other, we were clearly worlds apart. Here everything was about the food, drinks and culture. Living.

On Palindromena everything was about death.

I didn't blame Ray for preferring this place.

"Where is Elysea?" Ray asked. His eyes were bouncing around the market, arms jittering. He wanted to be out and among it all. Not stuck with me.

I brought my wrist up to study the echolink. While the two blue circles were visible, the blinking dot of the echolocator had disappeared.

"It's not working." I shook my arm, as though that would help.

Ray pointed to the gloomy clouds ahead. "The electricity in the storm must be interfering with its sensor. We need to split up. You take the north; I'll take the south. If I don't see you, meet back at the boat in two and a half hours."

I agreed and Ray disappeared.

The storm continued to roar overhead. The metal floor shook beneath us. Wasn't it dangerous being out here in the storm, surrounded by metal? Although, what other choice did they have? It wasn't like they could take shelter on the island.

Ray had once told me that his mother believed thunder was

the voice of the Old Gods. "They only use it when we refuse to listen to their subtler messages," he'd said.

"Don't storms rage weekly?" I'd asked.

He'd laughed then. "We're not very good listeners."

I was wondering what message Ray was hearing in tonight's storm.

Flashes of lightning lit the crowd's faces as I maneuvered through the horde.

"Have you seen Tempest Alerin?" I asked a lady with a russet-brown complexion and braided black hair.

"Elysea Alerin's sister?" The corners of her lips turned downward. "Poor girl."

I didn't ask which girl she pitied. "Have you seen her tonight?"

She startled. "Elysea's dead."

I grunted in frustration. "Have you seen her sister? Tempest."

She pointed to the far edge, where the platform overlooked the ocean. "She walked that way not too long ago."

"Thank you!"

I moved quickly toward the stalls at the far end of the Spring Tide.

Music began thumping in between the cracks of lightning. Everyone stopped what they were doing and turned to the middle of the market. Almost everyone. One person hadn't shifted from her seat.

Tempest. She sat at a bar near the platform's edge.

I scanned the crowd but saw no signs of her sister.

I cleared my throat when I reached her. "Tempest Alerin," I said.

She stilled. For a moment, she didn't shift, as though she wished I would disappear.

A bulky olive-skinned barkeep raised his chin at me from the other side of the bar, his muscles straining against his shirt, a knife in his hand.

I forced a smile and took the stool beside Tempest. "Enjoying the food?" I asked with false levity.

"She's not here," Tempest replied hotly. "She's gone."

The barkeep came over, and I pulled out some Notes. "A ragar. Thanks, man. Liquid courage." I grinned, hoping he'd think I was only hitting on a pretty girl at a bar. I tried clearing the cobwebs from my mind to remember how to act normally.

"Sure thing," he replied with a knowing grin at Tempest.

She made to jump off the stool, but I grabbed her wrist. "Don't you want to stay for a drink?"

"I'm underage," she shot back, her eyes furious.

I didn't let go. "I'm interested in speaking with your sister." I kept my tone light. If anyone overheard us, it would sound like harmless bar chat.

"She's not here," she repeated through gritted teeth.

The bar was packed, raucous voices shouted over the sound of the music and storm.

Our conversation was sheathed by the noise.

"Tell me where she is, and I'll let you go," I said.

She jutted out her chin. "My sister isn't going anywhere with you."

Drums pounded in between the thunder.

Find her. Find her. Find her, the drums said.

"I'm not leaving here until I have her."

She bristled. "Why? Why can't you let us go? Why can't my sister have her last hours in peace?"

Would she come with me if I told her my life was linked to Elysea's? "That's not what you agreed to." I couldn't risk telling her the truth.

"What do you want?" she asked. "Notes? I can give you over a thousand. Take it all."

How did a girl her age have that many Notes?

"I wish it were that simple." I really did. I wished everyone could walk away from this alive, but that was not the promise of Palindromena.

"Notes make everything simple. You should know that, working at Palindromena. Notes are all you care about."

I loosened my grip on her wrist. "I'm sorry, Tempest, I am. I'm sorry your sister died, but you knew what you were getting into when you signed up for Elysea's revival. You have your twenty-four hours at the facility and then Elysea must return to the way she was."

"All I have to do is say one word, and Daon will slice you in two." She jerked her chin at the blade in the barkeep's hand.

"Palindromena's security fleet are docking as we speak," I lied. "You have nowhere to go. You're out of time."

"I'll take my chances." She squared her shoulders. "And I still have plenty of time."

I ran my hand over the echolink at my wrist. "I'll make you a new deal: you both come back to Palindromena and you can have the remaining time with your sister, as originally planned. There won't be any penalties for what you've done." That would never work, but she didn't need to know that.

Tempest appeared to consider my offer.

"I don't blame you," I said. "The revival process isn't easy. I *do* understand."

She nodded, and I found myself loosening my grip on her wrist even more. Then she pulled free of my grasp. We both stumbled off our stools. I made to grab for her again but someone else had joined us.

"Hello," Elysea said, stepping in and blocking her sister from view. "Looking for me?"

She had something tied around her head to conceal her identity, but when she stood next to her sister, there was no question who she was.

"Elysea." I let out a breath.

I'd found her. And there was still plenty of time to get her back to Palindromena before her hours were up.

"What are you doing?" Tempest demanded of her sister.

"I thought I'd come say hello," she said with a half-hearted grin. She didn't look nearly as confident as she tried to sound.

I pulled out my tablet, hoping there was a signal so I could message Ray for help.

"Don't," Tempest pleaded. "Let us go. *Please.*"

"Don't worry, Tempe," Elysea said. She turned to me. "I'll go back with you."

Perhaps Elysea had felt she'd had enough time back in her old life. Maybe my mother was right. People needed to say goodbye. It wasn't about living forever; it was about closure.

"But before I go, I want one thing," Elysea said. She unwound the scarf from her face, then raised her voice over the crowd. "Daon, can I have a bowl of your ceviche?"

The barkeep looked over with a smile, ready to greet his new customer. When he saw who it was, his knife stilled, its tip pointed upward. Thunder lit the sky; Daon's sharp blade glinted in the night.

"E-Elysea?" he stuttered. "How?"

Oh shit.

"No," I whispered.

"Did you miss me?" she asked with a grin, although she looked like she might cry. "Tempe told me it's been a while."

The barkeep looked as though he was about to burst into tears.

"Stop!" I reached for Elysea's arm.

"What's going on?" the barkeep thundered.

179

Tempest pointed at me. "He's trying to kill us!"

The barkeep's shocked expression turned sour. His fingers wrapped around his fillet knife and he took a step toward me. "You threatened my girls?"

I put my hands out. "No, it's not what you think. I'm from Palindromena, and Elysea—"

"He's already killed me once!" Elysea cried. "Don't let him do it again!"

"What?" the barkeep roared.

It was an outright lie, but it was enough to ignite the barkeep's fury. He tossed the knife at me. As it sliced through the air, a thought crossed my mind. Maybe I deserved this. Maybe the girls should get away.

The knife dug into the counter, scratching my arm and pinning my shirt to the wood.

The crowd scattered in various directions. A few people screamed.

"Go!" the barkeep shouted to Elysea. "Get out of here!"

I pulled against the blade to free myself. But I was too late. The Alerin sisters were gone.

CHAPTER TWENTY-ONE

TEMPEST

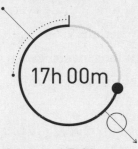

17h 00m

Monday, 7:00 p.m.

WE DASHED THROUGH the crowd, my hand gripping Elysea's so she didn't reconsider and return to Daon's side. Outside the bar, people seemed unaware of the commotion; the storm and music masked our getaway. The crowd had swelled like a rain cloud about to break.

I glanced behind us. Daon's eyes were full of pain. He didn't want Elysea to go. Did he realize he'd never see her again?

Elysea faltered, but I grabbed her arm and tugged her along.

A tinkling of bells signaled that the dancers would soon arrive. Even if she didn't mean to, Elysea veered toward the stage—as if the bells had summoned her. I hated pulling her away.

The drumming picked up speed, and a troupe of dancers glided into the market, dressed in the color of the ocean with bells tied at their wrists and feet.

Among the dancers, I spotted someone walking through the

crowd with purpose. He had cropped black hair, skin the color of the setting sun and was wearing a T-shirt with the Palindromena logo on the front. While everyone else watched the dancers enter, he searched the crowd with determination.

It had to be the reinforcements Raylan had mentioned. The guard stopped to talk with some patrons, and they pointed toward Daon's bar.

I darted behind a stall, hauling Elysea in behind me. I bit down on my lip, breaking the skin. Lingering citrus from the ceviche seeped into the wound.

We'd broken Palindromena's protocol, and they weren't going to let me—*us*—get away with it.

"This isn't good," I said, inclining my head toward this new threat.

Her eyes were wet with unshed tears. "You don't think we can get by him?"

"I've traded with nearly everyone in this market over the last two years. There's no way I'll go unrecognized."

She gripped my hand. "*We'll* go unrecognized." I appreciated that we were in this together, but that didn't help right now. Perhaps we should split up and hope for the best?

I peered around the stall. In the middle of the market, Elysea's old troupe continued dancing, unaware their beloved teacher stood mere feet away.

"Marsa lives not far from the market," I said.

Elysea blinked back her tears. "Marsa?"

"She bought Mom's treasure chest."

Elysea nodded absentmindedly. She was retreating. These past several hours had been too much for her. *I needed to get us out of here.*

We could try to sneak past, but with everyone on the lookout for us and the crowd so packed, it would be like harpooning fish in a barrel.

Elysea wrapped the scarf back around her face. While it was true everyone knew me, they also knew Elysea. More so. Before she'd died, she danced at every night market.

I removed her makeshift disguise.

"What are you doing?" she asked.

"We may have some enemies here." I gestured to the Palindromena guard as he stalked the market. "But we also have friends."

"Like Daon." Her voice was soft, hurt—a punch to the heart.

"Yes, friends who would do anything to protect you if they knew you were alive."

She worried the scarf in her hands. "What are you thinking?"

Dancers swirled blue fabric on banners, mimicking the motion of the sea, their faces dusted with blue paint, their eyes shiny black gems. They took turns leaping in and out of the lowered stage and into the crowd, their splashes and sprays illuminated by the lanterns and lightning. They looked like otherworldly sea creatures. A part of the ocean. The ocean that gave, and took, life. As it had taken Elysea's.

"Wait here," I said. "I have an idea."

Elysea was exactly where I'd left her, hidden among the shadows of a stall selling glowing alcoholic spirits—infused with powdered coral. The stall owner claimed drinking the liquid would bring you closer to the Gods below and protect you from the vicious storms and whirling tides.

"Where are we going?" the young dancer asked as she followed me. She wore a crown of cream shells and golden pearls, contrasting against her black hair and rich brown skin. She couldn't have been much older than ten and was as slight as a thread of seaweed. But she would help us. All I had to do was mention Elysea's name and she followed me through the crowd. Elysea's students were loyal, even after her death.

I gestured toward where my sister stood in the shadows. The dancer gasped as Elysea stepped under the light of a coral lantern.

"You're alive!" The girl's dark brown eyes sparkled like the moonlit sea.

Elysea held out her hand. "We need your help, Karnie."

Karnie looked between the two of us before setting her jaw. "What can I do?"

"Tempe?" Elysea asked, not knowing my plan.

"We need clothes." I gestured to the girl's costume. "And makeup."

"A disguise," Elysea said with a smile, so as not to scare her.

The girl took in a startled breath. "Are you in trouble?"

Elysea glanced at me before replying, "A little bit. We need to get out of the Spring Tide, but there are people looking for us."

"Who?" Karnie asked. She gave me a pointed look as if this were my fault. I suppose it was.

"They don't want Elysea to live," I said flatly. "They think she should be dead. Again."

Karnie sucked in a breath. "So you *were* dead, but now . . ."

The side of Elysea's mouth lifted. "I'm alive."

"Palindromena." Karnie's voice was hushed. Clearly the girl had never seen someone revived before. I was glad for her.

"Will you help?" I asked bluntly.

"I will," she said, then flounced away as though she hadn't broken from her performance.

"You could be nicer to her," Elysea admonished.

I snorted. "We don't have time to make friends."

"The only reason she's helping us is because I'm her friend."

I turned away, knowing she was right. Being nice had always come easy to Elysea. She instinctively knew what to say, while I worried over my response and always seemed to stumble.

When Karnie returned a short moment later, she wore a blue sash around her waist. She unraveled the material to reveal two costumes.

"I spoke to the troupe, Elysea," she said, her eyes bright with excitement. "They'll help you and your sister in any way they can."

I took one of the costumes from her outstretched hand. "Thank you."

"Anything for Elysea," she replied firmly.

"Thank you, Karnie," Elysea said. "Ready?" she asked me.

I didn't like being the center of attention; I could easily do the wrong thing. But what choice did I have?

"Ready."

———◦———

Once our faces were coated with blue paint, we moved toward the stage.

Elysea took the lead, knowing the steps of the routine; she'd choreographed it, after all. I waved a banner above my head in time to the beat, feeling ridiculous. Surely someone would spot my incompetence from the crowd. I'd always been a horrible dancer.

This was a terrible idea.

While Elysea remained focused, my eyes darted through the audience. Some watched attentively, while others tuned the entertainment to the background, distracted by the lightning streaking across the sky, or studiously observing the bottom of their glass—a temporary reprieve from any ailments.

Elysea's eyes locked on mine, and I noticed she was smiling. For the first time since she'd been revived, she looked happy. She loved being in the spotlight. One last time. I hadn't brought her here for a final goodbye, but here we were. Trust Elysea to see the positive in all this.

She spun her hands above her head before shifting her shoulders, rolling her limbs as though she were submerged in water. Was it my imagination, or did she appear more fluid than before? Had the ocean become a part of her when it had taken her final breath?

And was it my imagination that all eyes turned to her, unable to look away?

Even with the blue streaked across her face, her expression radiated warmth. Happiness. Life. This was the Elysea I knew, not the timid shell of a girl I'd been with the last few hours. Elysea had never been the bravest, and yet she was always willing to stand out in a crowd.

I tried to mimic Elysea's movements; her banner moved like ripples upon a glassy sea. I remembered all the times Elysea had tried to teach me how to dance when I was little. While she'd never given up, I'd always been a lost cause. No one could match her fluidity. Even if the troupe hadn't been told about Elysea's return, they would've recognized her. Her dance called to them. They gravitated toward her, then spun away again, mimicking the magnetic pull of the tide.

Thunder cracked. Time stood still. All eyes focused on the dancers.

That was when I realized the idiocy of my plan.

Everyone's gaze had shifted to Elysea as she moved down into the sunken stage. Including Raylan and the Palindromena guard. I wasn't sure if they recognized her or were drawn in by her performance.

I staggered toward my sister, my steps out of time. She twirled in the lowered middle section of the stage, her feet flicking up water. The other dancers remained on the upper level and swirled around her, a barrier of blue. I moved faster, in time with my quickening breaths.

Then I caught Raylan's gaze. He visibly jerked, as though he was waking from a stupor.

Gods below.

I'd screwed up. We were supposed to complete the dance, then retreat with the troupe offstage, but now we were trapped as the crowd surrounded the circular stage.

"Move," I said, pushing one of the dancers out of the way so I could descend the stairs to Elysea. The dancer let out a small yelp but didn't stumble.

Our audience watched from above, blocking us in. The cold water lapped at my ankles. I swished my banner around, caring less and less about my performance.

"Elysea," I hissed at her. "They've found us."

I searched for Raylan once more, but I couldn't see him or his backup. Had they called for more reinforcements? How were we going to get out of this fishbowl?

She didn't break her stride, lifting a leg above her head as she twirled.

"They're descending the stairs," she said, speaking through a broad smile.

I followed her gaze. They hadn't disappeared after all.

They pushed their way through the dancers. Our only barricade.

"What do we do?"

She lowered her leg and said, "Time for the finale!"

"Finale? We're surrounded! We're trapped! Who cares about the dance?" Sweat curled between my shoulder blades, beneath my diving skin. While the suit kept me warm in the water, it was suffocating me now.

"Don't fret." Her smile didn't falter. "The finale is always the best part. I've got a new move I want to debut."

"Now's not the time!" I shouted over the roar of the crowd— or was that the thunder or my heart thumping in my ears? Sweat ran down my brow and into my eyes, blurring my vision.

The dancers moved toward us, their steps as one, banners held high. They circled around Elysea and me, getting closer and closer.

"Get out of the way!" I heard someone cry over the music. *Raylan.*

The air fizzled with humidity and anticipation.

"Do you have your breather in your bag?" Elysea asked, throwing her hands to the ceiling.

"Yes." I'd topped it off at the day market after I'd sold the plant. Mom had taught us never to leave the Equinox without oxygen, for you never knew what might happen out on the water. "Why?" I knew she didn't have one. The dread in my stomach turned into a swirling storm.

"Just don't panic."

The tempo of the drums increased. Faster and faster and faster. The dancers spun around us, and I thought of the kids from school.

Water witch. Water witch. Water witch.

And I wished I was. Then perhaps I could get us out of here.

Raylan stood on the lip of the stage. His eyes burned into mine. The blue, which had seemed calming back at Palindromena, now was lit from the inside. A blue blaze.

He wouldn't give up until he had Elysea.

I dropped my banner to the floor. We were doomed.

The dancers whirled like a storm cloud, Elysea in the middle. They threw their banners high into the air, covering the coral lantern bowls and dousing the light. The crowd gasped in the darkness. Raylan yelled my name. The dancers spun. The blue powder smeared on their skin glowed like the coral it was made from.

In the absence of light, you could see the powder hadn't been applied without skill. Patterns danced across their skin, and as they weaved around and around, the lines blurred together like a school of fish. In the middle, Elysea's face glowed, her eyes pools of black. Her grin shone in the dim.

The dancers lowered their banners, revealing Elysea to the crowd. She threw up her arms, and two claps of thunder crackled on either side of the bridge, as though she had conjured them herself.

Then she disappeared.

CHAPTER TWENTY-TWO

TEMPEST

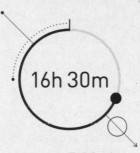

16h 30m

Monday, 7:30 p.m.

ONE MOMENT Elysea was standing in front of me. The next moment she'd disappeared. Like when she'd drowned. She'd been in my life, had *been* my life; then she was gone.

Forever.

"Elysea!" I shrieked.

Something twisted deep inside my chest.

The dancers continued twirling around the stage as though nothing had happened.

"Hurry!" Someone shoved my shoulders. It was Karnie. "Get down there."

"What? Where?" Then I saw it. A black hole had emerged from where Elysea stood seconds ago. *No*—not a hole, an opening in the stage. An opening to the waters below.

Now I understood.

I pulled my breather from my oilskin bag and shoved it in my mouth. There wasn't time to attach my dome. With a quick nod to Karnie to show my thanks, I closed my eyes and jumped into the opening.

The ocean was cool and calming—a reprieve from the humidity up on deck. The sound of the drums continued, reverberating above, sending pulses down into the water.

I screamed as two dark eyes surrounded by a glowing blue face appeared in front of me. My breather fell from my mouth.

A hand held the breather back up to my lips. A hand covered in glowing powder, powder that was now dispersing into the water. *Elysea.* She appeared as what I imagined the Gods below looked like: ethereal, beautiful, powerful and in control.

I inhaled slowly through my breather.

Elysea motioned for me to follow her. I didn't know how she could see anything; there was no coral to light the way, making it impossible to tell how much distance we'd traveled. Yet she continued to swim as though she knew where we were going.

Looking above, there was the smallest amount of light visible through the mesh floor. The Spring Tide continued on. Were we being followed? I couldn't hear anything but the muffled sounds of steady drums. Would Raylan jump into the water after us? The Director had said he was a fisherman; he wouldn't be afraid of the obscure waters.

Elysea turned; the powder had nearly disappeared from her skin. With what little light was left painted on her hand, she pointed above.

I glanced up again. There was nothing but black. When I looked back to her, she was gone.

Quickly, I kicked to what I hoped was the surface. When my head pierced through the water, I removed my breather.

"Up here," Elysea called. In the moonlight, it looked like she was standing on the water. That couldn't be right. She gestured to her feet. I paddled over to her, and my hands hit something hard. Metal.

It was a grate, sunk a few feet into the water. *Ah.* I knew where we were: the children's swimming pool. I pulled myself up onto the ledge. The large rectangular metal lattice was barely visible. It gave kids confidence to learn how to swim in the ocean while protecting them from the depths.

"What in the Gods below was that?" I asked, wringing the water from my costume and hair.

Elysea's teeth gleamed in the moonlight. "My new act. Did you like it?"

"Like it?" I huffed. "I thought you'd disappeared!"

She laughed. "That's the idea."

"How long had you been working on that, before—" I halted.

"Before I died?" I wasn't sure if she could see me nod in the dim. "I was planning to reveal it in the summer."

"When the water's warmer."

"And not so dark."

Of course. In summer, you'd still be able to see as you made your way under the bridge and to the nearby shallow pool.

"I'd been practicing for months," she said, a melancholy tone

193

in her voice. "It took a while to be able to hold my breath for long enough to make it here."

I rubbed my arms in agitation. "That was dangerous. You could've drowned." Again.

She gave me another smile. "But it worked."

There didn't appear to be anyone else around. No one would bring their kids to learn to swim at night. It was a genius plan, really.

"I'm supposed to wait for ten minutes and then swim back for my reemergence," Elysea said, studying the silvery moonlit water.

"You're kidding."

"Obviously, I won't tonight." I could hear the sadness in her voice, even if I couldn't see her expression clearly.

There wouldn't be a next time for Elysea. She'd never be able to finish her performance, to see the shock on people's faces when she resurfaced or hear the thunderous applause. Tonight was all she had. An unfinished routine performed out of desperation.

The desperation to stay alive for a few more hours.

<hr />

Marsa lived on one of the outer arms of the Reef, not far from the Spring Tide. There was no reason for Raylan to track us there. They didn't know we were trying to find the map to our parents' location. But the Equinox was only so big. And I wasn't sure how many Palindromena guards had followed us here. We had to collect the map and get out.

Like everyone on the Reef, Marsa was assigned two poky rooms. But she lived alone, her kids now grown. When she'd taught us at school, she was known for being an eccentric but not unkind woman who collected different-colored rocks, rather than relics that could be sold or traded.

"Rocks *are* relics," she'd say. "With little land left, what's more important than rocks?"

People liked to say she had rocks in her head. Some claimed she weighed the Equinox down with her collection and Old World ideals, and with such strict weight laws, they had tried to get Marsa expelled from Equinox. But the Conservators admired her appreciation for the land and instead inspected her home regularly to ensure her belongings did not supersede each household's limits.

I'd liked listening to Marsa and her stories. Stories from before her time and before her parents' time. She told tales like the layers in her rocks, each word and sentence building upon the next. It was her tales, not the relics, that were valuable.

I rapped on her door and waited while Elysea hid nearby.

When the door opened, Marsa smiled, revealing a few missing teeth. She swept wisps of gray hair back from her forehead with a wrinkled white hand.

"Come in," she said. "You're late."

Before I had the chance to say anything in response, she spun around, retreating into her house.

CHAPTER TWENTY-THREE

LOR

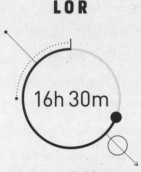

16h 30m

Monday, 7:30 p.m.

MOMENTS AFTER the Alerin sisters disappeared, the dancers removed their banners from the lanterns. Still, the girls were nowhere to be seen. One moment they were there, and the next they were gone.

Shit. Shit. Shit. Shit.

I'd allowed myself to be swept up in the performance. I'd allowed myself to imagine a different life. Somewhere like the Equinox, where no one knew who I was. A life I could carve on my own, stepping out of the Queen of Death's long shadow.

It was one thing to hide from your past and not know the world you were missing out on—and it was another to have it stare you straight in the face. A constant reminder of what you lost.

"Where did they go?" A hand landed heavily on my shoulder. I flinched, thinking of the knife-wielding barkeep. But it was Ray.

I didn't know how to explain my stupidity.

After I'd fled the barkeep, I'd slipped through the crowd to a gathering in the middle of the Spring Tide. At first, I'd been mesmerized by the girl descending onto the stage. She moved as gracefully as a leaf in the wind. The entire crowd had paused to watch. I didn't blame them. The girl was beautiful, even more so with blue dust all over her face. Her long dark hair trailed behind her like another limb, seemingly flowing in time with the music. If I'd ever believed in magic, it would've been then.

The crowd had *ooohh*ed and *ahhh*ed when she kicked water in time with the lightning bolts. That was when I realized there was something different about this performance. Something the audience hadn't seen.

Or *someone* they hadn't seen for a while.

But I'd been too late, and the girls had disappeared. Again.

When I didn't reply immediately, Ray pointed to my slashed sleeve and the drops of blood on my forearm. "What happened?"

"We have to find them," I said, ignoring his question. "You didn't see where they went?"

He shook his head. "I'd never seen anything like it and I've attended every Spring Tide."

I could see the memories of his past here had worn him down. There was no sign of his trademark grin. I hated it. It was one thing for me to glimpse a life I'd never live, but it was worse for Ray. He knew this life. He knew it down to his bones. It was his, once.

The troupe danced off the stage, continuing through the crowd as though nothing had happened. I grabbed the arm of one of the dancers. A sapphire ribbon was interwoven into her blond hair, blue splatters on her pale cheeks.

"Where did they go?" I gritted my teeth. I couldn't contain my fury. "Where did you hide them?"

The young dancer looked up at me and smiled. "Who?"

"You know who I'm talking about!"

Ray shook his head. "Let her go, bud. They're just kids."

I released the dancer, ashamed at my outburst. My pulse thundered in my ears as loud as the drums. *Dum dum dum dum.*

Like the tick of a clock.

The echolink showed seven thirty p.m. We had an hour to find the girls and get off the Equinox.

"Do you have a signal?" Ray asked.

"No. The storm is still interfering with the echolocator."

"We have time." He gave me a stiff nod, as though he was trying to convince himself as much as me. "We got this."

But time was slipping away. Just like the Alerin sisters. Right through our grasp.

They were water witches, I was sure of it. My grandmother used to tell me the tale of beautiful raven-haired women who lived and breathed water. They would crawl out of the sea and slip into your bedroom at night to drown you with a kiss.

As a boy, I'd vowed never to kiss a girl, in case she was a water witch in disguise. The vow lasted until I was fifteen, when a friend of Calen's visited from the Equinox.

"We need to find them," I repeated, shaking the thoughts of raven-haired beauties from my mind.

"We will." He glanced around the bustling market. "They're not going to hang around the Equinox with us here."

"Where else could they go?"

He scrubbed his hand though his cropped hair. He'd told me he used to wear it long, as did many people on the Reef. But he'd cut it after his accident. A fresh start. Or at least, that had been the idea. "I don't know," he said. "But we have to stop them before they leave."

I wished I could throw the echolink into the ocean. But that wouldn't stop the countdown. That wouldn't bring Elysea back to Palindromena. That wouldn't save Ray.

Sixteen and a half hours to go.

I was done playing nice.

CHAPTER TWENTY-FOUR

TEMPEST

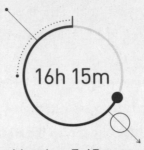

16h 15m

Monday, 7:45 p.m.

HOW DID MARSA KNOW I was coming? Did the Gods below warn her?

Marsa was known as a devout believer, who spent her days with her head underwater, searching for messages. Messages about what, I wasn't sure.

Marsa looked back over her shoulder to see I'd hesitated in the doorway. She crooked a pale finger, beckoning me to follow.

Her quarters were the same size and configuration as mine, but with tiny fish strung from one end of the living room to the other. Rocks of all different kinds and sizes lined the wall. Aside from a few chairs, there wasn't much else in the room. She must have kept it uncluttered to remain within the weight limits. I scanned the room for the treasure chest.

"Want some dried sugarfish?" Marsa asked, waving a bony hand around her. "Do you prefer one week old or one month old?" She gestured from the left to the right. "I have everything in between. The older the fish, the sweeter the flesh."

I scrunched my nose.

"Oh yes"—she smiled—"the smell. I lost my sense of smell years ago. Happens on the Reefs, you know."

I'd heard that could happen. After years of salt clogging your senses, you could eventually lose your sense of smell and taste.

"You were expecting me?" I couldn't see the treasure chest. The wooden planks nailed to the wall that made up her shelves strained beneath her rock collection. I could see why the Conservators would keep an eye on it.

Marsa smiled, the tip of her tongue sticking through the gap in her bottom teeth as she spoke. "I see and hear all." She turned away, then let out a ragged laugh, which turned into a hacking cough.

She was playing with me.

I wouldn't be waylaid by this woman's game.

"Take a seat." Marsa pointed to a chair with a few low-hanging sugarfish above it. She moved the fish aside for me to sit.

"Er, no, thank you," I said when she held out a handful of the dried fish.

Marsa sat opposite me and started chewing on the tail of one. "More for me, then. What can I do for you, Tempest Alerin?"

"You remember me?" It had been years since I'd been in her class.

Marsa threw the head of the sugarfish out the window. The head would nourish other fish below. "I know every child on the Equinox."

"I see."

Marsa had been let go from the school a year ago, after a boy nearly drowned while in her care. The principal had said it was negligence, but Marsa had claimed she'd seen something. Something that distracted her while the kids learned to swim.

She saw rocks float.

"Are you here to lift those anchors?" Marsa asked, tilting her head to scrutinize me.

"What?"

"You're not a light child," she said, as though that explained it. "Not a pumice." She looked behind her to her rock collection and shook her head. "Definitely not like a pumice. They're a porous light rock, you see. But you wear anchors around your feet."

"Right," I said as though that made any sense. "Actually, I was wondering—"

"I know grief," she interrupted, her eyes narrowed. "Gods, do I know grief. You think it wears you down, but no, it turns you into a fortified version of yourself. Although that fortification is often surface level. With the right amount of pressure, at the perfect angle, it can be shattered like a rock." She tilted her head. "What has shattered you, my dear?"

What was she talking about?

"I'm looking for something," I said, ignoring her question. "Daon sold you an item of my parents'. A treasure chest."

"Do you want it back?" Her wan face crumpled in disappointment.

"No. I just want to look at it."

"Why?" Marsa asked, crossing her arms over her chest.

"It was my parents'. I—I want to see it. One more time." I leaned forward. "Please," I added.

"I'm sorry," Marsa said, her eyes dancing about the room. "I'm not sure where I put it."

She wouldn't look me in the eye. Clearly, she was hiding something. But why would she want an old wooden chest that was falling apart? Unless she thought the gems embedded in the lid were real?

Then Marsa glanced at a metal box in the corner, the size of a fishing barrel, covered with a woven seaweed blanket. It was one of the few pieces of furniture that wasn't covered in sugarfish. It had to be important.

I darted toward it. I didn't have time to waste, and Marsa clearly hadn't had a visitor in a while. She wanted someone to talk with. Or talk *at*.

I pulled off the blanket and lifted the lid.

"No!" Marsa said, standing from her chair. Her bones creaked in protest at the sudden movement.

I pulled out a soft crocheted toy from the box. It looked like some kind of Old World land animal, long forgotten, with rounded ears and a bushy tail.

I continued riffling through the box while Marsa stood immobile in the middle of the room, her hand pressed to her mouth.

I had to find the treasure chest. It had to be in here. Some-where. Then I saw what Marsa was trying to hide.

I processed it in pieces. The white of a cracked shell. A small finger bone. A round, bulbous skull. I jerked back in fright.

"Oh Gods," I whispered. "What did you do?"

"Don't tell anyone," Marsa said. Her breath rattled out of her body in shaky gasps.

I dropped the toy. Realizing now what it was part of. A tomb for a baby.

Marsa finally started moving, and I flinched back from her. She covered the open box with the blanket. "Please don't tell anyone."

I opened my mouth, but shut it again. I didn't know what to say. Whose baby was it? And why had she kept the bones? In her own house?

"I didn't hurt her," Marsa said, her wrinkled hands clasped together. "She was my girl. My only girl."

"I—I—" I wanted to get out of here. This was too much. I didn't want to be reminded of what happened once we were dead. I didn't want to learn of Marsa's grief when I could barely handle my own.

"I have two sons," Marsa said. "And a daughter." She sighed, closing her eyes. "I *had* a daughter."

I felt ill. Ill for being here. Ill for knowing Elysea would soon be returning to death. Ill over the sight of bones. A re-minder of what we would all become. One day. But one day was tomorrow for Elysea.

I held my hand to my mouth and stepped backward toward the door.

"I shouldn't have done that," I said.

"No. You shouldn't have," she replied. "She was an illegal, you see." I didn't need to know the details, but I found myself pausing to listen. "But I didn't want to leave the Equinox, nor would I terminate the child." She picked up the toy I'd dropped and caressed its ear. "I thought I could hide her from the world."

I couldn't breathe. The air was thick with regret and longing.

"When I went into an early labor, I couldn't go to the doctors." She shook her head. "I gave birth in this very room."

I gasped, unable to imagine it.

"She lasted only a few weeks." Marsa smiled sadly. "The salt was too much for her small lungs."

"Crystal lung," I said in understanding. Newborns and the elderly were at risk of developing the condition. Their weaker lungs couldn't fight off the salt-riddled environment we now lived in. "I'm so sorry, Marsa."

"Thank you." She stood and moved to her bedroom.

I wasn't sure if she was coming back. I wasn't sure what to do. When she returned, she was holding the chest.

"I'm sorry too," Marsa said. "I should not have lied to you about it."

I wanted to snatch the thing out of her hands, but her expression gave me pause. This woman had been just as devastated by the loss of her daughter as I'd been over losing my parents and Elysea.

"I won't tell anyone about your baby," I said. "I promise."

She smiled, showing her missing teeth. "I know you won't. We all need ties to our loved ones. *This* is yours."

I took the chest out of her hands and lifted the gem-encrusted lid. I felt around the inside for the hidden compartment. There was a groove at the back, near the hinge. I pressed it. The false lining fell open and a small satchel tumbled out. I nearly cried with joy.

I swiftly moved the satchel into my pocket and handed the chest back. "Thank you, Marsa."

"Are you sure? You don't want to keep it?"

But I could see the way she was eyeing the stones on the lid. It meant more to her than it did to me.

Now that I had the map, I could let the treasure chest go.

I hurried back to Elysea, the truth in my hands.

But what if our parents *had* died that night and this map brought us nothing but more grief? What if there was some other explanation for Elysea finding Mom's necklace and Dad's echolink?

"Do you have it?" Elysea emerged from the darkness.

"Yes." I held out the satchel. She clutched it as though it were a lifeline. I supposed it was the closest she'd get.

"Marsa gave the chest over without question?" she asked.

"More or less."

I didn't want to talk about what I'd seen in Marsa's quarters. My stomach turned at the thought of her giving birth and then listening to the poor baby's ragged breathing, unable to call for help. She'd loved the little girl so much she couldn't part with her.

I glanced at Elysea. It was a feeling I could relate to.

The old woman had clearly lost her senses, collecting rocks to fill the emptiness in her heart. I wished there was something I could've said to console her, but after so many years, what more was there to say? Her baby never would've survived with crystal lung. Doctors still hadn't found a cure.

Would Marsa want twenty-four more hours with her baby, if she could've had the chance?

"You didn't open it?" Elysea asked, holding up the pouch.

"No. I wanted to wait for you."

She squeezed my hand, then loosened the drawstring.

As she'd said, Mom's necklace was inside, as was Dad's echolink. We stared at the black screen. And just like that, we were two young kids again, daring each other to touch Dad's echo. Elysea quickly pocketed the echolink. She pulled a piece of folded paper from the pouch. The map. She weighed it in her hand.

"Aren't you going to look?" I asked.

"Yes . . ." But an unspoken question hung between us. *What if their location is farther away than the time remaining?* It had to be close to eight p.m. That only left us sixteen hours.

We held a collected breath as Elysea unfolded the map.

"The Islands Cavalcade," she whispered, running her fingertip across the crude drawings of the distinctive spiral shape.

"Our parents left the Equinox to go live on the party islands?" My mom was a botanist; my dad, the Head Warden. If they were really fleeing something, why would they go there?

Elysea hung her head, her hair shielding her face from me. "The islands are a few days' journey from here." If our parents were still alive, she wouldn't make the reunion.

"No," I said. I traced my fingers over the red lines denoting the narrow passage of water between the Equinox and the Islands Cavalcade. "Not if we cross the Untied Sea."

She startled. "No, Tempe. That's too dangerous. Most boats, and their crew, don't survive the journey."

"If we travel via the Untied Sea, the Islands Cavalcade are only six hours from here. That will give us plenty of time to see if Mom and Dad are there."

"No, we can't. It's not worth the risk."

But it was. And I would face the Remorans—the scavengers of the seas—if I had to. I would reunite my family before it was too late.

"It's the only way, Ely." I placed my hand on her arm. "I want you to see Mom and Dad. You deserve the truth as much as I do."

She stared at me for a moment and then threw her arms around me. "Thank you, Tempe," she said into my hair. "I wish

I remembered everything about the night I died. But whatever happened, I'm sorry. I should've told you about the necklace and echolink as soon as I'd found them. I never should've gone out without you. We only had each other, and I left you." She sniffled. "While I can't change what I did back then, *we* can still do this. We can find Mom and Dad. You won't have to be alone anymore."

My tears flowed freely now. I hugged her close.

I might not have known why my parents left that night, but I knew who my sister was.

We were in this together.

LOR

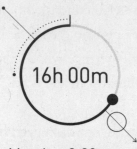

Monday, 8:00 p.m.

AT 8:00 P.M., the skies finally opened, delivering the storm it promised.

Rain poured down as we ran toward the harbor, our feet slapping the metal gangways. We hoped to cut the Alerin sisters off at the pass. We had thirty minutes before the Watchtower would float Ray's boat into the open ocean.

Countless vessels crowded the harbor; there was no way we could find the girls' boat without the echolocator.

We decided to depart and anchor not far outside the Watchtower to wait. Anyone leaving the Equinox would have to pass us by.

"Stop it," Ray muttered as I paced the deck. "You'll wear a hole in my boat and I can't afford another one."

He was trying to use his boat's transmitter to boost the signal of my echolink. Supposedly, it would make for a stronger signal in the storm that showed no signs of easing.

My hair was plastered against my forehead, and rain

streamed down my face. It felt like the sky was crying. I hoped it wasn't an omen. If I'd believed in any kind of Gods, I'd have thought that they were trying to warn me. This day would not end well.

Luckily, I believed only in what you could see and touch.

With the humidity broken, the sun long set, and the constant rain, I started to feel cold. My Palindromena T-shirt clung to me like an icy second skin. It was a foreign feeling. I hadn't felt anything other than the temperate climate of the Aquarium for years. My body didn't know how to respond. So it decided to react badly.

I pressed my shaking hands against my sides. "Have you got anything yet?" I gritted my teeth to stop the chattering.

"No," he replied, tweaking something on his boat's console. Because of the swirling rain, he was as saturated as I was, even under the narrow helm. But he didn't appear to be affected by the cold. He was probably wearing one of those diving skins under his clothes, like most people did on the Reef—even if they didn't plan on swimming.

"Why are you so annoyingly calm?" I asked.

He didn't turn around. "Have you ever heard of a riptide in the ocean?"

"Of course." Just because I wasn't a diver didn't mean I wasn't aware of the dangers. My grandfather hated the sea. For the early years of my life, he'd warned me away from it, even though our cottage overlooked the beach. He'd taught me the ocean was a cursed expanse that caused only death and destruction. It wasn't until he died, years later, that I first ventured into the blue depths. While it had felt like dishonoring his memory, I'd needed to feel something other than solid ground. I'd needed to feel like escaping the island was a possibility. But within seconds, I'd been knocked off my feet.

I then looked to the cliffs for a reprieve.

"A riptide," Ray continued, "seems all calm and innocent on the surface—a break between the waves—until it drags you out to sea to die."

That was when I could see the tension between his shoulders. He wasn't calm at all.

"If I stop and worry about it now," he said, "it's game over. I lose my job, and my parents will lose their home." While he didn't say it, I was most concerned about him losing hope. Where would Ray go if he didn't have the Equinox or Palindromena?

"Anyway," he said, "we still have some—"

"If you say *time*, I'm going to push you off the boat."

Ray laughed before falling silent.

"That was a stupid thing to say," I said. He hadn't been in the ocean since his accident. "I'm sorry. I'm the worst friend."

"Shut up."

"Look, Ray. I know it's been—"

"Just shut up for a second!" He crouched over the screen on the console.

"What do you see?" I sucked in a breath. Hoping. Waiting.

He turned, and my heart leaped in my chest.

"They're here."

I whirled around to the harbor. A small vessel was coasting toward the Watchtower. The boom lifted, and the boat switched into high gear.

"Start the boat!" I said.

Ray pushed down the accelerator. "Already ahead of you."

The girls' boat flew across the water and turned to the left. Away from Palindromena.

"Where are you going now, Tempest?" I whispered. "What's your plan?"

Ray's boat bounced up and down on the churning waters, and rain pelted our faces, making it difficult to see. At least we had the echolocator. If the blinking dot of Elysea's heartbeat was any indication, she was either terrified or excited. Did she know we were following them?

But their boat was smaller, faster. While the *Surf to Turf* barreled directly into the stormy waves, the girls' boat glided along the surface.

"They're getting away!" I shouted over the roar of the wind.

"This is a fishing boat." Ray's brows were low over narrowed eyes. I'd never seen him look so serious. "It's built to carry the weight of a catch, not for speed."

I watched the Alerins' boat lift a few feet out of the water and soar above the waves.

"How are they doing that?" I asked.

"It's based on Old World aircrafts," Ray said. His voice held a hint of wistfulness. "It has wings that allow it to rise out of the water at high speeds."

"It can fly?"

He laughed and shook his head. "No. The wings are still in the water, but when the boat picks up speed, the air lifts its body up from the surface. It allows it to cut through the waves with no drag."

That sounded like a flying boat to me.

The wind billowed the sails and helped our vessel pick up the pace. But we couldn't close the distance.

"Their boat is too fast," Ray muttered.

"What can we do?" We couldn't get another boat; we'd have to contact Palindromena for that.

"We're too heavy. I have too much fishing equipment."

I couldn't ask Ray to throw his equipment to the bottom of the sea. I wouldn't ask him to sacrifice his life savings for me.

I had messed up. Not him.

"Actually," he said, "there might be a way." His eyes darted to the side of the boat.

"What?" I'd do anything.

"The sea-blazer. It's quicker, lighter. You could catch up to them."

"I've never ridden a sea-blazer."

"I'll go, then. You stay here."

"No. I'll get them." I'd driven land rovers all my life. How different could it be?

"Okay, then. Do you still have your tablet?" he asked. I

tossed it over to him, and he typed something in. "I've entered my boat's signature so you can contact me when you find them. Catch up to them, get on their boat and kill the engine. I'll come get you." He clapped me on the back. "Be careful out there, okay?"

"I'll be fine." But my mind drew me detailed images of razor-toothed creatures lying in wait. I cursed my grandfather for showing me all those illustrations of deep-sea creatures. Both real and imagined. My mind couldn't discern the difference right now.

Ray lifted an eyebrow. "Just don't fall in. That's all I'm saying."

I examined the sea-blazer. "Not planning on it."

I lowered myself onto the seat, and Ray unlatched it from the side of boat. "Good luck," he said, pushing the vehicle away with his right foot.

I rotated the throttle and pressed the accelerator down. The sea-blazer rumbled like a disgruntled creature before lurching ahead. My foot slipped, but I gripped on to the handlebars. I straightened myself back on the machine.

I was wrong. The buoyancy of the sea-blazer was completely different than a land rover. Nothing tethered me to the surface of the ocean.

And I loved it.

I twisted the accelerator all the way up and tore through the waves. Before long, the Alerins' boat appeared on the horizon.

Then what? I couldn't help but ask myself. *Are you willing to hand Elysea over to be put back to death?*

This girl had already died. This wasn't the same as with Calen. I wasn't responsible. Elysea was supposed to have spent her twenty-four hours in Palindromena, let her sister say her piece and then be returned to her tank, none the wiser. It shouldn't have been a painful process. That was one of the reasons Wardens wanted clients to hide the truth from the revived. Knowing they were going to die would only torture them.

I pushed the thought to the back of my mind and twisted the throttle again. The loud engine drowned out any concern. All that mattered was getting Elysea back to Palindromena. Everything else was out of my hands.

And her sister?

Well, I couldn't think about that. I wasn't responsible for Tempest's grief. If she hadn't broken her sister out of Palindromena, then none of this would be happening.

As I neared their boat, I vowed to the Gods below, the Old Gods or whoever was out there that I would return to Palindromena with Elysea. I would return to the quiet of the basement. Ray would keep his job, and I would be safe.

I would be selfish. One last time.

CHAPTER TWENTY-SIX

TEMPEST

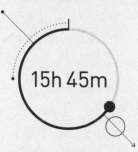

15h 45m

Monday, 8:15 p.m.

WE KNEW we were being followed as soon as we passed the Watchtower. Even in the storm, we could hear the growl of an engine, trailing us. But they didn't have a Quicksilver.

Raylan was about to see how fast the *Sunrise* could go.

Our boat lifted out of the ocean with a jolt and flew along the black water.

"Ha!" I laughed, seeing the other boat disappear behind us. I threw my arm around Elysea. "Mom and Dad were right about this boat. No one can surpass us!"

She gave me a timid smile, reminding me it was too soon to talk about our parents. We still didn't know if they were actually alive.

I returned to the console, checking that our navigation was set to the coordinates scribbled on the map. I steered the boat toward the moon.

The night grew silent; we'd outrun the storm. The stars

glimmered above like a school of tiny flarefish clustered together.

Elysea huddled at the end of the boat, her hand trailing in the water. After everything she'd been through, she still wanted to be connected to it.

"You don't fear it?" I asked.

Elysea glanced up, her face drawn. "Fear what? Death?"

I shook my head vehemently. I didn't want to talk about death. Especially hers. "The ocean?"

She lifted a shoulder. "I don't remember my drowning. I don't remember being scared or knowing I would die—and that water would take my last breath. The sea is all I've ever known. Water is in our veins. How can I fear it?"

All this talking of drowning made me dizzy. I sat down beside her to remind myself she was still here. For just under sixteen more hours.

"*Are* you scared?" This time I did mean death. And she knew it.

"Yes." She twirled a piece of her long hair around a finger.

My chest felt tight, and I struggled for a breath. It felt so close to drowning. But now that I'd started, I needed to know. I needed to know something that would make her impending demise easier to take. That was what Palindromena was for, after all. The time to discuss anything left unsaid. Time to heal.

"Do you remember anything after you drowned?" I asked.

Those who believed in the Gods below said you would be

reunited with your loved ones in a realm beneath the sea. A realm where you could breathe underwater. And those who believed in the Old Gods said you would go to a place in the sky. I wasn't sure what to believe. But I hoped whatever the truth was, Elysea wouldn't be alone. She would be safe and happy.

"I don't remember anything," she whispered. "Nothing at all."

My eyes stung, and I turned away. Was there nothing after death?

A high-pitched mechanical buzz cut through the night. I squinted to see what was behind us.

A sea-blazer.

Raylan.

Why? Why couldn't he let us be?

"Get the ropes!" I said, jumping into action.

Elysea ran across the hull and untied the ropes from the mast while I undid my side. We let go, and the sail launched into the sky with a snap, nearly throwing us both overboard. The boat picked up pace with the addition of its sails.

A light bloomed behind us. It hit the stern, marking our boat for all to see.

"He won't give up." Elysea let out a sigh.

"Apparently he never heard the word *no* as a kid," I grumbled. "Well, someone's got to teach him. Take the wheel, Ely. Let's dance rings around this guy."

She smiled. "You know how I love to dance."

The sea-blazer sidled up next to us.

"Pull over," Raylan yelled over the roar of the engine and waves. His hair dripped in rivulets down his blanched face.

Elysea twisted the boat away in response. But Raylan easily followed.

She then spun the wheel, and the boat lurched. I held on to the *Sunrise*'s mast. No one could maneuver a boat better than Elysea. She'd outrun storms on a lesser boat.

We cut across the ocean, shifting whenever the nose of Raylan's sea-blazer neared. Elysea laughed. She was enjoying this. Of course she was. Even though she hadn't felt any time pass, she'd missed the ocean.

Raylan continued to match us move for move, the tip of his sea-blazer nipping at our heels.

Elysea's laughter was cut short as Raylan veered his sea-blazer in front of us. While the *Sunrise* was swift, the sea-blazer was nimbler. And although it was dark, I was sure I could see fury lighting the Warden's eyes.

There had to be some maneuver he couldn't replicate.

"Move over," I said to Elysea, grabbing the wheel from her. I spun the *Sunrise* around.

"What are you doing?" she asked. "We can't go back."

"I'm not going back. Hold on." She clung to the helm.

I twisted the boat suddenly to the left. Raylan copied. Then I swung right. The *Sunrise* tilted vertically, leaving only the right wing still in the ocean. I gripped the wheel as we glided beside Raylan at an almost ninety-degree angle. Water rained down on him from the underbelly of our boat. I grinned triumphantly at his startled expression.

I straightened the wheel, and the *Sunrise* righted itself. I pushed a button on the console. The *Sunrise* dropped its hull into the water as the wings were retracted, sending a cascading wave out behind us. Raylan attempted to dart away, but his sea-blazer was caught in the swell.

I pressed the button again, and the wings extended back out. We sped across the water, leaving Raylan behind.

"Nice move, Tempe," Elysea said.

I grinned. "I might not be able to dance, but I know how to make an impact."

When we didn't hear the hum of the sea-blazer start back up, Elysea slowed the engine.

"What are you doing?" I asked, trying to push the accelerator forward. She held her arm out to block me, her eyes focused behind us.

"He's gone," she said.

"Yes." I frowned. "Wasn't that the idea?"

"No. I mean, he's no longer on the water. His sea-blazer must've been toppled by the wave."

"So?"

"We can't leave him out there."

"He'll be fine. He can tread water until his boat finds him. The whole point was to get away from him, wasn't it?"

"I don't want him to drown." Her voice was quiet.

"Fine." I sighed.

It wasn't easy to find the sea-blazer. Its front light had been

221

blown out by the wave. We steered forward gingerly, until something hit the side of the *Sunrise*. Metal sliding against metal.

"There!" Elysea pointed to the starboard side.

I peered over the edge. The sea-blazer was bobbing upright, seat empty. "I can't see him. He's not there."

"That means he's gone under." Her voice shook.

My chest constricted. While I hated what he wanted to do to my sister, I didn't want him to die. "We won't be able to find him in the dark. He's gone."

But Elysea was already pulling off her dancing costume.

"You're not going in there," I said. "Absolutely not."

She didn't stop.

I shook her. "You're not risking your life for him!" I'd just gotten her back. I needed all the time with her that I could get. "I'm wearing a diving skin. I'll do it."

I had my shirt up over my head when I heard a voice.

"I suppose I should be grateful." It was Raylan. He stood on the far side of the *Sunrise*. His clothes and hair were sopping wet; the longer strands of his blond hair had been swept aside to show a steely gaze. He must've pulled himself aboard while we searched for him.

He'd played us. His abandoned sea-blazer was merely a distraction.

He moved closer, and I stepped in front of Elysea.

"Stay where you are!" I shouted.

He held up his hands. "I have no weapon. I don't want to hurt you."

I snorted out a laugh. "No, you just want to drag my sister back to Palindromena. Get off my boat!"

"The sea-blazer's dead, water in her engine from your wave." He jutted out his chin toward the ocean. "I have nowhere else to go."

I crossed my arms. "I have no problem with you returning to the sea. You can swim back to your boat." But there was still nothing in sight. He'd likely die before he made it back.

"Elysea, please," Raylan began. "You must understand, I—"

"Don't talk to her!" I snapped.

Elysea stepped around me. "You can stay on our boat," she said. "But we're not going back to Palindromena with you."

His shoulders drooped a little. "You have to. You're running out of time."

I pointed at him. "You can't make us. *We* have a boat. *We* have the numbers. *You* have nothing."

"That's not entirely true," he said, something lighting his eyes. "I know *where* you are. And I have *this*—" He reached behind him.

So he did have a weapon after all.

"Please, don't!" Elysea cried.

Before he could use it, I dove toward him, my arms connecting around his middle.

"Oooof!" he cried, taken by surprise. He slipped on the wet metal hull, and we fell to the deck. I grabbed for the weapon he was holding behind him, but his arm was like limp seaweed.

He had hit his head against the mast when he fell. He was out cold.

I pulled his arm around and found a digital tablet, like the one Selna had used. There was no weapon. Guilt rushed over me.

"Is he okay?" Elysea asked, her steps cautious.

Gods, I hoped so.

I lifted his wrist to check his pulse and let out a breath. "He's alive, just unconscious."

Elysea stared at the echolink on his other wrist. "Should we take it off?"

"Maybe." But neither of us moved. We didn't want to invite more bad luck.

Instead, Elysea picked up the tablet. "Send coordinates to Raylan Bassan?" she read out loud. "What does that mean?"

"Raylan?" I repeated. "But this is—" I looked at the boy slumped around the mast. If *this* wasn't Raylan, then who was he? There must've been some mistake.

I took the tablet from Elysea's hands.

You have a new message from Raylan, the screen said. I clicked to read it.

Lor! Did you cut their engine? Where are you?

I deleted the message and looked at the unconscious boy on the deck.

Who was this Lor and why was he so intent on dragging my sister back to Palindromena?

224

CHAPTER TWENTY-SEVEN

LOR

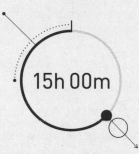

Monday, 9:00 p.m.

I WOKE TO a swaying boat and a pounding headache—possibly a concussion. The last thing I remembered was confronting the Alerins. And Tempest's furious expression as she ran toward me.

I groaned and tried to sit up. The image of a girl with long black hair swam in front of me. My first thought was of a water witch. I blinked a few times. The girl held a steel rod in her hand like a bat.

"What did you do to me?" I managed to slur. I tried to move but found myself tied to a metal post behind me. "You've taken me captive?" I wanted to laugh—this entire day was absurd—but nothing came out.

The girl twisted the rod in her hand, and although she looked like her sister, I knew it was Tempest. I was tied up in a narrow room with pieces of diving equipment scattered around. The boat's cabin. The porthole to the outside was black. I couldn't tell if it was the sky or the sea.

"Killing me won't solve anything," I said. Why did I say that? I should be bargaining for my life, not offering it up on a plate.

She leaned in. Her eyes swirled in front of me. I definitely had a concussion.

"You better start telling the truth, Palindromena boy," she said.

"Don't call me that." I twisted away from her. Although she wasn't exactly the most dangerous-looking person in the world, she held my fate in her hands. And right now, her hatred was focused on Palindromena. I needed to distance myself from that place.

"What should I call you, then?" Her top lip curled as she spoke, her hand on her hip. "Which is it, Raylan or Lor?"

How did she find out? And where *was* Ray? Would he continue searching for me if he found the overturned sea-blazer, or would he assume I'd drowned?

"I can explain."

She tapped the metal rod in her palm as she waited. "Please do."

I sighed, my head hanging forward so my hair covered my eyes. It was easier to talk without looking at her. "I was helping a friend. His name is Raylan."

"The Palindromena guard at the Spring Tide?"

"He's not a guard. He's a Warden. He needed someone to fill in for him, so I took his place for your sister's revival. I was doing him a favor."

"Are you even a Warden?"

"No, I look after the tanks in the Aquar—in the basement of Palindromena." What I wouldn't give to be back there right now.

"So you don't know a thing about this?" She waved her hand around. "And yet you said you understood what I was going through. You told me what to do with Elysea. You made me trust you."

"I'm sorry." And I really was. Not only did I wish that Ray had overseen his client so none of this had ever happened, but I wished Tempest had had a proper Warden. Perhaps she never would've broken her sister out if she'd had that support.

"Have you even been through the revival program, or was that also a lie?" she asked, using the rod to tilt up my chin so I couldn't avoid her scrutiny. She didn't believe I was telling the truth. I didn't blame her.

Something softened around her expression. She was hurt. She had trusted me because of the story I'd shared. Because of Calen.

"That was true." I considered telling her about the connection between me and Elysea, but that would lead to more questions. Questions I wasn't willing to answer. Right now, she thought I was her enemy and was unlikely to believe anything else I told her.

Her eyes searched my face. She sighed and then stepped back. I wasn't sure if she'd found what she was looking for.

"I'm sorry," I said again. I was apologizing a lot today. "I didn't want to lie to you, but I had to protect my friend. Surely you can understand that?"

She barked a harsh laugh, and that softness I'd seen was gone. "Protecting my dying sister and lying for a friend are not at all alike."

"Maybe not. But we'd both do whatever it takes for the people we care about." Hopefully Ray would keep searching for me.

She pressed her lips together before replying, "Don't pretend you know anything about me."

She was right. I didn't. I'd only read the file on her sister and how she'd drowned. I didn't even know why Tempest had broken Elysea out of Palindromena or where we were headed now.

"Where are you going?" I asked.

She put a hand on her hip. "That's none of your business." Clearly it was, seeing as I was coming along for the ride.

I spotted my tablet clipped into her diving belt.

She pulled it free. "Want this back?" she asked tauntingly. Before I could answer, she smashed it on the ground.

There went my chance to signal Ray.

I let out a heavy breath. "What are you planning to do with me?"

Her forehead smoothed, as though she hadn't thought that through.

"We're not going to hurt you," came another voice.

Elysea.

She climbed down into the cabin and took the rod out of her sister's hands. Tempest didn't argue. "Stop scaring him. It's not going to help."

Tempest shrugged as though she had nothing better to do.

"Where are we headed?" I asked Elysea, hoping she would see sense and let me go.

Although letting me go didn't solve my problem. I needed Elysea to come with me.

"To the Islands Cavalcade," she replied.

Tempest threw up her hands. "Don't tell him that!"

"Why not?" she asked. "It's not like he can go anywhere or tell anyone."

It was true. Without the tablet, I couldn't message Ray my location. I was stranded here.

"Why the party islands?" I asked. Maybe someone there could help me.

"Our parents are there," Elysea said, earning another glare from her sister.

"I thought your parents were dead?" That was what the file had said.

"So did we," Tempest said.

Now I understood. They wanted to be a family again, before Elysea died, before her gifted hours were up.

If I stayed tied to this boat, then they might just get their wish.

CHAPTER TWENTY-EIGHT

TEMPEST

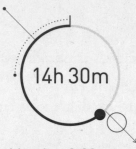

14h 30m

Monday, 9:30 p.m.

THE PALINDROMENA BOY made me uncomfortable. I don't know why. There was something about his blue eyes, and the way they tracked my movements. Like he was studying us. Studying me.

Elysea and I returned to the deck.

I checked the time on the boat's clock. "It's nine thirty," I said. "We have fourteen and a half hours to find Mom and Dad. That's plenty of time."

As long as Mom and Dad were actually at the party islands.

"How long till we reach the Untied Sea?" Elysea asked. She'd taken to carrying the map around everywhere with her, and had put on Mom's necklace. The echolink was unsurprisingly absent on her wrist.

"A few hours," I said, studying the boat's echolocator on the console. The Untied Sea ran in a diagonal line from the northeast to the southwest. A warning flashed across our screen as the boat drew closer to the end of Palindromena's jurisdiction.

We were lucky to have a Palindromena-sanctioned boat so we could come and go as we pleased. Was that why our parents had left the *Sunrise* behind?

Once we crossed the sonar perimeter, we were on our own.

"The *Sunrise* is quick," Elysea said, staring out at the horizon as though she could see where the Untied Sea began, and the hundreds of boats that littered the ocean floor. "We'll be fine."

But she didn't sound very confident.

"Do you wish I hadn't done it?" The question burned in my chest like I'd swallowed salt water. "Do you wish you hadn't come back?"

"No." She gripped my hand. "I'm glad to see you again. I'm glad we're here together. Whatever happens next, I'm glad."

I grimaced. I still didn't know how to take this change in plan. For years, I'd wanted the truth about Mom's and Dad's deaths, and now we were journeying across the ocean, hoping to see them again. I should've been exultant, but I was terrified of everything falling down around me. I now understood why Ely had kept the truth from me when she'd first found Mom's necklace. It would have broken me. It still might.

Elysea's hand felt reassuring in mine. I had her. For now.

"What about you?" I asked.

She frowned. "What about me?"

"If you could do anything right now, what would you want to do?" I doubted it would be traversing the Untied Sea.

She glanced away. "I don't want to think about that. It's easier not to."

I understood. Thinking of the what-ifs would not make her death any easier to take. For two years, I'd known she'd been taken too soon, but she'd only learned the injustice of it. Dwelling on her old life would make this harder.

"The storm is closing in behind us," Elysea said, pointing at a charcoal smear on the horizon. "Can we outrun it?"

"I'll do my best," I said, turning the boat away from the wind. Picking up speed, the boat lifted out of the water and sped along the surface of the ocean like the soaring birds of the Old World.

※

We couldn't outrun the storm after all.

"We have to go belowdecks," Elysea said as the rain fell from the sky like a waterfall. "We're going to get sick."

"And die?" I asked, punishing myself as soon as I said it. "Someone needs to stay up here to direct us." As much as I loved the *Sunrise*, she wasn't the best in bad weather. There was a fine art to keeping her upright, and in these winds, that meant someone staying at the wheel and not using autopilot mode.

"I can steer," she said. Because it wouldn't matter if she got sick. She was going to die anyway. "You should go to the cabin and keep an eye on Lor."

I glanced at the boat's clock.

Fourteen hours.

"No," I said, bumping her aside. "I'm better in storms. I'll stay up here. You go down and get some sleep."

"Tempe, I'm not going to spend my last few hours sleeping. I'll stay here with you."

I swallowed roughly, a lump in my throat preventing my reply.

She placed her arm around my shoulders. "Together until the end."

"We'll get to the islands. We're not far."

But the storm worked against us. We'd had to collapse the sail, the wind pushing the boat sideways. We were losing precious time, although neither of us wanted to say it.

"Remember how Mom used to talk about traveling the world?" Elysea asked. Her voice was strengthening the more she spoke about our parents.

"Yeah. She wanted to visit the other few islands down south and study their plants."

She shook her head. "Not only that, she wanted you to see the Reef that is half submerged." She grinned. "She always said you were most at home in the sea."

Except now I couldn't think of being beneath the surface without seeing Elysea's face, still and lifeless.

"Promise me you'll go there," she whispered after a moment of silence. "Take that trip with Mom that she always planned."

The rain pelted our boat with a *plink, plink, plink*, my tears mingling with the stream.

"Tempe?" she asked.

I managed to steady my voice before I replied, "We don't even know if they're still alive." And if they were, was that what I wanted? Was that my future? To finally be reunited as a family, mere moments before saying goodbye to my sister forever?

"They're alive." She clutched Mom's necklace to her chest. "I'm certain of it."

I wished I felt the same. But right now, nothing was certain. Holding on to hope was like trying to retain water with one hand.

I could feel my control falling away. "Then why didn't they come back for me? Why did they stop leaving messages two years ago?"

She faced me. Her eyes looked almost black in the night. It was like staring in a mirror. "They were running from something that night," she said. "Perhaps they wanted to come back, but couldn't? What I know for sure is that they wanted us with them. They never would've meant to hurt us."

I held a hand to my side, feeling winded.

"Did *I* hurt you?" I could barely get the words out. I knew I had. I'd revived her, blamed her for our parents' death and then expected her to return to her grave, never allowing her to set foot outside the recovery room. And now she had to face down the bitter squall of death, head-on.

Of course I'd hurt her.

She shook her head and smiled. "If anything, you're healing me, Tempe."

Gods below, I was glad it was raining.

How would I say goodbye, now that I had my sister back? How could I ever give her up?

I wrapped my arms around her. "I'm so glad to have you here," I whispered. "If only for twenty-four hours."

"I feel the same way."

We held on to each other as the *Sunrise* battled the storm.

CHAPTER TWENTY-NINE

LOR

13h 45m

Monday, 10:15 p.m.

MY CONCUSSION BECAME the least of my concerns as the storm rocked the boat side to side. I took back any kind words I'd ever said about the ocean. It was a hideous thing that wanted to shake the life out of you. I hoped Ray had taken shelter and wasn't following us into the storm blindly.

Although I couldn't tell what time it was, with my hands tied behind my back, it had felt like an hour or so since I saw either Elysea or Tempest. Meanwhile, I'd vomited eight times. Mostly all over myself.

"Hi," Tempest said tentatively as she descended the stairs into the cabin. She looked like she'd been crying, her skin sallow and her eyes and cheeks red. Or maybe that was the wind and rain.

I desperately wanted to wipe the latest spittle of vomit from my chin and T-shirt. "Hi," I croaked.

She stepped around the pools of bile as she checked my binds, probably worried they'd come loose while I'd been thrown about by the storm.

"Are you okay?" she asked, pulling back. She didn't quite look me in the eye, but I appreciated her concern. Something was changing within her. I hoped her walls were breaking down, but perhaps she was simply breaking.

"Out of all the hostage situations I've been in," I said, "this one is top-notch."

She tilted her head and narrowed her eyes. "You've been held hostage before?"

I laughed. "It was a joke."

"Oh" was all she said.

I tried not to let my desperation show. Somehow I needed to convince her to take her sister back and abandon this attempt at a family reunion. The scientists would be expecting Elysea to be in her room at the end of the twenty-four hours. If she wasn't there, they'd realize something went wrong. They'd investigate what happened and find out it was me—not Ray—who'd stepped in as her Warden. Ray would lose everything, and the scientists would uncover the truth about me.

I was Nessandra's son. And the secrets both my mother and I had been keeping would rise to the surface. We were both killers.

Perhaps that was what we deserved, but I still wanted to live.

"Are you all right?" I turned the question around on her.

Tempest rolled her eyes. "Don't ask me that."

"Okay," I said. "Stupid question. I'm sorry."

"Sorry you want to take my sister back to Palindromena?

Or sorry you want to steal her final hours from her?"

I heaved a breath. "I'm sorry about everything. Truly." I never should've left the Aquarium.

"Just stop." She rocked back on her heels. "I don't want to hear any more of your lies."

"I promise, no more lies." But I couldn't look her in the eye.

She squatted opposite me. "Then tell me why it matters so much to return Elysea to Palindromena? Why can't you let her d-die out here with me?" She stumbled over the word.

"It's my job," I said, shoulders slumping. It was the safest explanation. Telling her about our connection was still too risky.

She tilted her head again, her eyes searching mine. "Do you really care about your job so much?"

This time I held her gaze. "No, but I care about Raylan's. He needs the money. You don't understand."

"Then explain it to me!" Her voice echoed throughout the small cabin.

"Raylan's my friend." My only friend. "When I let you escape, his whole future was put in jeopardy. And it's not merely a job. It's money for him to try and heal his foot. It's security for his family and their home on the Equinox. Letting you and Elysea go tore everything he ever wanted away from him."

"Funny," she deadpanned. "I'm supposed to care about your friendship with Raylan when you don't care about my sister. The one person who's cared about me since my parents died five years ago. She's my only family."

How could I make her understand?

"I do care about your sister. And even though you've taken me captive and threatened me with a metal rod, I care about you too. But your sister died, Tempest. She wasn't meant to come back. She's been living on borrowed time. And that time is running out." I clenched my teeth. "I'm sorry you got caught up in Palindromena's schemes to control this world. I really am."

"Are you saying you don't agree with what Palindromena does?" she asked.

I closed my eyes for a moment. If only she knew exactly how much I resented what my mother did. She had gotten more and more desperate over the years. She didn't see the line between life and death as final anymore, and because of that, she'd lost perspective. When my grandparents died, she'd lost her connection to reality. The island was all she had left of them, and she would do anything to protect that and their legacy. But while my grandparents' focus had been on the crops, with the revival program as merely a way to fund their research, my mother was obsessed with finding a "cure" for death—so that no one would have to suffer grief. And she was willing to do whatever it took.

"No," I said finally. "I don't."

Tempest blinked a few times in confusion. "Then why do you work for them?" I opened my mouth, but she added, "And don't say I wouldn't understand."

I couldn't help it. I grinned. But it was fleeting.

I debated lying to her, but I needed her to see it from my perspective. I needed her to care about my well-being, and not just her sister's. In this instance, the truth might help my case.

"My mother is the Director of Palindromena," I said. "It was easy to get a job there. It was expected, actually."

"Nessandra is your mother?" She seemed surprised. She studied my appearance as though she were looking for the resemblance.

"Yes."

"How long have you worked there?"

"Two years. Before that, I was just a kid, like you."

She snorted as though she doubted there were any similarities between us. "You couldn't get a job anywhere else? Doing *anything* else?"

I grinned grimly. "Not really. My mother *should've* sent me to the school on the Equinox so I could study a useful skill—or at least learn about the wider world—but she decided it would be best if I learned by her side." I shifted restlessly against my binds. "I was never going to follow in her footsteps. I didn't like being stuck inside. I've always wanted to explore the world." And the cliffs were as far from my mother as was possible without leaving the island.

"I wasn't good at school either," Tempest said. "After my parents died, I didn't see the point in learning about the different Reefs across the world, the history of our planet or how the New World came to be. We never learn from our mistakes, so what's the point in knowing the past?"

I hoped that wasn't true. I was desperate to be a better man. A better friend. Although I was currently tied to a post, so clearly that wasn't working out so well for me.

"You don't think we've learned from the Great Waves?" I asked.

She shook her head. "The Equinox's population continues to grow to the point of unsustainability. We fish more than necessary and have stripped the Old World clean. And yet, it's never enough. We're just like our ancestors. Always wanting more than we have. What have we learned?" She turned the question around on me, one brow raised.

I would've hoped we learned to value what we had—and what little land was left. But maybe she was right.

"You're a diver," I stated—it was clear from this boat and its equipment. "You're a part of stripping the Old World clean. Isn't that hypocritical?" I wanted her to see that our jobs don't define our beliefs.

She shrugged off my accusation. "I love diving—it's not about what I find down there. It's not about the Notes I earn. It's about the world beneath. But no one focuses on what's in front of them. They only care about what they can find and what Notes can be made. While our ancestors may have lost everything in the Great Waves, something beautiful has arisen in its place."

A smile crossed her face as she talked about the sunken ruins. A look that made me wish I could see what she had.

"I think that's important," she said. "While everyone

mourns our life on the land and tries to bring it back"—
she gave me a pointed look, no doubt a dig at my mother—
"I like what we already have. I like the water and the world
below."

I smiled at her contemplative look. Her guard was completely down again, and she was beautiful.

I pushed that thought away. It wouldn't do me any good.
I needed her to not see me as her enemy. She needed to see
my side. Understanding her, getting close to her, was not a
part of my plan.

Tempest seemed to process my change in demeanor. She sat
back against the hull of the cabin, opposite me.

"If you don't like what you do," she said, "then what is it you
care about? Aside from dragging poor innocent people back to
Palindromena so they can die on a metal gurney rather than
surrounded by their loved ones."

I laughed, surprising both of us. "You're a real joy,
Tempe."

The corner of her mouth lifted. Whether she was smiling at
my reaction or me calling her by her nickname, I wasn't sure.
But I hated that I wanted to see her smile again.

"Well?" she demanded, locking that smile away.

"I used to climb the cliffs surrounding the facility."

She squinted at me, no doubt wondering why I looked so
pale. She didn't know I'd spent the last two years hiding from
the world.

"The island is so small," I continued. "I wanted more than the land we were given."

"Some people would argue that you're lucky to have any land. Most of us don't touch earth in our lifetime." I could tell it wasn't so important to her. Like Ray, it was the ocean she loved.

"I know. I know I'm lucky," I said. "But I want more. I want to travel the seas, see what else is out there." I halted, realizing I'd said *want*, and not *wanted*—as though it were still an option for me. "Atop the cliffs, I used to imagine that I wasn't stuck. That I could choose a different life."

"What's stopping you?"

I couldn't tell her about Calen; that wouldn't help her see me as anything other than a murderer. "My mother was an only child," I said. "She grew up on the island without any other children to play with. Her parents were her entire world. Until she had me. Before my grandparents died, I promised them I wouldn't leave her, as I was all she had left." Aside from her company. "What about you?"

"What about me?"

"Would you leave the Equinox, if you could?"

She shook her head. "Why? The Equinox is my home."

"You've never wished for anything different? For *more*?" I asked.

She kept her eyes locked on mine. A shiver ran down my back from her intense gaze. I was drawn toward her involuntarily, as though she *was* a water witch, and I, a doomed sailor.

"I wish for my sister to be alive," she said suddenly, breaking the spell. "I wish for my family to be reunited. And I wish you would leave me alone."

She moved to the far end of the cabin, wrapped her arms around her legs and hid her face from me.

As I watched her withdraw, I wondered how I was ever going to get through to her. And also worried what would happen once I did.

CHAPTER THIRTY

TEMPEST

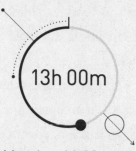

13h 00m

Monday, 11:00 p.m.

BENEATH THE DARKEST WATERS lay an illuminated temple. It was fragmented, shattered by the Great Waves. But in the cracks, the brightest lights emanated, coral growing from within. As though the water that had splintered the structure allowed it to become all the more beautiful.

I swam toward the temple. Although I didn't have a breather on, I could easily take in a lungful of air.

I should've realized then that I was dreaming.

I'd found it. The temple of the Gods below. I knew as soon as I laid my eyes on it.

Swimming to the entrance, my heart thundered in my chest. I would ask the Gods for more time. I would ask them to save my sister.

The temple was a labyrinth of stone corridors with the walls made entirely of coral. The color I'd seen from outside the temple.

When I reached the main room, I saw a shadowy figure upon a golden throne.

I swam closer. The God was a shadowed deity, a giant towering high above me. Its edges dispersed in the water, so you couldn't quite tell where the being ended or began. Like a squid ink blot. It was a part of the ocean, and the ocean was a part of it.

Light filtered down from an opening in the temple's ceiling and highlighted a crown made of spiky coral and black pearls on its enormous head.

Suddenly there was no water in the temple. I could speak to the God. I knelt at its feet.

"My sister," I said. "Please don't take her from me."

The giant deity tilted its head down toward me. Where its eyes should've been were two large holes. Its face was a skull.

It opened its mouth to reply. But instead of words, it bent down and swallowed me whole.

I was surrounded by black. By nothingness. By death.

I opened my mouth to scream, but it was full of water.

I woke to the boat juddering as if it had been shoved. Hard. Had another storm hit?

My eyes, crusted together by the salt on the wind and my tears, didn't immediately open.

I was still half asleep, unsure if the jolt was real or had happened in my dream.

"What was that?" Lor asked. He was sitting on the other side of the cabin. His light brows sitting low over his blue eyes.

I couldn't remember falling asleep. I hadn't slept properly since before I'd found the plant. Fatigue had weighed me down, body and mind. I wished there were somewhere else to rest. I didn't want to be down here with Lor.

"How long was I asleep?" I asked.

Lor glanced at his binds, unable to see the echolink tied behind him, and shrugged. "Less than an hour?"

The boat shuddered again and stopped. The ever-present hum of the engine cut out. I could only hear the waves lapping against the hull.

"Crap," I muttered, wiping my eyes and stumbling to my feet.

"What's wrong?" Lor scrambled to his knees as best he could while tied to the post.

"We're being boarded," I muttered.

I climbed up on deck to check on Elysea, and sure enough, another boat had sidled along next to us. While the storm had eased, a thick mist of rain had settled in, blurring the night. I pushed my hair back from my face.

"Are you all right, Ely?" I asked.

Before she could answer, a pale woman with sharp cheekbones and a fierce look in her eyes placed one foot on our hull, bridging our boats together. Her hair was streaked a luminous coral-blue.

"Hello, friends," the woman said, her voice low and melodic. "My name is Qera. I do apologize that this visit is at such an ungodly hour."

I bared my teeth, fury flooding my veins. "Get. Off. Our. Boat."

"Now, now." She splayed out her hands. "Is that how you welcome visitors?"

"It's how I treat Remorans," I spat.

Qera wore a long cloak woven from thick, stiff seaweed. She was draped in jewelry and had a silver loop through her narrow nose and a gemmed stud in her upper lip. Her blue hair was pulled back from her face and tied high above her head. Fish bones adorned her locks, in some sick imitation of a crown that the sovereigns of the Old World used to wear.

Behind Qera stood her crew. Their clothes were worn; skin peered through holes in shirts and trousers. Clothing clearly recycled from boats they'd attacked, then ransacked.

Remorans. The vultures of the ocean.

We must've crossed into the Untied Sea while I was asleep.

"Such anger," Qera said with a grin. "Are you from a Reef?" She pointed to my diving skin. "Let me guess. The closest is the Equinox. Am I right? You're a long way from home, *girls.*"

The way she said *girls*, she made it sound like we were easy pickings. Not if I had anything to say about it. We hadn't come this far only to be defeated by Remorans.

Remorans refused to live on any Reefs or the few isles that peeked their heads above the swollen seas. They flourished on the water, rejected any governing and banded together to pilfer everything from anyone they came across. They didn't dive because they didn't have to.

Despite the cool, salty breeze, they were barefoot. Each Remoran held a harpoon tilted in our direction. Not a direct threat, but a warning, if we didn't comply. And from the looks of the harpoons, it was either rust or blood that tainted each tip. I wouldn't have bet on rust.

The *Sunrise* bobbled, taking the tall woman's weight as Qera boarded. "This is a three-person boat," I said, pulling Elysea behind me. "You can't board without sinking us to the bottom of the ocean." The boat was constructed to sink if it took on extra weight in an attempt to control the Equinox's strict weight restrictions. No one could be smuggled into the harbor without the Watchtower knowing.

But the Remoran vessel was different. Cobbled together from scraps of stolen boats, most likely from Reefs like the Equinox—and other Remoran ships. Nobody was spared from their vicious greed. Panels for soaking up the sun's rays cluttered the deck and spread out along two wide wings. The sheer size of it allowed them to cross the turbulent seas and attack anyone that crossed their path. The bow had hundreds of spears attached to the front. A vessel of death.

"I only count two of you," Qera said, pointing between me and Elysea.

I couldn't help but glance at my sister. Why had Lor stayed silent? This was his one chance to yell for help. Did he want the Remorans to take our boat? Did he want them to turn us over into the water, so we drowned?

I held my breath. I'd seen boats try to smuggle people

onto the Equinox, only for the boat to sink before they reached the harbor. The Watchtower never sent anyone to help. Sometimes the crew would survive the waters. Palindromena would take those who didn't.

Our boat tilted; water lapped across the silver stern.

But then the vessel bobbed back up. I frowned. We had four people on board. Why hadn't we started to sink?

"Let's not waste time," she said to the man on the boat behind her. "I have other people to see, and boats to harvest. Climb on board."

My nails bit into my palms. "You wouldn't dare!"

Another bump, and the Remoran boat smashed into our hull, the spears tearing into the side of our vessel. Any further damage, and we'd take on water.

"But I always dare. Don't I, boys?" Qera said with a grin. Was it my imagination, or were her teeth sharpened? I'd heard that Remorans had resorted to eating human flesh when they were unable to find any fish and stumbled across someone trying to cross the Untied Sea.

I hoped it was merely the shadows of the night, tainting my thoughts.

"Yes, you do. As do I," one Remoran with a hooked nose replied. "I dare to hope for a new shirt." His own shirt had worn away to almost nothing, revealing sections of leathery pale skin. He eyed my outfit hungrily.

"And I hope for some supper," another Remoran said. He had a long coppery beard and a highly freckled face. He snapped his jaw at us. Laughter rippled among the crew like a rising wave.

Perhaps the tales of cannibalism weren't simply stories to keep children from wading off too far on their own.

"What do you want?" Elysea asked, standing tall beside me.

"It's a fairly long list," Qera said, splaying her hands wide. Her wrists were so thickly adorned with bracelets they looked like metal shackles. "What *don't* I want is the more appropriate question." Her crew laughed again. There had to be around twenty of them. We didn't stand a chance.

Qera stepped closer, and I couldn't help but flinch back in disgust. She stunk of fish guts and seaweed.

"We don't have many supplies," Elysea said. "We're not traveling far." That was mostly true. We hadn't had time to pack for the trip.

"I'm sure we can find something else of value." She grinned, and there was no mistaking her pointed teeth up close. "Can't we, boys?"

They snickered and aimed their spears at our chests.

"Step aside, girl." Qera tried to push past me to reach the cabin below. "Where's your power generator?"

I couldn't let them take our power. With the sun gone, we needed our backup generator to get to the Islands Cavalcade. Or else we'd never find Mom and Dad.

"You don't want our boat?" Elysea asked. I shushed at her to keep quiet.

Qera showed us her pointy teeth again. "Are you offering?"

"We'll die out here," I said, hoping she had some humanity left. "If you take our power, we don't have a chance. There's nothing around here for miles."

"Not our problem," she replied. "You wander into Remoran territory, you pay the price. Sometimes that price is your life." She shrugged like it was nothing.

We never should've risked venturing into the Untied Sea.

The Remorans knew not to cross Palindromena's perimeter or face the wrath of their fleet. They couldn't fight off high-tech boats. While the *Sunrise* was Palindromena-built, it didn't have any weapons.

Qera's crew sniggered behind her. Another Remoran stepped on board. This time the boat did tilt. We had half an hour, maybe less, before we joined the dead below.

"Move," the Remoran with the tattered shirt said, shoving me to the side to reach the boat's controls.

Qera's crew unfurled a wire and threw it across the water. The guy with the tattered shirt plugged it into our charger.

"Don't do this," I pleaded. "We'll give you anything— anything else."

Qera narrowed her eyes at me. "I don't need anything else." She turned back to her crewman. "Flick the switch."

My heart leaped in my chest.

"Take it all." She grinned.

The boat hummed as the transference of energy began. The Remoran crew thumped their fists and feet against their boat.

"Ten minutes!" the Remoran with the hooked nose and ratty

shirt hollered over the fracas. He flicked the gauge next to the steering wheel. "Then we'll be fully charged and ready to go."

I glanced at Elysea. *What do we do?*

"Now, now," Qera said. "I'll give you my breather. Fair trade?"

"Fair?" I snapped. "We'll never survive the waters! You're condemning us to death!"

"You have a diving skin," she replied.

"You piece of—" I went to tackle her, but Elysea held me back.

"Don't," Elysea said. "They'll hurt you."

I shook her off. We needed to do something. In ten minutes, we'd be dead in the water. Elysea shot a glance down to the cabin, which didn't go unnoticed by the Remoran leader.

"What do you have down there?" Qera asked.

Elysea moved to block her path. "Nothing of interest."

Why was she protecting Lor? She should've been worried about getting us out of here. She didn't have a diving skin; she was still wearing her dancing costume.

Although I wasn't sure what we could do. The Remorans were armed, literally, to the teeth.

Qera grinned. "Wrong answer, friend."

She pushed past Elysea, and we ran after her.

"Stop!" Elysea said. "Don't—" But she didn't finish her sentence.

I halted halfway down the stairs, confused at what I saw.

The cabin was empty.

"Don't *what?*" Qera asked.

"Nothing," Elysea said with a shake of her head.

How had Lor gotten free? I should've known he'd leave us for dead if he could. We never should've kept him on board.

The Remoran leader took a step toward us. "What's going on here?"

Elysea shook her head, backing up the stairs until she ran into me.

"What are you hiding?" There was a gleam in Qera's eye; she hoped she could find something more than power.

"Nothing," I repeated with a nod to Elysea. "Take a look around and see."

"I'll do that," Qera replied. "Thanks for the suggestion."

I thought about locking her down in the cabin, but we'd still have an entire boatful of Remorans to deal with. And I didn't want to anger them further.

"Qera!" a voice called from above. "Get up here. Now!"

"I'm busy!" she shouted back. "Can't do anything themselves," she said to us conversationally. "*Men.*" She shook her head with a sigh.

"But our boat," another Remoran yelled, "she's sailing out to sea!"

Elysea and I exchanged a glance.

Lor.

LOR

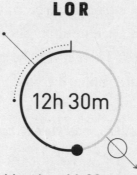

Monday, 11:30 p.m.

SOMETHING WAS WRONG. I knew as soon as the boat shuddered.

When Tempest said we were being boarded, I'd hoped it was Ray. That somehow he'd found me, even though the girls had smashed my tablet. But then something banged against the hull.

We were being rammed.

Ray would never do that.

Loud voices carried from up on deck. I heard the word *Remoran*, and my blood turned cold. As someone who'd lived on Palindromena my whole life, stories of the Remorans were as terrifying as the myth of a giant sea creature that roamed the ocean, eating everything and anything in its path.

The Remorans would eat these girls alive. Perhaps literally, if the stories were true.

I had to get out of here.

I pulled against my binds, but the knots were tight. Tempest was a sailor; of course she knew how to tie knots. But I was a climber. I knew ropes intimately, especially their weaknesses.

I pulled again and again until my shoulders ached and my wrists were rubbed raw. There had to be another way.

I glanced around the confined cabin. There were a few diving supplies, flotation devices if the boat was to go under, but not much else. This boat was clearly built for speed; there wasn't even a sleeping quarter.

I pulled against my binds again.

"Shit." Something cut into my wrist. I twisted around. It was my echolink. While the edge of the band wasn't that sharp, the pressure had dug the metal into my skin, splitting it open.

My blood made the rope slick.

But it gave me an idea.

I twisted my wrist and pressed the edge of the metal band against the rope. I rubbed my wrist back and forth a few times. The rope began to fray.

"Yes!" I moved my wrist more quickly.

When half the rope's thickness had worn through, I took a deep breath and pulled as hard as I could. The rope snapped, and I was free.

And it sounded like I was just in time. Someone had boarded, the extra weight lowering the boat in the water. I opened the nearest porthole and looked out into the black. Goose bumps prickled along my arms.

I'd never been a good swimmer. I'd never needed to be. But I didn't have a choice.

I squeezed through the porthole and into the water below.

The water wasn't too cold, but I couldn't see anything. I clung to the hull and maneuvered myself around to the other side to see what we were up against.

A large winged vessel had pulled up beside the Alerins' boat. Or more like, pushed *into* the boat. Even without any light, I could see the damage to the hull. The Remoran crew were encouraging a tall woman with blue hair and pale skin who had boarded the girls' boat.

I tried to focus on the Remorans, rather than the thought of what might be in the water with me. I couldn't help but imagine a razor-toothed creature with its mouth open, grazing my heels.

I'd never liked the ocean at night. It hid too many secrets. Why Ray loved it, I'd never understand. But I didn't have time for fear.

I pushed away from safety and headed toward the stern of the Remorans' boat. The crew were rowdy, gathered at the bow, thrilled with their catch. It was the perfect time to act unseen.

I lifted myself up on the back of their boat. I said a quick thanks to the heavy supplies I had to lug around the Aquarium for keeping me strong. Once on board, I crouched low as I approached a tacked-on helm, the only thing that stood between me and the crew. I crept closer—so close I could smell putrid fish guts wafting from the Remorans' clothing. All they had to do was turn to see me.

My breathing sounded so loud in my ears, I was surprised I hadn't been discovered yet.

Inside the makeshift helm were the vessel's controls. It looked like they'd been pieced together from other machines, including land rovers. While I didn't know anything about steering a boat, I'd been driving and fixing rovers since my feet could reach the pedals.

I quickly unscrewed the steering wheel and searched around for something to jam the ignition. Luckily, the boat was a mess. Littered with all kinds of garbage, including bones scattered across the floor.

Repressing a shudder, I picked one up. I hoped it was a fish bone. As I crunched the bone under my shoe, the crew roared. I peered over the open window of the helm, but no one was watching me.

Quickly, I pressed the ignition, then shoved the splintered bone into it so it couldn't be shut off. The engine sputtered to life. They didn't have much power; that must've been why they crashed our boat.

The girls' boat, I corrected myself.

"Hey!" one of the Remorans said from nearby. "Did the boat just start?"

I ran from the helm and dove off the back of the vessel, the steering wheel in my hand.

As I returned to the girls' boat, the crew's previous cheers turned into cries for help.

A Remoran man jumped onto his vessel as it sailed out to

sea. As I hauled myself up on deck, I heard a snap as the cord connecting the two boats broke in half.

"Hi there," I said.

Three heads swiveled toward me. Tempest, Elysea and the blue-haired Remoran woman. The boat dipped with my added weight. I needed to get rid of the Remoran. Now.

I waved the wheel in the air. "I believe you may be missing a part of your boat."

The Remoran watched as her vessel sped away, her crew held captive.

"What did you do?" she asked.

In response, I threw the steering wheel into the water—in the opposite direction that her boat was sailing.

"I suggest you go after it now," I said. "Before it's too late."

The Remoran leader bared her sharp teeth before diving into the water after her steering wheel.

"Quickly," Tempest said to Elysea, moving into action. "Get the *Sunrise* up and running before they come back for us."

Elysea pulled the plug from the console and threw it into the ocean. She started the boat and the hull lifted up and out of the water.

The Remorans would never catch us now. I hoped Ray wasn't still following; I didn't want him encountering the Remorans on his own.

"How did you get free?" Tempest asked when we were a safe distance away. She probably wanted to tie me back up.

"Does it matter?" I replied. "You needed help."

Her face was hard. She still didn't know whether she could trust me. "I suppose you want us to thank you?"

"Not if I have to ask for it." I squeezed the water from my clothes and hair and rubbed my hands together to generate some warmth. I hadn't been in and around the ocean this much in my entire life.

Elysea leaned around her sister and untied the bloodied ropes from my wrists. "Thank you, Lor. There's a spare T-shirt down in the cabin, if you want to change into something dry."

"Thanks," I said.

Tempest didn't say anything, but I could feel her eyes on my back as I went down to the cabin to change.

———

Half an hour later, Tempest tapped the boat's echolocator. "We're out of the Untied Sea. We did it!"

Elysea grinned, patting her sister on the back. "We *all* did." She glanced at me.

I made to reply, but the words stuck in my throat. "What is that?" I managed to get out, pointing ahead.

Multicolored lights appeared in the water like a fragmented rainbow. Elysea slowed the boat.

"Coral," Tempest said with a smile. She darted to the edge for a closer look.

"There must be a large ruin below that's close to the surface," Elysea said.

I leaned beside Tempest to have a look. I'd never seen the Old World, but I'd imagined it many times when surrounded by the glowing tanks of the Aquarium. Even so, I never could've pictured anything like this.

The few illuminated lights in the water turned into thousands as we moved slowly over the ruin. The coral looked like splotches of fluorescent paint. Looking straight down, I could see the vast shape of a building with hundreds of archways and turrets.

"I wonder what else is down there," Tempest said. The pink and blue lights reflected in her eyes. She smiled at me. My heart squeezed. She was too beautiful for words.

"We don't have time to look," Elysea said, sadness in her voice. "It will have to remain undiscovered."

Tempest pushed back from the edge with a sigh, but I couldn't look away.

The Old World *was* beautiful. Tempest was right. And although I wasn't a great swimmer, I wished I could dive down there and see it for myself.

Elysea shifted the accelerator down.

The dappled lights blurred together as we picked up speed. Soon we were gliding on empty black water again. I mourned the loss of a world I would never get to explore.

After a few minutes, Tempest took over the controls from her sister. "Go get some rest," she said. "We should be at the island in a few hours."

"I'm okay," Elysea said with a yawn.

Tempest pointed her toward the cabin. "Go."

Elysea chuckled in defeat. "Thank you again," she said to me as she walked by. "We owe you."

Before she descended the cabin stairs, she stumbled, her legs collapsing underneath her.

"Elysea!" Tempest cried, abandoning her post.

I pulled Elysea up from the deck. Her brown hair had splayed around her face like a halo. Her eyes had rolled back into her head.

"Oh Gods," Tempest moaned. "Oh Gods. Is she—"

She couldn't say the words. I placed my fingers at her wrist. But I could feel a faint pulse, while mine thundered in my ears.

"No," I said. "She's okay." But her heartbeat didn't feel steady. And neither did mine.

"Then why did she collapse?" Tempest's voice took on a level of hysteria. "We're only halfway through our time. What's wrong with her?"

"I don't know."

I glanced at my echo, but the second circle was blinking. I shook my wrist. Why wasn't it—

Something clawed at my chest. My arms went slack. Elysea fell from my grasp and my vision went black. As black as the deepest depths of the ocean.

CHAPTER THIRTY-TWO

TEMPEST

12h 00m

Tuesday, midnight

I WASN'T READY for Elysea to die. I wasn't ready to see the life drain from her eyes. This was worse than before. Much worse. I hadn't seen her in death; I hadn't seen her body. Daon had offered to identify her instead of me.

While I'd imagined her lifeless many times, it was different seeing it myself. Now I couldn't turn away. And the vision would haunt me forever.

"No, no, no, no, no." I urged her to wake up, but she wouldn't. We were supposed to have twelve more hours. We were supposed to reunite with our parents.

Lor was out cold beside her. What in these cursed waters had happened?

I brought Elysea's head onto my lap. My tears fell onto her still face.

I wouldn't remember my sister as alive; I wouldn't remember all the precious times we'd spent together. I wouldn't remember her laughter, her voice, her dancing. I would only remember her lifeless body.

Her death would erase all that I loved about her.

"Please," I whispered over both Lor and Elysea. "Please wake up. Don't leave me here alone."

In all the times I'd prayed to the Gods below, they'd never listened. I begged that they would this time. Just this once.

Aside from my panicked breathing, all I could hear was the hum of the *Sunrise*'s engine and the boat slicing through the still water. The rain stopped, the clouds parted and the moon shone down onto the deck, lighting Elysea's face. I wanted to turn away. I wanted to dive off this boat and sink down into the world below. I wanted to hide from her, from everything.

Then Elysea's eyes flicked open, and Lor groaned.

I pulled Elysea upright. "Are you all right? What happened?"

She took in a shuddering breath, her eyes darting around the starry sky. "I don't know." She placed her hand to her chest. "My heart . . . I think it stopped." Terror lit her eyes.

Once I was convinced she could sit up on her own, I moved to Lor. His eyes darted behind his lids. His arms trembled. He was stirring.

One circle on the echolink screen disappeared, then re-appeared again.

Lor jerked awake with a gasp. I stumbled back on the deck.

"Where am I?" he asked. The blue of his eyes was muted,

washed out. His skin the color of a rain-laden cloud. He looked like he was dying.

"You collapsed," I said slowly. A thought nudged at the edges of my mind that I couldn't quite grasp. "After Elysea did."

Lor glanced down at his echolink and shook his wrist. I flinched at the sight of it.

"There must be some kind of glitch," he said.

"Glitch?" Elysea asked, exchanging a look with me. "What glitch?"

Although I didn't want to, I inched closer to him. The black screen of the echolink beckoned.

"The tether must be under strain, or something." He said it almost to himself.

"What's a tether?" I asked.

He looked up from studying his echolink. "A what?"

"*You* just said it. What's a tether?"

He shook his head, but I wasn't going to let him lie to us again.

"Why did you faint after Elysea?" I asked.

"Sympathy?" he suggested with a small shrug and a laugh.

It wasn't funny. "Do you expect me to believe that?"

"Tempe." Elysea's face was grave. "Let's give him some space. He's not well. Can't you see?"

"Yes, I can." My voice was stern. "And I want to know why. Why do you look like death, when it's my sister who will die in less than twelve hours?"

He dragged his hands over his face. "I haven't told you the entire truth," he said from behind his hands.

Why wasn't I surprised?

"Then start," I snapped. I wasn't going to wait for Elysea to pass out again so he could keep his secrets. "Why did Elysea collapse just now?"

He pulled his hands from his face, his eyes boring into mine, his jaw clenched. "I don't know. That *is* the truth."

I could sense there was more. "But?" I prompted.

"But I know why *I* collapsed after her," he said.

Somehow I knew what he was going to say the second before he said it.

"Your sister and I are connected." He gestured to Elysea. "What happens to her happens to me. If her heart faltered, then mine did too."

And for the rest of my life, I would never forget his expression when he said, "In twelve hours, one of us will die."

CHAPTER THIRTY-THREE

LOR

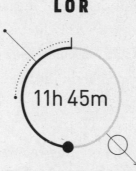

11h 45m

Tuesday, 12:15 a.m.

I REALLY DIDN'T KNOW why Elysea's heart had weakened; all I knew was that I had to get back to Palindromena. *Now*. Or both of us might die.

"What are you talking about?" Tempest asked. I couldn't see her irises. Her black hair curled around her shoulders like seaweed, and her eyes were as shadowy as the ocean on a moonless night. Was she the goddess of death coming to collect? Or a water witch who would drag me to the bottom of the ocean?

"Your sister and I are tethered." I sat upright. The feeling in my body had returned. I wasn't dead. Not yet. But I was tired. A bone-deep tired. "What happens to her happens to me."

But it was worse than that. We weren't simply connected. If I didn't get Elysea back before the twenty-four hours were up, then one of us would die. And it could be me.

I let out a stuttering breath. I should've listened to Ray.

He had wanted to involve Palindromena's security to ensure Elysea was returned in time, even if that had meant losing his job. He'd wanted to save my life. But I hadn't listened. I'd thought we could find her ourselves, before Palindromena discovered she was gone. And it hadn't been just about Ray. I'd wanted to keep some semblance of the life that I had down in the Aquarium.

"What do you mean, Lor?" Elysea asked.

I'd hidden the real reason we needed Elysea back at Palindromena for long enough. I'd thought telling the sisters the truth would turn them against me. That they'd see a glimmer of hope and take hold of any possibility for Elysea to live on. Now I didn't have a choice.

"The revival process is not a one-way street," I said. "A life can't be restored without borrowing from someone else. That's why Palindromena hasn't revived as many people as they can. And that's why it lasts only twenty-four hours. They need to borrow life from someone or, rather, *share* it." I pointed to Elysea. "We are currently sharing a pulse. My heartbeat. I am your tether to life."

"I don't understand." Tempest's brow furrowed further. "Explain."

"Before you were revived," I said to Elysea, "an incision was made to implant a sensor that was linked to my echo." That had been part of the prerevival process Ray had run with the scientists before giving me the echolink.

Elysea ripped off the faux infirmary bracelet, and sure

enough, there was a small raised square beneath her skin.

"Then all I had to do was put on the echolink and press the sync button just before noon." I glanced at Tempest. Did she now realize she'd been with me the moment I'd revived her sister? "My heartbeat jump-started your dormant one, like a jolt of electricity through our echolink connection. Once your heart was restarted, we share the pulse, keeping the same rhythm." I pointed to one of the blue circles on the echo's screen. "This isn't simply to monitor the countdown—it's a sensor that keeps our hearts in sync. You're using my heart as a form of bypass to ensure yours keeps pumping blood throughout your body." I tapped the second circle.

Elysea placed her hand on her chest.

"Because we share a heartbeat, what happens to Elysea happens to me," I said. "That's why when she collapsed, I did too. At the end of the twenty-four hours, the tether will be broken, and the Warden goes back to their life and the recipient dies."

"How is the tether broken?" Tempest asked.

"We need to unsync our heartbeats," I said. "Palindromena will essentially stop the patient's heart."

Tempest gasped. "You kill them?"

I crossed my arms. She didn't understand. "If we don't stop the patient's heart at twenty-four hours, then one of us will die anyway."

"*One* of you?" Tempest narrowed her eyes. "Don't you mean the patient? Elysea?"

"Maybe, maybe not. There's no guarantee. Toward the end

of the twenty-four hours, our hearts will fight over the pulse until one wins." I avoided looking at Elysea. She'd remained quiet this entire time. I wondered what she was thinking. Did she think it was worth the risk? A fifty percent chance at living? Had I been right in keeping this secret from her?

"Then the twenty-four-hour thing is fake?" Tempest demanded, her cheeks flushed, her eyes glistening. "My sister can live past tomorrow?"

"No. Two hearts tethered together puts a strain on both hearts. One will weaken and fail. Palindromena imposes the twenty-four-hour rule to ensure it's the Warden that lives and their patient that returns to their previous state."

"You mean death," Tempest sneered. "That's why no one is allowed to leave the facility, and that's why you've been following us. You don't care about your job, or your friend. You're trying to save yourself! You want to take Elysea back to Palindromena to ensure she dies and not you."

"I don't want to die," I said. "Is that such a terrible thing?"

She huffed but didn't reply.

"Why twenty-four hours?" Elysea asked quietly. "Why can't we share a tether for longer?"

"It's to do with the cycle of the body called the circadian rhythm," I said. "The body essentially resets itself after twenty-four hours, which disrupts the bypass and breaks the tether."

"What will happen to us when the time runs out?" Elysea asked, her green eyes downcast. "If we're not untethered?"

"One of us will die. Instantly."

Elysea shifted away, holding her hand to her mouth. "I don't want you to die."

Thank whoever might be watching us, Gods or no Gods. The girl has a conscience.

Tempest turned to her sister. "What are you suggesting?"

"I can't be responsible for his death, Tempe," she said. "It's not worth the risk."

"Why does it have to be one or the other?" Tempest squeezed her eyes tight. "I don't want you to die if there's a chance we can stay together."

I could understand her pain. She'd discovered her sister could possibly return to her normal life. Be reunited as a family. For good.

"I won't kill him," Elysea whispered. "I can't be responsible for that. I've died already. I should be the one to offer my life up for him."

"You don't want to live?" Tempest's voice wobbled. She was avoiding my eyes.

"You know I do," Elysea replied. "But we both know we can't have someone die for us to be together."

Tempest took in a stuttering breath. It was an impossible situation. "I don't want to let you go," she said. "Not again. Never again."

Elysea went to her sister to console her, whispering something to Tempest before returning to me. Elysea was beautiful, yet she wore her beauty like an uncomfortable mask, as though she didn't want anyone to notice. It was only when she danced at the Spring Tide that she appeared at ease in her own skin. Was this because she'd known she lived on borrowed time? Or was she always this unsure?

"I'm sorry we ran away," she said to me, her face soft and understanding. "I never would have if I'd known I was putting another person's life at risk. Take me back to Palindromena. We'll fix this."

I wasn't sure what she wanted to fix. We could never fix her death. But that wasn't my fault or responsibility. Bringing this girl back to Palindromena was my only concern.

Or it had been. But now that I'd started to know the Alerin sisters, I didn't want to separate them. At least, not right now.

"How far away are your parents?" I asked.

"Why?" Tempest asked with a growl. Her walls were back up. In the last few minutes, she'd thought she was going to lose her sister, found hope and now faced losing her again. I'd want to yell at someone too.

"Perhaps we could do both?" I said. "We could travel to the Islands Cavalcade, then return to Palindromena to untether."

That would allow the Alerin girls a few hours with their parents. It was the least I could do. After everything I'd already put them through, chasing them across the ocean, ruining their final hours together. And what was to come, with the untethering process, was much worse. They would have to say goodbye for good. That was when the real pain began. Something Palindromena didn't advertise.

Elysea looked up, her expression cleared. "You'd allow me to do that?"

"That's what the revival program is for," I said. "To say goodbye."

"We have eleven and a half hours remaining, and we're still about two and a half hours from the party islands," Elysea said, her eyes unfocused. "With a few hours on the island and then about four hours to return to Palindromena. That's cutting it close."

It was, but it was doable. We were already so close to the island, to the sisters reuniting with their parents. I couldn't take that away from them, even with my life on the line.

I glanced at my echolink, hoping we wouldn't both end up dead.

"It will be enough time," I said.

"Tempe?" Elysea asked, her voice soft. "What do you say?"

Tempest shook her head. "What can I say? No matter which way we turn, we face death. There's no escape."

Elysea gave her sister a sad smile. "We always knew death was the outcome here. When we get to the island, we'll have our answers."

Tempest's shoulders sagged. I thought she might collapse when she said, "But I won't have you."

I wanted to turn away. I didn't want to witness the pain

between them. I hated knowing that I was causing it. But it was my life or Elysea's.

"We all have to say goodbye, eventually," Elysea said, pulling her sister's hands from her face. "We can't follow each other into the dark, no matter how much we might wish it. And I only want what's best for you."

"What about you?" Tempest asked. "What about what's best for you?"

"My time was already up. This extra twenty-four hours is a blessing."

"That doesn't make it any easier," Tempest replied. And I knew it would be harder now, knowing that Elysea *could* live and I was the only one standing in the way of that.

And Tempest was right. Twenty-four hours with your loved one didn't make it any easier to say goodbye, no matter what Palindromena promised.

There was no closure. There never would be.

CHAPTER THIRTY-FOUR

TEMPEST

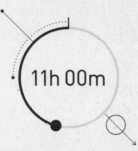

Tuesday, 1:00 a.m.

I WATCHED the water foam behind us as we cut along the black ocean.

It had been an hour since Elysea had fainted, and my hands were still shaking. Eleven hours to go. Eleven hours until we said goodbye. How would I let her go now that I knew she could live? Truly live. But she wasn't willing to take the risk. She wasn't willing to take someone else's life.

Could I?

And I couldn't believe that Dad had risked his life every day to bring back patients. What had gone so wrong that he had to flee the Equinox and never return?

I heard Elysea's soft steps behind me. I squeezed my eyes tight.

"I can't believe after all this, you're willing to give up," I said. How many times would I need to say goodbye?

"You know it's not that. But I was already dead, Tempe. I wasn't in pain." I turned around. She lifted a shoulder. "I wasn't . . . anything. It's not Lor's responsibility to sacrifice himself for me."

"You think he deserves to live more than you do?" I still didn't know much about him, but I knew my sister deserved better than this fate.

I'd been hiding from my grief. I'd focused on my anger instead. My belief that Elysea had wronged me and my parents was a coping mechanism. A way to convince myself that I didn't want—or need—her in my life. It had been easier to deal with her loss.

But now I knew the truth. I'd wanted to revive her because I missed her. I'd wanted her back. For almost two years, I'd pretended it was for retribution. I had lied to myself.

Not anymore.

Elysea's eyes had grown fierce. "Who decides that, Tempe? Who decides who lives and who dies? Whose life is more important than another's? We all have family; we all have friends. We're all loved. Who says I'm more important than Lor?"

"I do."

I turned into the wind, fighting back tears, letting the air cool my heated cheeks.

"Don't worry," she said. "Everything will be all right when you're back with Mom and Dad."

"We don't know for sure they're even out there!" My voice cracked. "And even if they are, I don't want to lose you." I was done pretending Elysea's death hadn't broken me. I needed her. She'd been my compass, my anchor. Without her, I'd be swept away in the tide. "What will I do without you?"

She turned my shoulders to study my face. "What you've been doing for the last two years. You'll go on living."

"Living?" I scoffed. "I haven't been living. I've been surviving. One day to the next. Until the day I would see you again. That's not living."

She squeezed my arm. "Then you need to try harder. For me." She sat down on the edge of the boat, pulling me with her. "We are blessed to have this time together. I wasn't meant to come back. You know that."

I gritted my teeth to try to stop the tears. Her hand in mine was solid and warm. She felt real. She felt alive. If only my wish to keep her were enough. If only the Gods below listened to my prayers.

"We need to focus," she said. "We can't waste time on conversations like this. I need you to be strong. For me."

I realized then that she was shaking. The more I pushed, the more upset I became, the more I flared with anger, the bigger toll it took on her.

Elysea *needed* me. I'd always thought I needed her, that she was my strength, my backbone, my steel. But I would be her downfall. If I couldn't show her I could be strong, then she wouldn't die in peace. She only feared death because she feared me being alone.

But not anymore. If she needed me to be strong to get through this, then I would be strong. For her.

I knew how to pretend. I'd done it for the last two years. I'd pretend I was strong until the last moment, before it was too late. Before nothing more could be done.

I would pretend. Until her last breath.

———⋘⋙———

Lor had retreated below. We hadn't tied him back up. We didn't need to. Now we knew he needed us more than we needed him. He wasn't going anywhere.

"Is everything all right?" Lor asked as I approached. He grimaced. "I mean, of course it's not, but—"

I waved his explanation away. "Yes."

"I'm truly sorry, Tempe," he said, using my nickname. And although I had introduced myself as Tempe rather than Tempest, I hadn't expected him to use it. It made me feel uncomfortable.

"Here." I handed him a compressed fish bar and a water canteen.

He gulped down the water and ripped into the bar.

I sat against the hull, my legs spread out in front of me. The rhythmic thrum of the waves eased my mind. I could do this. I could stay focused. I would be strong. For Elysea.

After consuming the bar and all the water, Lor leaned back. He looked slightly less pale.

"Thank you," he said. "I know I lied to you, but I really do know how hard this is."

"Today has been the worst and best day of my life." I'd never been so aware of the air moving in and out of my lungs. Of being alive. "Being back with Elysea has been wonderful, and horrible."

"There's no easy way to face death."

"What would you do if you were me?" I asked.

The side of his mouth lifted. "I'd probably push me into the sea." He sobered quickly when I didn't laugh. "But I appreciate you're much nicer than that. You're not a killer."

I pressed my lips together. I'd been nothing but bitter and cruel to Lor since we escaped Palindromena. Back in the waiting room, I'd thought I could trust him. That he wanted what was best for me. He had that sort of face—a *kind* face—that made you drop your walls. Still, he'd been lying to me.

Even now that I knew the truth and *why* he'd lied, it was hard to lower my defenses. But I wanted to. He was the first person in a long time who seemed to care about my sister and me—even though he would inevitably take away Elysea's life.

It was complicated. How I felt was complicated. Even so, I found myself returning to him. And I knew that meant something, even if I didn't want to admit it.

"No, I'm not a killer," I said. "But I feel like I'm killing Elysea. I brought her back from a place where she felt no pain, and now she knows her life is going to come to an end. *I* did that."

Lor kicked his legs out, mirroring me. "You wouldn't want to know when you were going to die?"

I grimaced. "Definitely not."

His eyes scanned my face. "But then you can make the most of your time left."

"Knowing your time will be cut short is a curse. It taints everything you do. Everything you say. Every single moment."

"Does Elysea see it as a curse?"

"Of course she doesn't," I said. "She sees it as a gift; she doesn't blame me. She's a good person."

"And you don't think you are." It wasn't a question.

"Do you think *you* are?" I threw it back at him. It was easier than answering.

He sighed, tugging his sandy-blond hair. "I want to be."

He was so confusing. At times he seemed confident. But now he seemed unsure of himself. Who was the real Lor? Was he still pretending to be someone else? How could I discern the truth?

"When was the last time you saw your parents?" he asked, changing the subject.

"I don't want to make small talk with you," I lied, crossing my arms over my chest.

I wished he'd stop looking at me. I felt as though he could read what I was thinking. It made me uncomfortable. Keeping my thoughts hidden meant I could also hide them from myself. I didn't want my true feelings to be exposed. I couldn't handle them right now.

"Then why are you still here?" he asked, a smile creeping

onto his face. He was a study in contrast: light hair and fair skin against the bright blue of his eyes and red lips. I hated to admit it, but he was handsome. Especially when he smiled.

I bit my lip. "I'm here to keep watch." Another lie.

"Ohhhh," he said with an exaggerated sigh and nod. "I see."

"What?"

"You're avoiding Elysea."

I tucked my legs underneath me. I couldn't keep still. "No, I'm not. She's my sister, and she has only about ten hours left to live. Why would I be avoiding her?"

He gave me a sad smile. "I work at Palindromena, remember."

"So?" What did he think he knew about me or how I was feeling?

"Sometimes it's easier to avoid what hurts us, and right now, looking at Elysea reminds you of how you're going to lose her soon, again."

I stared at him, teeth gritted. I wished I had the power the kids at school used to claim I did. I wished I was a water witch. I wished I could control the ocean, go back two years ago and drain the water from my sister's lungs.

I expected him to shift uncomfortably under my stare, but he didn't flinch.

"I know I was never really your Warden," he said, "but if you want to talk to me about this, you can."

"*This?*" I snapped. "You mean how you're going to steal my sister's last breath?" Heat rose to my cheeks.

I was surprised to see his eyes were glassy. "Would you sacrifice your life for someone else?" He wasn't taunting me; he seemed genuinely curious.

I hadn't thought I'd known the answer, but it came out without thinking. "For my sister? Yes."

"Even if it meant leaving your loved ones behind? Your mom and dad?"

"*If* they're actually still alive. We don't know what happened the night they supposedly died. And if they didn't die, we don't know why they never returned for us. Maybe they prefer their new life?" The words were like bitter seaweed in my mouth. I didn't want to think that was true, but I couldn't understand why they'd stopped leaving clues two years ago.

"If you think that, then why are you searching for them?"

"Because it's the most important question I don't have an answer to. I was only twelve when my parents died. It forged me, made me who I am today. But if they truly didn't die, then everything I've known for the last five years has been a lie." I raised an eyebrow. "Wouldn't you cross the ocean to find out the truth? Find out the truth to the one moment that defined you?"

Without my grief, without my anger over losing Mom and Dad, who would I be? The only thing keeping me going was this question. The unknown.

I'd worry about my future later.

Lor's gaze didn't stray from my face, but a flurry of emotion shifted behind his eyes. What was he thinking? What wasn't he saying?

"Yes," he said simply. "I would."

As I left the cabin, another truth was impossible to ignore.

Lor was still lying.

CHAPTER THIRTY-FIVE

LOR

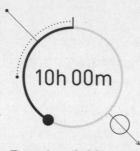

10h 00m

Tuesday, 2:00 a.m.

TEMPEST WENT BACK up on deck to be with her sister. I tried to ignore the countdown on my wrist.

Ten hours.

That better be enough time to return to Palindromena and get this horrid thing off.

I was lucky Elysea had agreed to come back. She could've taken the risk and hoped she'd live on. For the first time in my life, I felt as though someone—or something—was watching over me. Something other than death.

I wondered what Ray was doing right now. Had he honored my wish to not get Palindromena security involved? Or was the entire fleet currently searching for me? His job now forfeited?

Elysea came down to visit a short while later. Her movement was graceful, fluid. As though she was already submerged. As she would be again soon.

"We don't have much water left," she said, handing over the refilled canteen. "How are you feeling?" She tapped her chest, over her heart.

"Steady," I said. The echolink showed two bright rings around its face. We were back in sync. For now. I still wasn't sure if we'd actually make it to the party islands, as I didn't know what had caused the disruption to the tether. I didn't want to lose connection again. Next time it might be for good.

I took a tentative sip. "Thank you."

She sat beside me, keeping a clear distance between us. Was she scared of me? I wouldn't blame her, knowing her borrowed life would eventually return to me.

"Are you all right?" she asked.

This girl was willing to give up her second chance at life; she deserved the truth. "I've been better."

My body felt weak and disconnected. I wished Ray were here so I could ask if he'd ever felt this way during a revival.

Elysea held a hand to my perspiring forehead. "You look like death." She realized what she'd said, and snatched her hand back.

"You can't catch it," I said with a laugh.

The corner of her mouth lifted. "But I will, in the end."

I'd never thought I could hate Palindromena and what my mother did more than in this moment. I didn't want to take Elysea from the world. But what choice did I have?

Elysea twisted away and leaned her head back against the hull. "Tempe says we'll be at the island in under an hour." She fiddled with something in her hand. A piece of paper. A map? She always seemed to be carrying it with her.

I didn't know how to reply, so I went with "That's good."

"Have you always lived on the isle?" she asked after a moment of silence.

"Yes. Born and raised."

She smiled. There was no denying she was extremely pretty. Like her sister. But where Tempest was stormy and strong, Elysea was ethereal and soft. A different kind of water witch. But just as dangerous.

"What's it like?" she asked.

"Living on the isle?"

She sighed. "I can't imagine it, living somewhere that's still. Living somewhere that doesn't change with every weather system. Not hearing the constant slap of waves and hum of diving boats. Not knowing the persistent taste of salt. Not waking with it on your lips."

"I don't know any different," I said, reminding myself of the life I had wanted to return to. I pressed my hand to the hull, feeling the hum of the engine and thrum of the current around us. But my wants and needs were changing. How could I go back to the Aquarium after all this? How could I go back to being alone?

Ever since I'd put on that damned echo, I'd been thinking

more about my future. I wanted to live beyond today, but now when I pictured what that looked like, the Alerin sisters clouded my thoughts. Especially Tempest.

Elysea watched me with her large eyes, willing more.

"Island life is calm, I suppose, as least it is compared to what I saw of the Equinox. People move slower at Palindromena. They appreciate the nature around them. They're not as busy. They're not as rushed." Which was ironic, considering how important time was there.

Her eyes focused on the porthole behind me. "Where do you think we go when we die? Do you think we return to the land of our ancestors, or do we float around in a black ocean of nothingness?"

I wasn't ready to talk about death. Not to Elysea. Not when she was facing the reality of it so soon. "I don't know."

"Will it hurt?" she asked after a moment. "When I die?"

I didn't want to tell her the details. The revived weren't supposed to know the truth.

"No." I wasn't sure what I was saying no to. No to everything. No to this whole situation. But there was no way out, not for either of us.

"No?" She didn't blink. Didn't flinch. She wanted the truth.

I swallowed roughly, bile rising in my mouth. The taste of fear.

"Palindromena will take care of you." I wanted to ease her uncertainty.

"What happens toward the end?" I didn't miss the tremble of her bottom lip.

"You'll feel faint." I stared at the far side of the hull, unable to look at her. "Your body will tire around the one-hour mark as your heartbeat gets weaker. Palindromena's scientists will step in before the hour is up." It was hard to swallow. I cleared my throat. "They'll stop your heart. But it's painless—you won't even know it's happening."

I couldn't say any more. My voice threatened to break.

Elysea touched me, making me jump. She squeezed my arm. "Thank you for being honest." Her eyes were clear. I thought she'd cry, yell or take back our deal. But she seemed accepting.

"I'm sorry," I whispered. "I wish it didn't have to be this way."

She gave me a small smile. "I'm sorry for breaking out and causing all this trouble."

"I understand why you did it."

"It's not all bad." I must've made a strange face, as she added, "I mean, it's bad, but at least I get more time with my sister. And I'll see my parents again. Hopefully."

I wished I could see the bright side of this situation. I'd never forget my part in Elysea's demise. I'd be haunted by the grief I'd caused.

Most of all, I'd remember Elysea's sister. *Tempest.* The storm of a girl who'd glimpsed a calmer life, only for it to be stolen again.

Tempe wouldn't forget me, and I wouldn't forget her.

CHAPTER THIRTY-SIX

TEMPEST

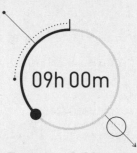

09h 00m

Tuesday, 3:00 a.m.

I WOKE to an inky darkness and blinked in confusion.

Nothing but black.

Had we sunk to the bottom of the ocean?

But it was warm here, like an embrace.

Hair tickled my skin. I let out a sigh in understanding. I wasn't facing oblivion, and neither was Elysea.

Not yet.

"Elysea," I said. "Your hair."

A groan rumbled against my cheek as Elysea shifted. "Sorry," she said, pulling her curls from my face.

Finally, I could see.

We'd both fallen asleep up on the deck, our backs against the control console. I didn't think I could sleep with everything that had happened, but I was physically and emotionally exhausted.

I rolled my neck, releasing the stiff sleepiness from my bones.

"How do you feel?" I asked her.

"Good," she replied. Her eyes were bright, her skin returned to its normal warm olive tone, her lips pink. Rest had done her good. I swallowed hard, unable to look at her for too long.

I checked the time on the boat's console.

3:00 a.m.

We'd been asleep for half an hour.

"I should check where we are," I said. I'd set the autopilot mode before we'd sat down.

The stars had revealed themselves while we'd slept. And the moon lit the water like a watchtower light. It shone on the broken horizon. A shadowy mass lay straight ahead.

"The Islands Cavalcade," I whispered. The thought of our parents living and breathing on that piece of land was enough to steal the air from my lungs.

"Where?" Elysea pulled herself up to take a look.

I pointed to the land in the distance.

Elysea squeezed my hand. "We've made it, Tempe."

———

I directed the boat to the middle island—the largest—as the map suggested. Elysea was holding on to Mom's necklace at her neck, her eyes closed, lips trembling. I didn't have to hear the words to know she was saying a prayer to the Gods below.

Let our parents be here. Let them be alive. Let us be together.

If only for a few hours.

I guided the boat toward the pier that circled the island. Unlike Palindromena, there weren't any other boats in the area aside from a collection of complex-looking rafts. I'd heard most people who lived on the Islands Cavalcade did not venture beyond the island chain.

The *Sunrise*'s bow nudged the brick jetty as we pulled in. No voices came over the intercom. Didn't they care about people coming or going? I supposed as an island, they didn't need to worry about weight restrictions. You couldn't sink land to the bottom of the sea.

I wondered why no one had ever privatized these islands. And how did they manage to keep their crops all for themselves, when every other island was required to share their produce with the nearest Reefs?

Whether they were still here or not, I couldn't help but wonder why our parents had chosen this place as their destination.

Countless lights were embedded in the island's rock. And even though the sun had yet to rise, we could easily make out the island's shape, which was unnaturally round and wrapped in a purplish moss. Music echoed from somewhere in the middle of the island.

Atop a towering circular wall were a cluster of colorful tents. They glowed like coral with torches of flickering firelight burning between them. Where did they manage to find so many different-colored fabrics? Were they from the Old World?

"It's so pretty," I murmured, looking up at the sheer cliff.

"The Islands Cavalcade," Lor said, squinting. "A nonstop party for everyone who lives there."

I ignored his comment. I was hesitant in having Lor join us; something about his presence made me increasingly uneasy. But Elysea had insisted.

"Where should we start?" Elysea asked. She'd pulled her hair back into two braids and tucked the strands up underneath like she used to when she was practicing for a performance.

"Let's find where the music is coming from," I said. "It will take four hours to travel back to Palindromena." I nodded to Lor. "Which leaves us five hours here."

"Four," Elysea said, smiling at Lor. "To be safe."

"Then we leave at seven, before the sun rises." I looked between Elysea and Lor. "Agreed?"

"Agreed," Lor said.

I jumped off the deck and latched the boat to one of the empty ports. "Then let's not waste any more time."

We walked around the circular moss-covered wall until we found a narrow passageway that burrowed deep into the island. The music echoed from down the chasm.

"This way," I said, stumbling a little. I caught myself on the side of a cliff.

"Are you all right?" Elysea asked, bracing me against her.

"Of course," I said, wishing I had some Land Legs to stabilize my body and mind. Both Elysea and Lor didn't appear to be affected. They were used to the steadiness of Palindromena.

She took hold of my hand as though I was the one who needed protecting.

As we traversed the crevasse, I caught Elysea's eye. She was shaking her head.

"What's wrong?" I asked.

"Doesn't this look familiar?" She didn't tear her gaze from one side of the vertical cliff. Looking up made me woozy. I wished there was time to sit down and rest.

"You've been here before?" Lor asked.

Elysea shook her head. "I've never been anywhere but the Equinox."

"And Palindromena," I reminded her.

She pressed her lips together. "It reminds me of some-thing—"

I took in our surroundings. There was less vegetation in the passageway leading to the middle of the island, probably due to the shadowing from the cliffs. I spotted a pink flower. It reminded me of the flowers Mom used to pick from her fields to take home and place behind my ear. I pulled the plant from the cliff, taking half the vine with me.

"What in the cursed waters is this?" I whispered.

Behind the vine was a wall. A concrete wall. Like those of the Old World below. I looked straight up, realizing the vertical cliffs weren't rock faces at all.

"It's a building!" I said with a gasp. "This isn't an island."

The cliff faces on either side of us were concrete walls. I dug my heel into the sandy earth beneath my feet. It didn't take long to reach something harder. More concrete.

"Cursed waters," Elysea whispered, looking around. "You're right. But that means the chain of islands—"

"Are the remnants of a dead city." I finished with a sigh. The Islands Cavalcade was another ruin that had been claimed and repurposed. Now it made sense why they'd never been forced to share their crops. Crops couldn't grow on Old World remains.

"How has it remained intact?" Lor asked, studying the wall. "Surely the Great Waves would have destroyed this building as they did with the other Old World structures?"

"Does it matter?" I said, bitterness twisting in my belly.

A crease had formed between Elysea's eyebrows. "I hoped that maybe there was more out in the world."

"More than death?" I butted in. "This entire planet is a graveyard." I tapped my fingers against my thighs. "Come on. That's not why we're here."

We continued through the gap in the building until we reached a vast circular opening. It was a field of grass—most likely carried as seeds from Old World birds, before they'd died out. Around the field was a series of stone steps leading up to the tents at the top ledge, which we'd seen from the sea. A bonfire blazed in the field, with hundreds more torches lining the stone steps, enveloping the building in an amber haze.

The circular shape suddenly made sense.

"It's an Old World amphitheater," I said. "For performances. It must've been dislodged in the Great Waves."

A sprawling red tent sat in the center of the field. It appeared to be held up by the giant rib cage of a dead sea creature. And even though it was three thirty in the morning, people spilled out of the tent with cups and food clasped in their hands. Anyone who wasn't eating or drinking was moving to the music.

It took a while for me to pinpoint exactly where the music came from as the circular building reverberated the sound. Dozens of people sat up on the stairs of the amphitheater, singing in staccato rhythms, while others thwacked drums made from old pelts strung between a circle of animal bones.

"It's some kind of festival," Elysea remarked from beside me.

"Or not," I muttered. "This *is* a party island. Isn't this all they do?"

"Where do they get everything from?" Lor asked. "How do they survive without an island—a real island—to provide for them?"

"I'm not sure," I said. The people here didn't appear to be wanting. They chatted animatedly, their hands carving through the air as they spoke. Some wore shells twisted into their curly thick black hair; others had pale golden hair with pinked tips. And the children who ran by all had rounded bellies. This was clearly a thriving place.

Something sweet permeated the atmosphere, mingling with the ever-present salt. Like at Palindromena, it was a relief to smell something different. It helped settle the swaying in my head.

"What are they burning?" Lor asked.

I watched clouds of magenta-colored smoke rise into the air.

"Karpa," I said of the deep-water fish. "It's bitter to eat, but it smells sweet when it's cooked."

"And it creates a powder," Elysea added, nodding to the wisps of pink cloudlike ash emanating from the pyre, covering the children as they squealed in glee. "It's often used to paint with or dye clothing on the Equinox."

Lor looked at his borrowed red T-shirt. Perhaps he struggled to see the point in colorful clothing, but it was the small things that kept our culture alive, vibrant. It was a tie to the Old World. Although we'd given up much of what belonged to our ancestors, we couldn't let all our traditions be washed away.

Children reached into the cooled ash and rubbed it between their hands. They chased the other kids, who screamed when powder was smeared in their hair and across their faces.

"It looks like fun," Elysea said, a hand to her chest. There was a subtle sway to her movements that had nothing to do with being on land. She could feel the music calling to her. She wanted to join in.

"Shall we?" Lor asked, nodding toward the crowd of hundreds gathered around the tent. They'd yet to spot us as we'd stalled in the shadows.

I grabbed Lor's wrist to study his echolink. He flinched at my touch. "Eight and half hours left," I said. "We don't have time to search for Mom and Dad in the crowd. We need to find out if they're here. Now."

Elysea turned to me. "What are you suggesting?"

I pointed to the drums. "We don't need to find them. *They* need to find us."

CHAPTER THIRTY-SEVEN

LOR

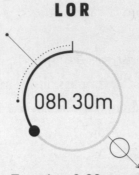

08h 30m

Tuesday, 3:30 a.m.

ELYSEA AND I could barely keep up with Tempest as she found the nearest stairs and started climbing to where the musicians played on the balcony. She was angry—but then again, Tempest's default setting was angry. This time, I could understand her frustration. All those days I'd spent at the top of the cliffs in Palindromena, I dreamed of all the islands I would one day visit. It was disappointing to know that the only thing out here was more ruins. I hoped for all our sakes that her parents were here.

The only person who didn't seem disappointed was Elysea. Since we'd stepped onto the field and she'd heard the music, she couldn't wipe the smile from her face. I remembered her dancing at the Spring Tide. She'd been so carefree—even as Ray and I were closing in. Even knowing she had mere hours to live.

This girl knew how to make the most of her time. To live her life. I didn't want to tell her what her sacrifice would be for. For the life I lived. I would have to return to the Aquarium, to my books and the dead. I wouldn't see the sun again. I wouldn't travel the ocean. The world wasn't something I could explore.

Then why couldn't I stop following these girls? Why was it so hard to imagine saying goodbye in just over eight hours? Especially to Tempest. She had a hold on me, and I would follow wherever she led.

"Come on, Lor!" Elysea called back. "You're slowing us down."

Even though I knew I shouldn't be a part of this family reunion, I climbed the stairs.

When we reached the musicians, Tempest wasted no time and started slapping a crude drum made from a pelt over bones. She had no rhythm, but I had to give her credit. She wasn't fazed by other people. She said and did exactly what she wanted. It was a freedom I'd never had, even when I wasn't hiding in the Aquarium. I'd always been uncomfortable in the spotlight and in my mother's shadow. Before Calen's death, I did everything my mother wanted. I didn't leave Palindromena. Climbing had been my one act of rebellion. Something my mother didn't want me to do, but was still contained to the island.

But now I wanted more.

My yearning for the wider world hadn't died within me that day on the cliffs. I'd merely been suppressing my desire for two years. And the desire came roaring back, stronger than ever.

I wanted to live. Truly live.

I took a steadying breath and stood beside Tempest. It didn't take long for her enthusiastic, and angry, addition to the song to be noticed by the crowd below. The musicians next to her stopped playing, wondering what she was doing. Soon, the amphitheater echoed silence. But Tempest played on.

She let out three short, sharp beats. Bringing the crowd's attention to her. Everyone looked up to see what the commotion was about.

"Please be here," she whispered. There was a tremble in her voice. "Please."

Elysea had tensed as she searched the faces of the crowd. I held my breath. I wanted them to have closure.

While most people in the crowd had turned away to resume what they were doing, two figures stood still. A tall, lean man with graying hair and olive skin next to a shorter woman with brown curly hair that framed her sandy complexion. Even from a distance, you could see their faces marred with shock.

"Mom!" Elysea cried out suddenly. "Dad!"

We'd found them.

<hr>

Tempest and Elysea started clambering down the stairs. I was close behind, unsure where else to go, and because I needed to hear the reasons these people left their kids—these two amazing girls—behind.

Once we'd reached the bottom of the stairs, Elysea took off at a run. She wasn't alone; her parents also sprinted toward us.

It was a flurry of arms and hair and laughter as Elysea collided with her mother. Tempest stood at a distance, watching with cautious eyes.

"You're alive!" her mother cried. "Thank the Gods below!"

Tempest exchanged a surprised look with me. I shook my head in bewilderment.

"You found it," her mother said, holding something at Elysea's throat. "You finally came."

"Elysea!" her father called her over. "Come here!" He had tears running down his face as he looked at his two now-grown daughters. Elysea disentangled herself from her mother's embrace, then launched herself at her father. He caught her with a laugh.

"I missed you!" Elysea said. Her shoulders shook as she cried happy tears.

"Tempe." The girls' mother turned to her youngest. "It's so wonderful to see you after all these years." She was wearing a bright purple dress with rows and rows of shell necklaces that jangled as she moved. Up close, there was no doubt this was the girls' mother. Her daughters had inherited her large eyes, bow lips and thick dark hair.

But Tempest stood her ground. "What do you mean, *you're alive?*" She didn't meet her mother's open arms. I could understand her wariness. She wanted to know what had happened before getting her hopes up. "How could you have known Elysea died when you've been gone 'all these years'?"

Her mother glanced back to Elysea. "No," she said, shaking her head vehemently. "No, no, no. Please tell me you're all right, Ely?"

Elysea pulled herself from her father's embrace. "I'm so sorry, Mom. But I'm here now. Because of Lor. He brought me back."

Suddenly all eyes were on me. The drumming music around us faded into the background. I could've heard a drop of water fall into the ocean.

"Lor *Ritter*?" Mr. Alerin asked. He narrowed his eyes. "Nessandra's son?"

I gritted my teeth and nodded. This moment had nothing to do with me. It was like being back at Palindromena. Witnessing final goodbyes. "I'm Elysea's Warden," I said.

"Oh Gods," Mrs. Alerin whispered. "I'd hoped you survived, Ely. I couldn't find you in the water, so I hoped that—" She collapsed to the grass and sobbed into her hands.

"Survived *what*?" Tempest demanded. "What *is* going on?"

"Maybe we should go back to our tent," her father suggested, his voice trembling from the revelation of Elysea's death. His hands clutched the edges of his shirt as though he needed something to hold on to. "Let your mother have a moment."

"A moment?" Tempest threw up her hands. "We don't have time—don't you understand? Elysea died, and she'll be dead again soon. We came here to find out what happened the night you disappeared. We thought you were dead for years! Why didn't you come back for us? Why did you leave in the first place? Why won't you . . ." Her lip started trembling. She turned away with a hiccup.

Elysea left her father's side and put her arm around her sister. "It's okay, Tempe."

I was used to Tempest's fury, but suddenly now, I was angry for her. Why were her parents playing this game of keep-away? Why not tell their daughters the truth? What could they possibly have to hide?

"We didn't mean for you to think we were dead." Her mother wiped the tears from her face and glanced up at her daughters. "The night we left, Elysea told us it was too much of an upheaval, and that she didn't want to come. We thought you'd both decided to stay on the Equinox and we wanted to respect that."

Elysea's cheeks flushed. "I'm sorry, Mom. I was confused. I should have—"

"It's not your fault," Mr. Alerin interrupted. "We put you in a difficult position by asking you to leave without giving you the information you needed to make a proper decision."

"What information?" Elysea asked.

"Why we needed to leave the Equinox that night, and never return," he said.

"And *why* was that?" Tempest asked. She'd stopped crying,

her hands fisted at her sides. The fire behind her eyes was back. A water witch poised for revenge. "Tell us!"

Mrs. Alerin managed to stand and took hold of her daughter's shoulders. She gave her a sad smile before she replied.

"We left to save your lives."

CHAPTER THIRTY-EIGHT

TEMPEST

08h 15m

Tuesday, 3:45 a.m.

OUR PARENTS LEFT to save us? From what?

"What are you talking about?" I demanded.

"Your father and I"—Mom stood a little straighter on the grass—"came into some trouble." Her eyes leveled on me. She looked exactly as I remembered her, perhaps a little more sun-weathered and covered in numerous shell necklaces, but otherwise, she was the same. It had taken all my willpower not to throw myself at her when she ran across the field. The twelve-year-old me, the one who'd cried every night for years over her death, wanted to be held by her. To convince myself she was real. The seventeen-year-old me, and the logical part, advised against letting her in.

I couldn't take another step forward until I knew the truth.

"We both loved working at Palindromena," Mom said. "Deren helped ease the pain of grieving families, and I helped nurture new crops to feed the Reefs. We were doing something worthwhile. Something to help our struggling world. The little that we could."

Elysea looked at our parents with such hope, while cradling Mom's necklace in her palm, as though their words could take the pain of the last five years away. I bit the inside of my cheek. I wished I could be as understanding.

Dad placed his hand on Mom's shoulder. "As Lead Botanist, your mother made all the decisions to sustain the crops. We were paid well. You girls were never going to have to worry about your future. But we had made promises to Nessandra." His eyes shifted to Lor. "We promised to protect Palindromena above all. Even our families. It was their security policy so no one would break the rules. Rules that ensured Palindromena's survival."

I felt like I was teetering, but this time it wasn't because I was on land. I was so close to the truth.

"What are these rules?" I asked.

"Never tell a patient they were once dead," Mom said. "Never let a patient leave the recovery room, let alone the facility. And never tell anyone how the revival procedure actually works." All the memories of my parents whispering late at night about what they did at the facility whirled in my mind.

"For twenty years, we didn't break the rules. Until five years ago," Dad said. "I was working late on some paperwork. There was only one active revival in the facility. In the middle of the night, the client found me, screaming that her husband was dying and that she couldn't find her Warden. Her husband was only twelve hours into his revival and he should've had plenty of time. Something had gone wrong." Dad took a deep breath as if the memory was fresh and painful. "Her husband was flatlining. I later found out that the Warden had gone for a midnight swim and gotten caught in a rip tide. As his heart faltered, so did his patient's. At the time, I didn't know what to do, so I tried to locate Nessandra.

"But I couldn't find her anywhere. Even as Head Warden, I only had access to certain areas of the facility. But this was an emergency. Ensuring the peaceful twenty-four hours of a patient's revival was a Warden's responsibility." He ran a hand through his graying hair. Unlike Mom, he looked different from what I remembered. Skinnier. Less cheerful. Haunted.

"Security allowed me access to the research labs to find Nessandra. I'd never been back there. I'd never had to." He took a deep breath. "When I found her, she was untethering a patient. At least, that was what it looked like at first. The man was living, but after she touched his echo, he was gone." That was Elysea's future, but my sister didn't flinch at the words. "I then realized there were two other men in tanks. I asked what was going on."

"Nessandra said she was testing a theory," Mom chimed in. "She had tried using two men to tether to the patient, instead of one. She had tethered the men's pulses twelve hours apart, in hope to bridge the gap at twenty-four hours when the body resets itself. She hoped she could permanently revive a patient, as well as keep the other men alive. She wanted to 'cure' death." Her lip curled in contempt. "But no one survived."

"Both the Wardens and the patient died?" Elysea asked. She considered Lor, but he wouldn't meet her eyes.

"No," Dad said. "It's worse than that. I didn't recognize *any* of these men. I asked Nessandra who they were, and she told me they were three fishermen whose boat had up-turned close to the island. One had drowned, becoming her test subject, but the other two had still been breathing. Because Palindromena had rescued them from the water, she claimed they were hers. No one would come looking for them. Their families would think they'd also drowned, as so many people do."

All those people who disappeared in the waters. All those tales of being taken by a ravenous sea creature. How many were because of Nessandra? How many people had she taken to become batteries for the dead? How many people had she murdered in the name of "curing" death?

Elysea covered her mouth with her hand. My knees wobbled and I felt faint. This was the company we trusted with our future. The company we paid our taxes to. The company we trusted with our loved ones once they were gone.

"Nessandra tried to convince me what she was doing was worth the sacrifice," Dad said. I glanced at Lor, and he flinched at the mention of his mother's name. "But it was never *her* sacrifice. She'd killed two innocent men. Men who had fallen into the sea and needed to be rescued, not experimented on. But she was so focused on her goal to eradicate death, she decided it was worth the cost."

"Queen of Death," Lor murmured, so softly I almost didn't catch it. Did he know this about his mother? Was this the secret he'd been keeping from me? "She didn't want anyone else to suffer like she had when her parents had died."

Dad shook his head. "I told Nessandra that I couldn't be a part of it. I told her she needed to stop what she was doing. That it was wrong." He laughed cruelly. "She said I needed to fall into line. That my job did not allow me an opinion on her research. So I told her that I would tell the world about what Palindromena was really doing out on the water with their retrieval boats. She would lose everything. That was when she turned security on me."

"She tried to have him killed," Mom said. I gasped.

"I grabbed your mother, and we fled Palindromena. But we were being followed. We made a rash decision. We couldn't return to the Equinox. We knew Elysea was out diving that night for your birthday, Tempe, so we headed to the *Sunrise*'s location."

Elysea looked at the paper in her hands. "You gave me this map and told me to get Tempe and leave. But you wouldn't tell me why."

"I was so frantic, I wasn't thinking clearly," Dad said. "I knew Palindromena's fleet wouldn't be far behind and we needed to lead them away from you. We didn't want you to get hurt." He shook his head. "If I could do it all over again, I would do it differently."

Mom put her arm around him. "It was the only decision we could make at the time."

He nodded hesitantly. "After Ely left, the fleet approached. Nessandra ordered the vessels to fire their cannons at us, decimating our boat. Nessandra thought we were dead, but we'd managed to jump from the boat before it exploded. We clung to the debris for a few hours, until a small fishing vessel found us. We gave them thousands of Notes to keep our secret and bring us here." Dad gestured to the amphitheater. "It's not far from the Equinox, but it's outside Palindromena's jurisdiction. We planned to wait for you to arrive before moving on to another Reef. But you never came."

"As we said before, we thought it was your decision," Mom said. "But after six months of waiting for you to arrive, we started to worry that something went wrong. We wanted you to know we were alive and that we were still waiting for you."

"So we used a raft to get to the closest Reef and borrowed a boat to journey to the Equinox," Dad said. "But when we crossed Palindromena's perimeter, the facility was notified of an incoming vessel that wasn't one of their own and came to investigate. We hoped we could reach you, but Nessandra's fleet was too fast. When she saw it was us, she fired the cannons at our boat, not caring who heard. But in the night, the detonation sounded like thunder. No one came to our aid. We had to retreat."

I swallowed sharply. Had I heard the gunfire and simply thought it was another storm?

"What about this?" Elysea held out Mom's necklace in her palm.

"Over the next few years, we continued trying to cross the perimeter, but we never made it to the Equinox before Nessandra's boats found us," Mom said. "One time we were so close." She brushed Elysea's hair behind her ear. "We saw the *Sunrise* on the horizon, not far from a dive site. But Nessandra wouldn't let us come to you. The next night, I dropped my necklace into the waters above the ruins, hoping you would find it and know we were still alive. And that we wanted you to follow the map to our location."

"When you still didn't come to us, we returned a few months later," Dad said. "And I left my echolink behind."

I squeezed my eyes shut. Our parents had wanted us to be together, but Nessandra had kept us apart all these years. The same woman who had comforted me at Palindromena, saying she was sorry for my loss.

Elysea put her arms around Mom's waist. "Is this true?" she asked Lor, grimacing. "You take people from the ocean for your experiments? People who are still alive?"

Lor crossed his arms. "They're not *my* experiments. They're my mother's. And I don't agree with anything she does at Palindromena."

"But you knew about this?" Elysea asked, her voice cracking.

"I—" He swallowed. "Not entirely, no."

"Stop lying," I said. He'd been hiding something from me on the *Sunrise*, and he was still holding back.

Something flickered behind his eyes. Anger. "I'm not."

I didn't want to look at him anymore. How many times did he have to lie until I realized I couldn't trust him?

"Why did you stop leaving us clues?" I asked Mom and Dad. "I never found anything of yours."

Mom pressed her face into Elysea's shoulder. "We stopped coming back two years ago."

My scalp prickled in forewarning.

"Two years?" I asked.

But Mom wouldn't elaborate, her breath coming in gasps, tears running down her face.

"A few weeks after I left behind my echolink, and you still hadn't joined us, we returned one last time," Dad said, his forehead crinkled and eyes red.

I exchanged a look with Elysea, but her face had drained of color. Her eyes were glassy and unfocused.

"I remember now." Her voice was so quiet I almost didn't catch it. "I'd been keeping watch at the dive site at night for almost two weeks after I'd found Dad's echolink. I still hadn't told Tempe, in case I was wrong." Elysea closed her eyes, as though imagining the scene. "When you finally showed up, you weren't alone."

"Nessandra," Dad said, fury twisting his usually cheerful face. "As always, she was notified when we crossed the perimeter. We'd hoped to beat her to the dive site, but our borrowed boat couldn't compete with a Palindromena-built vessel."

"She was furious we kept returning," Mom said, her entire body trembling. "We told her we just wanted to be with you girls, but she thought we were planning to destroy Palindromena. She wanted to convince us to stay away, once and for all. That was when she spotted the *Sunrise*."

"No," I said, realizing what they were about to say.

"We tried to stop her," Dad said, "but her boat was quicker than ours. She rammed into the *Sunrise*, throwing Elysea into the water." He placed his hands on Elysea's shoulders. "Mom dove in after you, but she couldn't find you." Mom had dissolved into tears now. "Nessandra said if we didn't depart immediately, she'd go after Tempe next."

I couldn't move. I couldn't breathe.

"We had to leave." Dad rubbed the bridge of his nose. "We had to protect you, Tempe. We had to let Nessandra win."

Now it made sense why my parents had reacted that way when they first saw Elysea. They thought she'd somehow survived the accident.

I couldn't even look at Lor. His mother had destroyed my family.

I wanted to curl into a ball and cry and cry and cry. My parents had been so close to reuniting with Elysea. How could the Gods below allow this?

Elysea didn't move. She was in shock.

But I remembered my vow. To be strong. For her.

I took a step toward my parents. "There has to be something we can do to save Elysea. Dad, you were a Warden—isn't there some way to extend her life?"

Dad shook his head. "I wish there was. If I knew of anything, I would do it."

"How long do you have left, Ely?" Mom asked through her tears.

Elysea smiled grimly at Lor. He checked his echolink and said, "Less than eight hours."

"So, what?" I looked between them all. "We accept that Elysea has a few hours left to live. You're all okay with that? After everything you've done to protect us from Nessandra?"

Dad shook his head. "No, of course we're not okay with it. But we can't risk your life, Tempe. Because of what we did, Elysea has hours left to live."

"Because of *Nessandra*," I snarled. "But we're together now; we can all fight her."

"It's too risky," Mom said. "We should cherish this time that we have together." She sounded like my sister.

"Ely?" I asked. But I could tell by her face that she'd given up. The memory of that night had exhausted her.

"Tempe, sweetheart." Mom reached for me, but I didn't want to be coddled. I wanted everyone else to burn into action.

"I need some time by myself," I said, walking away.

I should've said space. Because time was the one thing I couldn't get more of.

CHAPTER THIRTY-NINE

LOR

07h 50m

Tuesday, 4:10 a.m.

THE QUEEN OF DEATH. That was what the employees called my mother. Before I started working down in the basement, I thought my mother followed my grandparents' guidelines. A life merely borrowed for twenty-four revived hours. But after working in the Aquarium for a few months, I saw a pattern. My mother would bring in bodies through the Aquarium's back doors, but they wouldn't end up in tanks. I assumed the people were dead, but deep down, I knew they weren't. I never questioned her, as I was afraid of the answer, but now I knew and couldn't hide from the truth. She was experimenting on the living.

Was the real reason patients were given something to forget their most recent memories because my mother had a hand in all their deaths?

We still had seven hours and fifty minutes left, and yet I felt exhausted, as though it were the final hour. My mother had killed Elysea. A wonderful girl with a loving family. I wouldn't blame anyone for hating me for simply being related to her.

"I'm sorry," I said to the Alerins as Tempest walked away. "I wish there was something I could do. Something to help Elysea. To help all of you."

Elysea smiled. "I know you do, Lor." She turned to her parents. "I'll go after her."

"Maybe I should?" Mrs. Alerin suggested, watching Tempest's back as she strode to the entrance of the amphitheater.

Elysea shook her head. "It should be me."

She bounded off after her sister. Even without trying, she looked like she was dancing.

Which left me alone with Mr. and Mrs. Alerin. Just when I thought things couldn't get any worse.

"I'm sorry for what my mother did." Sorry didn't even cover half of it. What did you say to parents who were forced to leave their daughters behind, live in exile and witness their child being killed? All because of your mother?

Mr. Alerin squeezed my shoulder, his eyes downcast. "I knew some of the secrets Palindromena was hiding, even from its own employees, and I did nothing," he said.

I felt as though I'd been kicked in the stomach. For my entire life, I'd done nothing. For two years, I'd known my mother had crossed a line and I hadn't stopped her. I'd allowed my mother to keep her secrets. And she'd allowed me to keep mine.

Were we really so different? After all, she wasn't the only killer in the family.

Mr. Alerin let out a bone-deep sigh. "Do you drink ragar, Lor?"

I didn't, but on this occasion I would.

—————

Minda and Deren—as they introduced themselves—took me inside the expansive red tent. There were tables and chairs with enough food to feed the hundreds of people on the island, and then some. People were drinking, eating and talking loudly. The air was hot and sticky and couldn't have been further from the Aquarium.

"Where does all this food come from?" I asked, watching as people sucked on clams, chewed tails of roasted fish and tucked into bowls of seaweed stew. "You don't have any crops for trade."

"We eat only what can be sourced from the ocean," Minda said. "And because we have very few boats in the area, the marine life isn't scared away."

"And that's sustainable?" I asked.

Minda smiled. "We feast like this every few months, but we also fast to ensure we don't over-fish the ocean, and allow species to repopulate. We're careful to take only what's needed."

"And everything else we use"—Deren waved a hand around—"was found here. This Old World amphitheater was built on top of a towering building, years before the Great

Waves hit. Because the clothes, tents and cooking implements weren't submerged, they've lasted much longer."

"And what exactly are you celebrating?" I asked.

Minda laughed. She sounded a lot like her daughters. "Being alive."

Deren handed me a mug of steaming hot ragar. I took a tentative sip. The fermented drink burned my tongue and made my eyes water. The fire settled somewhere in my chest, and I bent over and let out a rattling cough.

Deren slapped me on the back. "First ragar?"

I nodded, trying to catch my breath. Ray would be laughing his ass off if he were here right now. It made me miss him. He would love this place. I hoped he wasn't too worried about me, although I knew he would be.

"Is it always this strong?" I asked.

Deren smirked. "This is actually a weak batch."

"Don't mind him," Minda said, passing me a plate of roasted white fish flesh with a side of stew. "Eat up, you look famished."

"Thank you." I wasn't sure why I deserved their kindness. I took a seat at one of the empty tables. Deren and Minda sat opposite me.

I shoveled the food into my mouth to avoid any awkward conversation.

"You look so much like your mother," Minda said, her hand at her chest. "I'm sorry, you must hear that all the time."

I swallowed the fish. The food helped settle my stomach. "Not really, no." No one had seen me for two years to make the association.

"How are things there?" Deren asked, his expression guarded.

"The same," I said. Two years ago, when I'd realized my mother was doing more harm than good, I stopped talking to her. Since then, I'd retreated even further.

I continued to let her hurt people.

"Then she's failing," Minda said. She didn't need to clarify who she was talking about.

"Yes." I'd hate to think what my mother would resort to next.

Deren patted my arm. "Being a Warden isn't an easy job. We can't thank you enough for letting Elysea come see us for her last hours."

"I didn't." I couldn't let these nice people think their daughters were here because of me. "Tempest broke Elysea out of Palindromena. I followed them. And then they took me captive." I laughed, because what else could you do at this point? "When they discovered one of us would die after the twenty-four hours, Elysea wanted to return to Palindromena immediately, but I wanted them to have their reunion with you."

Minda stared at me for a long moment, and I thought I'd said the wrong thing. Then her expression cracked, and tears tracked down her face.

I'd definitely said the wrong thing. I was still rusty with the living.

"I'm so sorry." But they were just words. I wished I could actually be of some help.

"No," Minda said through her tears. "Thank you for telling me that. I'm happy to know Tempest protected her sister."

That she did. But who was protecting Tempest?

I let Deren and Minda talk in hushed whispers for a while and ate my food in silence. The ragar burned less the more I drank it.

Elysea found us at the table a short while later. "Tempe needs some time," she said with a sad smile. "She's sorry."

I wondered if Tempest was truly sorry or whether Elysea had amended her response to not upset her parents.

"I understand," Minda said.

"Before I forget—" Elysea pulled something from her pocket and handed it to her father. An echolink. "This is yours."

The echo shook in Deren's trembling fingers. It represented the very thing that had taken him from his family, and what would eventually end Elysea's life.

"Thanks, Ely." He moved his hands under the table, removing the echo from sight. Would he destroy it like I wished I could destroy mine?

Elysea nodded and sat next to her mother. She leaned her head on her shoulder. They looked so alike—brown hair, green eyes, olive skin and round cheeks.

I looked away, the guilt rising, and poured myself another ragar. I hoped the burning liquid would dull the ache building in my chest.

The amphitheater was a stadium of stars. At least, that was what it looked like as my vision blurred. We'd only been on the Islands Cavalcade for two hours, but I was already mourning the thought of leaving this place. The sights, the music, the food, the people—the life. It reminded me of the Spring Tide. It reminded me of what it was like to truly live. I took another sip of ragar.

I'd only had two glasses, but it was enough. I could feel a weightlessness in my mind. Akin to floating. I wanted to close my eyes and let the waves take me. I wanted to forget. I wanted to forget the Aquarium.

"Lor!" Elysea said as I stumbled away from the tent and toward the pyre. "Are you drunk?"

She had tied various colorful scarves around her waist to make a skirt and had been dancing with the younger children by the pyre. I was glad she was enjoying her final hours.

I held two fingers close together. "A little. Where's Tempest?" It had been nearly an hour, and she hadn't reappeared. It was now five in the morning; we only had two hours left on the island. "Doesn't she want to enjoy the party?"

"No," Elysea said. "Not really."

"That's a shame; I miss her."

Elysea chuckled.

I hadn't realized I'd said the last part out loud. "I think I should stop drinking." I placed the mug on a table nearby. I needed to be in control of my tongue. It was too easy to get comfortable around these girls.

Deren and Minda were never far, keeping a close watch over Elysea while they still could. The more time I spent with them, the more I liked them. And that wasn't the ragar talking.

"She's still off on her own," Elysea said. It took me a while to realize she was answering my initial question of Tempest's whereabouts. "She doesn't want to join in the celebration. She says there's nothing to celebrate."

"You're alive," I said, gesturing to her with a grand sweep of my hand. "And you weren't over a day ago. That's reason to celebrate."

She laughed again. "I think you should get some food and sit down." She didn't need to say it. I needed to sober up.

I wandered away from the bonfire. I should've gone back to the tent, but I wanted to sit in the dark; the radiant pyre was giving me a headache. Or perhaps that was the ragar.

Then I spotted her. She was off in the field, hugging her knees close to her chest, watching Elysea rejoin the children in their dance around the flames.

"Tempest!" I exclaimed. "You're here!"

"Go away." She didn't even look at me.

"No. I will not."

"I don't want you here," she said. "Can't you understand that?"

I could. I knew I looked like my mother, and any reminder of her was not what Tempest needed. If it weren't for her, we wouldn't be in this mess. But being alone wasn't good for Tempest either.

"Then close your eyes," I said, plonking myself down next to her.

She turned and gave me a strange look. "You're acting odd."

I shrugged one shoulder. "You don't really know who I am."

I'd meant the old me, but she said, "I guess I don't."

"I wish I could make up for what my mother's done to you. I wish I would have stopped her."

She gave me a quizzical look. "*Could* you have stopped her?"

"No, probably not."

She sighed and turned away from me.

"We have a little under two hours," I said, checking the echo. "Why don't you join your sister? Enjoy yourself?"

"Before you take her life away?" She shook her head. "Tempting offer."

I ran my hands down my face with a groan. "You never let it go, do you?"

"My sister's death?" Her eyes were hard. "No. Never."

"But your sister has." I pointed to Elysea as she leaped around the pyre. It looked like she was disappearing and emerging from a cloud. "Isn't that what matters?"

"My sister and I are very different," Tempest said. She was worrying her bottom lip between her teeth, her eyes focused on Elysea. "And she doesn't have to concern herself with what happens after her death. *I* do."

"Trust me. It's not easy to know you're dying."

She looked me over then. "Do you feel all right?"

It was the first real concern I'd seen from her. "Yes."

Her cheeks reddened, as though she realized what she'd asked. She'd let her guard slip.

"Elysea wants to enjoy her time left. She wants you with her."

Tempest pushed a hand through her black hair. "Elysea should want more than that. She should want to live. And she should want revenge."

"Isn't it easier that she accepts what's going to happen to her?"

She raised an eyebrow. "Easier for you."

I let out an exaggerated sigh. "Aren't you tired of keeping up your walls, Tempe?"

She blinked. "What are you talking about?"

I gestured to the celebration. "You could be a part of this, if you wanted."

"And what makes you think that I want to be a part of it, Lor *Ritter*?" The way she said my last name, it was as though she was cursing me. I really hoped she wasn't a water witch after all.

"Everyone wants to live. But what you're doing right now, it's not living. You're all"—I spun my hands in circles—"anger and hatred and frustration. That's not living." I should know. That was how I lived my life too.

"You don't know who I am." She repeated my earlier words. It was true, we really didn't know each other. But I wanted to.

"Remember when I told you not to waste the revived hours, or you'd regret it?" She didn't reply. "I'm reminding you not to do that now. As your Warden." She needed to see the truth, before it was too late.

"But you're not a Warden!" Her hands slapped the grass. "Why do you care what I do? After midday you get to return to your normal life, with your murderous mother, and I lose my sister. Forever."

"I won't go back to her," I said, meaning my mother.

"You won't?"

I shook my head, a little too enthusiastically, and now I felt light-headed. "I've spent too long in denial. I can't hide any longer."

"Where will you go, then?"

Even though I would return Elysea to Palindromena before anyone found out what had happened, I couldn't go back to the Aquarium. Not anymore. I was fighting for a life that I wasn't truly living.

"I like your family," I said, changing the subject. "You're good people. You don't deserve what my mother has done to you. Especially your sister. But, most of all, *you* don't deserve it. Grief is the hardest on those left behind." I knew that all too well.

She took in a shuddering breath, as though she were about to cry. "Thank you," she said, her voice steadying.

We didn't speak for a few minutes.

While the silence was comfortable, the ragar wouldn't let

me stay quiet. "If you didn't know today was her last day, what would you do?" I asked.

She glanced at the pyre, a smile playing at her mouth. "I'd dance with her, even though I'm a terrible dancer."

"I remember," I said, thinking of her Spring Tide performance.

She shot me a furious look and I smiled. "Dancing abilities aside, you should go to her. Palindromena isn't completely wrong in what they're trying to do. My grandparents started it, did you know that?" She shook her head. "When they discovered how to revive a living thing for twenty-four hours, they saw the opportunity to help people. But the one fishbone in the stew is that the client knows it's their last hours with their loved one. You can never fully enjoy the revival, knowing your goodbye is inevitable."

"Are you suggesting I pretend she's not going to lose her life in a few hours?" She brushed her hair over her shoulder; it fell like a dark waterfall. My fingers itched to touch it.

"What have you got to lose? You can either spend the rest of your time here, with me, or you can make the most of the time left with your sister."

"Well, I certainly don't want to spend more time with you."

I thought she was being serious but then I saw the glint in her eyes. She gave me a tentative smile.

"Go, then." I waved her away with a returning smile.

I hated that I missed her as soon as she left.

CHAPTER FORTY

TEMPEST

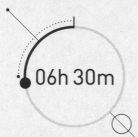

Tuesday, 5:30 a.m.

TIME. Time—that was what it always came down to.

As much as I didn't want to heed Lor's words, he was right. This was all I had. Just an hour and a half left with my family whole again. Why waste it?

I wanted to stay angry at him, I wanted to hate him because I hated what his mother had done, but I couldn't. It was clear he was as horrified by her actions as we were. If I ever saw Nessandra again, she would get a piece of my mind—and, most likely, my fist too.

Before I joined Elysea at the pyre, I sought out my parents. They were sitting around a small table, their gaze intensely focused on my sister as she danced.

"We had a happy life," I said. "We looked after one another."

Mom twisted in her chair. "Tempe!" She held out her arms. "Come sit with us."

I pulled a chair to their table. It hadn't escaped me that, like the drums, all the furniture was made of bones. Fish bones. That was one thing this world had in abundance. Death. And yet, everyone around us was enjoying life. They had built something out of the skeleton of the Old World. Something thriving.

"We didn't live in mourning," I added. "Of course we missed you, but Elysea pushed me to keep going. To keep living. Would you expect anything different?" I laughed as Elysea jumped through the air, as though she were weightless. She had a trail of kids following her, attempting to match her moves.

Dad reached around Mom and gripped my hand. "We have no doubt you girls did what was best for each other."

"We can never convey how sorry we are," Mom said. Her eyes glistened. "You must know that we never wanted things to turn out this way?"

"I understand now." I rubbed the bridge of my nose, wishing my tears away. "I'll just miss her, you know?"

Mom wrapped me in her arms. She smelled the same. Even without her plants at Palindromena, she smelled of earth and sweetness. "I know, darling. We will too. We *have*, all these years. But you have us now. We can live here, together."

I looked around the amphitheater, imagining my life as one large celebration. It didn't fit who I was, who I'd become. I wasn't the same girl who hid behind her mother's legs when she was little. And I wasn't the teenager who preferred the company of underwater skeletons. I *was* stronger now. I would worry about *after*, when the time came.

I gave Mom a squeeze and gave Dad a kiss on the cheek before heading to the bonfire.

Elysea was teaching the kids one of her routines.

"Tempe!" she cried when she saw me. She left her ragtag troupe and grabbed my hands. "Will you dance with me?"

"You know I can't follow your moves."

She grinned. "Then dance however you feel!"

I wanted to cry or rage. But neither would help Elysea. I did my best to move to the rhythm.

While I was clearly terrible, she smiled as though I were the best student she'd ever had. It gave me more confidence. I held on to her hand and tried to mimic her movements.

After a few minutes, I forgot to care how awkward I looked compared to Elysea. I let go of everything. For a moment. And it was freeing. It was like diving underwater. Complete control but also complete abandon.

"Lor!" Elysea cried, snapping me back into myself. "Come dance with us!"

"No," I said, pulling my hand from Elysea's. But she held firm.

Lor appeared out of the darkness. He'd sobered since I saw him last, but there was a relaxed way to his movements that made me think he was still a little affected by the ragar.

"No," I said again.

"Don't be mean," she whispered.

Lor approached us cautiously, as though I might bite. I wished I still wanted to, but the fury had ebbed from my body. That was the magic of Elysea.

"I don't really dance," he said.

Elysea beamed. "Wonderful! Neither does Tempe. You can *not* dance together."

She put my hand in his, and I flinched as though I had touched the fire. His skin was soft, delicate. Not the product of working the ropes on a boat, scavenging dive sites or climbing the cliff faces of Palindromena.

Had he lied about that too?

"Hello," he said.

"Hi." I stilled my movements.

Elysea danced away.

"I'm sorry." I dropped Lor's hand. "I really *don't* dance."

Lor's expression was somber. "Neither do I."

We stood for a moment, looking at one another, the music and dancers twirling around us as the fire crackled nearby. I thought of the Spring Tide. Of how we'd been caught in a storm. And I felt trapped again. The music pounding in my head. And Lor's eyes, vibrant blue in the firelight.

But this time everything was different. I didn't want to escape. Not really.

I wasn't used to making new—or *any*—friends. But I tried to imagine what it would've been like if I'd met Lor under different circumstances. If he hadn't been Nessandra's son, or Elysea's tether. How would I feel then? Would I want to dance with him?

As we stood there, he gave me a tentative smile. For whatever reason, he seemed to want to be near me as well. And for the first time since Elysea was revived, I felt connected. Connected to this world. And extremely aware of every breath between us.

He stepped toward me, his hand seeking mine. His lips parted. "Tempe," he said. "I . . ." But he didn't finish the sentence.

Everyone disappeared in that moment, and all I saw was Lor. The real Lor. He'd stopped trying to apologize, he'd stopped trying to be my Warden, he'd stopped *trying*. He just was.

He stood there, his hand held out to me, his eyes burning and a question playing on his lips. There was a confidence within him, as well as an almost painful desperation to break through to me. I hadn't met this boy before.

And he was beautiful.

I stepped back. I could see what Elysea was trying to do. She didn't want me to see Lor as the enemy. She wanted me to understand he, too, was caught in a terrible situation.

I wished it were that easy. I wished I could forgive him for his part in this. But he still held Elysea's life in his hands. And in a few hours, he'd snuff it out.

I turned away, but Lor reached out, his fingers grazing my arm. "Wait," he said.

I stopped but didn't look back. "What?"

"Is there anything I can do?" His voice was soft, barely audible over the music.

I was about to say he could die so my sister could live, but I didn't mean that. Now that I'd seen the real him, it couldn't be unseen. I couldn't wish that boy harm.

I twisted to face him. "I want you to promise my sister won't be in any pain."

He pressed his lips together. "Of course."

"Good. And after Elysea is gone, I never want to see you again."

His breath hitched but he seemed to understand. He would always remind me of my sister.

"I'm sorry," I said.

And I was. Sorry for what could have been.

I left him by the pyre. I had an hour remaining with my family. They were all that mattered now.

CHAPTER FORTY-ONE

LOR

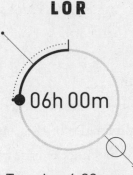

Tuesday, 6:00 a.m.

I WATCHED TEMPEST walk away. My heart aching over her words.

After today, I would never see her again. Although I didn't blame her, I wished there was something—anything—I could do.

While I hadn't been driving the boat my mother used to crash into Elysea, I still felt responsible. I'd known my mother was experimenting on the living in her reckless pursuit to cure mortality. Was it too much of a leap that she'd turned to murder to silence those around her? I was nineteen now; I wasn't a helpless little kid anymore. I had some power. Didn't I?

My mother had always claimed the Reefs needed Palindromena's crops to survive, but after visiting the self-sufficient party islands, I knew that wasn't true. They didn't receive medicine or vitamins. And yet they were still surviving.

No. They weren't merely surviving. They were thriving.

They spent their days with friends and family, celebrating being alive. Sure, you would get sick of seafood and seaweed stew, but it was better than nothing. And everyone here looked healthy and happy.

Everyone but Tempe.

I'd been watching her dance with her sister before I'd approached the pyre, and for the briefest moment, I'd seen happiness light her face. It had knocked the breath out of me. She was beyond beautiful. And not because she was smiling, but because she let her walls down; she allowed herself to be in the moment—enjoy the music and her sister's company. I saw the real Tempest. Who she must've been before she lost everyone she loved.

But it was a fleeting moment.

She had returned to the grief-hardened girl. I understood. I was angry too. At my mother, at Palindromena, at myself.

I pushed through the crowd to get some air. The smoke was settling in my lungs, and it made my chest feel tight.

I sat down in the grass, suddenly exhausted. I couldn't see where Tempest had gone, but I could make out Elysea's silhouette by the fire. I wished I could help the Alerin sisters, I did. I didn't want another person's death on my hands—even if I wasn't directly responsible. I closed my eyes and tried imagining Elysea taking her last breath. I tried imagining Tempe saying her final words of goodbye. But I couldn't.

Maybe it was because I wasn't really a Warden. I didn't

know how to cope with the end of the revival process. But I knew it was worse. I cared that Elysea was going to die. I cared that Tempe would be grieving again.

I saw the desperation on Tempe's face as the final hours counted down. She knew she would never be the same. That she *hadn't* been for the last years her sister was gone. And I knew how that felt. I didn't want her to go through what I'd been through. I didn't want her to watch her sister die.

I might not believe in the Gods below, but I felt deep down that it was my fate to be Elysea's tether, meet Tempe and her family. It was my fate to help them all, because I'd failed Calen.

Today, I'd been delivered an opportunity to do something good. I could never heal the hole I'd torn through Calen's family, but I could try to heal the Alerins.

But how? Reviving a patient meant stealing the life from someone. And that was the problem. It would always require a sacrifice. A life for a life. If only there was someone who wasn't really using their life.

Like me.

I laughed. What a stupid thing to think. Perhaps the effects of the ragar hadn't worn off like I'd thought.

Or maybe I wasn't being stupid, after all . . .

There had to be someone who was alive, but not entirely. Someone who had a heartbeat, but wasn't really living. While there were lots of bodies in Palindromena, they were all dead. Except . . . except for the *Lifers*. They were people who'd been in boating accidents, but had never woken up. Nor did their heart stop. While they were technically brain-dead, they still had a pulse. My mother kept their bodies in case she wanted more subjects to test on.

Even so, a patient couldn't be revived twice. Once Elysea's heart was stopped, it couldn't be restarted. Unless we switched the tether from my pulse to a Lifer, before Elysea's heart stopped beating. We could then stop the Lifer's heart so Elysea would live on. I could use their life for something good. And the Lifer could finally be at rest and free from my mother.

Something prickled under my skin. Excitement. Hope.

I could save Elysea.

All I needed was someone who could perform the tethering process. And I knew just the person.

But first, I needed to get back to Palindromena.

⸺⸻⸺

Although it was nearing sunrise, the party showed no signs of slowing down. I searched for Tempest and her parents, but couldn't see any familiar faces. Cups of ragar were pressed into my hands as I moved through the pulsing crowd, but I pushed them away. I needed to stay sharp.

I headed toward the pyre and wormed my way through the rings of dancers to find Elysea in the middle.

"Elysea," I called over the music. "I need to speak with you."

She smiled and tried to draw me into the dance, but I shook my head. "It's important!"

She gestured to her ears as though she couldn't hear what I was saying. But she must've read the seriousness on my face, as she made her way over. "Is everything all right?" she asked. "Is it time to go?"

I checked my echolink.

6:15 a.m.

"Almost. But come with me, I have an idea."

It was easier to explain my plan to everyone at once.

We pushed back through the dancers. My height allowed me to see over most of the crowd.

"I need to find the rest of your family," I said. I had to lean down for her to hear. "Do you know where they are?"

"Tempe said she was going to get some food." I could barely make the words out.

Inside, the tent was quieter now. Most of the food was gone. Tempest was sitting with her parents at one of the tables. They had their heads close together, talking in hurried whispers, but looked up as Elysea and I approached.

I took a deep breath. I hoped they would hear me out.

"I think I can save Elysea."

CHAPTER FORTY-TWO

TEMPEST

05h 30m

Tuesday, 6:30 a.m.

I DIDN'T BREATHE for the entire time Lor explained his plan. The sun was about to rise, we had to leave, but I was rooted to the spot. When he'd finished, tears were streaming down my face. Elysea was still as the ocean on a calm, clear day. I wanted to throw my arms around her, tell her she'd live, but I could see the doubt behind her eyes.

"I've never heard of such a thing," Dad said. We'd been making plans for me to live here before Lor had found us. Now our plans could include Elysea.

"I call them Lifers," Lor explained. He looked completely sober now, his blue eyes clear and pale face flushed. "They're kept in one of the back rooms in the basement. They're essentially brain-dead, but very much still alive. We can tether their pulse to Elysea's and then stop their heartbeat, allowing Elysea to live." Was it still considered killing someone, if these people could never wake up?

Would they want their heartbeat to be used to help someone else live? *I would.*

"Elysea?" I asked. "What do you think?"

"You said you're not sure it will work," she said to Lor cautiously.

"No. It's never been done before, but I have a friend who has been studying the revival process. He's the best chance we've got."

Elysea exchanged a glance with Mom and Dad. "I don't know," she said. "I don't want to place this burden on anyone else."

"You won't be. These people are already essentially dead. It's just their heart that continues pumping. And they're stuck in the tanks until my mother decides to get rid of them or use them for another test. This way, their death can be for something good. They can finally be at peace."

"Just think of it," I said. "All of us, together." My future unraveled out in front of me, and for once, it was not a storm on the horizon. It was the sun rising.

Elysea rubbed her temples. "I don't want to think about it." There were pink streaks in her hair from the pyre ash. "I don't want to get my hopes up."

"You're tired," Mom said, pulling out a chair. "You should rest."

"We don't have time to rest," I said, standing next to Lor. "We have to get Elysea back to Palindromena as soon as we can. Right, Lor?"

He blinked, stunned that I was finally on his side. "That's right."

Elysea had already agreed to travel back to Palindromena; there was no reason for Lor to lie to us now. Warmth unfurled in my chest when I looked at him. I could trust him.

"Your mother will let you do this?" Dad asked. He was skeptical. He had a right to be after everything Nessandra had done.

"I'm not planning to ask for permission," Lor replied, his voice resolute. It was clear he wanted to distance himself from everything his mother had done. Reviving Elysea permanently was the first step.

"Why are you questioning this?" I asked. "This is the miracle we've been hoping for! Sent up from the Gods below themselves, and yet you all look like you were slapped in the face with a familfish."

"Tempe—" Dad began. But I could tell by his tone that he was about to say something negative. I didn't want to dwell in the darkness, for once. Lor had provided a lifeline, and we were going to take it.

"Isn't it worth the risk?" I asked.

"We took a risk leaving you that night five years ago. And when we tried to return to you two years ago," Mom said with a shake of her head. "Look how that turned out."

"It's not the same." I couldn't understand why they weren't leaping at the chance. "Elysea is already dead. What have we got to lose?"

"You," Mom said abruptly.

The air left my lungs. "What are you talking about?"

"We have to protect you," she explained. "If Nessandra knows you've spoken to us, she'll fear for her company. After she hurt Elysea, there's no telling what she might do."

"Then come with us!" The longer we debated this, the less time we had to set up the new tether.

"The *Sunrise* only holds three people," Dad said. "Any more, and she'll sink to the bottom of the ocean. We could take our raft to the closest Reef to borrow a boat, but it will take longer than the remaining five hours."

"I'll protect them," Lor said with a firm nod to Dad. "I'll make sure nothing happens to either of them. I promise you."

Mom and Dad exchanged a glance. I could understand why they didn't want us leaving, but this was the only opportunity to reunite our family for good.

I thought about offering my place on the *Sunrise* to one of them, but I needed to make sure Elysea arrived safely at Palindromena and Lor's friend performed the tether. I was the one who'd brought Elysea back to life; I needed to see this through to the end.

"If you promise," Mom said eventually. She stood, holding out her hand to Lor.

"I promise you," he said, "with my life."

When Lor put his hands in hers, Mom pulled him into a hug.

"Look after my girls."

CHAPTER FORTY-THREE

LOR

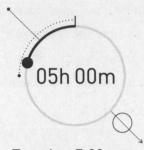

Tuesday, 7:00 a.m.

I WOULD FIX THIS. I would. I would do whatever it took to save Elysea. I had the power to undo one of my mother's mistakes.

Even with the lies, the heartbreak and a five-year separation, I could see what the Alerins were. And what they could be again. Seeing them together was like diving into salt water with an open wound. I had to mend it.

I had five hours left.

The Alerins made me realize that I'd never had what they had. My mother was different. She'd put her research above everyone else, myself included. In her effort to ensure no one else suffered from grief, she'd caused an insurmountable amount of suffering to innocent families. Today I would end all that.

Elysea and Tempest stood in their parents' embrace on the dock while I climbed aboard the boat. I glanced away as they whispered words of love and goodbyes—if things didn't go to plan.

I typed *Surf to Turf*'s signature into the *Sunrise*'s communication system and composed a message.

Where are you, Ray?

I held my breath and pressed send. I hoped he was on board.

I received a message almost instantly.

BUD! Where am I? his message read. Where are you? I thought you were dead!

Not yet, I replied. It wasn't funny, but Ray would appreciate my attempt at humor.

Did you find Elysea?

Yes. We'll be back at Palindromena at 11:00 a.m.

THAT'S CUTTING IT CLOSE, he wrote back.

I know. But I have an idea. I need you to meet me at the back entrance to the Aquarium around then. Bring the revival gear.

I'm afraid to ask why.

Then don't, I replied. Just be there, and make sure no one sees you.

I clicked off the messaging system.

Tempe detached herself from her parents first and made her way to the helm.

"Will Raylan be there?" she asked, her jaw set, eyes bright. She'd changed since I'd told her my plan. Something had shifted. For the first time in two years, I'd given her hope. And in turn, I'd given myself hope.

"Yes," I said.

"Then let's go."

Elysea wiped her eyes and reluctantly pulled away from her parents.

"Be safe, girls," Minda said, with a quick glance to me.

I gave Minda a nod.

She would see her daughters again.

<hr />

Tempe captained the boat for the first hour before going belowdecks for a nap. With the still wind, we were making good time across the Untied Sea. We were going to make it. I was sure of it.

I stood beside Elysea, keeping watch for any Remorans. We didn't speak. What was there to say?

The sun sat heavy on the horizon; it looked as though we were sailing straight into it.

I held my hand up against the glare.

"Go rest," Elysea said. "You look like—"

"Death?" I offered with a laugh.

Her lips curled into a smile. "Yes."

I let out a deep sigh. "Just half an hour."

She waved her hand at me. "*Go.*"

Tempe had curled herself into ball on the cabin floor, facing the wall. She murmured in her sleep, and rolled over.

I took a step back, stunned. She looked so different.

Her brow smooth and jaw relaxed. She looked younger. Happier.

She always looked as if she carried a storm with her. And she tore into a room as though she were a ravaging wind. But there was something raw about sleep, something revealing. Her angry mask was gone. I glanced away. It wasn't right for her to be lying vulnerable, not knowing I was there.

I lay on the opposite side of the boat, next to where I was once tied up, and stared at the ceiling. I hoped this would work, but if it didn't? What would I do then?

I pushed the thought away. I couldn't think like that. Not yet. We still had time to fix this mess. Ray would figure it out. He'd been studying revivals ever since he injured his foot. I had to trust that all this had happened for a reason. And it wasn't so Tempest could watch her sister die and then walk out of my life forever.

I also had to push thoughts of Tempest away. I couldn't think about how beautiful she was. How it hurt to see her cry. How thoughts of her filled my head more and more. This wouldn't do me any good.

I had to focus on getting Elysea a new tether.

For the first time in my life, I whispered words of prayer to the Gods below, not knowing if they existed, listened or cared. But wasn't that how everyone prayed? With faith that they weren't alone and no evidence to prove it?

"Don't let this end in death," I said. "Let her live. Ease their pain."

And though I heard no answers and saw no signs of the Gods below, a voice in the back of my mind reminded me that everything always ended in death.

CHAPTER FORTY-FOUR

TEMPEST

03h 00m

Tuesday, 9:00 a.m.

I WOKE to the vibrations of the *Sunrise* buzzing against my cheek. I hadn't meant to fall asleep, but the hum of the engine and emotional exhaustion had made me forget my excitement and apprehension.

Lor was sleeping on the other side of the cabin, his arm flung across his belly, his face tilted to the ceiling. His eyelids flittered.

I sat up and scrubbed my hands over my face. I hadn't been asleep long enough for salt to encrust my lids. I crept to Lor's side and checked his echolink.

9:00 a.m.

That left us two hours to get to Palindromena, and an hour to retether Elysea. I hoped putting my trust in Lor wasn't foolish.

Lor began twitching beside me, his arms jerking, his legs leaping.

"Calen!" he screamed, bolting upright, his hand reaching out for something that wasn't there.

I flinched backward. "Are you all right?"

Lor's chest was rising and falling rapidly. His focus bounced around the room as though he was reminding himself of his surroundings. "Yes."

Clearly, he wasn't. His blue eyes were haunted. By what?

"Who's Calen?" I asked, shuffling closer.

He covered his face with his hands. "My best friend."

"Your friend who died?" It seemed like weeks ago when we'd first talked about Lor's experience with a revival.

He nodded, hands still over his face, but his breathing was steadying.

"How did he die?" I asked.

He peered through his fingers. "We were climbing a cliff . . ." He let out a tortured sound and shook his head. "It's my fault he's dead."

"Do you want to talk about it?" I asked. "I know I'm not a trained Warden, but then again, neither are you."

He dropped his hands and grinned. "Thank you, Tempe."

"For what?"

"For being here," he said. "And for not hating me because of what my mother did to your family."

"You assume too much." But I said it lightly to show I was joking.

He grabbed my hand and squeezed it. "I'll do my best to save her, you know that, right?"

I could see by the intensity of his expression that he would. But that didn't mean his plan would work. If he failed, I knew Elysea would sacrifice herself.

I didn't want to have this conversation. I wanted to hang on to the hope that everything would be all right. "I should go check on Elysea."

"Stay for a moment." He pinned me with his gaze. "Please. I don't want to be left alone."

Something stabbed in between my ribs. "Neither do I," I whispered.

He rolled onto his back to face the ceiling, keeping my hand in his. "Tell me something." His voice broke. "Tell me something good."

"Good?"

"Something other than this place." He gestured to the cabin ceiling. "Something to make me—us—forget."

But there was nothing outside this place. Nothing other than water. It had been, and always would be, this way. Still, his gaze burned against the side of my face as I considered. What was good? What made me happy? And why had it been so long since I'd thought about that?

I'd been happy back at the Islands Cavalcade. I'd been happy in the short time I'd danced with Elysea. And even though there were tears, I'd been happy to see my parents. To be in my mom's embrace. But I couldn't talk about them now. It was too raw, knowing the four of us might never be together again.

So I said, "There's this place on the Equinox. A place where Elysea and I used to go when we were younger, when we wanted to escape everything. We first discovered it not long after my parents disappeared."

He closed his eyes. "Tell me."

I watched his blond lashes flick against his pale skin. "At night, we'd swim under the Equinox, holding our breath until it burned, until our arms and legs felt like jelly. We'd pretend we were colorful fish," I said, remembering the rainbow diving skin I used to love as a kid. "Only then did we surface. We'd climb back onto the Equinox and scale the side of the Conservator's hall up to the roof where the lightning rod is. It's the tallest point. From there you can see everything."

"Ah," he said in understanding. "You imagined what was beyond the Equinox."

"No."

A frown appeared between his brows. I'd never wanted to leave the Equinox. The Equinox was my home. It always would be. I wanted everything to go back to the way things were. I wanted my parents back. And Elysea. I wanted to return to the time when I was happy.

"Go on," he said.

I took a breath. "There's this amazing view from the rooftop." I closed my eyes and thought about all those times Elysea and I had climbed up there. "The Equinox is close to many sunken cities, and if you look down upon the ruins below and let your eyes blur, the ocean looks like the night sky, and the coral its stars. It's as though those cities aren't lost after all. As though there's life below. And it's breathtaking."

I felt Lor shift to sit up, his warmth pressing against me. I opened my eyes. He was watching me, a small smile on his face.

"What?" I made to snap, but it came out breathless.

He was so close, his blue eyes drew me in. Each ring was a different color, the darkest toward the center. I was held captive in his gaze. And that was exactly where I wanted to be.

"You see beauty in this sunken world," he said. I quirked an eyebrow, but he continued in a whisper. "You make this world beautiful."

My breath caught somewhere in my chest as his eyes flicked to my lips.

"No, I don't," I whispered back. "I mean, I don't believe this world is beautiful." Dark and deadly, yes, but not beautiful. Beauty was easy, peaceful, enchanting—something you longed for. That was not our world.

"You've lived much more than I have," he said, "than I ever will."

Was he talking about dying? Did he think he'd fail?

"Lor, I—"

But I didn't know what to say. I'd been cruel to him. I'd pushed him away. Called him a liar. And, in my worst moments, hoped he would die so Elysea could live. But he was looking at me as no one outside my family had ever looked at me. As though I mattered.

"It's okay," he said, his hand brushing the hair back from my face.

But it wasn't okay. If he failed, one of them would die. And I couldn't bear losing either of them.

"It will be okay," he said, inching toward me. "Maybe not all water witches are bad." He whispered the last part, as if to himself.

Water witches? But he said it as though it was a beautiful thing, and not something to fear.

He watched me closely, as if asking a question. *Can I?*

I was scared to say yes, but something deep within me, like the pull of a tide, drew me toward his anticipating lips.

My skin blistered at the touch of him. I wasn't sure who had ignited who. He tasted like the sea, smoke and brine.

His hands snaked up and into my hair. I breathed him in between kisses, needing him, needing this, needing life.

Then I remembered who he was and the hold he had on my sister and my future. I pulled myself free of his warmth and fled up the stairs, not looking back.

A lump formed in my throat as the island of Palindromena rose on the horizon.

We'd made it through the Untied Sea without running into Qera or her friends. Perhaps she was still trying to catch her boat. The thought made me smile.

The boat's clock showed we had an hour and fifteen minutes remaining.

What happened if Lor failed? While I'd only met him yesterday, he was a connection I'd made, all on my own. The first in my life. And when he looked at me, I felt alive. I didn't want to let go.

I'd always been difficult to get to know. I was uncertain and anxious, stuck in my own head, always worrying what people thought of me. I'd learned it was easier to keep people at a distance than try to befriend them and be rejected.

When my parents disappeared, I'd hardened my heart against everyone and everything—to survive. Everyone outside Elysea. I didn't want them to know the real me. The vulnerable me. Someone who couldn't lose another person they cared about. And then I lost Elysea.

Then why was it so different with Lor? Was it because I saw my grief reflected in him? Or because he didn't shy away from me? Or was it that he always seemed to want more time? With me.

Whatever it was, even in this most impossible of situations, I felt like I could breathe. I had hope. And that was because of him.

"Are you all right?" Elysea asked. Her shoulder brushed mine, and I forced myself not to lean into her warmth. How could she be asking about me at a time like this? I would be a shaking mess if I were her, and she was still, her body calm. Only her eyes were wide with concern, concern for me.

"I'm—" There wasn't an answer other than *I'm a mess*, but I didn't want to put that on her. "Fine."

"You don't have to pretend with me, Tempe," she said.

But I did. "We're almost there. Everything will be all right. Soon."

She gave me a small nod, but doubt clung to her like a storm cloud, darkening her expression.

"What will you do tomorrow?" I asked, trying to convince her that there would be one.

She turned from the island on the horizon toward the Equinox. Although we couldn't see it on the water, we could feel its pull. The lure of home. Of comfort. And happiness.

"What will *you* do?" she asked instead.

"Don't evade the question."

She tugged the ends of my long hair. "I'll be with you, silly."

I swallowed down my fear. "And what will *we* be doing?"

She smiled wider then. "Whatever you want."

"Ely, I love you." I gripped her hand in mine. "You know I do. But do you ever think you worry too much about me?"

"Too much?" She frowned. "You're my little sister."

"I *was*. I'm older than you now. I've lived two years alone, and I survived." She flinched at the reminder. "I want you to tell me what *you* want to do. I don't want you to only worry about me. I want you to live your second life. I want it to be all about what you want."

"If this works—" she began.

"It will," I interrupted. I couldn't think any other way right now.

Elysea sighed and sat down on the edge of the boat. I put the *Sunrise* into autopilot and sat beside her.

"I want my old life back," she said. "But I've been dead for two years; will people accept me?"

"Of course they will," I said. "We already saw that at the Spring Tide with Daon and Karnie. Everyone has missed you; they'll be thrilled to have you back in their lives."

"Poor Daon," she said. "I should've told him how I really felt before I died."

"You have to stop worrying about everyone else!" I grabbed her shoulders. I wanted to shake her. "You have to look after your own heart."

She touched her chest. That was the wrong thing to say.

But before I could correct my wording, she said, "I love Daon with all my heart, I do. But I love him as I love you. And that won't change. Not for him, or for anyone else." She smiled. "I see the way you and Lor look at each other, and it makes me realize I can't see myself feeling that way about anyone."

I wanted to deny how I felt about Lor, but I'd only be lying to my sister and myself. "That's okay, Ely. It's your life."

"I have you, Mom and Dad, my dancing, and Daon's friendship." She lifted her chin. "*That's* what I want."

I put my arm around her. "Everyone loves you, Ely. We've been broken without you. *When* you come back to the Equinox"—I raised my eyebrows to make the point that it was *when* and not *if*—"everyone will be thrilled to have you back. But you must put yourself first, for once. Let *me* take care of *you*." I pointed to her heart.

She looked up, tears in her eyes. "You've always taken care of me. I know you don't see it that way, but when Mom and Dad left, I needed you. You're my best friend, Tempe, and I never would've survived those years without you. Whatever happens next, please know that."

I opened my mouth to reply, but Lor appeared from below.

Elysea jumped up to the helm. "We're almost there," she said to him.

"Pull in around the back of the island," he said. "We don't want to be spotted entering the main harbor."

"There's another entrance?" I asked, taking my place beside my sister.

Lor avoided my eyes when he replied, "Through the caves. It's where the retrieval boats go when they've pulled a body from the water."

My stomach swirled. That was where Nessandra would've taken Elysea after she'd killed her.

Elysea followed Lor's instructions and steered the boat around a large boulder. Behind lay a narrow opening to a cave, which tunneled deep into the isle. An entrance hidden from the open ocean.

The *Sunrise* slipped into the crevasse like a fish darting between rocks. Elysea looked back at me with a tight smile. I knew what she was trying to say. *We'll be okay.* But I wasn't

356

sure what okay was anymore. Was it saving Elysea? Was it finding a new tether? Was it returning to Mom and Dad? Or the Equinox? Or was it seeing that look in Lor's eyes again, to feel his lips against mine?

What did I really want?

Time.

Why was there never enough to figure everything out?

Elysea flicked on the lights, illuminating the cave. The engine purred, echoing between the banks of the fissure. The rocky ceiling couldn't have been more than a few feet above the *Sunrise*'s mast. As the sides of the *Sunrise* were scratched and snagged, my chest tightened in sympathy.

When we reached a gray sandbank, Lor jumped from the boat and Elysea lowered the anchor.

"Let's go," he said, gesturing toward a door carved into the stone innards of the isle. He was rushing. He could feel death knocking at his door.

I clutched Elysea's hand, until I was sure both our knuckles had gone white.

"There won't be anyone else down here," he said, misjudging our hesitation. "The Aquarium was my post. My mother is used to me avoiding her. She won't be here." He glanced back to the door cut into the wall behind us. "I'll get us in and out without anyone knowing. Trust me."

That was the problem. I *did* trust Lor. But even if I did trust him, it didn't mean we would succeed.

CHAPTER FORTY-FIVE

LOR

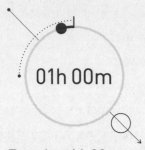

01h 00m

Tuesday, 11:00 a.m.

WE ONLY HAD an hour to find someone to tether with Elysea. Even without looking at the echolink's screen, I could feel the time ticking down. Each heartbeat was a second lost.

I could no longer look Tempe in the eye. I didn't want her to see I was scared. Not of dying. I knew death all too well. I'd grown up around it. Some people had friends and family. I had my mother and the dead.

But I was scared *for* her and what would happen if I failed.

As we stepped through the door from the cave and into the Aquarium, I wanted to turn back. I hated this place now more than ever. I knew now what I had to do. Once Elysea was re-tethered to a Lifer, I would end the revival program for good.

"Cursed waters," Tempe whispered. "What is this forsaken place?"

The tanks glowed in the low light, illuminating the bodies. It was dehumanizing. How did I ever spend a second down here, let alone two years? How did I ever consider this a life?

"This is where we store the dead." I cleared my throat. "I mean, this is where we keep the patients before they're revived."

Elysea's eyes were round like moons. "*I* was down here?"

I nodded, but couldn't speak. I wouldn't return her to this place. And I wouldn't return myself.

I wanted more. I wanted the world outside, I wanted to learn to sail, to climb cliffs on other islands and continue to get to know the Alerin sisters. I wanted Tempe to look at me the way she had when I'd kissed her.

She wanted more from this life, too. I was sure of it. And I wanted to be a part of that life. I wanted to give her more.

And I wanted a life of my own. I wanted for Ray to know everything. I wanted to be the friend to him that I hadn't been to Calen. I had to be alive to do that.

"Do they stay down here forever?" Elysea asked. Her hands were shaking.

"No," I said, finally finding my voice. "We keep the bodies for ten years, and if no one comes to revive them, then they are buried in the temple below the ocean, or . . ." But I didn't want to talk about the furnace. That was where Elysea would go if we failed.

"Let's keep moving," I said instead. We didn't have time to discuss the proper ways of dealing with the dead.

"Where?" Tempe asked.

"We need to find a suitable tether," I replied.

"What makes a good tether?" Elysea asked, skimming her

hand along the sides of a tank. The girl inside had her face to the ceiling as though she were deep in thought.

"Someone who's a similar age," I said. "Relatives are also good tethers, as they usually have a similar pulse, which is easy to tether to."

"That's why you were chosen as my Warden," Elysea said. "Because we're a similar age."

"And that's why I could cover for Ray; he's only a year younger than me," I said. "Follow me."

I opened the door to the room at the back of the Aquarium where the Lifers were kept. There were only four tanks. Four people. There were two elderly men and a younger man and woman. Their tanks were side by side, their fingertips floated out toward the glass, as if they were reaching for one another.

Elysea watched their faces with sad eyes. "What happened to them?"

I pressed a screen below the tank of the younger man.

"*Boat crash. Serious head injuries,*" I read from the words that had appeared. "*Heartbeat irregular and unstable.*" That wasn't going to work.

"What about her?" Elysea asked, her hand pressed against a tank.

The woman wasn't much older than Elysea.

As I moved toward the tank, my chest tightened and my vision dimmed. I fell to my knees. Elysea collapsed alongside me.

"Ely!" Tempest cried. She propped her sister up under her shoulder.

Elysea opened her eyes. "I'm okay," she said weakly.

"What's happening, Lor?" Tempest asked.

"I don't know." I brought my heavy arm up to look at my echo. Both blue circles were fading. If Elysea were in the recovery room like she was supposed to be, she'd soon be taken away and her heart stopped. "We should still have over forty minutes."

Something else snagged in my chest, and it wasn't my heart. It was Tempest's expression. She was worried *for* me.

Where was Ray? Had the scientists already discovered Elysea missing and detained him? I couldn't do this alone.

I pulled myself up to read the notes on the tank.

"*Drowned,*" I read. "*Heartbeat steady but patient won't regain consciousness.*"

This could be it!

I pressed my forehead against the glass. "Please," I whispered. "Please work."

"Lor?" Tempe asked, her voice unsteady, soft.

I tried to nod, but my head felt too heavy.

I couldn't let them down . . . I would try to . . .

"Lor!" someone shouted.

Raylan.

But before I could reply, a cry croaked out of my throat. I slid down, my legs collapsing underneath me.

My head fell back, hitting the floor with a whack.

CHAPTER FORTY-SIX

TEMPEST

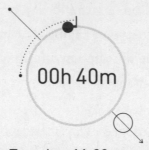

00h 40m

Tuesday, 11:20 a.m.

MY HEART SQUEEZED as Lor fell. The other boy, who I'd last seen on the Equinox, rushed to his side. This had to be Raylan. He threw a medical bag to the floor and lifted Lor by the shoulders to sit him upright.

"Is he dead?" he asked me.

"I don't know! It's only eleven twenty. We're supposed to have forty minutes left."

"Shit, shit, shit, shit," Raylan said, pulling at Lor's arm to read his echolink. "His heartbeat is fading."

"What?" I asked. "Why?"

Raylan shook his head. "I don't know. It must have something to do with Lor's heart."

But Lor's heartbeat was what kept Elysea alive. That would mean—

"Tempe," Elysea called softly, her head in her hands.

"Are you okay?" I asked.

She pulled her hands away, and I gasped.

Water leaked from her eyes, nose and mouth. There was no ignoring the smell. Salt.

"What's happening?" I asked Raylan.

"Her lungs are returning to their previous damaged state," Raylan said. "She'll die the way she previously did. She'll drown. But this shouldn't be happening so soon. We should've had more time."

Elysea collapsed to the floor with a sigh.

I crouched next to her, pulling her head onto my lap. Her lungs sounded waterlogged as she struggled for breath.

Oh Gods. Oh Gods. She's dying. She's going to die in my arms.

"We're supposed to have forty minutes left!" I wasn't sure who I was yelling at. I wasn't ready. I'd never be ready.

Lor groaned. His eyes flicked open. "What happened?" he mumbled.

Raylan checked Lor's echo again. "Your heartbeat is fading. We can't keep you two tethered. We need to get your mother. She'll know what to do."

Lor clutched at Raylan's shirt to sit more upright. "No. She can't know."

"It's your funeral." Raylan grimaced. "Sorry, poor choice of words."

I brushed Elysea's braids back from her face as she coughed up seawater. "It's going to be okay, Ely. Hang in there."

"I have an idea," Lor said softly. Raylan leaned down to catch his words. "You need to retether Elysea to a new pulse." He pointed a shaking finger to the young woman in the tank.

"To her. Before Elysea's heart stops. Or mine does." He gave him a wry smile.

"No," Raylan said. "That's too dangerous. I'm not trained for this. I'm not a scientist!" He scrubbed his hands over his cropped hair. "Anyway, they're about to realize something's wrong when they don't find Elysea in her room. It's over, bud. Let me take the fall. Let me get your mother. Please."

"No." Lor gripped his friend's hand in his. "I trust you. You got this."

Raylan stared at Lor for a moment before turning to me. "You," he snapped. "Help me get that lady over here, and I'll set up the tether on a new echo."

"Go," Elysea croaked, pushing me away. "Help him."

I had to climb into the tank to pull the woman from the water. It was freezing. I didn't want to touch her; it didn't seem right. But with Elysea coughing up foamy seawater, and Lor barely conscious, I didn't have a choice.

"Lift her over the edge," Raylan said, leaning down into the tank.

I maneuvered the woman to her feet, the water making her buoyant, then lifted her arms up so Raylan could help pull her over the other side. He placed her on a gurney and wheeled her toward his bag. Inside were numerous echolinks. He pulled one out and began programming it, his fingers moving swiftly across the screen. He then snapped the echolink onto the woman's wrist. A blue circle appeared.

"I'm synced into her pulse," Raylan said. "But we have to be quick. The crushed coral in the tank was keeping her alive, and she won't last long outside the water."

"I hope you know what you're doing," I muttered.

"Me too. Me too." He pointed to Elysea. "Now bring your sister over here."

I knelt down to lift Elysea from the ground. My feet slipped on the water around her. I crashed to the floor. Raylan appeared at my side and helped me drag Elysea over to Lor.

I cradled her face in my hands. Her eyes flicked open.

"My heart . . ." she said faintly, hand flapping at her chest.

"I know, I know." I willed myself not to cry. "We're figuring it out. Just hold on, okay?"

I wished I could give her my strength. My heartbeat.

Raylan helped Lor sit up against the back of one of the tanks, then pressed something on Lor's echo. "Thirty minutes left!" His voice wobbled on the announcement.

This was it. This was the moment. We either said goodbye or this ridiculous plan worked.

Elysea stirred against me. "I'm so sorry, Tempe," she said.

I squeezed her hand. "Sorry for what?"

"For leaving you, again." She gave me a sad smile. At first, I worried seawater was again leaking from her eyes, but no, they were tears.

"Don't be silly—you're going to be fine. Everything is going to be fine."

And yet everything about this was wrong. We were dealing with things beyond our control, which *should* have been beyond our control. But no one hesitated. If someone gave you the key to life, how did you turn it away? And this wasn't just anyone. This was my sister.

I hoped the Gods below would forgive us for meddling in their business. I prayed they would let my sister live.

Raylan placed an echolink on Elysea's wrist, over where the plate had been hidden under her skin. A faint blue circle appeared on the screen. Her pulse *and* Lor's. He then threaded a cord from Elysea's echolink to the woman's on the gurney beside us.

"Step away," he said to me. "I don't want to confuse the sensors with whose pulse we're trying to sync to."

I kissed Elysea on the cheek, then stood back. Lor's blue eyes caught mine. He gave me a tight smile. He was looking better than Elysea. It was clear now who was going to survive. And he knew it.

I closed my eyes and let out a deep breath. I had to believe this would work. I *had* to.

"I'm ready," said Raylan, picking up the woman's wrist. "I'll start the tethering process to this lady. Lor, stay with me, bud."

But Lor didn't reply. Both he and Elysea went slack.

"Ely!" I reached for her.

"Don't touch her!" Raylan cried. "Unless you want to lose your life instead."

I watched her eyelids flicker. Before I could ask what had happened, a shriek echoed through the room.

Beside us, the woman on the gurney had jolted upright. Her eyes open. Her mouth, midscream.

She was alive.

"No!" I shouted, seeing both Lor and Elysea lifeless, while the woman thrashed and wailed.

"Stop, stop, stop," the woman said, pulling at the echolink on her wrist. "Please stop." She tried to climb off the gurney but slid to the ground.

How long had it been since she'd used her muscles? Years?

She pushed herself up and crawled toward us. Raylan ran over to her, and pulled the echolink off her arm. Her eyes closed, and she became still once more. But her chest rose and fell. She was well and truly alive now.

"What did you do?" I scrambled over to Raylan. He was studying the woman's echolink.

"I don't know," he muttered.

"You clearly did it wrong."

"No," he protested. "I didn't."

"She's not brain-dead!" I pointed to the woman slumped on the ground. "We can't steal her pulse; we can't stop her heart."

"I need to get Nessandra," he said. "The protein in the coral must've sufficiently healed the damage to the lady's brain. That's why she's recovered. Nessandra's the only one who can help us."

"No," I said.

367

Nessandra had tried to kill my father. She'd killed my sister. She'd never help us.

"What other choice do we have?" Raylan's eyes filled with tears. It was clear how much Raylan cared about Lor. "It's the only way to save them both."

When I didn't reply, he said, "Once the scientists find Elysea's recovery room empty, they'll lock the facility down and we'll lose any chance of fixing this. We need Nessandra. Now!"

"All right," I said. "I'll get her. You make sure these two are still alive when I get back."

"Hurry. You have fifteen minutes!"

Upstairs, a normal day at Palindromena was underway. The sunlight pricked my eyes, in contrast to the darkness of the Aquarium below.

The tree in the middle of the foyer glowed in the sunlight. How could everyone walk around like nothing was wrong when they played with life and death every day?

Like on the Islands Cavalcade, I didn't have time to search for Nessandra. She would have to come to me.

I rushed to the black-bark tree and clambered up its branches.

"Hey!" someone said from underneath me. It was a security guard.

In seconds, I amassed quite a crowd.

"Get me Nessandra!" I yelled from atop the tree, staying clear of the security's batons. "Tell her it's about her son, Lor."

"Get down," the security guard growled at me.

"Not until you get Nessandra."

"Now, now," a calm voice came from behind me. I swiveled to see we'd been joined by the Director. The Queen of Death herself. "There's no need to make a scene, Tempest. I'm here now. Why don't you come down and tell me what the problem is?"

Looking at her, it was hard to imagine she'd killed my sister and driven my parents away. She looked so put-together, so friendly, so understanding.

A million secrets were hidden behind that smile.

I wanted to slap it off her face.

"It's about your son," I said, refusing to budge until she knew the severity of the situation. If I came down now, security might throw me out before I had a chance to speak. "Lor is dying."

An odd expression crossed her face. "I think you're confused," she said, holding out a perfectly manicured hand. "Come down before you hurt yourself."

"Not until you come and help Lor."

"I'm afraid that's not possible," Nessandra said with a glance to the crowd listening in around us. "My son is dead. He has been for over two years."

I nearly fell out of the tree.

CHAPTER FORTY-SEVEN

LOR

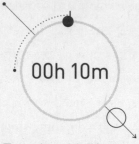

00h 10m

Tuesday, 11:50 a.m.

I WOKE to Ray's worried face peering down at me. I sat upright.

"How are you feeling, Lor?"

"I'm fine. Is it done?" I asked.

Ray glanced away. I looked beside me. Elysea was slumped over.

Shit. Had we failed?

Ray shook his head. "I couldn't work out the retethering. And that lady"—he gestured to the woman we'd selected from the Lifers—"is not brain-dead. In fact, she's got quite a good pair of lungs on her and isn't afraid to use them."

The woman was now sitting in a wheelchair, her head drooped to her chest.

"I gave her a sedative," Ray explained. "She was going to hurt herself. The good news is that she's alive and she'll be staying that way. But that's the only good news I've got."

"What are you saying?" I asked. Was it all over? "Where's Tempest?"

Something hot curled in my stomach. Fear.

"You have ten minutes left. Actually"—he jerked his chin to Elysea—"*she* has ten minutes. Your vitals are much stronger." He pointed to the blue circle on my echo. "You've won."

"Fuck."

"Yeah." He ran a hand down his face. I'd never seen him look so worried. "I'm so sorry, Lor. I know you didn't want her to suffer. But you have to remember, it's your heartbeat, after all. She was just hitching a ride."

"And Tempest?" I couldn't imagine she'd leave her sister alone, with only minutes to go.

He gave me a sheepish grin. "We needed some help."

"What are you talking about?"

He didn't have to answer. My mother stormed into the room, Tempe following close behind.

"Lor!" my mother cried, running toward me. She wrapped her arms around me. "What did you think you were doing? Tethering with someone! How could you risk your second chance?"

"Second chance?" Ray frowned. "What is she talking about?"

"Lor is dead," Tempe said. "Or at least, that's what everyone is supposed to think. He died two years ago while climbing with friends. His best friend, Calen, was used as a tether to bring him back. Nessandra couldn't say goodbye to her son, and she killed Calen so Lor could live on. Am I missing anything, Lor?"

Her walls were back up. All the warmth and softness I'd seen in her, gone.

"I'm sorry." I glanced at Ray. "I wanted to tell you—"

"*That's* why you hide out down here?" His eyebrows were high. "You're supposed to be dead?"

I nodded. "Both Calen and I fell from the cliff and into the water that day, but only Calen survived. Our friends brought us to my mother for help. But she revived me with Calen's pulse and then killed Calen."

"That's why this"—my mother gestured between me and Elysea—"was flawed from the start. Lor's heartbeat is weaker because he was once revived. I'm surprised both of them made it this far."

"I can't believe it," Ray said. "I knew you were hiding something, but this? Why in cursed waters didn't you tell me? I never would've asked you to cover for me!"

"I'm sorry, Ray! I wanted to tell you, but I didn't know how." I buried my head in my hands. "I stole my best friend's life and I've been hiding out down here so that no one would recognize me; my friends saw *me* die, not Calen. If I was walking around like nothing happened, then they'd know what I'd done."

My mother sighed. "What *I* did, Lor. Is that why you agreed to all this?" She gestured to an unconscious Elysea. "As some sort of punishment? It was my decision to bring you back. *I* decided to stop Calen's heart. It's been two years; when will you let it go?"

I wished I could wash away my culpability so easily. But I couldn't. I had to face what I'd done. For once.

"No, Mom." My eyes filled with tears. "When I woke up, I knew what you were planning to do. I saw it in your eyes. Your determination. And I saw the fear in Calen's. We *both* knew." I rubbed my running nose with the back of my hand. "I didn't stop you. And when you told Calen's mother that he later died from complications of near drowning, I didn't correct you. I just hid from the world." From everything.

After my revival, I'd refused to speak to my mother. She had planned to invent a story about a new procedure that had brought me back, a few months after Calen's death, so no one would make the connection. But I'd refused.

Initially I stayed down in the Aquarium so no one would realize what had happened with Calen, but after a while, I didn't *want* to leave. I didn't deserve to.

"All this doesn't matter right now," my mother said, reaching for my hand, my echo. "We need to make sure you live."

"You killed Elysea!" Tempe roared. "You're not touching her again!"

Nessandra shook her head. "You don't know what you're talking about."

"I saw my parents," she said. "They told me the truth!"

Nessandra shook her head again. "It was an accident. I just wanted to scare your parents away. Your sister wasn't meant to die. I'm not that cruel. Lor, tell them."

But I wouldn't justify my mother's actions any longer. "We don't have time for this!"

"We can't use the other lady," Ray interrupted, exhaustion lining his voice. "I tried to connect Elysea's pulse to hers, and she woke up. There's nothing we can do without another tether."

Tempe whirled around on him. "So we let my sister die?"

"She was already dead," Nessandra said. "This is the way it's supposed to be. The way it has been at Palindromena for fifty years."

"Are you serious?" Anger flared red on Tempe's cheeks. "Lor was dead, and look at him now! You broke the rules for your own family. Why can't we do the same for mine? You owe me that! After everything you did to my parents. After everything you did to my sister—accident or not. You ruined my life! Fix it *now*!"

My heart shuddered at her words.

My mother's expression, however, didn't shift. She was used to being calm under pressure. "There's nothing that can be done. I'm sorry, but I'm telling you the truth."

I pulled myself to stand and took a cautious step toward Tempe. The more time went on, the stronger I became. Elysea would be dead in minutes.

I never wanted this. I'd wanted to protect Tempe from the grief I'd felt over Calen's death.

"I'm so sorry, Tempe," I said.

She shook her head. "No, no. I don't want anyone's apologies. I want a solution." The anger from her voice had cooled. Her shoulders curled inward, protecting herself.

I wanted to hold her, just for a minute. But I didn't think she'd let me. I placed my hand on her elbow instead. "I wish there was one."

Tempe met each of our eyes. No one said anything. "Why are you all looking at me! Do something! Anything!"

My echolink buzzed against my skin.

Five minutes remaining.

"You killed my sister!" Tempe said, rushing toward my mother.

My mother took a step back, hands in the air. "I did what was necessary to protect Palindromena. To protect the future of our society. One life for hundreds of thousands. It isn't a question."

But we'd seen a different way of life on the Islands Cavalcade. We didn't have to abuse the dead to keep on living. Couldn't my mother see she had lost her humanity in this futile attempt to thwart death and grief?

Tempe's shoulders began to shake.

"There are five minutes left, Tempe," I said, not wanting to speak this truth. "You should say goodbye while you still can."

Tempe slumped next to her sister and lifted her face. "She's unconscious," she said. "I can't even do that."

"She's not gone yet," I said. "She can hear you."

Tempe clasped her sister's hand in hers. "Ely, you're the one person who made my life make sense. I was always a fish out of water"—a soft smile played at her lips—"but with you next to me, I was never alone." Tears rolled down her cheeks, but she didn't brush them away. "I will miss you forever, but I promise to do better. I promise to live my life the way I should have when you died two years ago. Without fear, without anger and without regret. Because that's who you taught me to be, and being anything less would be an insult to your memory. You will forever be a part of me. Guiding me. You will always be my coral pathway, leading me through the dark."

My throat closed and my breath shattered.

Tempe was right. Not making the most of our lives was an insult to the departed.

I'd taken Calen's life and I'd squandered it. I thought I was doing the right thing by not being out in the world, but I should've made the most of that time. For him. Because he couldn't.

The minutes continued counting down on my wrist. This was it.

I crouched behind Tempe and placed my hand on her shoulder, ready to be rebuffed, but she didn't shrug me off.

"I didn't know your sister for long, but she was one of the most generous and caring people I've ever met. She loved you so much, and I'm sure, if she could, she would want you to know that."

"Thank you," she said, and then she turned to press her face into my shoulder and cry.

I held her, hoping I could bring some comfort.

I'd never known a love like Tempe had for her sister and her parents. My mother loved in a confused and twisted way. A possessive way. Her grief was selfish. She couldn't let me go the day I died.

But I wouldn't be selfish. Not anymore.

While I'd never known a love like the Alerin sisters', I could imagine it. I could imagine living on the Equinox and attending the Spring Tide with Ray and watching Elysea dance. I could imagine holding Tempe close, as we *not* danced to the music together at the Islands Cavalcade. I could imagine the heat of the pyre reflected in her eyes, and in my heart.

And yet, I could never be anyone but the boy who had drowned and stolen someone else's life. I'd had my chance to live, and I'd been reckless. And Calen had paid the price.

It was time to make it right.

Elysea could offer the world far more than I could. She could truly live her life. Live without remorse. Be with her friends and family. She had shown me that in this past twenty-four hours. Out of the two of us, *she* deserved to live.

"I'm so glad I met you, my beautiful water witch," I whispered against Tempe's hair. "I wish we had a thousand tomorrows together. I wish we didn't have to say goodbye."

She pulled back, her eyes red and concerned. "What are you talking about?"

I wiped the tears from her cheeks. "I'm going to do the

right thing." I would fix my mother's mistake. "Be happy, Tempe."

I glanced over my shoulder at Ray and my mother. "I've been living on borrowed time," I said. "And it's time to give it back."

As the last second counted down, I pressed the blue circle on my echo.

Stop heartbeat? the screen asked.

I let out a long breath, thinking of all the tomorrows I'd never have, and clicked *yes*.

CHAPTER FORTY-EIGHT

TEMPEST

00h 00m

Tuesday, noon

AN ALARM SOUNDED on Lor's echolink, and he collapsed against me.

"Lor?" I asked. "Lor! Oh, no, no, no, no."

Please no. Please don't let him be dead.

"Lor!" Nessandra cried. She pulled him off me and shook his shoulders. But he didn't move. He didn't blink. He didn't breathe.

Nessandra removed the echolink, leaving behind two small holes in his skin. She pressed her fingers to his wrist.

"Lor," she said again, this time more to herself. "He's gone."

I slumped forward, my hands crushed to my chest. I couldn't breathe.

Raylan approached with heavy steps. "Why would he do that?" he asked, his voice like gravel.

Nessandra twisted to look at me, pure hatred on her face. "You did this to my boy."

I crossed my arms to try to stop shaking. "I never forced him or even asked for his life for Elysea's." I had wanted to in the beginning, but couldn't.

Why would Lor do this? He'd been down here in this kind of purgatory, not living his life for the past two years. He deserved to live.

"What's happened?" Elysea asked. She blinked at us, the color returning to her face.

Even though I was heartsick over Lor and felt like I might be ill, I threw myself at her, wrapping my arms around her. She was alive. She would *stay* alive.

Lor had kept his promise in the end.

Nessandra wailed as she cradled Lor's head in her lap. His eyes stared upward. Seeing nothing.

I turned away, tears rolling down my face. I could see from Elysea's expression that she understood. She pressed her face into my neck.

"Why, Lor?" she whispered.

For us, I thought. *For us.*

She didn't raise her head. I felt the sprinkling of her tears as they hit my skin.

I wished I could block out Nessandra's cries, but I couldn't. And I shouldn't. Lor deserved our grief. He had died so Elysea could live.

Eventually, I pulled away from Elysea. We needed to get out of here. We needed to get away from Nessandra. This entire place was cursed.

I helped Elysea to her feet.

"Are you ready to go home?" I asked her.

She nodded, but Nessandra said, "She's dead. You can't return to the Equinox."

Nessandra wasn't looking at us, her focus on her son. I glanced away, unable to look at his glassy eyes and pallid skin. I wanted to remember him as he was.

"We're going back to our parents," I said, not telling her where they were. "We're heading far away from here."

Nessandra shook her head and looked up. Her mascara was running tracks down her cheeks. "You're not leaving."

"Nessandra," Raylan begged, his voice clogged from tears. "Let them go. There's been enough sadness today. Enough death."

"No." She shook her head again. "Not until you do something for me. For Lor."

I hesitated. Was this a trick? "Do what?"

"You need to save him." Her voice went from hard to pleading. "Please. Please save him."

"There's nothing we can do," Raylan said, his hand hovering near Nessandra's shoulder. "You've always said a person can't be revived twice."

"That's right," she replied. "The heart can't take it. We've tried to tether to another Warden, but the heart doesn't restart. It won't resync."

My chest grew tight. Why was she saying this? How did this help?

"But it's a fault of the heart, not the technology," she said defensively. "If the heart was stronger—or if it had never been used in a revival, then it wouldn't be a problem." She gasped, her hand at her chest.

"What is it?" Raylan asked.

Her eyes glimmered, a smile bloomed on her face. "If Lor had a different heart, then we could revive him."

I stepped in front of Elysea. "What are you suggesting?"

She waved me away. "I'm not going to hurt your sister. But we need a new heart. One that hasn't been revived before."

"No," I said. "Lor wouldn't want someone else sacrificing their life for his."

When would this agony end? This cycle of death.

Nessandra's narrowed her eyes at me. "You've known my son for a day. You don't know how he really feels. He was confused. He wanted to help you." She looked down at Lor's motionless form, brushing his hair back from his forehead. "But he wants to live more. He deserves to."

"And who will give up their life this time?" I asked. "Whose heart will you take?"

That was what it always came down to. A life for a life. Elysea was right. Who were we to decide who lived and who died? But that was what Palindromena had been doing for decades. They'd been playing God. It was time for it to end.

"Mine," Nessandra said. "*I* will sacrifice my life. I will donate my heart to my son."

I sucked in a breath. I would've doubted her, but there was no denying the love she had for Lor. Even if her way of loving was different from mine, it was clear from the way she looked at him that she would do anything to bring him back. But no one was asking the question of whether we *should*.

"This is absurd," I said. "Death isn't a game!"

"A game?" Nessandra's eyes bored into mine with such ferocity that I flinched. "My child, my *only* child, the only person I have in this entire sodden world is gone. Because of you. Because you decided to bring your sister back. You played the game first, Tempest. And now you're telling me to give up on him?"

"I want Lor to live," I said, avoiding looking at his prone form, "but we can't kill you, Nessandra." Even if she did deserve it. "It's not right."

"A mother should never outlive her child," she said softly.

We stood quietly, unsure what to say. How did you respond to someone who was willing to give up their life?

Raylan was the first person to break the stunned silence. "From what I've learned about the heart," he said, "it won't start beating on its own. Once transplanted, we'll need to somehow restart it. We still need some kind of bypass."

"Yes," Nessandra said, pleased that he was indulging her. "We'll need a form of electric shock to get his new heart to start."

"You mean we need another tether?" Raylan asked.

"Not necessarily," Nessandra said. "Not if we can jump-start his new heart with a rhythm that's familiar to both the heart and the body."

"How do we do that?" Ray asked. "Lor's pulse is gone."

"Yes." Nessandra nodded sagely. "But not entirely."

"What are you talking about?"

"Calen," she said. "He used to be tethered to Lor via his echolink. Echos work on electricity generated by the heart and can hold a charge long after the person dies or is untethered. Calen's echo will still have Lor's pulse in its memory, which we can use to generate an electric shock to restart Lor's new heart with its old rhythm. The chance that his body accepts the transplanted organ will then be infinitely improved."

"I'm not a surgeon," Raylan said. "I can't do this." And it was clear from his expression that even if he was qualified, he didn't want to.

"I understand," she said. "We have many scientists here familiar with the heart. I'll arrange the operation." But was she telling the truth about sacrificing herself? Could we trust her not to turn on us? On Elysea?

I looked at my sister, but she didn't reply. Her eyes were focused on Lor. His lips were turning blue. A sob bubbled up from my chest, desperate to break free.

But I wouldn't let it. Just like I'd been strong for Elysea, I would be strong for Lor.

Elysea reached out and gave my hand a squeeze. We were

still in this together. Now we had to save Lor, as he'd saved us.

"Okay," Raylan said. "Where's the echo? I'll run the tethering process now."

Nessandra hung her head, her short blond hair falling across her face. Her shoulders started to shake. At first, I thought she was crying. Did she know how ludicrous this plan sounded? But then I realized.

She was laughing.

"Nothing is ever easy in this world," she said, looking up from Lor's body to Raylan. "The echolink was buried with Calen so no one would find out what happened with Lor."

"Buried?" I repeated.

She looked at me. "In the burial temple. Under five thousand feet of water."

She was right. Nothing in this sodden world was ever easy.

CHAPTER FORTY-NINE

TEMPEST

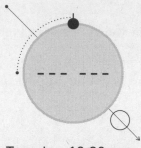

Tuesday, 12:30 p.m.

AFTER WE'D PUT Lor into a tank for preservation, Nessandra led the way through a series of corridors burrowed beneath the island. I focused on the roar of the waves thundering against the cliffs to distract myself from the image of Lor's lifeless body now housed in the place he'd longed to break free of.

Nessandra unlocked a rusted metal doorway and ushered us through. I knew Mom and Dad would hate that we were trusting Nessandra, but it was worth the chance to save Lor. Although I hadn't known him long, I wanted more for him.

Elysea, Raylan and I entered a dome-shaped room with diving equipment lining the walls. In the middle of the floor was an opening to the dark waters below.

"The entrance to the temple?" I asked.

"If you swim directly down, you'll find it," Nessandra said with a nod toward the opening.

"Swim?" Raylan asked. He looked unnerved. "Isn't there some kind of machinery to deliver the dead?"

Nessandra looked at him. Her pale cheeks were red from crying. "We usually have to swim down with a coffin. You're lucky you don't have to do that," she said harshly. She pointed to the diving gear. "You'll find everything you need there."

"Why don't you go?" I asked. "You know where Calen is buried. Wouldn't it be quicker?" Could we really trust her? After everything she'd done? What if she sealed the entrance, locking us and the secret to Palindromena below?

"I can't swim," she replied.

"You're joking." Our world was almost entirely made of water. Everyone needed to know how to swim.

"I've lived on the island all my life," she said with a small shrug. "My parents warned me away from the water. It's a dangerous place."

"And you decided to make it worse?" I let out a harsh laugh. "Pulling people from the water who could've been resuscitated to use for your experiments? What if that had been Lor out there on the ocean?"

She turned away from me. "Swim straight down, and you'll find the temple."

Elysea touched my shoulder. "Come on, Tempe. We have to do this." She stepped into a black diving skin from the collection hanging on the wall.

"Where is Calen buried?" I asked, pulling on metal flippers. Unlike Mom's old ones, these were made from cut metal, not blunted knifes.

"In an unmarked grave," Nessandra said. She passed me a breather. "I buried him to recognize his sacrifice for my son, but I didn't want the grave marked in case his mother ever asked for an autopsy. I'm not exactly sure where he'll be, as I didn't transport him myself."

I nearly asked her how many unmarked graves there would be. Who else had she hidden down there? I bit my tongue. Nessandra was willing to give her heart to her son. We needed her on our side.

I dangled my legs in the water. I could feel the slight chill through my diving skin. Elysea sat beside me.

"Are you sure you want to do this?" I asked her. "I can go alone."

"I'm not leaving you," she said. "Never again."

I squeezed her hand. "Never," I agreed.

"I'm coming too."

I turned to find Raylan pulling on metal flippers and grabbing another breather. He wore an echolink on his wrist. "It will help us keep track of time," he said to my quizzical expression. After today, I never wanted to see one of those things again.

"Is that a good idea?" Nessandra asked. "You haven't been in the water since—"

"I'm going," he said, cutting her off. "Lor's in this mess because of me. He took my shift so I could go to the Equinox and see a doctor about my foot. He needs my help."

Nessandra patted Raylan on the shoulder. "Thank you, Ray. There's an audio link in the diving hood so we can all stay in contact. You'll have two hours of oxygen. Don't waste it."

Elysea's brows pinched together. "I'm so sick of count-downs."

I gave her a sad smile. From the moment we were born, time was our master.

"Just a little longer," I said. Then the rest of our lives could continue.

Nessandra passed each of us a flashlight. "It's dark down there," she said. Something about her expression made me think she wasn't talking about the lack of light. "There's no coral."

I pulled some iridescent blue stones from my oilskin bag. I shook them in my hand.

"You still do that?" Elysea asked with a smile.

"Of course." It wasn't a childish ritual to me. I was showing my respect to the water, the Gods, and whatever lay in wait beneath the surface.

I nodded to Elysea. We could do this.

I let the stones fall.

One last dive.

CHAPTER FIFTY

TEMPEST

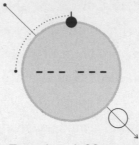

Tuesday, 1:00 p.m.

ALTHOUGH IT HAD only been just over a day since I was last in the ocean, it felt like an eternity. It had been the longest time between dives since I was twelve years old, when my parents disappeared and Elysea and I were tasked with earning Notes.

I let the oxygen fill my lungs and the weight of the water soothe my mind.

Lor wasn't lost to us yet.

Our weighted flippers eased us down toward the ocean floor.

"Are you all right, Elysea?" I asked, speaking around the breather in my mouth.

"Yes," she said. "Just keep swimming."

"Raylan?" I asked, swinging the flashlight in his direction.

He was working one leg more than the other, trying to balance himself as we fell.

"I'm fine," he huffed.

I wished I knew what had happened to him, but now wasn't the time to ask.

We continued our descent in silence, our flashlights lighting only a few yards ahead. According to Nessandra, it would take us around thirty minutes to reach the bottom. We'd then use the remaining air for the return trip. She said we wouldn't need to use any oxygen while in the temple. It didn't make sense, but I told myself to trust her. For Lor's sake.

We fell and fell and fell.

Then our feet hit something solid. A plume of sand billowed up around us, blocking our view. When it settled, Elysea let out a gasp.

"The temple," she said.

Our flashlights bounced around the large structure, lighting elements in sections.

Marble pillars. A tiered, sloping roof. Carvings of the Old World engraved onto a golden door. A forest of trees. A mountain. A horned beast.

Everything we'd lost.

The temple reminded me of my dream of the Gods below. But there was no coral to light the way, as though the Gods had forsaken this place. And anything to do with Palindromena, despite what the facility claimed.

We swam across the ocean floor, my breaths coming quicker and quicker as we approached the entrance.

"How do we open the door?" Raylan asked.

For a moment, I thought he was asking me, then a voice crackled in our domes.

"There's a square on the left side of the door," Nessandra said.

"There." Elysea pointed to a glass panel on the shell-colored marble walls.

Raylan pressed it, and the golden doors opened. We tumbled forward as the water sucked us into a room. The doors automatically closed behind us and the water began to drain through a vent in the wall. Once it was only a puddle on the floor, we pulled off our domes and breathers. I folded up my dome and attached it to my diving belt.

Raylan removed his flippers, revealing an angry and swollen foot. His face had turn ashen, like driftwood on the ocean.

"Are you going to be okay?" Elysea asked. She knelt down to have a look, but he stomped toward a second set of doors.

He tapped his wrist. "It's one thirty. Let's find Calen."

Inside, the temple was musty but dry.

From what we could see with our flashlights, the building was one large room with an arched ceiling. Rows and rows of stone coffins lined the floor and walls and were stacked on shelves at the back. I could see why it was expensive to be buried down here. They'd run out of space.

At first, I thought the ceiling was painted black, until I saw a school of flarefish flit by. It was like living underwater—a suggestion the Old World government had made when the waves first struck. But it was impossible to keep enough oxygen down here for a whole society.

I could already feel the lag on my lungs. I wanted to put my breather back on, but we'd need the remaining oxygen to resurface.

"Find the unmarked grave," I said, starting with the row of caskets closest to me.

Elysea took the back wall, and Raylan studied the sides, while I focused on the coffins in the middle. Raylan's limp was more pronounced. He gritted his teeth in determination. He was a good friend.

The caskets had names, the date of the person's death and a message detailed on the stone covering. I scanned for any blank lids. But it was dark in here; I had to shine my flashlight across each lid, one by one.

"Here!" Elysea called. "This one is unmarked!"

She pointed to a coffin on the bottom of a shelf and I ran over. It had nothing engraved on the lid.

"I have one too," Raylan called out. "Over here!"

"Cursed waters," I said. It was as I feared. How many people had Nessandra killed for her experiments and hidden in this place? The only way to find Calen, and his echolink, would be to check each one.

We tried Raylan's coffin first.

I prayed to the Gods—wherever they were—that this was Calen's so we could get out of here. It was too quiet. Too dark. And yet somehow less gloomy than the Aquarium.

Where Lor had spent his final two years.

Don't think about that. Not now.

"This is so wrong," Elysea said, pulling at her braids. "These people should be left in peace. That's why they're here."

"So is reviving people from the dead and experimenting on them," I muttered as we pushed the stone lid to the side. "We don't have a choice."

The lid scraped noisily, echoing in the large chamber.

Raylan shone his flashlight into the open casket. "Dirt," he said in surprise. "Why is there dirt in here?"

I lifted a handful and shrugged. "It must be a sign of respect."

I dug in deeper, feeling around for something. Hoping for bones. It would be easier to deal with. I didn't want to think about what else I might find. Something not quite decomposed . . .

But there was only dirt.

The coffin was empty.

"There's no one in here," I said, moving my hand around to double-check.

"Maybe it's an empty casket?" Elysea suggested. "That's why there's no name on the lid?"

"Must be. Let's check the one you found, Ely."

We went to the back wall, and between the three of us, we moved the coffin from the bottom of the shelf so we could open the lid.

"Hopefully this is it," Raylan said. He was chewing his bottom lip, his voice desperate. No one wanted to spend hours down here, checking casket after casket.

I took in a deep breath. "Ready?" I asked.

Elysea and Raylan both nodded and we shifted the lid across to reveal—

More dirt.

I placed my hand into the soil and felt around. I pulled my hand back as though I'd been stung. "It's also empty."

"Could it be another unclaimed casket?" Elysea suggested hopefully.

"Nessandra," Raylan called out. "We can't find it!"

Her voice came back, smooth and controlled. "Keep looking. He has to be in there somewhere."

But something twisted deep in my stomach. Something was wrong.

I approached the nearest coffin with a name written on the headstone.

KIYA BERCE

AGE FORTY

BELOVED MOTHER AND SISTER

"Raylan, help me with this," I said, pointing to the lid.

"Why?" he asked.

"Just help me, okay?" I didn't want to voice my concerns. I wanted to be proven wrong.

He shifted the heavy lid to the side. Elysea's hot gaze burned on my back as I reached into the dirt.

"What is it, Tempe?" she asked.

I tilted my head back and groaned. "It's empty too."

"No. That can't be right." Raylan reached in and felt for himself. He shook the dirt from his hand. "Where are all the bodies?"

"In a better place." A familiar voice came from behind us, from near the entrance.

We spun around, our flashlights bouncing around in the dark until they landed on a figure in a long seaweed coat.

Qera. The Remoran.

She was flanked by two other Remorans, spears aimed in our direction.

"Or should I say, in a more *useful* place." She grinned, showing her sharpened teeth. "Nice to see you again, girls. And welcome to my temple of iniquity."

CHAPTER FIFTY-ONE

TEMPEST

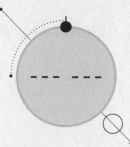

Tuesday, 1:45 p.m.

THE METAL TIP of Qera's harpoon gleamed under the light from our flashlights. The two men beside her were nearly half a head shorter than her imposing height. I recognized one as the bearded man with numerous freckles and the man with half a shirt who'd boarded our boat.

"Who in the cursed waters are you?" Raylan asked. He jutted his chin at Qera.

"Apologies," she replied with a bow. "I'm Qera, Queen of the Remorans." She gestured to the men on either side of her. "This is Teyva and Arnyx." They waved with their harpoons, vicious grins on their faces.

"Remorans?" Raylan repeated, his voice breaking. "What are you doing here? This is Palindromena territory."

"We're doing what we Remorans do best," she said. "We're taking what's no longer being used. But where's the other boy you were with?" Her forced friendliness slipped for a moment.

"The pale one? I'd like to thank him for his little prank."

Her two guards let out a cruel chuckle. They were out for blood.

I gritted my teeth. "Where are the bodies? What did you do with them?"

Qera shrugged, her necklaces jangling. "Why do you care?"

"This is a sacred place," I snapped. "You shouldn't even be down here."

"And yet you were the one caught with your hand in a coffin, my dear."

"We're looking for someone," Elysea said.

"Well, you won't find anyone here." Qera spread her arms wide.

Now it made sense why we had crossed the Untied Sea without issues. The Remorans were *under* the water, not on it.

"Why would you take the bodies?" I asked, clenching my fists. "What purpose could you possibly have for them?"

She leaned her hip against a tomb and checked her nails. "If you must know, it's getting harder and harder to acquire materials from the Old World. Nearly all the dive sites have been pillaged, and hardly anyone risks journeying into our territories anymore. And while we can't cross Palindromena's perimeter, no one said anything about going *under* it." She smirked. "Down here we've found plenty of materials for a new kind of vessel." Her eyes looked black as the night.

Elysea gasped. "You're using bones to build a boat?"

She grinned. "We all do what we gotta do to survive, am I

right?" Qera said, nodding at the open coffin beside us. "You must be here for a similar reason."

"It's nothing like that," I said. "We're here to help someone, not because of greed."

"Greed helps me," she replied. "And I'm a someone." Her crew laughed at her inane joke.

"How long have you been raiding the temple?" I asked. How long ago had she taken Calen's body? Had she found his echolink?

"*Raiding* is such a horrible word," Arnyx said as he scratched at his belly through a hole in his torn shirt.

"So true," Qera replied. "I much prefer *procurement*. And it's been a while since we procured something new. Since you wouldn't give us your boat's energy, maybe you can offer me something now?"

As she took a step forward, the men closed in behind her. It was clearly a threat, not a question.

I tried not to shrink back. "We don't have anything. We didn't find what we were looking for."

Qera shook her head, the bones rattling in her blue hair. "We've emptied the place. But I'm thinking you might have something else on you. Your diving gas, perhaps?"

"My breather could do with a top-off," Teyva said with a thoughtful tap to his bearded chin.

My hand instinctively went to my dive belt, where my breather was hooked.

"We'll never make it back to the surface," I said.

She twirled her harpoon around. "The way I look at it, you owe us. I offered you my breather for your boat, but instead you betrayed me. And your friend did a lot of damage to my vessel."

"We don't owe you anything!" Heat rose to my cheeks. We needed to get out of here. But how?

"I'm a forgiving person, aren't I, boys?" Qera said. The Remorans agreed reverently. "If you have something better to offer, I'll leave you with your diving gas. This time."

I glanced at Raylan and Elysea, but their faces were blank. We didn't have anything on us that we didn't need to return to the surface.

"Do you have the echolink?" Nessandra's voice came over our hood's audio, startling all of us. "You've been in the temple for thirty minutes."

We stilled. We didn't dare breathe.

Qera then slapped her thigh and started laughing. "Well, this is good news, isn't it, boys?" She noticed the echo on Raylan's wrist. "I love echolinks."

"Come any closer and we'll notify Nessandra," I said. "She'll bring the entire Palindromena fleet down upon you."

Qera cocked her head before taking a leaping step forward. "Reach for those hoods and I'll skewer all of you and eat you up for dinner." Teyva and Arnyx also moved closer. A few more steps and they could reach out and touch us with their harpoons.

I glanced to Raylan and he shook his head. It wasn't worth the risk.

"What use do you have for an echolink?" I asked, stalling. It wasn't like the Remorans were reviving people, were they?

"It's handy knowing the time," she said, "especially when planning our trips to the burial temple. Everyone at Palindromena are usually busy around noon with revivals. Although, we're *so* happy to have run into you." She grinned hawkishly.

"Go on." She held out her hands, and the two guards inched closer to ensure we did as she instructed. "Hand the echo over."

We didn't really need Raylan's echolink. It was Calen's we needed.

I gestured to Raylan's echolink. "You'll let us go if we give it to you?"

"You have my word," Qera said with a bow.

"The word of a Remoran is worthless," Raylan sneered. "Like tears in the ocean."

She raised her eyebrows. "Either you give me the echolink, or I pull it from your dead limp wrist. I'll let you decide."

The Remorans aimed their harpoons at our chests to prove exactly how we'd die. "I'll even help you into the coffins." Her grin was terrifying.

"Hello?" Nessandra's voice came over the hoods again. "What's going on down there?"

"Don't even think about it," Qera said, teeth bared.

I didn't want to die down here, and I certainly didn't want my body to become a part of this gruesome new fleet she was building.

"And it will go nicely with mine," Qera said.

"What did you say?" I asked, holding my breath. It couldn't be.

Qera jangled her wrist at me, and sure enough, under all the gold and silver bracelets lay a silver echolink.

It had to be Calen's. Where else would she have gotten Palindromena tech?

I could see Elysea had realized the same thing, her brows lifting. We had to get that echo.

"Does yours still work?" I asked cautiously.

Qera nodded. "It's sent from the Gods themselves."

Okay. Okay, think, Tempe, think. There had to be a way out of this temple, with Calen's echo. And without getting speared through the middle by Remoran harpoons.

"What if you give me your old echo, for our new one?" I asked.

Qera snorted. "Why would I do that when I can have both?"

We'd failed. We had nothing else to give her, and she clearly didn't want to part with her—Calen's—echo. I thought about trying to pry it from her wrist, but I would be skewered before I even reached her. We were out of options.

If only we could distract them.

But we had no weapons. And we couldn't escape while they blocked the entrance. As far as I could see, there was no other way out of the temple. Aside from the glass ceiling . . .

That could work!

If we broke the glass, that would provide a distraction to take the echolink and escape through the ceiling. But how?

"Hurry up," Qera said, her palm outstretched. "Toss me the echolink, and we'll leave you be."

I glanced around the room. There were a few stones on the floor, which must've broken from the coffins over the years. While they would shatter the glass, there was no way I could throw a rock hard enough. Neither could Elysea.

"Raylan!" Nessandra's voice was equal parts frantic and enraged. "Report back. Now!"

That's right! Before Elysea's revival, Nessandra had told me that Raylan had been a spearfisherman on the Equinox. He was broad and muscular.

He was our only chance.

"Raylan," I said, "give them your echolink."

He shot me an incredulous look.

"Fine. I'll do it." I grabbed his arm and leaned close. "Break the ceiling," I whispered as I pulled on the face of the echolink. The pins on the band retracted from his skin, leaving two punctures behind.

"What?" he breathed.

There wasn't time to explain.

"Take it," I said, and tossed Raylan's echolink over Qera's shoulder.

"That wasn't very nice," she grumbled. While she turned to pick it up, I ran for the rubble.

"Raylan!" I shouted before I tossed the rock. "Here!"

"What do you think you're doing?" Teyva asked, advancing on us.

But it was too late. Raylan had the rock in his hand. He pulled his arm back and threw it into the air.

It collided with the ceiling with a bang. For a moment, nothing happened. Then the ceiling cracked and groaned.

Seconds later, we were showered in water and glass.

CHAPTER FIFTY-TWO

TEMPEST

Tuesday, 2:15 p.m.

THE WATER CASCADED into the building, filling it almost instantly. Was this what it felt like to be in the Great Waves?

"Put on your breathers!" I cried to Elysea and Raylan as we were tossed about like leaves in a whirlpool.

Once I had the breather attached and my dome on, I allowed myself a breath.

The Remorans had been washed off their feet, but they wouldn't be far. If we were lucky, the wave would've knocked Qera out cold.

"Nessandra," I said over the in-hood audio link. "The Remorans are down here and they have Calen's echo. We need help."

"Remorans? *How?*" she asked, then cursed. "Never mind, I'll send down security, but it will take thirty minutes until they reach you."

Raylan's eyebrows knitted together. "They'll be long gone before that. As will Calen's echo."

"Then we'll deal with them," I said with a nod to Elysea. She pressed her lips into a firm line.

"I'm counting on you," Nessandra replied. It was the first time I'd heard doubt taint her voice. But we could do this.

The temple was now completely full of water. I would worry about what we'd done to this sacred place later. The dirt from the caskets we'd opened had muddied the water, and even with our flashlights, it was difficult to see. But the Remorans had to be here somewhere.

Something silver shot past my shoulder, tearing through my diving skin and into my flesh. I gasped in pain.

A spear.

My blood pooled around me.

I checked behind me to see that Elysea and Raylan were in one piece before swimming in the direction of the spear.

That left two weapons.

My heart thundered in my ears, and yet I felt more assured than I had on the boat when facing Qera. I'd spent nearly every day of the past five years in the dark, maneuvering around sunken buildings. The Remorans might rule the surface, but we were in *my* domain now.

I swam behind a casket. Raylan and Elysea followed.

"Turn off your flashlights," I said. "We need to split up. Ely, you stick to the left side. Raylan, you take the right. I'll swim down the middle of the temple." Hopefully I'd find Qera and the echolink. "And switch off your audio link. We don't want the Remorans to hear us coming."

Raylan and Elysea nodded and then all I could hear was the hush of my own breathing.

Elysea gave my good shoulder a squeeze. We clicked off our flashlights.

Swimming in pure darkness was disorienting. I hoped I was moving toward the entrance, but I had no real way of knowing. All I could hear was my breath coming in short gasps. I missed the glow of coral, although I needed the shroud of darkness.

Something whooshed through the water nearby. Another weapon down. Did it hit Raylan or Elysea on the way? I desperately wanted to turn on my flashlight to find out, but I didn't dare give my position away.

I nearly choked on my breather when a pale face appeared in front of me.

Qera. She had her breather in her mouth but no diving dome or weapon. It must've been her harpoon that had just been thrown. She grabbed for me, but I twisted out of the way.

Watch me dance, I thought. Elysea would be proud.

I kicked out my foot, connecting with her hip. But it wasn't enough to hurt her; the water slowed my movements.

She grabbed my leg and twisted the flipper off. It sank to the stone floor. I tried to right myself, but it was more difficult with only one flipper.

I thought of Raylan and kicked harder with my other leg to balance out. I reached for Qera's wrist. She elbowed me in the face, attempting to tear my dome loose.

Where were Elysea and Raylan? Were they okay or locked in their own battle?

A look crossed Qera's face; I hoped it was a look that meant this wasn't worth it. She flipped in the water and swam toward the entrance.

But I couldn't let her escape.

I kicked as fast as I could and launched at her, wrapping my arms around her shoulders. I reached for the echolink on her wrist.

There! I had it.

My fingers grasped the face, and I pulled.

Before it came free from Qera's skin, my breather started beeping frantically.

No oxygen left.

What?

I grabbed at my dome, releasing my hold on the echo and Qera.

In her free hand, she held my small diving tank.

She pretended to blow me a kiss and then kicked me in the stomach.

I spat out the breather and took the small breath of diving gas left in the dome. There would never be enough to travel to the surface. I was dead. And so was Lor.

Someone grabbed my arm. It was Elysea. She pointed to my hood and I switched on my audio link.

"Where did Qera go?" she asked.

I pointed to the entrance. Speaking would only use up more oxygen.

Elysea took my hand and tried to pull me along. I shook my head and showed her where my diving tank had been removed. The fear on her face was evident.

Instead of pulling me toward the entrance, she directed me straight up, toward the hole in the ceiling. I tugged away, gesturing back to where Qera had disappeared.

The echolink, I mouthed.

"No," she replied. "I'm taking you to the surface."

I shook my head again. *I won't make it.*

She stared at me for a long moment, her eyes glassy. She could go after Qera to get Calen's echolink, but I would die down here. Or she could pull me to the surface and try to save me. Still, there wasn't time for both.

I already felt the tightness in my chest. The small amount of oxygen in my dome was running out.

"I'm so sorry," I said, not caring anymore that I was using the last of my oxygen. "I love you."

"No," she said, and then swam away.

I turned on my flashlight. I might as well see before the darkness invaded permanently.

I thought of Lor. Would I see him again once I was dead? Did the Gods below truly exist? Why hadn't they protected me?

Two dark figures swam toward me. They flicked their lights on. Elysea had found Raylan.

"We're taking you up," she said.

"No." Raylan needed to go after Qera, if Elysea wasn't willing to. Before I could gesture to Raylan, Elysea grabbed one of my arms, and Raylan grabbed the other. They kicked toward the broken ceiling.

I wanted to struggle. I wanted to tell them that I'd never make it. But I also didn't want to die alone.

I kicked along beside them.

"Here," Elysea said, tapping my dome to get my attention. She then unclipped her diving tank and plugged it into mine. My lungs expanded in relief.

Air. Glorious air.

I looked at her, confused. Was she sacrificing herself? But then Raylan passed his tank to Elysea and I understood. While I didn't have enough diving gas to make it to the surface, if we shared the two tanks between the three of us, taking shallow breaths, then we could make it. Just.

But we couldn't follow Qera. We wouldn't get Calen's echo. We wouldn't save Lor.

CHAPTER FIFTY-THREE

TEMPEST

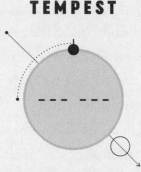

Tuesday, 3:00 p.m.

FIFTEEN MINUTES into our ascent, we crossed paths with Palindromena's security. They helped us reach the surface, where Nessandra was awaiting our return. Her previously neat hair was sticking in odd directions, and she'd been crying. Raylan had informed her of what had happened on the way to the surface.

The security guards pulled us from the water. We were all low on oxygen, our heads fuzzy, lungs aching. I rolled to the side and closed my eyes. It was too bright up here. I wanted to sleep. I wanted to cry. But for the first time, I didn't want to yell and scream. All anger had drained from my body.

We'd done everything we could to save Lor. And we'd almost died in the process. Sometimes the Gods below weren't on your side. Sometimes you couldn't turn back the tide.

I'd barely known Lor, but I knew, like he had, that we could've meant something to each other. Whether it was fate or luck that had connected us, he was gone. Truly gone.

I should've been angry, but it wouldn't bring Lor back. Anger hadn't helped me grieve Elysea. It hadn't helped me move on. Anger had been my anchor. It had tethered me to the darkness in the world, to the things I couldn't control. I had hidden from my grief. It had been easier that way. But it wasn't healthy.

Like Lor, I hadn't really been living.

It reminded me of how I'd told Lor that most people ignored the beauty that had arisen since the Great Waves. Even in the darkest of times, the coral burned bright. And I could either focus on the gloom or turn toward the light. The Gods below wouldn't turn my face or hold my hand. It was my choice. It was my life.

And while I wouldn't have Lor by my side to help, I had Elysea. And I had my parents. I was no longer alone.

⊷⊶

As much as I didn't want to spend another minute inside Palindromena, my torn shoulder needed tending to. Nessandra set me up in one of the recovery rooms and sent a doctor in to stitch me up.

Elysea waited in the corner of the room, making sure I didn't go anywhere.

Sometime after being treated, I drifted off. I woke to Elysea touching my uninjured shoulder.

"You have some visitors," she said, a smile on her face. Color had returned to her cheeks.

"Visitors?"

Elysea stepped aside to reveal our parents standing in the doorway.

I wanted to leap from my bed, but I was too woozy, so I held out a hand.

"Mom! Dad!" My voice wobbled.

Mom rushed to my bedside. Tears streamed down her face as she enveloped me in her arms.

Dad approached the other side of the bed. He smoothed my hair back from my forehead. "How are you holding up, Tempe?"

It was too much. I'd tried to be strong since Lor died—since Elysea died, really. But I couldn't hold it together any longer. I didn't want to. I'd been like that fractured glass ceiling. Enough pressure, and I'd broken.

I wept into my mother's embrace as my dad rubbed my back.

"You're safe," she whispered. "We're here, and we're never leaving again."

That made me cry harder. As much as I wanted to be happy in this moment, it was polluted by sadness. Lor would never have a happy reunion with his mother—whether she deserved that or not wasn't the question. *He* had deserved it.

"I'm sorry about Lor," Mom said. She must've heard from Elysea. "He was a nice boy."

"I couldn't help him."

Elysea patted my hand. "We did everything we could."

It didn't feel like it. So many moments could've gone differently, and if they had, Lor would still be alive.

"How did you get here?" I asked my parents. I wiped my tears away with the back of my hand.

"After you left, we took a raft to one of the closest Reefs and borrowed a boat to cross the Untied Sea," Dad said. "We couldn't stay at the Islands Cavalcade any longer. We'd let our fear keep us there." He exchanged a look with my mom. "And we needed to confront Nessandra about what she'd done to Elysea. We needed to ensure she wouldn't hurt anyone else."

"What happened?" I asked.

Mom clasped her hands together. "She's gone."

"What?" I clenched the bedsheet in my fists. "She was here an hour ago."

"She took one of the Palindromena boats," Dad said. "Security found the inbuilt tracking device on the pier. She'd ripped it out. She doesn't want to be found."

"Lor," Elysea said in understanding. "She couldn't face what she'd done here—to him or anyone." I wasn't so sure about that. Nessandra seemed like a woman who would fight, not run away. She wasn't the sort of person who'd give up.

"No," I said, realizing the truth. "She's gone after Qera. She still wants to save Lor."

Dad shook his head. "He's gone, Tempe. I'm sorry. There's no bringing him back."

"I know." Still, I could relate to Nessandra. It wasn't easy to let the people you love go. It wasn't easy to face grief. But I knew, if Nessandra kept running, it would only cause her more pain in the end.

"What does that mean for Palindromena?" I asked.

Mom pressed her lips together. "Your father and I will take over operations for the time being."

"And by operations, do you mean . . . ?" I let the question hang there.

Mom weaved her fingers through mine. "We will close down the revival program immediately. There will be no further tests on patients. But we will continue to tend to the crops."

"And everyone's okay with that?" I asked.

"Your mother was the Lead Botanist, and I was the Head Warden," Dad said. "With Nessandra gone and news spreading not only about what she did to Elysea, but her other experiments, the company needs a fresh start. Palindromena employs hundreds of people. No one wants to lose their jobs. We'll find another way to make Notes and keep the crops alive."

"What about Nessandra?" Elysea asked. "What about what she was doing?"

Mom ran a hand through her hair. "We want to bring her to justice, to have her answer to the families she ruined, but without her boat's tracking system, she'll be impossible to find."

"She has to have gone somewhere," I said. "She can't live out on the ocean with no supplies. She can't even swim."

"The main thing is that Palindromena's revival program is shut down," Dad said. "We will work on a way to give back to those families who were hurt. As a company."

It was a start. And sometimes, that was all you needed.

CHAPTER FIFTY-FOUR

TEMPEST

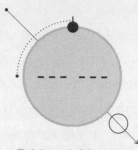

Friday, 6:00 p.m.

IT HAD BEEN THREE DAYS since Elysea and I returned to the Equinox to take up residence in our old quarters. Mom and Dad had spent most of their time at Palindromena, planning their restructuring of the facility from the ground up. They couldn't permanently return to the Equinox just yet, due to weight restrictions. The Conservators were looking for a solution in recognition of my parents' plan to create a more balanced relationship between island and Reef. They were thrilled to learn Nessandra had been replaced.

We had plans to spend the weekend together as a family, but tonight was for me and Elysea.

Explaining Elysea's and my parents' return to everyone on the Equinox was easier than expected. They were understandably excited, thinking Palindromena had finally found a way to bring someone back for good. But we told them about how Mom and Dad had been on the run from Nessandra, and the truth to Elysea's revival. Speaking about Lor's sacrifice was a way to keep his memory alive. And to ensure we never took what he'd done for granted.

Everyone was so thrilled to have Elysea back in their lives.

Elysea's reunion with Daon was more complicated. She was worried Daon would break up with his new girlfriend now that she was back in his life, so she finally sat him down and explained that she didn't feel that way about him. And she wouldn't feel that way about anyone.

In the beginning, it was incredibly awkward, as she wanted me in the room when she told him. But when she explained everything in her heart, I was overjoyed. Overjoyed that she had this second chance to be who she really was.

Elysea was always good at embracing life, but she'd often hid her true self. When she wasn't dancing, she was protecting me, worrying about me, providing for me. She never planned for *her* future. Now that we were the same age, she could have more freedom. And that was because of Lor.

I couldn't yet think about him or picture his face without tearing up. Without Lor, I wouldn't have Elysea. He would always be in my heart.

⟞⟋⟍⟝

At sunset, I headed to Daon's bar. I sat at the same stool where Lor had found me only days earlier, and yet I felt like a completely different person. Lighter. Happier. Elysea's life wasn't the only one Lor saved.

I couldn't help but wish Lor had met this version of me.

Daon tapped the sign hanging behind his bar. "Did I forget your age again?" he said with a grin, jolting me out of my thoughts.

I wiggled on my seat to get comfortable. "My birthday is only a day away, Daon. You know that."

"Still," he said with a dramatic sigh. "My rules are the rules."

I rolled my eyes. "Fine, then. I'll have a bowl of ceviche."

He pointed at me. "That, my girl, I can do."

As he was working on my dinner, I looked out over the ocean. I could barely make out the coral outline of where the buildings of the Old World began. Lor never had the chance to see it with his own eyes, but Mom and Dad had agreed that he would be buried down in the temple, after the ceiling was rebuilt and better security was installed against people like Qera. While Lor didn't get to visit the Old World in life, he would live in its remnants in death.

It was the best honor we could give him, even though he deserved so much more.

"Is this seat taken?" a familiar voice asked.

Raylan.

He looked well. Warmth had returned to his brown complexion since I saw him last.

I wiped a tear from my cheek. "Hi."

He gave me a sheepish grin. "I'm sorry I disappeared on

you two. I should've stayed, but I couldn't face that place after everything that happened. I couldn't imagine Lor not being there. I was—"

I waved his apology away. "Sit with me."

He took the stool next to mine and let out a breath. "It's hard, isn't it?"

"Being back here?" I asked.

"Everything," he said. "Moving on."

"We'll move on eventually."

"I should want to," he said, "but it doesn't seem right to forget him."

"No," I agreed. "We'll never forget."

I noticed he had a metal brace around his left foot. "How's it feeling?" He'd been in a bad way after we'd resurfaced from the temple.

"This helps," he said with a smile. "One thing I learned down there"—he didn't want to mention the temple, and I didn't blame him—"is that it's not impossible to swim; it just requires some training. While I won't be able to spend my days spearfishing like I used to, I can at least return to the ocean. I don't have to be afraid of it."

I was happy for him. I was sure Lor would be too. "What will you do now?" I asked.

I'd wondered the same thing about my future. I was used to diving every day to fund the revival procedure, and although I still had enough Notes for Elysea and me to live comfortably for a while, I found myself missing the water.

"I'm not sure yet," he replied. "I still need a job to help my parents, and the Equinox."

Daon gave Raylan a shot of ragar and half a shot for me.

"An early birthday present." He winked. "Don't tell your sister." Then he returned to the ceviche preparation.

"Perhaps I'll open a stall here," Raylan said, gesturing to the stalls around us. "I make a mean fish cake. Or at least, that's what Lor used to tell me." His face crumpled. "I miss him. Every day."

I nodded, unable to speak as I swallowed down my sorrow.

"What about you?" he asked, wiping his own tears away.

I took a sip of the ragar. It burned my tongue and throat. It was disgusting. I pushed the glass toward Raylan. I could see Daon laughing at me out of the corner of my eye. Jerk.

Elysea would soon be onstage, her first performance since her return to the Equinox. For a moment, I could imagine everything had gone back to the way it had been five years ago. My parents safe, my sister alive.

Hadn't that been what I'd always wanted?

I shrugged at Raylan's question and winced. My stitches pulled if I made any sudden movements.

"I think I want to travel," I said.

Raylan raised his eyebrows. "Really? I thought you'd want to stay with your family."

It was a shock to me too. The words had tumbled out of my mouth without a second thought.

"Not yet," I said. "But one day. I want to make more of my

life. I want to leave the Equinox and see what else is out there."

More.

That was what Lor had asked me. And he was right. I did want more.

We only had one life to live, and while there might be many dangers in our sunken world, one benefit was not being tied to one place. I had the *Sunrise*; I could go wherever I wanted. When I was ready. But first, I would enjoy being with my family. I would enjoy having more time.

Drums began to echo throughout the room, silencing my thoughts. The crowd quieted. Whispers spread like a wave upon the sand.

Although it wasn't Spring Tide, the place was packed. They'd come to see her.

Over the past few days, word had spread about Elysea's return. Rumors and mystery surrounded her reappearance. The girl who was once dead, who'd risen to dance again. I'd heard little kids refer to her as a water witch, which only reminded me of Lor.

I wish we had a thousand tomorrows together, he'd said. *I wish we didn't have to say goodbye.*

I squeezed my eyes tight and pushed back the thoughts that threatened to overwhelm me.

I couldn't imagine the pressure of having to perform for all these people, but when Elysea entered the market, she beamed. The crowd parted for their sea goddess.

That afternoon, we'd curled her hair and dyed the ends blue

with coral powder. I also helped weave hundreds of pearls into her brown locks. Her dress was made of threaded seaweed and shells. As she moved, she looked like the sea come to life.

She *was* a sea goddess.

The crowd clapped and hollered as she moved toward the middle of the market.

I grinned at the creation we'd made.

"She's stunning," Raylan said from beside me. "She belongs on the stage."

The music picked up pace as Elysea entered the middle of the crowd. Tonight, the stage was raised above her onlookers, not sunk into the water. It was only fitting for the girl who had risen from the ocean.

Elysea held the audience in the palm of her hand as she began to move. And it wasn't merely the gossip surrounding her reappearance. It was her presence. Her very being. It drew people in.

"She does," I said as my eyes filled with happy tears. I was so glad I hadn't let her go. That I'd fought for her. I would've done anything for her. That was what you did for the people you loved the most.

You crossed oceans. You searched seas. You sacrificed everything.

As Elysea moved her hands around her head, her eyes caught mine.

She smiled, and I smiled back.

Because of Lor, I had Elysea. But nothing lasted forever. Not the Old World, not the light of the coral, not the people you love the most. You have to hold on to every moment. Breathe every breath. For you never know when it will be your last.

And don't hold on to the pain.

Maybe not today. Maybe not tomorrow. But one day. One day I would also let Lor go. I would release the tears, the ache, the regret, the sorrow. I would let it all fall down into the great vanishing deep.

TURN THE PAGE
FOR A SNEAK PEEK OF

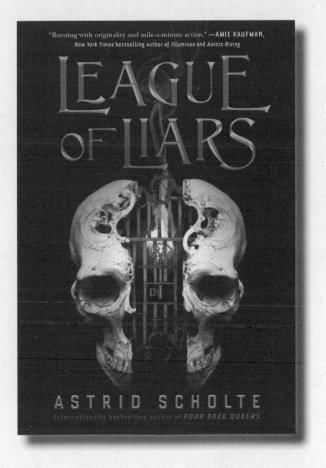

CAYDER

B ecoming a criminal is a choice," my father would say. "We either choose to accept the ways things are or try to force fate's hand."

Father always spoke in such definitive terms: Shadows were dangerous. Edem was illegal. And liars were cowards.

Well, then call me a coward, because some lies were necessary. Like the tiny detail of where I was working over the summer. What my father didn't know wouldn't hurt him.

Before I left the house, I checked to see if my sister had once again snuck in via the latticework outside her bedroom.

"Seriously, Leta?" I groaned at her disappointingly empty room. Apparently, I wasn't the only Broduck keeping secrets.

Over the last month, she'd been away more than she'd been home, and even Father was bound to notice her absence.

After inhaling breakfast, I joined the commuters gathered by the local trolley stop to Downtown Kardelle. Although the permacloud hung over the capital city, diffusing shadows into a safe gray, the group stood away from the buildings. Despite what Father said, shadows weren't inherently dangerous, but people instinctually shied away from what could linger within.

The 7:30 trolley announced itself by screeching around the bend. The carriage hurtled by, packed to the brim with commuters, the driver not even offering a wave of apology as he passed the stop.

It hadn't taken me long to learn the trolley never ran on schedule and I had to be thirty minutes early to arrive at work on time.

Last week marked the start of my three-month apprenticeship at Edem Legal Aid before commencing my final year at school. My mentor was none other than Graymond Toyer, the number one public defender of edem-based crimes. And an old friend of my father's. I needed Mr. Toyer's recommendation if I wanted to shorten the duration of my undergrad studies and apply to law school after two years instead of the usual four. And as my sister liked to remind me, patience wasn't one of my virtues.

That wasn't entirely true; she said I possessed *no* virtues.

I planned to eventually become a prosecutor for the Crown Court. The Crown Court was the highest court in the land and dealt with the most serious edem crimes. But studying the other side of the law would be invaluable as a prosecutor, ensuring justice prevailed for victims and their families. Families like mine.

As I glanced at my watch, something bright sparkled off the glass face.

A spot of sunshine.

Thanks to the machine in the center of the city that pumped

water into the air at the exact right temperature to generate a fog, it was rare to glimpse unobstructed sunlight. Occasionally, if the temperature unexpectedly changed, the permacloud would falter, allowing the sun to break through. With sun came the darkest shadows.

While most streets had been cleared of any substantial trees and the shadows they could cast, hundreds of lampposts lined the sidewalk to flood diffused light at nighttime. With nearly constant cloud cover during the day, the lampposts' shadows shouldn't be a concern.

But now, with the sun streaking though the cloud, the thin gray lines on the sidewalk turned black. And within the pitch-black shadow lay a shifting substance—as though something dark and simmering had been spilled onto the pavement.

Edem.

My first and only use of extradimensional magic was when I was ten. I'd been grounded by Father for accidentally breaking a vase—one of Mother's favorites—not long after she'd passed away. Desperate to escape my room and the oppressive manor, I'd smashed my permalamp, which kept shadows at bay. I welcomed the darkness, waiting for edem to appear. It didn't take long. An obsidian shadow trailed up my hands and wound around my arms.

"Free me," I'd commanded.

Edem allowed you to manipulate time and change your reality. My rescue was provided in the form of a ladder, plucked from yesterday, when the gardener had set up his window-cleaning equipment outside my bedroom.

While my father hadn't known I'd escaped—the ladder fading and returning to the past once I'd climbed down—he soon uncovered my crime when the Regency came knocking the very next day in full body armor, their silvery cloaks trailing behind them. The flash of silver reminded me of my mother's own cloak, and for a brief moment, I'd foolishly thought she had returned home.

The Regency were a trusted arm of the government who monitored and reported edem fluctuations to the monarchs of Telene. While the royals decreed edem law, the Regency enforced it. They tracked shifts in time and pinpointed the exact coordinates to investigate and arrest the person responsible. When they arrived at Broduck Manor that day, they quickly realized I'd been the culprit; a smoky gray design crisscrossed both my arms from where the edem had touched my skin.

Known as an *echo mark*, it indicated the use of edem. The larger the impact, the longer the mark lasted. Luckily for me, the gardener had not been on the ladder at the time it was stolen from the past and delivered into my present. Had the gardener fallen to his death, my echo mark would have been permanent. A death echo.

I hadn't touched edem since.

I glanced at the commuters around me. No one else appeared to notice the edem lying within the shadow. I planned to ignore it, until the man beside me moved into the patch of sunlight.

From behind, we could have been mistaken for one another: both in tailored suits, his hair not too dissimilar from my own structured dark brown coif. But his skin was much paler than my warm beige. I wouldn't have given him a second glance until he bent to the ground.

Surely he wasn't about to—

"Please." His voice was urgent as the inky shadows trickled over his skin like liquid, covering his fingers in darkness. "I can't be late. Not again. I'll lose my job. Please. *Help me.*"

Edem spread from the lamppost's shadow, across the sidewalk and into the cobblestone street. It pooled in the center of the road and began to rise into the shape of a trolley—near where a child was crossing the tracks. The trolley would run him down before he could even realize what happened!

The shadows began to solidify and turn red. In a moment, the trolley would be pulled into our reality from somewhere in the past or future. What would happen if there were people on that trolley when it disappeared? If they were now on the tracks, they could be killed when the trolley returned to its timeline.

I shoved the man away from the shadow. The shadows on the street dispersed instantly, the connection to the edem lost.

"Hey!" I gestured to the kid crossing the tracks. "You could have killed him!"

"I'm sorry!" the man cried. "Please don't tell the Regency! I was desperate!"

The trolley was always late, and yet this man was the only one who sought out edem. *He* had decided to act selfishly and damn the consequences. It was that exact kind of thoughtlessness that had killed my mother.

"I'm sorry!" the man said again.

The woman beside me had already opened a panel on the

5

nearest lamppost and pulled out a pair of shackles. She snapped them onto the man's wrists, locking him to the post before he could make a run for it.

The Regency had their own trolley line that ran throughout the city, allowing them to dispatch agents to sites of edem crimes and any attempted usage. Opening the panel alerted the Regency; it took only ten minutes for them to arrive at the scene.

Four Regency agents jumped off the small trolley in unison, their silvery cloaks falling down behind them with a *thwump*. They were dressed head to toe in a light gray—the color of Telene and the royal family—and safe shadows. Silver epaulets lined their shoulders, and rows of polished buttons ran down their front.

My mouth went dry. I was ten years old again, trying to explain to my father why the Regency were at our door. But this time, I wasn't about to be dragged from my home.

"What happened here?" one agent asked, his gravelly voice booming. His brown hair was buzzed short, and under his thick beard, his skin was pockmarked and pale.

"Please," the shackled man whimpered. "I didn't actually use edem!"

The agent turned away. "Who can explain what happened here?"

I swallowed down my fear and stepped forward. "Our trolley didn't stop," I said. "So this man attempted to find another form of transport." I nodded to the patch of sunlight that was already fading, along with the black shadow. "He nearly killed a kid who was crossing the street."

The agent moved toward me, and I forced myself not to shrink back. "And how was this disaster averted?"

"I pushed the man out of the shadow." I'd done what was expected of any citizen of Telene, and yet now, faced with the Regency, I felt like I'd made a mistake.

The agent nodded. "Well done, son. Our king thanks you for your quick thinking."

Before I could say anything further, the rest of the agents surrounded the man.

"Stop!" the man cried as they removed the shackles from the post. "I didn't do *anything*!"

I flinched as the agents shoved him into their trolley. I'd hate to see how they treated someone who had actually used edem.

The man looked back at me as the trolley departed. I swallowed down a lump in my throat.

I'd saved a boy's life, but at what cost?

I shook the thought free. The Regency *had* to be strict. It was the only way to protect our nation.

The man would have to argue his case before the court.

———

I finally arrived at Edem Legal Aid at ten a.m., my shirt and vest sticking to me like a second skin. I pushed the office door open with a little too much force. The door banged into the wall behind. Several people glanced up before seeing it was me and then returned to their typewriters.

"Whoops," I offered sheepishly.

The office clerk at the front desk furrowed his brows behind his minuscule glasses. A line of black hair ran around the back of his pale bald head, as though someone had taken a pen to it but had forgotten to color within the lines.

"You're late, boy," Olin said gruffly.

"I know, I know," I said. "A man on the street attempted to use edem, if you can believe it."

"We work at *Edem* Legal Aid," Olin said with a roll of his eyes. "I can believe it."

"Right, of course. He made me miss my trolley, and I had to run all the way to Downtown Kardelle to catch the connecting trolley to the Unbent River."

"That explains the smell." Olin wrinkled his nose.

I hoped he was kidding. Then again, I'd never even seen Olin smile, let alone make a joke.

I brushed past Olin's messy desk to reach my own by the window that overlooked the red-brown river.

"Hang on—" He held out a narrow envelope with a waxy crimson seal. "Mr. Toyer asked me to give this to you when you arrived."

The seal looked like a blot of splattered blood. A symbol of two chained hands with a bar down the middle was pressed into the wax.

The emblem of Vardean.

Vardean was Telene's only prison, where criminals from all over the nation were jailed for breaking the law, edem-related or not. While most kids would have pissed themselves over the sight of that emblem, I found it comforting.

After the Regency had discovered a naive ten-year-old had

8

been the cause of the edem fluctuation the night I'd escaped my bedroom, I was sentenced to a year at Vardean Reform. The boarding school was attached to the prison complex and housed any edem abusers under the age of sixteen.

While my year at Vardean Reform was meant to be a punishment, I'd thrived there. It had been a relief to escape both my father and the memories of Mother back at Broduck Manor. There, I'd learned the intricacies of the law. Something to focus on—something to push the grief away. Vardean was a pillar of strength and protected the good citizens of Telene from dangerous criminals. Over that year, my appreciation of the justice system had been born. In truth, I would have stayed at Vardean for the rest of my schooling if allowed.

"What's this?" I asked Olin.

"A letter from Vardean," he replied with another roll of his eyes. "Surely you recognize the emblem from your time there?"

Disdain dripped from each word. Many people looked down upon those who'd spent time at Vardean, even if it was the school and not the prison sector. Was that why Olin was so short with me? If Graymond could look past my childhood misdemeanor, surely Olin could too.

"Mr. Toyer was called in to Vardean to process a new client over the weekend," Olin said. "He's still there."

"But we were planning to go through appeals paperwork today."

"Would you prefer to stay here?" he asked, honestly confused.

"Is that a trick question?" I grinned and snatched the envelope from his hand, then ripped it open.

Dear Cayder,

Change of plans for today. Meet me at Vardean prison foyer at 10 a.m.

Don't be late.

Graymond Toyer

Not exactly illuminating, but Graymond couldn't divulge any details about his new client, in case the letter was misplaced. Confidentiality was an important part of practicing law; I knew that. And I was good at keeping secrets.

Slipped in behind the letter was a blood-red token with the prison emblem pressed onto its face. I ran my fingers across it. *A ticket to Vardean.*

"Graymond wants me to meet him there?" I'd been trying to get back to Vardean ever since I'd left. Without breaking the law, of course.

Even though my father worked at the prison as a senior district judge, he'd outright refused my suggestion of working with him over the summer. He'd forbidden me from pursuing a career in law, claiming he didn't want either of his children involved with Vardean. He wanted to forget what happened to Mother and refused to even mention her name.

Ever since her death, he had a single-minded focus for his job. My sister and I were merely annoyances and mouths to feed. Father thought I was spending my summer working at the Downtown Kardelle Library. Out of trouble. And, most importantly, out of his sight.

If I ran into him at Vardean, then my ruse would be exposed and he would ensure my apprenticeship with Graymond would come to an end. Graymond had promised not to tell my father what I was up to this summer—he knew how stubborn my father could be. But I couldn't pass up the opportunity to see Graymond in his natural habitat. Perhaps I'd get to see a trial in action!

Something prickled under my shirt's crisp collar. Anxiety *and* anticipation. "It's past ten a.m.," I said.

Olin was unmoved. "Then you better get going."

"Olin, my friend, you are the master of the understatement."

He finally cracked a smile. "Good luck, Cayder."

———

Vardean was an hour away from Downtown Kardelle by suspension tramway. The gondolas were made entirely of glass so if any criminals attempted to break out, they could be easily spotted by the prison guards posted at either end. And in the hundred years of Vardean, no one had ever escaped.

I sat alone in the glass gondola as it skimmed along the ocean; my father, the lawyers, judges, jury members and prison employees would have already made the journey earlier this morning. No one else was allowed access; even prisoners' families were prohibited from visiting.

I glanced behind me to see if I could spot Broduck Manor on the cliffs. Like most wealthy families, we lived on the coast called Sunshine Mile—named after the yellowish cliffs the homes were built on. The three stories of white stone stood out from the jagged golden rock. It looked like a beacon of hope, but it was nothing but a lie.

Broduck Manor used to be a happy home. When my mother was alive, my father had been a reasonable man and was known to smile and—sometimes—laugh. My sister and I spent our days playing inside the enclosed gardens, a sanctuary from the outside world. The house was full of warmth and love. A true *Sunshine Mile* home.

The manor had become its own kind of prison since Mother died, and Leta and I had attempted to break free in different ways. While I threw myself into my studies in hopes I could shorten my undergrad degree and apply to law school sooner, Leta had become increasingly obsessed with edem. She spent more hours out investigating superstitious nonsense about edem creatures than she did under Broduck Manor's ornate ceiling.

Leta claimed that our mother had also believed there was more to edem, and she wanted to prove her right. While Mother had never spoken such nonsense to me, I allowed Leta to continue her childish fantasies.

Mother used to work for the Regency and would travel to edem crime scenes to gather evidence for the court. Her last trip had been to a rural town called Ferrington, half a day's trip outside the city. While she was investigating a crime scene, a nearby farmer used edem to make it rain, conjuring a severe storm in seconds and catching my mother in the downpour. The sandy soil became a mudslide, and my mother was swept off her feet and into a ravine.

She died because one selfish man thought watering his crops was more important than the safety of those around him.

The Regency had been swift to arrest the perpetrator, and he was currently serving a fifteen-year sentence in Vardean. While the sentence wouldn't bring my mother back, at least justice had been served.

My mother's death had forever altered my course in life, but it had also given me a purpose.

The gondola rattled through the gray permacloud for a few miles before it dispersed. I sucked in a breath. I would never get used to the sight before me.

Out on the horizon, a black streak cleaved the sky in two. Like a static bolt of lightning, but where light should be, darkness reigned. Known as the veil, it was the source of edem and many kids' nightmares. A fissure between our world and another, allowing time-altering magic to seep through.

In front of the veil, a building with one central spire rose from the ocean.

Vardean.

Almost one hundred years ago, a ship crossed this exact section of ocean until it shuddered to a stop, the engine dying. The captain descended into the engine room to discover what had happened and found the entire room gone. Not destroyed. Gone. In its place was a black void—the veil. Returning to the deck, the captain found the other half of his boat had disappeared through the darkness, along with his crew.

The captain managed to escape on a lifeboat before the rest of the ship disappeared into the veil, never to return.

The ruling king and queen of Telene sent their top scientists to investigate the phenomenon. While one diver was near the veil, he discovered a dark substance under the shadow of a boat. He touched it, thinking the boat was leaking fuel. But when the liquid began to climb up his hand, he panicked and ordered it to go away. Misunderstanding the diver's intent, edem transported the man to another part of the ocean, hundreds of miles from his boat. The man was barely conscious when he returned back to the research base. Initially, his ranting about being magically transported out to sea was seen as delusions from exhaustion. But after some tests, the scientists discovered this liquid— edem—could manipulate time, and the consequences were always unpredictable and often disastrous.

These scientists became the Regency. At first, edem only appeared in black shadows close to the veil itself. But the more they did their tests, the more the veil grew and edem spread to Telene's shores. And while the Regency developed the perma-cloud to prevent dark shadows and their connection to edem, they could not control what people did inside their homes, forcing the king and queen to declare the use of edem illegal. But not everyone abided by the law. Before long, the fissure stretched up into the sky.

To this day, edem had not spread beyond Telene, but if people continued to break the law, it would eventually infect the shadows of the rest of the world. Before the veil, people moved freely between nations and shared their cultures and customs with one another. But as the veil grew, the neighboring nations shut their borders and halted any trade until edem could be brought under control. That was one reason Vardean, and the legal system, was so important.

The veil crackled behind Vardean—a sign that someone had recently used edem. I thought back to the man on the street today. Even with the threat of being arrested, people continued to risk imprisonment to change their fate. If I hadn't intervened, a boy would be dead, possibly dozens more. The Regency *had* to be strict.

The gondola descended toward Vardean and pulled to a stop. I stepped onto the station that connected to the prison via an enclosed metal bridge. A steady humming drowned out the sound of the waves, like the buzz of an engine or an overloaded lightbulb about to pop.

A young prison guard stood by the gated entrance. Unlike Regency agents, Vardean guards were employed by the prison itself. The guard wore black instead of light gray, and the only splash of color was the red Vardean emblem on her peaked cap and the piping along her collar like a plump vein. She looked like the typical guard I'd glimpsed while at Vardean Reform; the only act of rebellion was her bleached white hair, which hugged her brown face like a baby to its mother. She was pretty in the way that said she clearly couldn't care less what you thought.

"Morning," I said, flashing her my best smile.

"Stand with your legs and arms out," she commanded, her expression unmoved. I complied, and she ran a handheld metal detector over me. It made the hairs on my arms and the back of my neck stand up. Then she pulled my satchel from my shoulder and rummaged for contraband items.

She cocked a dark eyebrow. "Reason for coming to Vardean?"

I handed her my red token. "I'm with Edem Legal Aid."

"Aren't you a bit young to be an attorney?" Amusement lit her face, the apples of her cheeks lifting.

"I'm Graymond Toyer's apprentice, the number one public defender in Telene."

She laughed. "Not for long."

I blinked a few times, wondering if I'd heard her correctly.

She didn't clarify and pressed a button beside the gate. "Visitor for Graymond Toyer," she said into a mouthpiece. She inserted my token into a slot, and the gate retracted into the wall.

"You'll get the token back when you head home, Boy Wonder."

"Thank you, er . . . What's your name?"

She cut me off with a wave of a hand. "Does it matter? You won't see me again."

Why was she implying I was only here for a day?

"Well?" she asked when I didn't move. "Go on, then." She gestured toward the open gate. "Shoo."

I walked along a narrow corridor that led to a crowded room. Several passageways branched off the central foyer to courtrooms, interrogation rooms and legal offices, and the hallway to the far right led to the reform school. People bustled by with papers stacked under their arms. I recognized their expressions as the same one I wore whenever I looked in the mirror: determination.

The first time I'd entered this foyer, I was ten years old. I'd been surrounded by kids my age who'd each committed minor edem infractions. While everyone else shook with fear, a strange feeling of calm washed over me. Just as it did now. This was a place where everything made sense. This was a world where justice prevailed. This was a world I understood.

"Cayder," a low voice said from behind me.

I jumped, recognizing the voice. But it wasn't my father's scratchy growl.

"Mr. Toyer." I turned with a grin.

Graymond Toyer had warm brown skin and a neat speckled beard. His tailored royal-blue three-piece suit hung precisely on his broad shoulders, making me feel underdressed in my beige vest, white shirt and tawny pants. I would have worn my best had I known I'd end up at Vardean today.

"Sorry, I'm late," I said. "There was an incident at the trolley stop. I got here as quickly as I could, Mr. Toyer."

"Not to worry, son," he said, clapping me on the back. "And I told you to call me Graymond. *Mr. Toyer* is my old man."

I nodded. I knew Graymond from when I was a kid. He was always at Broduck Manor, working with my father in his study or helping my mother in the garden. My father's parents had passed before I was born, and my mother's family lived overseas, and so Graymond became like an uncle to Leta and me. That was until my mother died. Graymond hadn't visited since. Whether something had driven a wedge between my father and him or whether my father had simply shut Graymond out like he had his own children, I wasn't sure.

"What am I doing here?" I asked. "I mean, I'm glad to be here, don't get me wrong. But . . . well, why?"

Graymond laughed and walked me to the middle of the room.

Fine lines feathered out from around his mouth and brown eyes. He simply pointed upward.

Now that I was standing in the center of the room, I could see a circular opening in the stone ceiling. A metal elevator slowly descended with a *click click click*.

"I thought you might want to assist me with my new case," he said.

I bounced on the balls of my feet. "Really?"

"You've put in some solid hours back at the office doing dry paperwork, but I want you to see what the law is really about."

"Vardean." I'd always wanted to see the prison sector. As a student, it had been off-limits.

"No." Graymond frowned. "Helping our clients."

My cheeks burned; I felt like I'd failed some kind of test.

Graymond pushed the rusty elevator door open when it reached us. "Welcome to Vardean, Cayder."

The elevator rose toward the hole in the rocky ceiling, and my heart beat in time with the *click click click* of the elevator chain.

"First, I want to warn you . . ." Graymond leaned back against the elevator wall, his arms crossed. "I know that you plan to become a prosecutor once you graduate law school, but I expect you'll have an open mind as to what can land someone in here. It's easy to jump to conclusions and judge the inmates."

"Of course, sir."

He nodded, short and sharp. "Good."

The elevator entered the hole in the ceiling, and for a moment, all I could see was a bright cone of light surrounding us.

"What matters most to our clients is that we listen to the

story they tell us," Graymond said. "I know you're a hard worker, Cayder, but are you a good listener?"

Unless it was having to listen to my sister and her insistent conspiracy theories about the veil, then yes. "Of course."

"*Listen*, but do not judge. Does this make sense to you?"

"Suuuure," I said, dragging out the word.

"I say listen, as their *stories* are all we have. And yes, they are simply stories. Their point of view. What they saw. What they smelled. What they heard. And what they did and didn't do. Is it fact? Is it the truth?" He paused, and I wasn't sure if he wanted me to answer. "We don't know."

"But if—"

"We don't know, Cayder. My job as a public defender is to present the case as I know it to be true. The burden of proof is on the prosecutor—they must prove beyond a reasonable doubt that my client is guilty."

"What if your client *wants* to plead guilty?"

"Interesting you should mention that." He scratched at his beard that matched his cropped silvery hair. "My new client claims that he is indeed guilty."

"And you don't believe him?"

He tilted his head side to side noncommittally. "Let's see what you think."

The elevator pulled out of the rock and into the prison sector. The building looked like a swollen birdcage, with row after row of cells lining the walls. The ceiling was made of a glass prism, refracting hundreds of beams of light, preventing any dark shadows. Vardean was the one building where you could control the presence of shadows both day and night. The only place where time couldn't be altered, or a crime commited.

While I'd witnessed the occasional fight and nightly breakdowns in the dormitory, there was no comparison to the chaos unfolding before me. Criminals were screaming, crying, spitting and—from the smell of it—pissing and worse. Arms and legs reached out from the bars, desperate for contact or merely acknowledgment.

The yelling amplified as we stepped out of the elevator.

"They all have a story," Graymond said with a sweep of his arms, raising his voice over the racket. "Are you ready to listen?"

Now I understood what the guard had referred to earlier. A part of me, the sane part, wanted to walk back into the elevator and descend back to the foyer, get on the next gondola out of here and never return.

Another part—the part that longed for justice for families like my own—reveled in the sight.

My chest expanded. My head felt light and buoyant.

I was back.

TURN THE PAGE FOR MORE
FROM ASTRID SCHOLTE

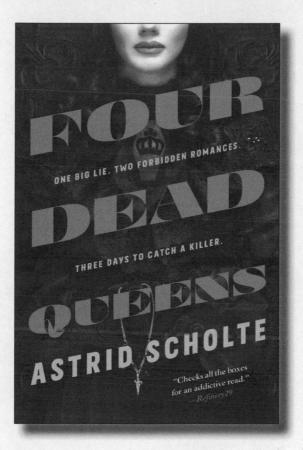

CHAPTER ONE

Keralie

The morning sun caught the palace's golden dome, flooding the Concord with light. While everyone halted their business and glanced up—as though it were a sign from the four queens themselves—we perched overhead like sea vultures, ready to swoop in and pick them apart.

"Who shall we choose today?" Mackiel asked. He was leaning against a large screen atop a building that displayed the latest Queenly Reports. He looked like a charming, well-dressed young man from Toria. At least, that was what he *looked* like.

"Choices, choices," I said with a grin.

He moved to drape his arm heavily around my shoulder. "Who do you feel like being today? A sweet young girl? A damsel in distress? A reluctant seductress?" He puckered his lips at me.

I laughed and pushed him away. "I'll be whatever makes us the most money." I usually picked my targets, but Mackiel had been in a good mood this morning, and I didn't want to tip the boat. He submerged easily into darkness these days, and I'd have done anything to keep him in the light.

I shrugged. "You choose."

He raised his dark eyebrows before tilting his bowler hat to further survey the crowd. The line of kohl around his lids made his deep-set blue eyes stand out all the more. Nothing escaped his scrutiny. A familiar smirk played at his lips.

The crisp Concord air was clean, unlike the acrid tang of seaweed, fish and rotted wood that pervaded our home down on Toria's harbor. It was Quadara's capital and the most expensive city to live in, as it shared boundaries with Toria, Eonia and Ludia. Archia was the only region separated from the mainland.

The stores on the ground level sold a variety of approved goods, including Eonist medicines, the latest Ludist fashions and toys, and fresh Archian produce and cured meat—all collated and distributed by Torian traders. Squeals of children, the murmur of business and sighs of queenly gossip bounced between the glass storefronts.

Behind the buildings rose an opaque golden dome, encapsulating the palace and concealing the confidential dealings within. The palace entrance was an old stone building called the House of Concord.

As Mackiel searched for a target, he held his middle finger to his lips—an insult to the queens hiding inside their golden dome. When he caught my eye, he tapped his lip and grinned.

"Him," he said, his gaze landing on the back of a dark figure who descended the stairs from the House of Concord into the crowded main square. "Get me his comm case."

The target was clearly Eonist. While we Torians were bundled up in layers to ward off the biting chill, he wore a tight-fitting black dermasuit over his skin, an Eonist fabric made of millions of microorganisms that maintained body temperature with their secretions. Gross, but handy in the depths of winter.

"A messenger?" I flashed Mackiel a hard look. The delivery would be of high importance if the messenger was coming from the House of Concord, the only place where Torians, Eonists, Archians and Ludists conducted business together.

Mackiel scratched at his neck with ring-covered fingers, a nervous habit. "Not up for the challenge?"

I scoffed. "Of course I am." I was his best dipper, slipping in and out of pockets with a feather-light touch.

"And remember—"

"Get in quick. Get out quicker."

He grabbed my arm before I could slip off the roof. His eyes were serious; it had been months since he'd looked at me that way—as though he cared. I almost laughed, but it lodged somewhere between my chest and throat.

"Don't get caught," he said.

I grinned at his concern. "When have I ever?" I climbed down from the rooftop and into the crowd.

I hadn't gotten far when an old man stopped abruptly in front of me and raised his hand to press four fingers to his lips in respect for the queens—the *proper* greeting, as opposed to Mackiel's middle-fingered version. I dug in my heels. My spiked soles gripped the well-worn cobblestones. I halted in time, my cheek brushing the back of his shoulders.

Dammit! What was it about the palace that inspired such slack-jawed stupidity? It wasn't like you could see anything through the

3

golden glass. And even if you could, so what? The queens didn't care about us. And certainly not someone like me.

I slapped the cane from the old man's hand. He stumbled to the side.

He turned, his face pinched in annoyance.

"Sorry!" I said. I fluttered my lashes at him from under my large-brimmed hat. "The crowd pushed in on me."

His expression softened. "No worries, my dear." He tipped his head. "Enjoy your day."

I gave him an innocent smile before slipping his silver pocket watch into a fold in my skirt. That would teach him.

I stood on my toes to find my target. *There.* He didn't look much older than me—eighteen, perhaps. His suit clung like a second skin—from his fingertips to his neck, covering his torso, legs and even his feet. While I wrestled with corsets and stiff skirts each and every day, I couldn't imagine his outfit would be any easier to dress in.

Still, I envied the material and the freedom of movement it allowed. Like him, my muscles were defined from constantly running, jumping and climbing. While it was not unusual for a Torian to be fit and trim, my muscles weren't from sailing back and forth to Archia, or from unloading heavy goods at the docks. I'd long been entangled within the darker side of Toria. Hidden beneath my modest layers and pinching corsets, no one knew of my wickedness. My work.

The messenger hesitated at the bottom of the House of Concord stairs, rearranging something in his bag. Now was my chance. That old man had given me inspiration.

I dashed toward the polished slate stairs, fixing my eyes on the palace with my best imitation of awe—or rather slack-jawed stupidity—on my face, my four fingers nearing my lips. Approaching the messenger, I snagged my toe in a gap between two tiles and pitched forward like a rag doll. Inelegant, but it would do the job. I'd learned the hard way that any pretense could easily be spotted. And I was nothing if not committed.

"Ah!" I cried as I crashed into the boy. The rotten part of me enjoyed the thwack as he hit the stones. I landed on top of him, my hands moving to his bag.

The messenger recovered quickly, pushing me away, his right hand tightly twisted around the bag. Perhaps this wasn't his first encounter with Mackiel's dippers. I stopped myself from shooting Mackiel a glare, knowing he'd be watching eagerly from the rooftop.

He was always watching.

Changing tactics, I rolled, purposely skinning my knee on the stone ground. I whimpered like the innocent Torian girl I pretended to be. I lifted my head to show my face from under my hat to take him in.

He had that Eonist look, evenly spaced eyes, full lips, high defined cheekbones and a proud jaw. The look they were engineered for. Curls of black hair framed his tan face. His skin was delicate, but hardy. Not at all like my pale creamy skin, which flaked and chapped in the winter wind and burned in the blistering summer sun. His eyes were on me. They were light, almost colorless, not the standard Eonist brown, which guarded against the sun's glare. Did it help him see in the dark?

"Are you all right?" he asked, his face giving nothing away.

Eonists' expressions were generally frozen, like the majority of their quadrant.

I nodded. "I'm so, so sorry."

"That's okay," he said, but his hand was still at his bag; I wasn't done with this charade just yet.

He glanced at my black boot, which had scuffed where my toe had caught between the stones, then to my knee cradled in my hands. "You're bleeding," he said in surprise. He did indeed think this was a ploy for his belongings.

I looked at my white skirt. A blotch of red had spread through my undergarments and was blooming across my knee.

"Oh my!" I swooned a little. I looked up into the bright sun until tears prickled behind my eyes, then turned back to him.

"Here." He grabbed a handkerchief from his bag and handed it to me.

I bit my lip to hide a grin. "I wasn't watching where I was going. I was distracted by the palace."

The messenger's strange pale eyes flicked to the golden dome behind us. His face betrayed no emotion. "It's beautiful," he said. "The way the sun illuminates the dome, it's as though it were alive."

I frowned. Eonists didn't appreciate beauty. It wasn't something they valued, which was ironic, considering how generically attractive they all were.

I bunched the hem of my skirt in my hands and began pulling it up over my knee.

"What are you doing?" he asked.

I swallowed down a laugh. "I was checking to see how bad it is." I pretended I only then remembered where he was from.

"Oh!" I rearranged my skirt to cover my legs. "How inappropriate of me." Intimacy was as foreign as emotions in Eonia.

"That's all right." But he turned his face away.

"Can you help me up?" I asked. "I think I've twisted my ankle."

He held out his hands awkwardly before deciding it was safer to grip my covered elbows. I leaned heavily against him, to ensure he didn't feel any shift in weight as I slipped a hand inside his bag. My fingers grasped something cool and smooth, about the size of my palm. The comm case. I slid it out and into a hidden pocket in my skirt. As soon as he had me on my feet, he released me as though he'd touched a month-old fish.

"Do you think you can walk?" he asked.

I nodded but swayed side to side. Novice dippers gave themselves away by dropping the act too soon after retrieving their prize. And my knee *did* hurt.

"I don't think so." My voice was light and breathy.

"Where can I take you?"

"Over there." I pointed to an empty chair and table in front of a café.

He held on to my elbow as he guided me over, using his broad shoulders to navigate the crowd. I fell into the chair and pressed the handkerchief to my knee. "Thank you." I tipped my head down, hoping he'd leave.

"Will you be okay?" he asked. "You're not alone, are you?"

I knew Mackiel would be watching from somewhere close by.

"No, I'm not alone." I put some indignation into my voice. "I'm with my father. He's doing business over there." I waved a hand vaguely at the surrounding shops.

The messenger crouched to look under the brim of my hat. I

flinched. There was something unsettling about his eyes up close. Almost like mirrors. Yet, under his gaze, I felt like the girl I was pretending to be. A girl who spent her day at the Concord with her family to enjoy the spoils of the other quadrants. A girl whose family was whole. A girl who hadn't shattered her happiness.

That moment passed.

Something flickered behind his expression. "Are you sure?" he asked. Was that real concern?

The cool of the metal case pressed against my leg, and Mackiel's hot gaze was on my back.

Get in quick. Get out quicker.

I had to disengage. "I need to rest for a bit. I'll be fine."

"Well, then," he said, glancing behind him to the House of Concord, his hand on his bag. As a messenger, his tardiness wouldn't be tolerated. "If you'll be all right . . ." He waited for me to refute him. I might have oversold my fragility.

"Yes. I'll be fine here. Promise."

He gave me a stiff Eonist nod, then said, "May the queens forever rule the day. Together, yet apart." The standard exchange of interquadrant goodwill. He turned to leave.

"Together, yet apart," I recited back to him. Before he had taken a step, I was up off the chair and among the crowd.

I clutched the comm case in my hand as I ran.

ACKNOWLEDGMENTS

The Vanishing Deep began all the way back in 2015 as a small nugget of an idea, and since then the book has transformed into something I'm really proud of. And it's all thanks to the following people:

My editor, Stacey Barney—thank you for pushing me to be a better writer and helping me find the truth and heart to my characters. This would be a very different, and lesser, book if it weren't for you!

I am extremely grateful for my wonderful agent Hillary Jacobson. Without you, I would still be querying and hoping and dreaming about becoming an author. Also, many thanks to my film and TV agent, Lia Chan at ICM, and my foreign rights team, Roxanne Edouard and Savanna Wicks at Curtis Brown UK.

A huge thank-you to the epic powerhouse team that is Penguin Teen: Jennifer Klonsky, Felicity Vallence, Caitlin Tutterow, Caitlin Whalen, Tessa Meischeid, Alex Garber, Kara Brammer and the rest of the crew that I've had the pleasure of working with. I'm so very lucky to be with Penguin Random House!

Thank you to my amazing Aussie publishers, Allen & Unwin, for making my lifelong dream of seeing my book in local bookstores come true! Special thanks to Jodie Webster, Sucheta Raj, and Sophie Eaton.

To Andrew, this book is not only dedicated to you for fixing *that* plot problem, but because you are calm like the ocean and strong like the tide. Thank you for your endless support, patience and those gorgeous chapter headings!

To Mum and Dad, thank you for always being so supportive of all my dreams over the years. I love how you've embraced my writing career, although I really wish you wouldn't check Goodreads! It's a scary place!

Hugs to all the Angelz! Thank you for being there for all the good times and the stressful ones. I couldn't ask for better agent siblings. Let's catch up again soon, yeah?

Dearest Amie Kaufman, I'm so blessed to know you. Thank you for your wisdom and kind words. Thanks to Sarah Glenn Marsh, Beth Revis, and Kerri Maniscalco for the amazing blurbs of *Four Dead Queens*. I'm incredibly grateful for *The YA Room*, *What Lucie's Reading*, *A Cup of Imagination*, *Claire Eva Reads*, OwlCrate, Midnight Pages, The YA Chronicles, Cre8tive Inspir8ions, @life_books_me, *Reading Anonymous*, and the Australian Writers' Centre—to name just a few. Many thanks to Jay Kristoff, Stephanie Garber, Adrienne Young, and Dill Werner for your support. And to my Aussie YA writing crew of Katya, Ella, and Sophie—thank you for the celebratory midday wines!

The reaction from friends and family continues to remind me how lucky I am to have you all in my life. A special shout-out to the TC girls and my US entourage, Jessica Ponte Thomas and Shannon Thomas, who are the greatest cheerleaders and friends.

Hugs and kisses to my precious cats, Lilo and Mickey, who keep me company on every draft, revision and deadline. One day I'll write a book for you.

In my acknowledgments for *Four Dead Queens*, I thanked Walt Disney for inspiring me. This time, I'd like to mention Disneyland, which has been a constant source of inspiration since I first visited as a baby. It just so happened to be the location of my second round of edits. I'm pretty sure some Disney magic was absorbed into the pages!

Lastly, I want to thank *you*, the reader. I would not be writing these acknowledgments if it weren't for your phenomenal support of *Four Dead Queens*. I've always wanted to be a published author and the realization that people I've never met are currently holding this book in their hands never ceases to surprise and often terrify me. Thank you for allowing my lifelong dream to become a reality. I owe you one. In return, I plan to write stories for many, many years to come.

I hope this book took you on a journey that was equal parts thrilling, heartbreaking, terrifying and beautiful—much like the process of writing a book!

Till next time!

ASTRID SCHOLTE was raised on a diet of Spielberg, Lucas and Disney, and knew she wanted to be surrounded by all things fantastical from a young age. She's spent the last fourteen years working in film, animation and television as both an artist and a manager. Career highlights include working on James Cameron's *Avatar*, Steven Spielberg's *The Adventures of Tintin* and Disney's *Moon Girl and Devil Dinosaur*. She lives in Melbourne, Australia, with her fiancé and two cats, Lilo and Mickey. Her debut young adult novel, *Four Dead Queens*, was an international bestseller and award winner. Up next is *League of Liars*. You can find her posting about books, cats and Disney on Twitter and Instagram @AstridScholte.

astridscholte.com